Yasodhara and the Buddha

ALSO AVAILABLE FROM BLOOMSBURY

Yasodhara and the Buddha

Vanessa R. Sasson

BLOOMSBURY ACADEMIC
LONDON · NEW YORK · OXFORD · NEW DELHI · SYDNEY

BLOOMSBURY ACADEMIC
Bloomsbury Publishing Plc
50 Bedford Square, London, WC1B 3DP, UK
1385 Broadway, New York, NY 10018, USA
29 Earlsfort Terrace, Dublin 2, Ireland

BLOOMSBURY, BLOOMSBURY ACADEMIC and the Diana logo are trademarks
of Bloomsbury Publishing Plc

First published by Speaking Tiger 2018
This edition first published 2021
Reprinted 2021

Copyright © Vanessa R. Sasson, 2018, 2021

Vanessa R. Sasson has asserted her right under the Copyright, Designs and
Patents Act, 1988, to be identified as Author of this work.

For legal purposes the Acknowledgements on p. 255–256 constitute an extension
of this copyright page.

Cover design: Ben Anslow
Cover images: Gold foil (© Katsumi Murouchi / Getty Images), Jujube, Ziziphus lotus
(Rhamnus lotus). Handcoloured copperplate engraving from *The Classes and Orders
of the Linnaean System of Botany*, Longman, Hurst, London. Richard Duppa (1816)
(© Florilegius / Alamy Stock Photo)

Bloomsbury Publishing Plc does not have any control over, or responsibility for, any
third-party websites referred to or in this book. All internet addresses given in this
book were correct at the time of going to press. The author and publisher regret
any inconvenience caused if addresses have changed or sites have ceased to
exist, but can accept no responsibility for any such changes.

A catalogue record for this book is available from the British Library.

A catalog record for this book is available from the Library of Congress.

ISBN:	HB:	978-1-3501-6315-7
	PB:	978-1-3501-6316-4
	ePDF:	978-1-3501-6317-1
	eBook:	978-1-3501-6318-8

Typeset by RefineCatch Limited, Bungay, Suffolk
Printed and bound in Great Britain

To find out more about our authors and books visit www.bloomsbury.com
and sign up for our newsletters

For Sheila
Queen, Teacher, Friend

Contents

Contents

Preface

By Wendy Doniger

Vanessa Sasson's *Yashodhara* retells a story about a man, a story that has been retold by countless other men for many centuries. As it is the story of Gautama Shakyamuni, who became the Buddha, Buddhists and non-Buddhists have retold it in many languages, from Pali and Sanskrit through the many vernaculars of Southeast and East Asia, and in all the European languages. (Herman Hesse's *Siddhartha* is the best known, and perhaps the best, of this last group.) Who owns this story? Recent concern for the inclusion of women has brought new attention to the much-neglected voices of women, particularly but not only nuns, in Buddhism. This move to broaden, in terms of gender, the scope of our understanding of the religions of the world has been, unfortunately, matched by a counter-movement that would narrow it, the theory of cultural appropriation, which would limit the right to interpret a religion or a culture to the people who created it, or who live by it.

Vanessa Sasson's novel is on the side of the angels (or Yakshas) in both of these issues. She re-imagines the thoughts and feelings of the woman closest to the future Buddha, his wife, thus broadening our own imagination of the tremendous effect that Gautama's enlightenment had on the people—including the female people—in his world. And, as a Canadian woman, she stakes her right to join all the other authors who have told their own versions of this story, and to respond in her own unique way to a great story that she has lived with, in so many of its incarnations, for many years.

The result is an extraordinary novel that flickers between a richly evoked and historically informed tale of ancient India (for Professor Sasson has studied the texts for years, and knows her stuff) and a vivid attempt to imagine how a woman in that place and that situation would have felt in a situation that is both culturally specific—a very Indian story about renunciation—and, alas, widely cross-cultural: her husband abandoned her, and even took away their child. Remarkably, these two worlds here melt together in a single story, simultaneously familiar and exotic, unique and universal. It makes for a thrilling and challenging read.

Introductory Note

This is the story of Yasodhara, the woman who was married to the one who became the Buddha. Yasodhara is not the focus of most early Buddhist texts. The literature preserves fragments of her life, but the focus is (unsurprisingly) usually on her husband. In this book, I have tried to bring together some of these early fragments into the shape of a modern novel, to tell her story from her perspective (as I imagined it). As the writing process unfolded, however, I came to appreciate how much information we are missing. The literature is genuinely scant where she is concerned—particularly regarding her youth. She is a key player during a few moments in the Buddha's life, but otherwise, we know little about her. We know she produced their one and only son, that she was left behind when he made his Great Departure, and that when he returned to the palace seven (or eight) years later, he took his son back to the forest with him. The Jatakas (past-life stories) refer to her regularly, suggesting that Yasodhara and the Buddha had been connected for lifetimes, but we do not know much more than that. Indeed, Yasodhara is so marginalized in some cases that she does not even receive a name. She is known simply as Rahulamata—Rahula's mother.

If one digs a little deeper, though, precious details rise to the surface that may enable us to imagine a bit more. The most significant of these may be the fact that Siddhattha and Yasodhara are described as having been born at the same moment in their final lives. It was this detail (found throughout the early literature) that stimulated the direction I have taken in this telling. Yasodhara and Siddhattha plunged into their final lives at the very same instant to land in the same neighborhood, just a few doors away from each other. The heartbreak she experiences after his departure (which is described dramatically in a number of sources) was grounded in the fact that the Buddha took his last steps alone, without inviting her to join. After countless lifetimes of shared experiences, he abandoned her without even saying goodbye. According to one account (preserved in the *Jatakanidana*), his Great Departure took place on the very day she gave birth! After his son was born, Siddhattha is described as walking over to her bedroom to see them. He stood at the threshold and considered entering, longing to touch his newborn son, but he realized that if he did, *she* would wake up and then he would no longer be able to leave. He therefore departed without touching his son or saying goodbye to his wife. His abandonment was dramatic and the outcome devastating. Yasodhara woke up the next morning to the news of his departure, told to her by someone else.

The *Jatakanidana* offers us one version of this extraordinary narrative, but there are so many others. I have spent the bulk of my academic career exploring this literature, enjoying the rich tapestry of their shared multi-life story, and I have yet to scratch the surface. Unlike biblical traditions, Buddhist storytelling is not limited to one sacred text. It boasts of an open, fluid canon, that continues to expand with each passing generation. Indeed, we would do better to think of the Buddhist canon as a library (and not as a book), with hundreds of volumes lining its illustrious shelves. The Buddha's story, where Yasodhara plays an ongoing part, has been told more times than anyone can track, and each telling is different. The skeleton of the story remains, but the details vary, the emphasis redirects. In the same way that a great storyteller never tells the same story twice, so too here. The *Jatakanidana* was probably produced about 1,500 years ago in Sri Lanka, and it is quite different from the late-medieval *Bhadrakalpavadana* of Nepal, or Thich Nhat Hanh's contemporary account, *Old Path White Clouds* (1987). Every time the Buddha and Yasodhara's timeless story is told, it shifts, so that one can spend a lifetime studying these narratives and never quite reaching the end of them. Just as every wine is slightly different, although made from seemingly similar grapes, so too is every telling its own creation, but produced from a similar set of building blocks. The connoisseur never tires of the subtleties.

The question that begs reflection (at least for me) is this: if the story was told one way in Sri Lanka 1,500 years ago, another way in medieval Nepal, and still another in twentieth-century France by a Vietnamese monk, what would the story be today? And somewhat audaciously, I wondered, what it would be like if I was the one to write it? What would I say?

Was I even allowed to try?

The scholar in me wrestled with these questions for a long time, and in the end it was the scholar in me who answered: the Buddha's story is one that invites continuity. Precisely *because* there are so many versions—none with final authority—there must be room for more. By telling the story one more time, in my own voice with my own perspective, I realized that I would be participating in a tradition that goes back thousands of years. I don't have the poetic skills of Ashvaghosa, or the exquisite flair of Newari prose, and I certainly cannot hold a candle to Thich Nhat Hanh's wisdom, but storytellers do not have to compete. Just because I will never dance like Baryshnikov does not mean that I am not invited to enjoy dancing anyway. I can try to see the Buddha's story from the inside—just as previous authors have—and experience the long history of hagiography with my own eyes.

And what I saw with my own eyes was mesmerizing. When I finally allowed myself to climb into the story and create a telling of my own, what I found broke my heart. I found Yasodhara facing suffering, living suffering, while her husband roamed the forest in a quest to solve it. She was living what he was trying to understand. Yasodhara was stripped of everything—her home, her husband, her status as a married woman, and eventually even her child. I saw him receiving all the glory while she was left with shattered remains. For a time, I was angry with him. What kind of a hero causes so much pain? What kind of paradox had I landed in, that he was idealized for solving the problem of suffering while he created so much of it at the same time? Could he not have done things differently? My protective impulse wrapped itself around Yasodhara and pushed the Buddha away.

But then I learned something else: I was not the first to feel the burning pain of Yasodhara's story. Although Buddhist hagiography focuses on the Buddha, and although these texts (unsurprisingly) idealize him, the early writers did not close their eyes to the suffering he leaves in his wake. Yasodhara's laments are part of the tradition too. When she discovers that he has gone, she challenges the Chariot Driver for taking her beloved away. She demands explanation, she charges in fury, she collapses with pain. Her abandonment was not lost on many of the early hagiographers. Buddhism has a long relationship with misogyny, little of which is subtle, but what I found as I wrote this book was something else: male authors taking on a woman's voice, crying her tears of pain, and expressing the loss that his Departure represented for her. They knew what the Buddha's departure cost Yasodhara and they took the time to express it. These male authors gave a voice to the pain that renunciation creates for the women left behind. They were sensitive in ways I had not appreciated until then. Although I may have been upset with the Buddha for having hurt Yasodhara, I grew to love the writers for their sensitivity to her plight. Indeed, I would never have experienced frustration with the Buddha if his story (in all its complexity) was not provided so compellingly by them. They provided me with a map that I had not appreciated until I tried to chart the course myself.

There is a lot more I could say about this project, but I believe it is time to let the story speak for itself. For the reader interested in learning more about the tradition upon which this telling rests, I recommend the notes provided at the end of the book. Each chapter is accompanied by a discussion about the sources used for each scene and points to additional research. The study questions may also serve to stimulate deeper consideration of the material and are offered for that very purpose.

I do, however, want to make one important caveat (the academic in me is desperate to make at least one) before I close: namely, that this book does not belong to the category of historical fiction (and this not only because the gods are regular actors in the story). Scholars have yet to determine with any material certainty when the Buddha lived (*if,* that is, he lived at all) and how much of his story might be true. Assuming Yasodhara and the Buddha did live once upon a time, their story presumably took place in northern India (or southern Nepal), somewhere around the fifth century BCE, but maybe in the fourth century, or maybe in the sixth.

Whatever the exact dates might have been, the time period feels too distant for me to reach. I cannot imagine northern India (or southern Nepal) in the fifth century BCE, if for no other reason than we have few sources narrating what life would have been like in those days. The earliest Buddhist writings that we do possess come later, beginning around the first century CE (more or less). The stories I have spent my academic life reading are based on the memories of a world five hundred years younger than the one the Buddha and Yasodhara probably knew. I cannot begin to imagine all the changes that took place during the time period we lost.

The story I have told here is, therefore, a story inspired by later hagiographies. It is not historical fiction, but perhaps what can be more appropriately labeled "hagiographical fiction" (if such a label existed). This book is my attempt at recreating a hagiography, inspired by hagiographies that belong to an earlier time. It is why, for example, I include a temple with a stone goddess. Temples with stone deities were not likely to have been a regular feature of north Indian religious life during Yasodhara's time period, but by the first century, when this book really takes place, temples had arrived. Likewise, I make reference to Durga, the *Ramayana*, Shakuntala and many other stories that were probably not in written form during Yasodhara's period, but were in circulation later and were most likely based on oral traditions that reached earlier into the past. Some of these stories were probably constructed in tandem with Buddhist hagiography, as narratives from different traditions mingled creatively in the Indian imagination.

In other words, some of the material in this book is based on early Buddhist literature. Some of it is based on what we know as early Hindu literature. Some of it may be historical, but most of it is not. And some of it has come out of the playfulness of my mind.

Prologue

I was shivering despite the heat. I gripped the wall for support as I reached for my shawl. The inlaid jewels felt so cold and hard against the palm of my hand. No matter how many pillows I had filled my room with over the years, I had never been able to soften the edges. The towering structure of palace life was built with too much stone. I folded myself into the white cotton cloth, trying desperately to quiet the trembling.

I could not go downstairs in this state. I didn't want to fall apart in front of everyone, but I knew they were waiting and my body was not complying. I could not make myself still.

I took a deep breath and readied myself to let go, but as soon as I did, I buckled and fell. "Great Goddess!" I cried out as I hit the marble floor.

My maidservant flew into the room and was beside me in seconds. "Your Highness!"

"I can't do this!"

I was trying to breathe but was failing miserably. "I don't want to lose my baby!"

Neelima was holding my hand, squeezing it with all her strength. "Breathe, Your Highness. You must breathe."

I tried, but there was no air. "Who asks such a thing from a mother? It isn't right!"

"I know," she mumbled as she tried to hold back her own tears. "It never is."

I was clutching a leg of the rosewood bedframe as though it might carry me to shore, but it did little to anchor me. The swirling was coming from within and no ship would have been strong enough to navigate against my pain. Looking up, I was met with high ceilings pulsating over my head, geometric carvings moving in all directions.

"What if he needs me out there?" I pleaded. "What if something happens?"

"He won't be alone. They will take care of him," she tried to assure me.

"But they can't take care of him the way I do! He needs his mother and they are taking him away from me!"

There was no response to that. We could both see the truth of my words. I looked around the room, looking for something to save me from the situation. Some argument that had been left behind that might convince them to change their minds.

"And they will be in the forest!" I added, suddenly remembering this piece of fear. "It's so dangerous out there! There are snakes and tigers and who knows what else!"

She held onto my hand as my worries spilled onto the floor.

"What if I never see him again, Neelima? What if he never comes back?"

"I don't know . . ."

"What kind of a man makes such a request?" I burst with anger. "First he leaves me, and then he comes back only to take away my only son! How can he do this to me?" If I had had anything in my hands at that moment, I would have thrown it across the room.

"How does he keep finding new ways to splinter me apart?" I sobbed into the darkness of my palms.

For some reason, this last question affected her differently. Perhaps it was because she had just met with him. She straightened her hunched frame, tucked a few wisps of gray hair that had escaped her headscarf, and looked me right in the eyes.

"Your Highness, I know that this is horrible. But I also know that you are brave," she replied. "You can face this."

"But I don't want to face this . . ." I said almost to myself.

"Of course not. But it is what you are being called to do. Master Rahula *needs* you to do this. He needs you to be brave so that he can be. It is time for him to receive his education."

"But why does his education have to take him so far away?"

"I don't know . . . but it is the way of things for him."

I took a deep breath as her words landed on my crowded heart. She was telling me what so many others had told me before. She was telling me what I did not want to hear, but what everyone else seemed to recognize. I looked into her weathered face, following the lines of history that were etched across her forehead. Her spotted hands resting on mine.

She was right. My own confusion was probably nothing compared with what he must be experiencing in his little seven-year-old self. I had to pull myself together for his sake.

Sensing my determination, she offered me one of her gnarled hands. "Let me help you up."

I took it gratefully. Her calluses were so thick they had turned into cushions.

"Are you all right?" she asked as I leaned against the bed. The silk sheets were bunched up in a corner. I had not let anyone into my room for days. Not even her.

"I . . . think so."

"Can I bring you a cup of something warm? Milk with a sprinkle of dried turmeric perhaps?"

I shook my head and turned towards the window. The sun was breaking through the sky, flooding my room with orange light.

"Tell them that I will be downstairs in a moment."

"Yes, Your Highness," she obeyed with a bow.

It was time. I ironed out my simple white clothing and adjusted my braid. I would not break again.

*

I walked carefully down the rounded marble staircase that led to the Great Hall. The trembling had subsided, but I was still a bit uncertain of myself. I held the golden handrail with one hand and lifted my robes with the other so as not to slip. When I reached the bottom, I exhaled with relief.

I could see bodies milling about in the courtyard ahead. Men dressed in orange rags moving silently. Ochre-colored shadows. I adjusted my braid one more time, smoothed out my white wrap and tightened my sash, and then crossed the Great Hall to the courtyard, with one objective in mind: to find my son.

He was sitting by himself by the edge of the lotus pool. "How are you, darling?" I asked as I sat down beside him.

He did not look up. His fingers were trailing through the water in between the flowers. A flock of black birds tore through the darkening sky, chasing the moon like lost souls. He did not notice them either. The servants would start lighting the oil lamps soon and then everything would be different.

"Sweetheart?"

Still no response.

"Rahula," I whispered as I placed my hand on the softness of his little neck. "Please look at me."

He trailed his fingers a little while longer, making pathways through the water. A frog watched him from the safety of a lotus leaf. Eventually, he looked up. His beautiful eyes were filled with the emotions he could not speak aloud. I wanted to fall into them. My mind fled into the past without permission as images of him from over the years paraded before my eyes. When had he grown so tall?

I placed a lock of hair behind his ear, as I had done so many times before. I loved caressing his hair. But a moment later, I recoiled at the realization that soon his hair would be shaved away. He would be so different. He would not really be my son anymore.

"How are you feeling, sweetheart?" I asked, as I attempted to put those thoughts aside.

He shrugged. "I'm all right."

"Are you ready?"

"I guess so." He turned towards the water again.

"Sweetheart, it's all right to feel a bit scared right now. You don't have to be so brave." He looked up at me. "You know," I added, "I'm scared too."

At these words, all of his restraint melted and he threw himself into my arms. "Oh Mother! I *am* scared! I don't want to go!" He sobbed against my neck. He was trembling, just as I had been a moment earlier. Every fiber in my being wanted to scoop him up and run away. Run from the men in orange robes who were forcing us into this separation. Run from the world that dictated such realities and called them wisdom. My baby was crying and I wanted to make his tears go away.

I inhaled the sweet smell of him. I would have renounced the entire world to be able to hold onto him longer, but I would not renounce his future to satisfy my desires. Slowly, ever so carefully, I pulled us apart.

"My most beautiful sweetheart," I whispered. "I am so sad. I cannot imagine living without you." I wiped away the tears that were dripping down my own cheeks. "But I won't hold you back. It is time for you to find your life."

"But I want to be with *you*!" he exclaimed.

"I know. I want that too, but you will be with your father. He will take good care of you."

He looked past me to where the men were, his father sitting straight and elegant at the center.

"I don't even know him," he objected.

"You will learn to know him."

"But . . . what if he doesn't like me?"

"That, my darling, is one thing I know you don't have to worry about," I said with a confident smile. "You are impossible not to love, my beautiful Rahula. And your father is a good man. You will see."

He wiped his tears, which I knew was a good sign. "But what if I never see you again, Mother?" he asked, as he voiced an all too familiar fear.

"I believe we will see each other again, darling. But if anything happens . . ." I stumbled against the words, but caught myself, "then I will see you in the next life. We will never be lost to each other Rahula. Don't ever forget that."

Men in orange robes approached. "Are you ready, young master?" asked one of them.

Rahula searched my face, looking for permission.

"He is ready," I answered for him.

1

Beginnings

I was born during the hottest season in the year. The clouds sat poised on the edge of release, teasing us with the possibility of rain, but not giving in. While they dallied, we were suffocating.

Most of my household had moved to the flat, clay-baked roof in the hope of some respite after I was born, but my father wanted a few moments to himself. We lived on the edge of the town, far from the bustle of hawking merchants and clanging noise. My father soaked in the quiet and approached the magnificent asattha tree that stood a few paces from our front door. He bowed to it with reverence, circumambulated it three times, keeping it by his right side, and whispered a prayer of gratitude for the delivery that was my birth. There would be all kinds of ritual celebrations to properly thank the gods for my safe arrival in the coming days, but that evening after my mother's many hours of painful labor, a silent prayer was enough.

The sound of clicking hooves reverberated from a distance. A rider bearing the royal flag was approaching. My father watched as this unexpected visitor drew near.

"Are you Dandapani?" the royal messenger asked from the height of his horse.

"I am," my father replied.

The messenger nodded, dismounted and pulled out a trumpet. He blew into it without producing any semblance of a melody, making a terrible racket that was sure to disturb the entire household. He was announcing his own arrival in case my father had not noticed.

"I come bearing a message from Maharaja Suddhodana, King of the Sakya Kingdom!" he declared with a well-rehearsed voice, as he lowered his instrument and tucked it under his arm.

News certainly does travel quickly, my father marveled to himself. He expected a royal message to arrive eventually—the king was, after all, family—but not on the very same day of my birth.

"Maharaja Suddhodana has received news of your daughter's successful arrival. He congratulates you and looks forward to welcoming your family at the palace."

My father imagined the moment when he would present me to the royal court for the first time. His heart swelled with pride at the thought of it. He pictured the festivities that would be thrown in our honor, flower petals raining over him as he carried his first child through a sea of boisterous applause.

The messenger's voice interrupted my father's fantasy. "The king would also like to announce the successful birth of the Prince of the Sakya Kingdom!"

What was that?

"I am sorry," my father stammered. "Did you say that the king's son was born today as well? The queen has delivered her child?"

"That is correct," replied the royal messenger.

Two little brown monkeys chased each other through the branches overhead, squealing with dangerous delight.

"But ... why wasn't this announced? I don't understand!" My father looked around in bewilderment, half-expecting a parade of elephants to materialize in front of him. "Where are the festivities? Why haven't I heard the sounds of conch shells blaring? Why is it so quiet?"

The messenger ignored his confusion and continued with his recitation.

"Unfortunately, the king requests that there be no festivities of any kind for the time being. The prince's birth is accompanied by complications that Maharaja Suddhodana is not prepared to announce. The entire Sakya Kingdom is asked to refrain from celebration. In fact ..." and here his royal demeanor expanded dramatically, "the kingdom is hereby declared to be in a state of mourning."

My father's face blanched.

"Mourning? But why?"

One of the monkeys launched a mango pit at the messenger's head before he could answer. It hit the messenger squarely between the eyes. In a flash, the messenger transformed into a petulant child, abandoning his required demeanor, stomping his feet and screaming at the monkeys who were racing away with what seemed like victorious giggles.

My father, however, barely noticed. "Why are we in mourning?" he repeated.

"Unfortunately," replied the royal messenger as he wiped the mango slime off his face, "that is not part of the message."

Without another word, the messenger climbed back onto his horse and rode off, rubbing the sore spot on his forehead and leaving my father far behind.

My father let himself fall onto the brittle grass. He could not understand what had just happened. The king had sired an heir, which meant that the kingdom finally had a prince. And the prince and I were born on the same day, which should have been an auspicious sign for both families, but obviously something had gone wrong. Enough to warrant placing the kingdom in a state of mourning . . .

He knew what that meant but he could not bear to think of it. Queen Maya was my father's sister, my paternal aunt. He could not allow himself to consider the possibility that seemed to be looming on the horizon.

He sank further into the grass as reality encased him. The kingdom finally had an heir to the throne, after years of waiting, but something had gone wrong. He kept repeating the words to himself, trying to make sense of them. Where was Maya, his beloved older sister? Why wouldn't more news be shared?

And then something else dawned on him. Something even more wrenching than the question of his sister: the kingdom was placed in mourning on the day of his daughter's birth. Was that a bad omen? Were the stars condemning his daughter before she even began? The protective impulse of fatherhood rose to greet him for the first time and it was more powerful than he expected.

And what about the celebrations? All celebrations were cancelled, said the messenger. That meant *our* celebrations as well. *That* was why the king had sent a message so soon. Whatever the women might have prepared would have to be cancelled.

The day I was born, the day that was supposed to be filled with celebration and congratulations, was now darkened. My father's long-awaited moment of public fatherhood, the moment when he would be able to parade me through the palace hallways with pride and joy, had been snatched away.

*

The queen's death haunted the king. She had experienced such an easy pregnancy. Everything was going so well. And they had waited so long to conceive a child together! The entire Sakya Kingdom had. How could he lose her now? He paced the length of his Throne Room for days, replaying their final moments together over and over in his mind. She knew that the end of her life was drawing near and she had asked him to let her go. She insisted on giving birth in Lumbini Garden.

"*But Maya, do you realize what you are asking?*" he asked her. "*We have plenty of gardens right here in the palace compound. Lumbini is a long road away! It's too dangerous to be going on a trip now!*"

"*I know what I am asking, Husband,*" *the queen replied.* "*But the Goddesses of Lumbini are calling. I must go to them. I am certain of it.*"

"*But . . . when would you return?*"

"*I will not return, Husband,*" *she explained quietly.* "*I will stay until the end.*"

King Suddhodana never saw his wife again. Her final scene had played itself out exactly as she said it would. She died in the garden not long after delivering their one and only child, surrounded by her maidservants at the base of Lumbinidevi's tree.

Try as he might, the king could not face the loss of her and celebrate the birth of his son at the same time. He could not imagine raising a prince without his wife, so closed the doors to the kingdom instead, outlawing celebration and stifling any happiness he might have otherwise felt.

He did make one exception to his rule, though: he requested an astrological reading of his son's chart. He gave them very little time to prepare, sending the astrologers into a last-minute scramble, but that was irrelevant to him. The king needed to understand who the child was. At the very least, he required confirmation that his son would play the part kingship required of him. The crown was a heavy burden to bear; without Maya by his side, it promised to be more isolating than ever. But if he could lean on his son, if he could depend on a future promised by the stars, maybe . . . just maybe, he would find the strength he needed not to fail.

The astrologers were invited into the Royal Nursery for the occasion—a room that overflowed with the queen's expectations, from the elephants carved into the great wooden beams of the ceiling to the vibrant paintings she had commissioned to cover the walls. There were images of monkeys swinging in trees, swans gliding gracefully on lotus-covered ponds, and a cluster of gods lounging on a bed of clouds, looking down into the room with loving guardianship. The floor of the Royal Nursery was littered with toys she had received during the pregnancy— toys the infant was still much too young to notice, let alone play with—but that everyone looked forward to watching him enjoy. Every detail of the room spoke of her hopes and dreams. The hopes and dreams that had been shattered with her death.

The astrologers entered the Royal Nursery soberly, all too aware of the mood they would be met with. They knew not to expect trumpets announcing their arrival. It was not a joyous occasion, even if it should have been. Chief Astrologer led the procession, followed by his junior acolytes who shouldered the tremendous scroll they had been slaving over.

"Well?" demanded the king before the door had closed behind them. "I am ready to hear your analysis."

Chief Astrologer cleared his throat nervously. "Of course, Your Highness," he said as he stumbled his way through the ceremonial greeting, touching the king's feet with his forehead. "But . . . might I make one small request before we begin?"

"A request? You were commissioned to provide a reading!" His anger shot out of him before he was even aware it was there.

"Of course, Your Highness," Chief Astrologer repeated. "We have prepared everything . . ." he stammered as he gestured to the scroll behind him. "It is just that . . . Would you be so kind as to grant us permission to look at the child before we complete the process? We would like to see if there are any unusual marks on his body that might help us finalize our discussion."

"Do you mean to tell me that the charts are still not complete?!" His anger exploded. "What have you been *doing*?! This is the prince of your kingdom, YOUR future king! A GOD in human body! Do you not consider this chart worthy of your time?!"

The king's rage ripped through the astrologers' confidence like a tornado. This was precisely what they feared would happen. None of them responded; they all stared at the floor, dumb with terror, unsure of what to do or say next.

Why does everything have to be so complicated, the king hollered to himself in frustration. *Why couldn't they just do what he had asked?* He wanted to punish them just for upsetting him, but . . . If the astrologers required an examination to finish their work, refusing the request would only delay the situation that much longer. He ordered one of the nurses to bring his son to the leader while the junior astrologers busied themselves with the chart.

Chief Astrologer was forbidden from laying his hands on the precious heir, so he moved around the nurse who was holding him, bobbing and weaving awkwardly as he tried to see if there were any significant markings. The junior astrologers, in the meanwhile, kept their distance and busied themselves with the scroll. They laid it down on a table and removed the embroidered silk it was wrapped in. They carefully unrolled the parchment, making sure not to touch any of the paint with their fingers, until it lay completely flat on its surface.

Although he was still frustrated with them, the king could not withhold his awe. The chart was unequivocally a masterpiece—and this despite the speed at which he knew he had forced them to work. The background was dyed a deep red and it was covered with rows of golden calligraphy. Exquisite depictions of the stars and planets filled the edges, producing an utterly mesmerizing effect. *The secrets of my son's future are embedded somewhere on that parchment*, the king marveled to himself. He was now more anxious than ever to hear what they had to say.

As soon as Chief Astrologer completed his inspection, the child was returned to his bed. Chief Astrologer summoned his helpers. They stepped away from the glittering scroll and joined their superior in a corner. Almost immediately, the discussion swelled into a heated debate, with arms waving and hysterical whispering as they argued about the signs they were trying to interpret, none of it being explained to the increasingly impatient king.

Just before the king exploded again, Chief Astrologer broke through the circle with his declaration. "We have reached a conclusion, Maharaja."

Finally, the king said to himself.

"After careful consideration . . ." he began.

The king's worried brows were arched in anticipation. A small bead of sweat was forming along his temple. This king wanted so much from them. How could he tell him the truth? The chart prophesied disaster for the royal lineage. The small prince swaddled in delicately embroidered cloth would not turn into the man the king wanted. According to the stars, the prince would achieve more than any man had ever achieved. He would, in fact, offer freedom to the entire world . . .

But in the process, he would break everyone's heart.

"After careful consideration," he resumed hesitantly, "we believe that your son may take one of two roads. It is not clear from the stars which of these your son will take."

"I am listening . . ."

"If, Your Highness, the Royal Prince chooses to live as a householder, he will become the greatest king the world has ever known. He will bring law to every corner of the land, make peace with neighboring tribes, and he will bring justice to every subject in his domain. He will be the kind of king that materializes only once every ten thousand years."

The other astrologers stared at their superior in disbelief. That was not what they had agreed to! Thankfully, they had enough wisdom to know when to remain quiet. The king, in the meanwhile, was swept away.

"Wonderful news, Chief Astrologer! Wonderful indeed! I knew my son was special!" he declared with his chest puffed up like a lion, all the pain and sadness he had been carrying melting like butter in a sacrificial fire. He clapped his hands for a servant and bellowed, "Someone get these astrologers gifts for their efforts! They have done excellent work!"

Chief Astrologer watched as the king hustled about enthusiastically and was quickly engulfed by the magnitude of the sin he had just committed. He had falsified his astrological interpretation in the presence of the king. *To* the king.

The divine protector of his own world. He was desperate to speak the one morsel of truth he had left.

"I am ... sorry, Your Highness," he interrupted uncomfortably, "but there is more to say."

"Excuse me?" the king replied as he turned back around. "You have said all I need to hear. He will be a great king! What more needs to be said?"

"I beg your forgiveness, Maharaja, but as I mentioned, there are two options presented by the stars. One is that he will become a great king, but a second option also reveals itself." Sweat was pooling in every fold of his body now.

The king stared at Chief Astrologer with what seemed like a trail of unconscious understanding. The servants behind him, who were on the verge of bringing in the pageant of gifts, froze.

"I see," the king replied slowly. "And what is the second option?" His voice was just cold enough to be threatening.

Chief Astrologer took a deep breath, swallowed, and finally delivered the half-truth he had been desperate to share.

"It seems, Your Highness, that it is also possible that your son chooses a life of religious homelessness ..." He waited for a reaction, but the king did not move. He continued with the last portion of analysis in a very quick burst. "If he does that, the prince will become the greatest sage the world has ever known."

The king's consternation lingered a moment. He attempted to imagine a world in which his son chose a life of renunciation but rejected the thought immediately. He shook the image right out of his head and slapped Chief Astrologer on the back.

"Well," he said, "we certainly don't want him to become a wandering mendicant when he has a throne to inherit, now do we?"

And with that, he escorted the astrologers right out of the room.

Without their gifts.

Monsoon Rain

"This heat is terrible," my mother complained as she fanned herself. "Shouldn't the rains have started already?" She was pacing the front yard as I suckled at her breast. The sweat was pouring down her back. "I don't know how much more of this I can take."

My father was checking the structure around the well, ensuring the bricks were stable and well attached. A neighbor's well had recently collapsed while their son was playing along its edge. He toppled and drowned before anyone could catch him.

"You're just frustrated because you haven't been moving enough lately. It will pass," he assured her without looking up.

"Maybe it's the nursing. Maybe it makes me more susceptible to the heat than usual. Normally I can handle the dry season, but this is unbearable." She kept pacing while wiping the sweat from her face.

"Why don't you sit for a bit?"

"I don't want to sit! I want to pace." She marched through the scratchy grass at an increasingly hurried gait, barely even looking over the parched remains of the herb garden she normally tended so carefully. Her temperature was rising and my father braced himself for what he knew would come next.

"You know what?"

Here it comes, he thought to himself.

"I *am* frustrated, but not just because of the heat. It isn't right that we are forbidden from celebrating our daughter's arrival. Don't you think the king has gone too far in all of this? The forty days of confinement ended ages ago. We should have met with him by now."

They had been over this topic many times already, but apparently they would be going over it again. He kept his eyes on his work.

"Don't you think he is exaggerating by extending the mourning period like this for everyone?" she continued, insisting he respond.

When no answer was provided, she stopped and turned toward him. "Why won't you say anything?"

He put down his tools and walked over to her. "I am frustrated too, Pamita. But he is grieving and there is nothing we can do about that. We have to wait."

She dropped her shoulders with resignation. She knew he was right, but she wished he wasn't. "I am sorry, Husband. I know Maya was your sister and that this loss is yours too. But I'm worried. What if it's a bad omen for our daughter?"

"That's why I suggested that we go to the temple and ask the priest to bless her on his own. It doesn't have to be a big affair. We can bring her for a blessing, but you keep refusing."

"Because the king needs to be there! He is the leader of our community and he is her uncle. I don't want to do this without him. He needs to come out of hiding so that we can finally honor our daughter as she deserves."

"Then we have to wait," he answered patiently.

"I will tell you something, Husband: if we had borne a son, the king would have made more of an effort."

That was his cue. Whenever the politics of women were invoked, he knew he was safer at a distance. He would not argue with her. He touched her cheek with the tip of a finger and returned to his work at the well without another word.

She was on the verge of saying one more thing when something interrupted her. A slight tap on her hand. She looked down and there it was: a little raindrop, glistening against her dry skin.

One drop did not make the rainy season.

Tap. Tap. Tap.

She had not noticed the dark clouds rolling in as she complained. Could it be?

She looked at her husband. He was squatting on his heels, waiting to see if it was just a flirtation.

Crack!

The sky tore itself apart, fresh water pouring out of the swollen clouds, drenching everything with sudden and utter abandon. My mother screamed with delight as she hugged my bundled body against her own.

"Do you feel that, little one? This is your first rain!" she exclaimed as she twirled me under the falling drops. "The dry season is finally over!"

My father laughed as he raised his arms to the sky. A moment earlier, the world was full of hurt, but now everything was becoming new again. He flew over to us and grabbed us in his arms. "What a relief!" he cried. My parents held each other tight, my little body squeezed in between them, as they relished the feeling of fresh rainwater on their faces. My father then pulled back and looked at his wife. "Do you feel better now?"

She laughed. "I feel so much better! With the rains, anything is possible!"

My father twirled us all together, basking in the relief that the new season promised. The cracked earth would soften and the crops would start to grow again. Vegetables would sprout, fruits would bloom and the rice would yield another harvest.

"Wait a minute!" he declared suddenly. "What am I still wearing sandals for?" He threw off his straw sandals, hiked up his clothing and danced in the softening earth. He wiggled his toes and stomped about theatrically. The dusty dryness was being washed away.

My mother spun me in her arms, "Great Goddess, how I missed this!" she exclaimed with her face lifted to the sky. One of the servants ran up to her and offered to take me back inside.

"Absolutely not! My daughter must welcome the Gods of Rain with us!" She looked around and realized that the rest of the servants were still inside. "And so should everyone else. Tell the others that they are ordered to celebrate!" she commanded with a stern smile. "We may not be allowed to celebrate anything else, but no one can stop us from dancing in the rain."

The servants must have been on the other side of the door waiting for permission to be granted, because the moment they heard her words, they came running. Soon, they were catching raindrops in their mouths like happy children, quenching the deadening thirst that everyone had been parched with for so long.

*

Reports of monsoon celebrations were brought to the royal ministers, causing them increasing concern. The ban against celebration had gone on too long. The community had become restless and needed release. The ministers needed to speak with the king, but he had made himself utterly unavailable. Since the queen's death, he spent all his time in one of his private gardens and would not permit anyone to disturb him. He had closed himself off from their counsel and no amount of pleading had any effect.

Chief Minister decided to take matters into his own hands. He understood the pain of loss, but the king could not mourn forever. He walked over to the king's private garden and stood at the gate in the rain, his palms pressed together in formal supplication. He knew it might be a long wait, but he was determined to stand there until his king saw him. He stood stock still as the rain splattered against his silk clothing—a trick of stillness his father had taught him as a boy when they went hunting together. He had mastered the art over time, successfully turning himself to stone as he waited for his prey. Chief Minister called upon that skill now, ignoring the agony it invariably caused. He would not undo his position until his monarch emerged from hiding. It was evening by the time the king emerged.

"What are you doing here?" the king asked, surprised by the intrusion.

"My most sincere apologies for disturbing you, Your Highness," Chief Minister began with a ceremonial bow. "I was hoping I could have a word with you before you retire for the night."

"I thought I made myself clear," the king replied as he washed his hands in the ceramic bowl that had been placed under a decorated awning. "I don't want to have a word with anyone. Matters of state will be dealt with in due time."

Chief Minister tried not to reveal his horror at seeing how dirty and scratched the king's hands had become. "Of course, Your Highness, but I believe there are some matters that require more immediate attention."

The king lifted his eyebrows, but did not respond. He dried his hands on the cloth by the bowl, turned his back on the minister and began his walk towards the palace.

Chief Minister did not want to invite royal wrath, but he had to try to reach his king. He would have to take his chances. Decision taken, he wiggled his toes quickly to undo their numbness and ran to catch up.

"You are persistent," the king mumbled without turning to face him.

"My apologies, Your Highness. I do not mean to be. But I do believe the issue is pressing."

The king turned around and considered the man standing before him. The rain was a gentle drizzle now.

"You may speak," he decided as he resumed his brisk stride.

"You are too kind, Your Highness," Chief Minister answered as he exhaled with relief. He had to jog in the wet earth to keep up. "I wanted to suggest that . . . perhaps it might be time to introduce the prince to the people."

The king wheeled around and stared at his minister with incredulity. "Are you mad? We are still in mourning. You should know better than to suggest such a thing."

"Of course, Your Highness. You are, as always, correct," he stammered quickly. "But think of the community. They are desperate to celebrate. Have you not heard the singing over the past few days . . .?"

"I do not need to listen to monsoon singing! I ordered the community to mourn! These celebrations are an insult to the queen and her memory!"

Chief Minister dropped his eyes to the ground, praying he had not overstepped. The king towered over him with glaring frustration, then wheeled around and began trudging his way back towards the palace, leaving Chief Minister behind like a broken casualty.

As the king was about to fall out of earshot, however, Chief Minister heard what sounded like the glimmer of redemption. "You may follow," the king commanded gruffly without turning around.

Chief Minister exhaled, hiked up his wet robes and ran again, following his monarch all the way to the palace, through the central courtyard and into the Great Hall. When they approached the round marble staircase that led to the royal family's private chambers, he expected some kind of acknowledgment, but the king still did not say a word, so the minister kept following, not sure what else he could do. Chief Minister followed him all the way to the entrance of the king's bedchambers. A servant was waiting by the door, ready to help him out of his muddied clothes.

"What do you suggest?" the king asked as he turned to face the minister before entering his room. The sounds of celebration were streaming through the open windows. Palace servants had apparently become uninhibited in their celebration too.

"I would like you to bring the prince to the royal temple."

The king looked at his minister with silent eyes.

"It is time to formally introduce him to the Goddess Abhaya, the guardian deity of the royal family."

The famous Pearl Pillars that flanked the broad, gilded doors to his personal chambers shimmered in the evening light, strings of pearls lining the columns from top to bottom. The king sighed as he reached for a strand and fiddled with it.

"And you are certain that this cannot be postponed?"

The minister turned his head towards the window as he listened to the people on the other side.

"I am afraid not, Your Highness."

*

The king sat on his throne, tapping his fingers. He could not believe how quickly the procession had been arranged.

"Is everything ready?" he asked the servant by his side.

"Everything is in place, Maharaja."

"Where is Queen Mahapajapati?"

The words "Queen" and "Mahapajapati" did not seem to fit together, but there was no choice. The Sakya Kingdom required a queen and she was the most obvious candidate.

She was Maya's younger sister, a royal courtesan until then. She had been confined to the Women's Quarters for years, an invisible body abandoned in a harem on the other side of the palace. The moment she received the news of her sister's death, however, Mahapajapati rushed forward to step in before anyone could stop her. When the child was carried through the palace gates, Mahapajapati was there to pull him into her arms.

"The queen stands just outside the door, Maharaja. She carries the prince and awaits your summons."

"Fine," replied the monarch. He did not like the fact of her, but royal responsibility trumped personal inclination every time. When she was put forward as his new queen, he accepted without even looking at her.

The king soared out of the Lion Throne and threw the broad wooden doors of the Throne Room open himself. The new queen was right where the servant said she would be. She jumped as the doors whacked against their frames but recomposed herself quickly.

Mahapajapati knew that her face, her very existence even, upset him. She closed her arms around her nephew, dropped her eyes and waited for him to forget her. Embroidered robes sailed past without a second glance.

The torrential rains had come and gone a few times already that day. By the time the king stepped through the palace gates, a light mist was all that remained. The sun peered at him from between the clouds, twinkling against the floating dust. He looked up and whispered a small prayer to the Sun God, and then looked outwards and was stunned by what awaited him: the short distance between his palace and the royal temple was lined with hundreds of people, each one of us drenched in monsoon attire, diamond water drops shimmering all over. We had been standing there since the break of dawn, unmoved by the water that fell with intermittent insistence.

The king noticed my parents, standing together with everyone else, the little bundle that was me in my mother's arms. He smiled discreetly and promised himself to take the time to formally recognize my arrival before long. But the sight of all of us together, all of us waiting to see the heir—nobility and peasants side by side—made the weight of royal responsibility feel that much heavier to bear.

*

The procession towards the temple was led by elephants that were decorated with all their festival adornments. Vibrant silks studded with gems covered their tremendous bodies and massive anklets chimed melodically, their painted trunks swaying as they moved. The smell of camphor and sandalwood mingled in the air producing a luxurious scent that draped itself over the entire display. Flowers of every local variety were strewn across the swept ground.

The king was mounted on the chief of the elephants, his new queen and son floating behind him in a bejeweled palanquin carried by sixteen strong men marching in unison. Drummers pounded their instruments with hennaed hands, bringing to life sounds that were ordinarily confined to the caverns of the deep. The king moved slowly through this succulent display, his head lowered in humble recognition of the part he had been entrusted with. As he approached the temple gate, the king turned towards the community and bowed gravely while the queen and prince disembarked. The royal family then climbed the stairs together, stepped through the atrium and entered the clearing that led into the temple. We were left behind as we watched them disappear into the privacy of another world.

"I wish we could follow them," my mother whispered to my father from the side of the road.

"I know. I would love nothing more than to be in there with them, to see the prince blessed in that most sacred of settings."

"I hope it doesn't take too long. The weather is turning again," she said as she tightened her arms around me.

They both knew the temple well. It was built with an open courtyard. Blue stone tiles covered the floor in an intricate design that created an impression of flowing water. The goddess' sanctuary was firmly rooted at the center, draped by an extraordinary jasmine vine. The perfume produced by its small white flowers was so strong in the rainy season that my parents could smell it from the road. Directly in front of the sanctuary, a stone lion with fangs exposed stood to attention, facing the closed curtain and guarding the goddess within.

"I have an idea," my father whispered. He disappeared into the crowd without further explanation.

My mother tapped me as she paced, wondering what kind of mischief my father was planning now. Her feet were hurting. She had been standing for hours and she yearned for relief. A few minutes later, he returned, looking rather satisfied with himself.

"What did you do?" she asked.

"You'll see . . ."

A little boy was suddenly tugging at my father's robe. He was wearing a dirty cotton garment around his waist that presumably was once dyed green but now had become an indescribable earth color of sorts. His torso was bare and his nose was running. *A street child*, my mother thought to herself. He did have magnificent bronze hoop earrings. She wondered how he had gotten hold of those.

"I have news, Uncle" the little boy declared eagerly.

"That was fast," my father replied, genuinely impressed. "What did you find out?"

Before he could answer, my mother smacked my father on the shoulder. "Did you ask this little boy to spy for you?" she asked incredulously.

"Of course I did. He's very quick and he can get in and out of the temple without rousing attention. It's perfect!" He looked at the boy with approval and asked again. "Tell me what you saw."

The boy closed one nostril with his thumb and blew his nose into the street to free himself of the ongoing drip. He wiped his hand on his dirty clothing (even dirtier now!) and drew himself up with pride. "Well, the king showed his son to the priest and they talked for a bit, but I couldn't get close enough to hear what they were saying. Then the priest began to prepare the sacred fire. I think that's going to take a while."

The sacred fire was the source of all cosmic power. When we sat beside it, all kinds of magical transformations became possible. The priest would be sitting just below the goddess' sanctuary, reciting the eternal mantras he had been entrusted with from birth. His hands would be dancing around the fire as he chanted, swishing mysterious objects through the air, flicking his fingers and throwing in bits of rice at various intervals. The royal family would be sitting to the side, watching the performance that spoke of a time before time, until they were invited to receive the fire's blessing.

"All right. Run back inside and return with news as soon as there is more."

"Yes Uncle!" the boy declared, and he hopped away like a little grasshopper.

"What exactly did you promise him?" my mother asked, eyeing her husband carefully.

"Nothing terrible. Just a few of your famous sweets. He looked so bored, sitting by the road all by himself. I think he would have done it even without the promised payment, just to have something to do."

She laughed appreciatively and turned her gaze towards the temple, now enjoying the game too. Sometime later, they caught sight of a sneaky little body racing between the guards' legs.

"The royal family has received the blessing. They all have red paste and ash on their foreheads now. It won't be much longer."

"Wonderful!" said my father.

"And I saw Abhayadevi!" he added enthusiastically. "She was beautiful!"

"Was that the first time you've ever seen her?" my mother asked.

"I think so . . . I don't know. But it was amazing! The priest pulled the curtain aside just as I arrived. She was all dressed up!"

My father smiled. It was a special privilege to be in the Goddess' presence. She was the Goddess of Fearlessness and she protected the royal family. Her tremendous black stone body would have been draped in raw silk and decorated with elaborate adornments like a princess.

"Seeing her is a blessing for you," my mother explained gently. She placed her hand on his head and whispered a prayer, the touch taking the boy by surprise. He did not think to bow, clearly not used to affection. Sensing his discomfort, my father redirected the scene.

"Have they announced the name yet?"

"I didn't hear it, Uncle, but I'll go back and listen some more," he declared, even more eager to please than he was before.

"If you come back with a name, I will double the amount of sweets promised!"

The boy's smile broadened and he licked his lips unconsciously. He ran back to the entrance so quickly, he almost tripped and fell into the mud. Both of my parents gasped, but he caught himself and kept going without slowing down.

"I hope we don't get into trouble for this," my mother said. "What if he gets caught?"

"It's just a little fun, Pamita. The poor boy was bored. At least now he has something to do. And sweets to look forward to."

She looked at him uncertainly.

The sky was growing so dark, it was almost black. My father tried to calculate the timing of the incoming weather. The clouds were thickening. He breathed out with relief when he saw the boy darting back towards him. He hoped the ceremony was almost over so they could begin the journey home.

"Was the prince provided with a name?" my father asked as the little one skidded to a halt.

"I think so . . . but I am not sure. The king looked upset with the priest."

"Why would the king be upset?"

"How should I know?"

Fair enough.

"Well, what was the name?"

"I didn't catch it . . . But I heard the priest explain it: I think he said something like *The One Who Will Do Everything* . . . or something like that. Does that sound right to you?"

The One Who Will Do Everything? *What name could that be*, my father wondered to himself. He looked at my mother, but she shrugged with similar helplessness. And why would a name like that cause the king to be concerned? Neither of them could imagine what the problem might be.

"Hey look! They're coming out!" the boy cried. The crowd cheered as the royal family made its appearance at the entrance of the temple. They stood together on the stone steps with fresh vermilion paste decorating each of their foreheads. The drummers swung into position and were about to lead their rhythm back to life when a tremendous crack of thunder ripped through the sky. Everyone looked up and watched as Sakka, the God of Thunderstorms himself, shook the clouds violently with his bare, muscled arms. Within moments, the earth was barraged by buckets full of monsoon rain.

The rain was so swift and violent this time that the entire community broke into a terrified run. The little boy shot down the road like an arrow, yelling "I will come for my sweets later!" People were racing in all directions as Sakka launched his weather at them.

My father began to panic, looking feverishly around for refuge. I was too small to survive a storm and he needed to get us out of the way.

"Dandapani! Over here!" The king hollered.

My father turned and saw the king waving. Mahapajapati was making frantic hand gestures too. Without another thought, he steered my mother towards the atrium at the temple gate, my little body gripped against her chest.

"This is most generous of you Maharaja," my father expressed with relief as he helped my mother onto the landing ahead of him.

"Of course."

My father shook some the water off his clothes instinctively, but halted in mid-movement. They were standing in the king's presence. Right behind him stood his little sister, Mahapajapati.

The new queen.

He stared at her in wonder. She was wrapped in what seemed like endless layers of red cloth. *Maya's absence must be overshadowing every aspect of her new life*, he thought to himself.

His eyes dropped and he noticed the little being she was carrying in her arms.

The prince.

His nephew.

"Your son is beautiful," my father whispered in the hopes that it was the right thing to say. He did not want to trespass into the king's privacy, but there they were, all together on a tiny platform, with nowhere to turn.

"He is indeed," the king replied with an undercurrent of sadness.

"Did he receive a name during the ceremony?"

"He did," answered the king. "His name is Siddhattha."

"Siddhattha," he repeated as he savored the name. *The One Who Has Attained It All*, he now understood. "That is a very powerful name."

The king swallowed. "It is."

The king then peeked over at me. Recognizing the opportunity, my mother revealed my little face from under the blanket so that he could see.

"What about this one, Dandapani? Has she received a name yet?"

"Only just a few days ago, Your Highness. She is Yasodhara," my father answered with a proud smile.

My parents never expected their royal introduction to take place under such circumstances. They were cramped in a little space as rain banged against the roof. There was no fanfare and no audience. None of the features a royal introduction normally included. And yet it was precisely in that strangest of settings that the king took it upon himself to finally offer his blessing. He stretched out his right hand and laid it on my head, whispering words of protection in a moment of perfect intimacy.

My mother bowed in gratitude, but a moment later she was bursting with joy. "This is the first time you met the king!" she exclaimed as she squeezed me with delight. "In fact," she added as she looked over at the prince, "this is the first time that the two of you meet each other." She brought me closer to the prince until our two heads touched.

"Daughter, this is your cousin, Prince Siddhattha," she said with the exaggerated tone adults reserve for their children.

The king placed his hands on both of our heads and added, "May you be a comfort to each other all your lives."

*

The storm was growing increasingly forceful, cracks of thunder shattering against the sky. The king looked out at the now virtually empty road. One family was still there. The man was desperately tugging at his ox-cart, but the wheels had sunk into the mud. Every ounce of the man's strength was funneled into stringy arms that were trying to save what little he had. The woman held onto her two children like bundles of flat breads tucked by her side. The children were sobbing as the rain continued its assault. The man kept pulling, imploring his oxen to make the cart move, pleading with them to listen to him, to get the wheels out of the mucky glue.

The beasts tried with all of their might, yanking at the reins with their massive gray necks and their arteries swelling with blood, but they were not strong enough. Eventually they collapsed, the weight of the cart collapsing on top of them, smashing against both of their heads at once.

Before he knew what he was doing, the king raced into the rain and threw himself into the scene. My father was right behind him and together they struggled to save the oxen, to help the man who had been carrying the burden of his family on his own. The king labored and pushed, pouring all of his fears and worries into the moment he had launched himself into. He could not accept the name the priest had delivered during the ceremony. He did not want his son *to attain it all*. He wanted his son to become the next king. He needed his son to take the throne. The astrologers' pronouncement was haunting him all over again.

The area was turning into a marshland quickly. The men persisted, heaving back and forth in unison, creating a chain of human effort until finally the cart was ripped off its prey. The beasts had not survived the accident. The king stared helplessly at the scene, while my father stared helplessly at him.

The king was completely drenched, his clothes tightening around him with the weight of the water. His jeweled turban had come apart and had fallen in the mud. My father walked over and retrieved the decorated silk carefully. It seemed so much more delicate all undone.

"Your Highness, let me take you back," my father suggested.

But the king did not respond. He kept staring at the dead oxen at his feet and at the man who was bent down beside them, oblivious to his royal presence. The owner seemed to be trying to hold in his own despair as the rain slapped him. He had lost part of his livelihood. Of this the king was certain. The wife stood silently to the side, processing what the loss would cost their family, calculating future realities in her head. The children stopped crying. They too recognized the gravity of the moment, despite the water that continued to barrage their small frames.

This is suffering, the king thought to himself. This is what he was supposed to prevent his subjects from experiencing, but it was already here.

It had always been here.

A servant was beside him, offering refuge with a golden parasol. The king finally allowed himself to be led away, my father following quietly behind. The king promised himself to send two new oxen to the man's village in the morning. At least that much he could do.

And then it dawned on him.

Pain. Suffering.

That was the problem. That is what leads men to the religious life. Without it, men were content with the world. But whenever pain manifested, the mortal world proved not to be enough. If he could raise his son without him ever encountering real pain, maybe then Siddhattha would not feel the need to *attain it all.*

Maybe then his son would become king.

Adjustments

My childhood was spent playing in the palace compound with the prince and the many cousins of our extended family. The king refused to let the prince out of his sight, so determined was he to shield his son from the realities of the world. The family was provided with an open invitation to visit regularly instead.

On one occasion, we were invited to help host visiting envoys from the Zhou Dynasty. Every morning for weeks, the cousins and I raced over to the palace as soon as the sun burst through the morning sky, eager to discover what new delights the king would lavish on his illustrious guests. There were theatrical performances, concerts, acrobats, and comedy routines that kept us riveted for hours. But even more fascinating than the dramatic displays were the visitors themselves who spoke strange languages in high-pitched voices and wore costumes that dazzled and mesmerized. One woman in particular fascinated me with her long wrap-around, embroidered dress. I weaved between adult legs, trying to keep her in my line of vision. Each time she turned her head, the row of dangling jewels from her headdress chimed and sparkled. Her gait was so delicate, she seemed to float like a cloud fairy.

My spying eventually caught her attention and she had me summoned over.

"Our lady noticed you staring," her interpreter said.

"I'm sorry . . . I didn't mean to be rude . . ." I stammered with embarrassment.

"She wants to know if you find her pretty."

I gaped at him. "But . . . But she is *more* than pretty! She is the most beautiful woman I have ever seen!" I blurted out despite myself.

The lady whispered something to her interpreter and he nodded.

"Our lady would like to give you a gift," he said.

My eyes grew wide with surprise. *Was I allowed to accept gifts?* I wondered.

Before I could debate the question with myself, the woman flicked her wrist and revealed a fluttering treasure in her hand. It was a fan with a spine of dark wood lined with gold and studded with tiny emeralds. The paper was painted with a bright red background and a green dragon clutching a pearl in its fanged mouth.

"This is for you," her interpreter explained. "The dragon is one of our protectors. He holds the pearl of wisdom."

She whispered something again and he continued. "Our lady wants you to have this gift to remember her by. She wants you to guard your own wisdom just as the dragon guards the pearl."

I nodded meekly, unsure of what she meant. She smiled, twirled her wrist to close the fan and placed the gift in my little hands.

"If you practice, you will soon master the fan just as she does," the interpreter encouraged me. "Now off you go."

I stared at the beautiful lady a while longer, marveling at every detail of her gilded presence, and then bolted with the treasure clasped firmly to my chest.

The visitors eventually departed after many ceremonial farewells and we returned to being the small royal family we had always been. The palace, however, seemed faded and bland without our foreign visitors. They had opened the world to us with their tales and ornaments from faraway landscapes. But they were gone.

Sensing the emptiness created by their departure, the king invited us to share the evening meal with him in the open courtyard before we made our journeys home. The children were sent to one of the playrooms while the adults went to change. The servants busied themselves with preparations, draping the marble courtyard floor with long rugs and covering these with piles of decorated pillows so that everyone would have room to recline. They fed the doves, causing them to coo happily in their resplendent cages, and they inspected the tiled lotus pool at the center of the courtyard to ensure its surface gleamed.

When everything was ready, the adults were invited to return. They took to the cushions and sat together in small semi-circles while one of the servants was sent to fetch the rest of us from our unsupervised freedom. The king sat to the side with one of his ministers, finishing the day's affairs in confidence.

I had been running around for hours and was famished. As soon as I heard that the meal was being served, I tucked the fan carefully inside my clothing and raced out of the playroom before the others even heard the call. The rich aromas were marinating the air and my stomach was gurgling with insistence. I charged into the courtyard and slammed into one of the servants carrying a steaming dish. Amazingly, he managed to catch himself before anything spilled, but he growled as I scooted between his legs.

The servants were delivering a pageant of spectacular dishes: cashews stewed in rich cream, greens fried with onion and garlic, lentil soup bubbling over with warm spices, and countless platters of cooked rice garnished with saffron and herbs. It was the very definition of abundance and I stared at it all with dripping desire. When the fried breads were deposited just a hand's breadth away from me, it was more than I could handle. I grabbed one and stuffed my mouth furiously.

"Yasodhara!" my mother exclaimed under her breath. "What are you *doing*?"

I stopped chewing and stared at her. I could feel the oil slithering down my chin.

"What?" I asked.

My mother got up and pulled me into the corner. Unlike most mothers, she never reprimanded me in public. She knew how hurtful it was to embarrass a child, even if most people did not think it mattered.

"Daughter," she scolded with a whisper, "I have told you one hundred and eight times that you are supposed to wait for the adults before you stick your fingers into the food! *Especially* in the king's presence! No one eats before him! You *know* that! How could you act that way in front of everyone?"

She yanked my hair into place, straightened out my clothing and wiped away the trailing oil with swift efficiency.

"You have an apology to make. You are going to go to the king, touch his feet as I have taught you, and ask for his forgiveness. Is that understood?"

I nodded meekly.

"Now go!"

She stood back as I made my slow way towards the king all by myself, with everyone watching.

"Maharaja," I muttered in a tiny voice as I bent down at his feet, "I am very sorry for ..."

For ...? I could not remember what I was supposed to be sorry for. It had all happened so quickly! I looked up at him, but he just stared at me with a quizzical expression. I turned around and looked at my mother, hoping she would help me, but she just tapped her fingers against her crossed arms, waiting for me to do what she had asked.

I turned back to his feet and begged my mind to remember. *I am sorry because ... because ...? Oh, yes!*

"Um ... I am sorry for eating the bread."

The king seemed to have forgotten I was there because he had already returned to his discussion before I finished my sentence. I stayed at his feet a bit longer, not sure if I was supposed to wait for a dismissal, but when none came, I decided that I should just go. He did not seem particularly interested in me or anything I had to say.

I walked slowly through the crowd of adults and took a seat at the far end of the courtyard by myself. A flock of giant bats lifted out of the surrounding trees and screeched their way across the evening sky. I watched them glide with their tremendous wingspan and wondered what I looked like to them, seated and small, so far below.

The adults quickly forgot about me and returned to their discussions. Servants moved around silently, offering guests cups of steaming water perfumed with pink rose petals. The food, however, remained untouched as everyone waited for the king.

The boy cousins suddenly crashed into the courtyard. The prince, Devadatta, Ananda and Anuruddha created a racket with their entry that sent the doves flapping hysterically against their cages. Most of the boys threw themselves onto the pillows and stretched out their legs as though they owned the world. The prince, however, grabbed a fried bread and bit right into it. He walked over to me as he chomped.

"What are you doing here by yourself?" he asked.

I stared at him, my mouth hung open with indignation. He was chewing a forbidden bread right there in front of everyone! Wasn't anyone going to react? He was eating before the king said he could! No one said a word, except for one of the aunties who chimed away happily with a statement about his marvelous appetite. But that was it. No reprimand. No formal apology. Nothing. I could not believe it.

I ignored Siddhattha and stomped over to my mother with fuming exasperation.

"Mother! Did you see that?" I hollered as quietly as I could.

"See what?"

"*Him*! Siddhattha! He's eating the same bread I was eating and no one is saying a word!"

One of the servants had already rushed over to him and was wiping his mouth while he continued to chew. He seemed utterly oblivious to the injustice he was generating.

"Daughter, leave it alone. This is not the time," she whispered.

"What do you mean? Did you *see* that? Look!" I argued as I pointed. "Why does *he* get to eat and I don't?"

I thought my mother was going to let me have it at that point, but she gently reached for my hand and brought me closer instead.

"Daughter, he is the prince. It is different for him. You know that."

"But it isn't fair," I complained.

And then I saw Devadatta also stuffing his mouth. "Look Mother: even Devadatta is eating and no one's bothering him! *He's* not a prince!"

She looked over and sighed. Devadatta was pushing an entire bread into his mouth while his other hand reached greedily for more. "You are right, little one. Devadatta is no prince."

"So why does he get to eat and I don't?" I demanded.

"Sweet one, some things in life are just like that. The rules are not the same for boys and girls. You have to learn to accept the difference."

"And boys just get to do what they want?"

"Not quite ... Boys have other things to learn," she replied enigmatically.

"But it's not fair!"

She looked over at me with the kindness of understanding. "Perhaps ... but that is just the way of things sometimes. Let it be now, Daughter. The king will begin his meal soon."

"But ..."

"Yasodhara, let it be. Patience."

*

After a good show of pouting and a solid meal, I dusted off my pride and joined the cousins in the garden for more play. I took out my fan and practiced opening and closing it with a flick of the wrist, but it would not work. The fan always wound up lopsided somehow, as though it refused to obey me.

When the night grew colder, Queen Mahapajapati ushered us back inside. She led the children to the Throne Room where the king would eventually join us. He had a pile of exotic gifts that he promised to distribute if we were good.

I wandered into the room distracted by my fan. Devadatta and Ananda, meanwhile, spotted one of the juggler's balls in the corner and were fighting over it. Other cousins were chasing each other in the corridor. The prince, however, was standing quietly in front of the Lion Throne, staring at it.

"What are you thinking about?" Mahapajapati asked Siddhattha as she walked up to him.

"I am thinking about Father's throne. Why does he sit there, Aunty?"

"Because your father is king and that is where kings sit." She pulled at a thread from her wrap that had gotten caught on one of her bangles. The jewels were always catching at things, making movement a frustrating enterprise. She never understood the point of all the decoration.

"But why is Father king?"

"Because *his* father was king."

"But why was his father king?"

Mahapajapati took a deep breath. "Because his father was also king." She finally freed the jewel from its snare. She shook her arm to give the bangles some room.

I put the fan down and watched the conversation with some foreboding. Devadatta and Ananda were in a full tug-of-war behind me. Ananda became distracted and Devadatta seized the moment to yank the ball right out of his younger brother's hands. Ananda flew backwards and landed on his bottom with a crash.

"But why was his father also king, Aunty?"

"Because all the men in your family have been king." She thought that would bring the line of questioning to an end.

"Oh."

But it did not.

"Well, why do kings sit on thrones?"

He certainly is an amazing little thing, she thought to herself. She had never known a child with so many questions. "Because the throne shows that he is higher than everyone in the land. He sits above us all."

"But he isn't higher than everyone."

Mahapajapati looked at her nephew with a curious expression. "What makes you say that, child?"

"Well, is he as high as the priests and the sages?"

"No. You are right. He is not higher than the priests and the sages. Our teachers are higher than the king, but the king rules the land they live in. So they are both high, but in different ways."

"Oh," replied the prince thoughtfully again. "So Father is not the highest in the world."

"No. I suppose he isn't, little one."

Siddhattha was quiet for a moment. The throne was the most elaborate seat in the kingdom, built out of solid gold and in the shape of a tremendous lion whose head roared out of the top. Palm-sized rubies shone out of the lion's eyes, the hand rests were the lion's paws and the seat was covered with real lion skin. It was the only place in the entire palace Siddhattha was prevented from claiming as his own.

Sensing his thoughtfulness, Mahapajapati took a chance. "When you become king, little prince, that seat will be yours." It was what the king would have wanted her to say.

The prince was quiet. She hoped he was imagining himself as king, seeing the future everyone was eager for him to grab with both hands. But instead, his eyes twinkled with alarming mischief.

"Well, why don't I just take the throne now?"

Before she could stop him, he bounded up the steps and threw himself onto the forbidden seat, beyond himself with excitement about the taboo he was breaking in plain view.

"I am king now, Aunty! Look at me! I am king! I am higher even than Father now!" He jumped and twirled, his dirty feet stamping the one spot in the whole kingdom he should have been terrified of touching.

Mahapajapati's hands flew to her mouth, as though stifling a scream she could not voice. She was horrified, but she had no tools with which to reprimand him and she did not dare approach the forbidden throne herself. *This was precisely what was wrong with his upbringing*, she screamed to herself in her head. It is what she worried about day and night. The king had ordered her to raise his son without any limitations. He was terrified of the predictions that were made during his son's birth and had convinced himself that if Siddhattha never suffered, he would never leave. He convinced himself—and tried to convince everyone else—that he could raise his son to become a king without having to raise him as a man. That somehow, the man and the king could be kept apart. And now his son was dancing on the throne, daring her to reprimand him. Daring everyone. Mahapajapati raised her eyes to the ceiling and begged Maya for the wisdom she knew she needed. There were so many things wrong in their household and she was given so little power to counter any of it.

Just then, the king arrived. His eyes fell upon the scene and all of our eyes fell upon him. He could not believe what he was looking at. There was his son, the prince he was desperate to make into a king, dancing on the Lion Throne with obscene irreverence as though he were Krishna dancing on Koliya's head. The order of the cosmos was being overturned with the smear of his son's little feet.

Siddhattha threw himself into one last twirl (for his father's benefit no doubt). When the movement came to its natural conclusion, he stood on his royal stage facing all of us, his chest heaving with the thrill of exertion and his feet planted wide and strong, the lion head peering over him with its gaping mouth.

Siddhattha understood full well the scandal he had produced. He maintained his position with a glittering smirk, holding his ground in his kingdom of trespass.

King Suddhodana exploded.

"WHAT IN ALL THE GODS' SACRED NAMES ARE YOU DOING ON **MY** THRONE???!!! GET OFF OF THERE AT ONCE, OR YOU WILL GET THE BEATING OF YOUR LIFE!"

The prince froze. I dropped my fan, causing it to clatter on the cold stone floor. Mahapajapati clutched at her heart. The king had never yelled at his son before. Everything was always "yes," until it had become a deafening and angry "no."

Siddhattha looked around the room at all the faces looking at him. It felt as though we had all stopped breathing. Even Devadatta was silent, while Ananda had a look of wild panic on his face. The rest of the cousins, who were still in the hallway, peered into the room cautiously. Siddhattha remained perfectly still as he looked at each of us in turn, but when his gaze reached his father, he began to cry. Confusion and pain were written all over his little round face.

At the sight of his son's tears, Suddhodana's anger slipped from his shoulders and fell to the floor. He raced over and pulled Siddhattha into his arms. He held him with all of his passion and buried his face on his son's shoulder.

"I am sorry I yelled at you, Son," he whispered as he rocked him in his arms. "I am so sorry!"

Suddhodana felt ashamed for the first time. Not just for the violent rage he had allowed himself to reveal in front of everyone, but for all the fear he felt crippling his heart. Fear that no matter how hard he tried, his son would never be king. Fear that his son would choose a life of religious homelessness instead.

"Son," he said as he pulled back to look at his child, "are you curious about the throne? Do you want to sit on it *with* me?"

Siddhattha looked at his father quietly and then turned to look at the looming Lion Throne.

"Come," he urged. "Come sit with me. It will be yours one day." He took his son's hand and stepped towards the forbidden seat. But Siddhattha remained where he was. He did not want to sit on the throne.

The Great King Suddhodana dropped his shoulders in resignation, turned around and walked away, his jeweled sandals chiming with empty notes. Mahapajapati shuffled quietly behind, playing the role of dutiful wife she knew was expected of her. The cousins stared absently for a few moments, but soon lost themselves in play again. Devadatta and Ananda picked up their argument where they had left off—an argument that had begun the day Ananda was born and that would continue for the rest of their lives.

But I could not go back to my games. I looked at Siddhattha who stood alone in front of the throne he had tried to overturn. His clothing was disheveled and his little turban was coming loose at the edges. One of his earrings was missing. I picked up my fan from the floor and walked over to him. The great lion bared his golden fangs with threatening domination as I approached.

I took Siddhattha's hand into mine and did not say a word.

4

Durga

We were playing in a palace garden one afternoon. The boys were showing off as usual, displaying their skills in archery, prancing about with their bows strapped over their shoulders, unconditionally convinced of their own superiority.

"It's a good thing you girls have us around," Devadatta taunted. "You should be grateful."

"That's right," Anuruddha added. "Without us, you wouldn't be safe."

The boys were taking turns shooting at the mark they had installed at the other end of the garden, applauding themselves each time one of their arrows landed on target. They commented on every detail of every shot with exaggerated enthusiasm, all the while looking over at us to ensure we were paying attention.

"That one really sank in well!" young Nanda cheered as he watched his older cousins succeed. He was Mahapajapati's son and he was forever caught between the towering shadows of his family members. He did not even try to shoot himself. Instead, he was commissioned with the task of retrieving the arrows; he spent the afternoon running back and forth between the archers and their targets like a well-trained dog.

Devadatta welcomed Nanda's comments with a satisfied smirk. There was nothing he loved more than praise. But when he looked over at me, he realized I was annoyed instead of appropriately impressed. The one thing Devadatta could not stomach was irrelevance; it didn't matter what kind of reaction he received so long as it was a strong one. If I refused to be impressed, it would have to be something else, but he would not rest until he got some kind of a rise out of me.

"What's wrong, little cousin?" he taunted as he approached. "Are you intimidated by us? Or is it that you wish you could join?"

"I have better things to do than play your silly games!" I retorted, having taken the bait, despite my better judgment. I hated the social limitations girls were forced to endure, and he knew it well.

"If you think these games are silly, why are you still standing here?" he pressed on. His eyes were glittering with intensity, making me feel like a trapped animal as he closed in.

"I can do what I want. Leave me alone!" I answered defensively.

He took a step closer and loomed over me, his height hiding the sun and blocking out the light. I wanted to get away, and yet at the same time, my pride was pushing me to stand my ground. To win.

"What are you going to do if I don't leave you alone?"

His mocking tone cut me like a knife and morphed whatever fear I had left into self-righteous fury. I raised my hand and was prepared to strike when Siddhattha suddenly materialized by my side. He hadn't come out with us initially, but here he was, standing beside me. He caught my arm in mid-air and lowered it gently.

"Why do you always have to be so mean, Devadatta?" Siddhattha asked.

"This has nothing to do with you!" he answered defensively. "Yasodhara was bothering us. She was interrupting our archery practice!" he complained. "I have every right to bother her back!"

He suddenly sounded so small, his self-confidence having melted into a puddle by his feet.

"I see," said the prince. "Well, by all means, then. Continue with your archery practice. It will be a pleasure to watch."

Devadatta was taken aback. He had not expected such a response. He expected a fight. He *wanted* a fight (which he almost received from me). He always did.

A shadow of an idea flitted across his conniving face.

"You know what, everybody?" Devadatta announced to the group standing around him. "My mother says that Siddhattha has never been taught a thing!" Turning back towards the prince, he goaded further, "You probably don't even know how to string a bow, do you? The king is so afraid you'll break that he won't let you near a weapon. You've probably never even touched one!"

Ananda, who had been watching the scene with increasing concern, reacted with surprising ferocity. He rushed forward and pushed his older brother with both hands. "Shut up!" Ananda yelled. "Mother didn't mean it that way and you know it!"

Devadatta was taken aback by his brother's intrusion and stared at him for a moment as though trying to decipher where the source of his brother's reaction lay, but in the end, he decided that Ananda was simply not worth his time. Without comment, he flicked his brother to the side as though he was swatting a fly and returned his attention to the two of us.

"Father is going to beat you when he hears about this!" Ananda hurled at him defiantly. Devadatta glared at him and his little brother folded right back into his shell.

Devadatta placed himself directly in front of Siddhattha, his legs spread wide. "You probably don't know anything at all, do you Siddhattha?" Devadatta chided. "My father says that you'll never become a man because you haven't learned anything. No one's taught you a thing. Maybe you *should* stay a while and watch us shoot? It might do you good to see what a man looks like in action!"

Although my temper had quieted with Siddhattha's arrival, these last insults were too much for me. I stepped forward before Siddhattha had a chance to respond and ripped the bow right out of Devadatta's insolent hands.

"You think *you're* a man?! You're nothing like a man! You're just a disgusting little worm!"

Devadatta was caught off guard by my reaction, but his own anger quickly rose up to meet mine. "What are you going to do with that bow, Yasodhara? You think *you* know what to do with it? Or are you confusing it with a stirring spoon? You know you can't cook with a bow, right, little girl?"

He repulsed me, causing me to lose all sense of reality. "I can shoot an arrow better than you can, you pathetic little creep!"

Before Devadatta could respond, Siddhattha stepped between us. "This has gone too far. Yasodhara, give me the bow and we'll go back inside. I saw Cook preparing some sweets this morning. We don't need to be fighting like this."

For a brief moment, I considered dropping the bow and walking away, but Devadatta quickly returned me to my rage. He ignored Siddhattha's attempt at diffusion and began to howl with exaggerated laughter instead.

"YOU are going to shoot an arrow? Are you kidding??!! This is too good! Oh please, please do it! I can't wait to see you in all your glory!" He was clutching at his stomach, howling with cruelty. "Please save me from my misery! My insides hurt from all this laughter! I won't be able to take it much longer!"

The other cousins began to laugh too. All of them except for Ananda, who was on the ground where he had fallen, defeated by his older brother's abuse. And Siddhattha, who was standing next to me, watching. I turned to look at him and held his gaze as I thought about what I should do.

I hated Devadatta. Someone had to make him pay.

Siddhattha put his hand on my shoulder. "Yasodhara, don't do this. Let it go."

"No. I will do what I want."

"You've never used a bow in your life," he whispered.

"I will be just fine," was my reply as I shrugged him away.

I lifted the bow and tried to close my mind to the sounds of laughter surrounding me. I tensed every muscle, beads of sweat forming in anticipation. I placed the arrow along the side of the bow, aimed at the mark the boys had been using, pulled the string back as I had seen others do hundreds of times before, and with a silent prayer on my lips, released the arrow in what I hoped was a perfect stroke.

I expected a rush of air and a whistling sound as the arrow sped dutifully towards its mark. I expected cheers and strong pats on the back. I expected to hear the arrow sink into the X that marked the spot. But none of that happened. The arrow twanged against my hand and shook like a broken lute. A painful vibration shot up my untrained arm as the arrow twirled towards the ground and flopped at my feet.

Devadatta had won.

I could not look up. I could not even look at Siddhattha, whose soft kindness I could feel reaching towards me. I could not meet anyone's gaze. I turned around and bolted out of the garden as quickly as my little legs could carry me, covering my ears to the heartless laughter all around. I tore through the palace gates, banging the Earth Goddess with every step, and did not stop until I was home.

*

My mother was sitting on the floor by the fire, pounding down an apricot pit when I charged into her. I threw myself into her arms with all the drama that is youth's privilege.

"Oh my," she cried out as I flung myself into her safety. "What has gotten into you?"

I could not answer. I sobbed onto her shoulder, dampening her delicate clothing with my tears, wiping my nose along her arm as only a child can do and as only a mother can receive. Eventually, though, I told her everything.

She listened quietly while she held me in her arms. When I was done, she did not reply. Instead, she got up and turned her attention to the pot that was cooking over the fire. She dipped a wooden spoon in and tasted. Whatever she was brewing, it put a smile on her face. She then returned to her seat, picked up her tools and continued attacking the apricot pit. She did not address anything I had said.

I peered into the bowl and watched her hammer down the hard pit methodically. "What are you doing?" I asked, looking for a new way to converse with her.

"Preparing a face scrub. You are welcome to try it with me if you'd like."

"What's it for?" I wiped my nose against the back of my hand.

"It clears the skin. Makes me beautiful," she said with a sly smile.

"Oh . . ." My mother was beautiful already. "An apricot pit can do that?"

She laughed. "No, not on its own. Once I have it down to a rough powder, I will stir in some honey."

"Honey?"

"Oh yes! I bought some at the market the other day. A merchant from the Northern Kingdom was selling big jars of it! He said it came from bees that live high up in the mountains, very far from here. He said the honey-catchers climb great boulders by rope to get it and that they have to dangle in mid-air while they pull the honey out. Can you imagine such a thing? I paid a fortune for it!"

She kept pounding away at the apricot pit, grinding it down into smaller and smaller pieces in her bowl with what seemed like growing excitement.

"Aren't you going to say something about what I just told you?" I finally begged. Where was my scolding? Waiting for it was worse than receiving it and I just wanted to get it over with. She was supposed to tell me how temperamental and proud I was. Remind me for the hundred-and-eighth time that I needed to walk away from such situations and not hold onto them until I self-destructed. But she did not say any of those things. Instead, she just kept pounding.

"Aren't you mad at me?"

She stopped.

"Mad at you?" she asked. "What for?"

"For being stubborn. For not walking away. For fighting with the boys and making a fool of myself!" I blurted out dramatically.

"A fool of yourself? When did you do that?"

"*When?*" I repeated. "*When?!* When I told Devadatta that I could shoot an arrow as well as he could. I had no idea what I was doing! Mother, it was totally humiliating! They laughed at me!"

She put down the grinding tool and finally gave me her full attention. "Their laughter must have been terrible. I am sorry you had to experience that. And of course you are stubborn and temperamental. You need to curb those tendencies. But there is nothing to be angry with you about."

"Why not?"

"Because, Yasodhara . . . You were not wrong." She looked at me with a very serious expression on her face. "In fact, you were entirely right."

That was the last thing I expected to hear.

"What do you mean?"

"What I mean is, girls *are* just as powerful as boys. The only reason you could not launch your arrow is because no one has ever showed you how. But it wasn't because you are not *capable*. There is a world of difference between the two."

"But it wasn't even just that," I complained, barely processing what she was trying to teach me. "The boys were making fun of us and telling us that we can't even protect ourselves. That we need *them* to be safe, to do the fighting for us!"

My mother looked at me but did not answer right away. Instead, she got up and poured some of her steaming brew into ceramic cups. She handed me one and settled back down with her own. She took a moment to appreciate the feel of the cup in her hand, blowing softly at the heat rising from the surface.

"Daughter, there is no way around some facts," she eventually said. "There are times and places for things. In some ways, men do the fighting for us. It is true . . ."

"Men like Devadatta who are going to lord it over us and make us pay for being girls?" I demanded angrily.

My mother sighed and put down her cup.

"Why does he have to be so mean, Mother?"

"Darling, I know he can be mean, but you really do need to develop more patience. Devadatta's father is a very difficult man. The cruelty you see in him is just Devadatta's hurt coming out. You know that. You've seen how his father treats him."

"But Ananda has the same father and he isn't like that at all!"

"No, he isn't. He is his brother's opposite. Ananda's hurt comes out in a different way. He is afraid of standing up, while Devadatta does not know how to back down. They are extremes of each other, but they are both suffering. You must be patient with Devadatta when he gets like that. He is your family and he will be in your life all your life."

I crossed my arms and huffed. I would never accept him, no matter how many years I had to be his cousin for.

"But this isn't about Devadatta. You need to see beyond him right now. This is about something much more important. You need to understand something about who you really are."

"Who I am?"

"Yes. Who you are as a woman."

"But I'm not a woman," I said with some embarrassment.

She smiled again. "Well, in some ways you aren't. That's true. But you are in the process of becoming one. Perhaps it is time you started taking yourself more seriously."

"What do you mean?"

"It is time for you to realize that women *can* fight. That women do. Just because we aren't taught to use weapons does not mean that we have no power."

I stared at her with wide-open eyes. The healing aroma of the ginger wafted out of the cup and reached for me. I stayed perfectly still as the heat stretched out to caress my cheek.

"A woman's power is not about handling weapons or going to war," she continued, "although sometimes it can be that too. But a woman's power is something else. It is not something you can see or measure. It is not in our muscles, but it *is* in our bodies. It is subtler than male power, but it *is* fierce."

She looked at me with a piercing gaze, almost willing me to understand the depth of what she was trying to teach me.

"You think there is power inside me?" I mumbled shyly.

"Yes, Yasodhara. I do." She placed her hand against my belly and added, "it is right here."

I closed my eyes and let her hand fill me. And then a new question rose to greet me. "How did you learn about this?"

She smiled. "My mother taught me the same thing when I was about your age. A long time ago. She told me stories about goddesses who were filled with a power of their own, who fought their own battles and lived in the high mountains by their own rules. And she taught me that I was them and that they were me."

She took another sip. "Those goddesses probably live not too far from where the bees made this honey." She motioned to my cup. "Taste it."

I took a sip and experienced a burst of sweetness unlike anything I had ever known before. The texture was thick but silky.

"What is this?" I asked. "Milk and turmeric and ginger and ... what's that other taste?" I wondered almost to myself. "Is that the honey that makes it so sweet? It's wonderful!"

She smiled appreciatively.

"You were right to fight Devadatta, Daughter. Women are much more powerful than he seems to know."

I put the cup down and focused on her knowing face. "We are?"

"Yes, we are. Our power is not always obvious, but it is there, inside of us. We have a great blaze of fire in our wombs that is the source of all of our strength. When you challenged Devadatta, you were telling the truth. You were speaking from the fire of power that all women carry inside them. Devadatta was the fool not to see the truth. *You* were right."

I tried to absorb this new perspective the way the milk had absorbed the honey.

"And by the way," she added, "today, *you* were the one protecting a boy, weren't you?"

"Huh?"

"You fought Devadatta to protect Siddhattha. You already know exactly what I am telling you. Boys are not the only protectors in this world. Sometimes we are the ones protecting them."

I leaned back against the wall.

All of that anger I had felt ... there was nothing wrong with it after all? I put my hand to my belly, just as she had done a moment earlier and tried to feel the power she was describing.

"Mother? Who are these goddesses you mentioned? Can you tell me about them?"

She smiled. "I thought you would never ask."

*

A long time ago, a terrible buffalo demon named Mahisa Asura was determined to overtake the heavens. So he dedicated himself to meditation and the practice of austerity for hundreds, even thousands of years, waiting for one of the gods to notice his efforts and reward him accordingly. Eventually, Lord Brahma's throne shook with the heat produced below and was compelled to respond. He descended from the heavens in his golden chariot pulled by celestial swans and asked Mahisa Asura the purpose of his zeal. The demon prostrated himself at the god's feet and asked for the boon of immortality.

Every demon asks for immortality. And every god knows they will. The demons are greedy by nature, always asking for more than the universe is permitted to give. "You know I cannot give you that, Mahisa Asura," Brahma responded patiently. "Ask for something else." Mahisa Asura pondered a moment and then, with a chilling gleam in his eye, requested that he be made so powerful, no man could ever kill him.

With the wisdom that only experience can provide, Brahma agreed. "Very well. You will meet your death at the hands of a woman instead."

The arrogant demon exploded with cackling delight. There wasn't a woman in the ten-thousand universes that would be able to conquer him! Inside the trap of his delusional mind, Mahisa Asura had achieved the impossible and become immortal.

Immediately, he swept into the heavens and threw all the gods out. He took over the Divine Palaces and installed demons at every gate. He took over the earth too, destroying the temples, terrorizing the priests and ransacking every last remnant of the gods he hated.

The gods were no match for his strength, causing them to escape in a flurry. They ran to the base of Mount Kailash and begged the mighty lord Shiva for an audience. He welcomed them into his sanctuary and listened quietly to their tales of anguish. When they were done, Shiva's fury blazed like wildfire, igniting each of the other gods around him, one after the other, until they had become a volcanic conflagration on the verge of eruption. When their bodies could no longer contain the lava bubbling within, it hurled out of them with earth-shattering force. Light exploded out of each of their foreheads and met at a still point between them, a ball of celestial power that no human would have been able to look at and live to tell.

When the dust settled and the light faded, Durga was standing before them.

She was magnificent. Striding atop a tremendous mountain lion, she faced the gods in her beautiful silk dress, decked in jewels, her thick black hair bound like a rope down her back. She smiled knowingly, eighteen arms in all directions.

Awed by her breathtaking presence, the gods fell at her painted feet. They implored her to fight on their behalf, to defeat Mahisa Asura and save the world from impending destruction. They bestowed an array of cosmic weapons into her many awaiting hands. She accepted the challenge with the exhilaration of a natural warrior and turned towards the heavens emitting a blood-curdling roar. The ten-thousand universes shook with the reverberations.

Moments later, she was floating before Mahisa Asura and his evil entourage in the sky, challenging him to battle. One look at her and he was laughing. "Who are you to challenge one so great as me?" he boomed. "You are just a woman, delicate and small. You are no match for me!"

She did not answer. Just fixed him with her cold, hard eyes.

"Come now," Mahisa taunted, "Let's not be so serious. Love is what you were made for. Put down your weapons and let me show you what a real man is capable of doing with you. Lie with me!"

Durga did not flinch.

"I have not come here for play. I have come to fight," she responded with unshakable resolve. "Raise your sword."

Mahisa Asura laughed, seemingly incredulous at the woman's arrogance. Who did she think she was? Did she not realize how powerful he was? But Durga remained as still as Mount Meru, watching her prey with lethal eyes.

"Demon," she whispered.

He looked up at her quizzically. He had no means of recognizing who she really was.

"RAISE YOUR SWORD!!!" her voice blasted against him.

He lifted his now trembling hands to his face. Desire morphed into hatred and he bellowed back with the madness that coursed through his demonic mind, "War is what you want, little girl? Well then, war is what you will have!"

He sprang at her like a crazed animal and unleashed the greatest battle in cosmic history. With each blow that fell, mountains toppled, oceans were whipped into whirlpools, and the earth itself seemed on the verge of cracking in half. But it was clear who the winner was before it even began. Mahisa shrank progressively until Durga managed to jump onto his back in her dainty sandals. She grabbed him with her steel fingers, raised one of the many arms at her disposal and sliced off his head as easily as if she had been slicing a cucumber. Not one hair of hers had fallen out of place.

Durga is never disheveled.

*

A few days later, a maidservant appeared at our door and begged my mother to follow her. Chief Minister's wife was in labor, but the midwife had yet to arrive. They needed help.

Without a moment of hesitation my mother swooped through the house making arrangements. She ordered specific herbs to be sealed into jars, clean cloths collected, her favorite knife wrapped and bound. She even pulled out her collection of precious oils, her hands moving quickly through the bottles, selecting concoctions that only she could decipher. The servants tried to keep up with every instruction she launched into the air.

"I think that is everything. Make sure to wrap the bottles carefully so that nothing breaks," she hollered as she raced into her room to change. "The parcels have to be sturdy to keep up with my pace!" There was not a moment to spare.

"You stay here, Daughter. Tell your father where I've gone when he returns," she ordered as she pulled her braid together. One of our servants kept trying to help her, but she was in too much of a hurry for intervention to be possible. I watched her soar through each movement with commanding grace. Of all the women in the village, she was the one summoned when others needed help.

"Can I come with you?" I asked timidly, half of my body hiding behind the doorframe.

She stopped and looked at me. "You want to come?"

I shrugged under the weight of her gaze. "Can I?"

She stopped for the first time since she had been summoned and sat down on the edge of her bed.

"Tell me why . . ."

I knew that the answer I would give would determine the outcome. I rummaged through the drawers of my mind for the truth.

"You told me the other day that I was becoming a woman. If that is true, isn't it time I learned what being a woman is like?"

"Ah, I see . . ." She let herself settle into the softness of the bed and leaned back. Taking a moment, despite the rush.

"Come here," she said as she patted the spot beside her.

I sat down stiffly, carefully.

"Daughter," she said as she took my hands into her own, "if you come with me, you need to be prepared. Birthing is not easy. And it is rarely safe. It might not go well and there will be a lot of blood. Are you certain that this is the right decision for yourself?"

I pulled back in surprise. "Are you asking *me* to decide?"

"Well, if you are nearing womanhood, it is time you make decisions for yourself. Are you prepared to enter the realm of the Birth Goddess?"

I tried to imagine the whirlwind of a birthing chamber: the noises, the blood, the screams. I had heard stories and knew some of what to expect, but I also knew that I did not know the experience at all.

"Yes. I am."

*

We crossed the town as quickly as we could, weaving our way between pedestrians, cows, and lumbering carts. Shopkeepers haggled with their clients while children played games in the dust, and monkeys spied from rooftops hoping to steal a morsel of food, but we could not stop to look at any of it. I knew that if I tarried, my mother would send me home without a second thought. So I kept my eyes on her heels and followed her through the streets as best as I could, avoiding the many piles of animal dung that had dropped along the way.

Eventually we reached Chief Minister's stately home. We could hear his wife in the throes of birthing before we even got inside. My mother handed her bags to the first servant she saw and aimed like an arrow for the birthing chamber without waiting for an invitation. No directions were required: she just followed the sounds.

She pushed open the door and entered the space as though the room was her own. I followed and closed the door behind me as quietly as I could. Chief Minister's wife was panting with a wild look of fear in her eyes. A young servant was standing behind her, frantically waving large peacock feathers in an attempt to cool her mistress down, but it was clearly not having any effect. Chief Minister's wife was drenched with sweat.

"How are you doing, Lalita?" my mother asked softly. She pulled a small cloth she kept tucked under her sash and wiped the woman's face.

"I'm frightened, Pamita. Where's the midwife?"

"She's on her way."

"This doesn't feel right! Something's wrong! This isn't like the last time when Kaludayi was born—it may have been many years ago, but I remember the pain of birthing like it was yesterday and this is not the same!"

"Tell me what you feel."

I leaned against a table with my arms crossed protectively over my chest and listened as the two women exchanged knowledge of things unknown to me—details about body parts and feelings surrounding inner mysteries. My mother was not a midwife, but she had watched many women give birth and I could see her concentrating thoughtfully as she tried to interpret the clues. She looked worried.

"Yasodhara, check the water on the fire to ensure it is boiling. If not, add some wood to bring the temperature up."

"Yes, Mother," I obeyed quickly. I was glad to have something to do.

"And once you are done with that, find out how to get some straw in here. We need a lot more before the bleeding starts."

My stomach lurched. Perhaps I wasn't as ready as I thought.

By the time I returned with the straw, the room was buzzing with activity. More pots were on the fire, servants were bustling about, and clean strips of cloth were being laid on the table. My mother had single-handedly brought the room to life. The birthing chamber had been transformed into a realm of directed activity. It was no longer the deadened space of fear we had encountered when we had first walked in.

The midwife finally arrived and my mother breathed out a sigh of relief. She could see the danger on the road ahead and she knew a set of hands more skilled than her own was required if the delivery had any chance of success.

The midwife did not apologize for her delay or even attempt to explain it. She walked right past us and began unpacking her things, laying them out on the table and pushing our carefully arranged strips of cloth to the side. She checked the water on the fire to ensure it had reached the proper temperature, threw a few herbs in as it simmered, and looked around the room to ensure everything was where it should be and that nothing was where it shouldn't. My mother did not introduce herself, nor did she expect an introduction in return. She simply stepped aside and waited to see what would come next.

I had heard stories about midwives but had never watched one in action before. They were said to be creatures of the margin, living along the edges of our lands in isolation. But whenever life begged for an introduction, midwives took center stage without a glimmer of hesitation. Midwives watched the Goddess of Childbirth trample around the threshold of existence, sometimes taking more than she gave. They meandered between the lines of life and death as no one else could, their hands plunging in and out of bodies and speaking to souls as they dangled in the in-between. The women who were capable of dancing with such fiery deities, of moving through them and embodying them as their hands swam through the blood of childbirth—they were not the women of everyday.

The midwife's attention directed itself to the woman laboring. She walked over to her bed and tugged at one of her long gray chin hairs, curling it around her finger unconsciously. She then placed her hands on the swollen abdomen, searching for life beneath the surface with fingers that prodded without apology. She muttered a few words under her breath—to herself or to the deities she shared her profession with, she did not say. When she was done, she returned to the table and fussed with her tools.

"What's going on?" Lalita called out desperately. "Did you feel the baby?"

"You will have to be patient, My Lady," the midwife answered without looking up.

"But what's going on? I feel like something's wrong!"

The midwife looked up and locked eyes with her patient. "Something *is* wrong. It will be up to the Goddess now." She returned to her instruments without offering anything more.

My mother approached the laboring woman. "Be brave, my friend. You know that these moments do not belong to us. You must be brave."

Chief Minister's wife nodded and closed her eyes, silent tears dripping down her cheeks. She understood that the God of Death was hovering right outside the door. Whether or not He chose to enter . . . that was not for any of us to say.

The birthing waves coursed through her body with increasing momentum and soon they crashed against her with violent intensity. The woman clung to my mother's hand and cried as her body ripped itself apart. Blood was falling out of her in big clumps, red splatters landing against every surface. The straw was soaked with color and her screams filled the room. Although I initially had tried to make myself useful, as the situation progressed I found myself tied to a small square of floor, watching with horror as the laboring woman tore apart.

My mother pulled away for a brief moment and walked over to me. "You don't have to stay for this part if you don't want to," she whispered.

As soon as she offered me permission to run away, I knew that I would stay. I shook my head and re-joined her in the work. I stood on one side and my mother stood on the other, both of us holding Lalita's hands warm and tight. We then lifted her to her feet and helped her lean into a squat, her body falling onto ours for support. The midwife lowered herself between her legs, doing all she could to catch what would come.

We absorbed her screams together as she tore through the Goddess' realm with broken wings. I held her until it was done.

*

The sky was breaking into a new day by the time we emerged from the room. My mother went to speak with the family. My father was standing by Chief Minister's side, bracing him for the news to come. Kaludayi, Chief Minister's son, stood stoically at his father's side. He was my age, but he seemed to have gotten older overnight. Perhaps I had as well.

I did not want to impose myself in the privacy of the family moment, so I slipped out the back door for the garden. It was a small space with a lovely bed of vibrant flowers all along the sides. A tree filled with blossoming yellow buds stood in the middle, creating a soft glow around itself, and a swing hung from one of its branches. I tucked myself onto the seat and wrapped my arms around myself, letting my feet dangle beneath. There was a soft carpet of lost petals covering the garden floor—remains of what had once been beautiful and now had passed.

"Are you ready, little one?" my mother asked, startling me with her sudden appearance.

"Oh . . . yes," I mumbled as I struggled off the swing abruptly. I was in such a daze. "How is the family?" I asked, as I tried to reorient myself back to the present.

"Very sad, which is to be expected. They have two funeral arrangements to make. It is time for us to leave."

"Right."

Every muscle in my body ached. I followed my mother home.

Festival Day

My life changed the day womanhood announced itself on my body. I became part of a new category and I was given new rules to live by. Bleeding required confinement and according to the elders, confinement was necessary because I was polluting when I bled. I had never thought of myself as polluting before. Thankfully, my mother did not either.

Not long after my first Bleeding, I summoned the courage to ask her about it. My mother and I were walking through the back garden, picking herbs for her next concoction. I asked her what she thought of the pollution others accused us of.

"Oh goodness, Daughter! You can't believe everything the elders say!"

"What do you mean? I thought we were supposed to listen to the elders." *Wasn't that precisely what the elders were for?*

She bent down and examined what looked like yellow weeds growing between a few rocks along the footpath. She rubbed the tips between her fingers. "How marvelous," she whispered.

"What?"

"Look," she said as she cupped one of the flowers in the palm of her hand. "Wild mustard flowers. I didn't plant these." She admired the little plant a while longer and then stood back up, wiping her yellow-tipped fingers along her gardening apron.

"You know, Daughter, the elders have many things to teach us and we must respect their wisdom, but sometimes ..." She stopped as she searched for the right words. "Sometimes ... things are a bit more complicated than what the elders are willing to say."

"What do you mean?"

"Well, a woman's Bleeding means many different things. It isn't just one thing."

"But I thought things mean what the elders say they mean."

My mother smiled at my consternation. She reached out and adjusted my hair, bringing the wisps that had escaped my braid back into place.

"Well . . ." she began. "What do the elders say about our blood?"

I recoiled at the directness of her question, but the topic clearly did not embarrass her.

"They say that our blood pollutes us. That's why we have to stay apart," I recited with attempted courage.

"Good," she said, like the teacher she was. "Now, what happens when we bleed?"

"We stay in our rooms, apart from the men. So we don't pollute them."

"Careful," she cautioned. "What we *do* is we stay apart. *Why* we stay apart is the question we are trying to answer, right?"

"Oh . . . right."

"And watch where you're stepping! You just walked right over my coriander!" I looked down at my feet and found a stringy plant staring at me from between my toes. I lifted my foot and apologized quickly.

"So," she continued, "what happens when we stay apart? What do we *do*?"

I thought back to the one experience I had had of confinement so far. What *did* we do? "I don't think we do very much actually," I said uncertainly. "We just sit together, right?" I maneuvered around the next collection of bright green plants more carefully.

"Do we have to work?" she asked.

"Work?"

"Yes. Do we have anything that we need to take care of in the household during that time, the way we are doing right now?"

"Well . . . no. But that's because . . ."

"Forget the word 'because' for the moment. The question is, what do we *do*?"

"Well . . . nothing. We don't work. We tell stories. We talk. And we rest. There is nothing else *to* do."

As soon as the words came out of my mouth, I realized what she was trying to show me. Spending time together during the Bleeding was one of the most intimate experiences I had ever shared with my mother. Since our Bleeding came around the same time, we sat together. We talked for hours with no one to disturb us.

But she was not finished with her questions. "And is there anything else we really *can* do during that time?"

"What do you mean?"

"Well, when we bleed, are we capable of moving around?"

"Of course not! We have to sit until the blood stops." The idea of moving around while bleeding was absurd . . .

And then I understood all over again.

"You see, darling," she said with a smile, "what we *do* is one thing. How the elders explain it can be quite different. They can say that it is because we are polluted, but that is not necessarily what is happening."

She bent down to examine a purple basil plant. She plucked off one of its leaves and handed it to me, inviting me to experience it. I rubbed it between my fingers and smelled.

"But then ... the elders have been lying to us?" I asked as the scent of basil filled me with its luxury.

She laughed. I could only think in black or white. The shades of gray she was suggesting were confusing.

"No, I don't think so, little one." She picked at the basil, choosing the leaves she needed with care. She handed them to me in a pile. "Only that *what* we do and what others say about it are two different things. The elders may *say* that we are polluted during our confinement, but it has never felt that way to me."

She pulled out a few unwanted weeds and tossed them to the side. "It is so sensible after all. Haven't you noticed? Our bodies require the rest, so we really cannot do things any other way. We have to settle down during the Bleeding. And when we do, we get to share our lives with each other."

"But then ... there is still something I don't understand, Mother. Why would the elders call us polluting? Why couldn't they just say what you said instead?"

She looked at me thoughtfully. "That is a very good question, Daughter."

"I don't want to be called polluting."

"I don't blame you. I don't know why they've chosen those words ... It is certainly unkind."

"I think it's more than unkind. I think it's cruel!" I blurted out, as the pain of the word "pollution" hit me.

My mother looked up at the sky, as though the answers she sought were floating somewhere above her. She rubbed her back with the back of her hands and waited, but the answers did not come.

*

I smile now when I think about how impatient I used to be. I wanted answers before I could even finish articulating the questions. I never had the patience to wait.

Nothing challenged my patience more than the unrelenting requirements that went into getting dressed up. My pleasure was to throw a simple cotton dress over my head and quickly tie my hair up with a piece of string. But after I had become a woman, everything changed. I was not allowed to be so impatient anymore. I had to take my time and delicately prepare the face that I would present to the outside world. The first time these changes became real to me was just before the spring harvest festival. I raced for the door, but my mother managed to get there before me. It was going to be my first public appearance since I had become a woman. She caught me by the sleeve and pulled me right back in.

"Oh no you don't Daughter!" she announced. "You will not be leaving the house looking like a hurricane today! We have work to do."

First was the bath.

She marched me outside and brought me to the natural pool of water that lay on the outer edge of our garden.

"Off we go," my mother declared as she yanked my clothing over my head. "I think we need to boil this piece of cotton before you ever wear it again!" She tossed my favorite dress to the side and plunged me into the water like a leg of lamb into a stew.

I sank under the surface, hoping she might forget me there, but she was, of course, right behind me, pulling me back out before I had a chance to swim away. She had her robe hiked up between her legs and her sleeves rolled up.

"Let's begin, shall we? There are layers of grime to remove and it won't be easy."

She had laid out a series of thick dried leaves that we used to scrub ourselves with, each one dedicated to a different part of the body. There was a rough, large one for the arms and legs, a round one for the back and chest, and a soft one for the face. She used each of these in turn, scraping away accumulated dirt until I felt raw and painfully exposed.

"Mother! It hurts!" I complained. "Do you really have to do that?!"

"Dear, you are as calloused as a peasant farmer. This is not the kind of skin a young Khattiya is meant to have. If you insist on tearing through nature like a wild boar, then you have no choice but to accept the consequences. I can't believe how dirty you manage to get yourself!"

She plunged me back into the water, rinsing away the dead skin she had just torn from my body and then retrieved me in time for the next step in the unforgiving process. My head was a nest of tangles. She pulled her fingers through my hair repeatedly, picking the strands apart and making disappointed clicking sounds with her tongue each time she came across something that did not belong on my head. I squirmed and screeched, but she ignored me. She had no patience for the way I treated my hair.

Back into the water I returned with her hand on my head this time. She kept me under for a few seconds, using the movement of the water to help undo the damage. I resurfaced, she picked and pulled, dunked me, and pulled me out again.

My mother then brought out a new soap she had prepared for the occasion. She had combined beeswax and grapeseed oil with hundreds of fresh jasmine petals. Lathered onto my skin and into my hair, it produced a delicious scent. I could tell how proud she was of this new recipe when she saw my face lift with pleasure.

After the last rinse, she finally considered me clean. I climbed onto the water bank with relief, but then was met with more scrubbing—this time it was sesame oil. I kept my eyes squeezed shut as her hands rubbed my skin unapologetically. Another handful of oil went into my hair, lubricating each and every strand into liquid sunbeams. By the time the procedure was over, I thought I smelled like food, but my mother was satisfied.

"You can take a few minutes while your skin absorbs the oil, but don't get too comfortable," she chided. "We have to finish your hair and get you dressed. There is still much to do."

She collected her things and walked back towards the house with what I was sure was a spring in her step. There was nothing she loved more than getting me clean.

I wrapped myself in the linen cloth she had left behind and lingered a moment by the water. I felt oily and lethargic. I lifted my eyes up to the trees around me. The pool was surrounded by tremendous banyan trees that my mother decorated with long sheets of bright red silk. Sometimes she painted the bark with red and orange dye; I could see traces of the colors lining the trunks. My mother often visited these trees in the early morning and prayed to them for us. She asked them to remember her family and safeguard our welfare. I stared at the towering tree-beings and wondered what it would feel like to have my own family, to have my own husband and children, and to sing to the spirits on their behalf.

When I returned to the house, I found my mother sitting where hair torture was traditionally inflicted. She had a comb, a handful of pins, and a full tray of flowers beside her.

Phase two was the hair.

I took my place in front of her and felt her trace the comb slowly through my lubricated strands that were now the color of deep darkness. The knots that usually infested my head were all gone, so there was no flinching from me and no fighting from her. The comb moved over my head like a sailboat over a calm sea.

She took her time, combing long past the necessary point, humming to herself softly, enjoying the moment of intimacy. I could feel her smile warming my shoulders as the comb glided through my perfectly clean and untangled hair. This was motherhood as it is dreamed of but so rarely touched. She took her time.

Eventually, I felt my mother's fingers get to more serious work. Ordinarily, my hair would have been bound with a simple braid, but today was special. My mother wove sections of my hair together into intricate layers and then brought all of them together into one thick braid. Combined with the many flowers she added to the design, the effect was masterful. Unfortunately, it felt like my skin was being pulled into my ears. I kept scratching my forehead, hoping to alleviate the strain and she kept slapping my hand away.

The last phase was the dress.

"I have a surprise for you!" my mother sang happily. She walked over to her bed and pulled a package out from under it.

"What is that, Mother?" I asked.

She looked at me with a sly smile, her fingers resting lightly on the ribbon holding the package together. She then pulled at one end of it with a theatrical wave of her arm. A magnificent length of silk cascaded out of it.

"Oh my goodness!" I exclaimed. It looked like the ocean had tumbled into the room. I had never seen anything like it. It was brilliant turquoise, embroidered with white cranes placed in various poses all along the edge.

"Am I going to wear that?" I asked.

"I have been saving this for you for a long time, Daughter," she said to me. "I found it a few summers ago in the town market." She caressed the silk as she spoke. "The moment I saw it, I knew it was yours. Your father could have killed me, it was so expensive! I can still hear his words: 'Pamita!' she thundered, imitating his voice and bunching up her shoulders the way he does, making me laugh. 'That's much too expensive! It will be stained before you know it!'"

She leaned against the bed and rubbed her back. "He tried a dozen different arguments, but he knew my mind was made up. He never had a chance."

I picked up a section of the material carefully, unsure of how to receive such a gift. I had never realized how important this moment was for her.

"But Mother," I stammered, "I think Father was right. It *is* too expensive. What if I do get it dirty? You know how terrible turmeric stains can be."

"Then don't eat anything with turmeric!" she replied light-heartedly. "But don't take your father's protests too seriously. He wasn't really worried about the cost. He just didn't want to imagine you all grown up. You know how he is. He wants his little girl to be his little girl forever. But there is a time for everything in life. There is a time to be a little girl and there is a time to become a woman. Your time for womanhood has arrived."

Before I could object again, she threw the material over my shoulder and began wrapping me up in it, moving it around my body in intricate patterns that I could not follow. When she was done, I realized what she had been envisioning all this time: the material was arranged in such a way that the cranes seemed to move along my body, encircling me.

"Do you remember the story of Shakuntala?" she asked.

I nodded.

"Shakuntala was one of your favorite stories as a child. You made me tell it to you over and over again. Shakuntala was abandoned at birth in a field, but the gods kept her safe. A flock of white cranes descended from the heavens to sit by her side until she was found.

"Every time you saw a crane as a child, you asked me if they were looking for her. In this dress, surrounded by the white birds of your imagination, I knew you would feel safe."

I stared at myself in the mirror, amazed by the transformation she had created. I would survive this day. My mother had made sure of that.

*

I stepped out the door of my mother's room, walking as carefully as I knew how, examining each step I took, trying desperately to avoid letting my dress become caught between the open toes of my jeweled sandals. I bumped right into my father's chest.

"Oh!" I exclaimed. "I am sorry, Father."

My father stared at me.

"I'm sorry," I repeated, "I was concentrating."

He remained silent.

"Father, why won't you answer me?" I finally demanded with a slight stomp of my feet.

My father lifted my chin with his hand and looked at me with pained tenderness. "Your mother was right. You are a woman now." Nothing in the world was softer than my father's heart.

"I promise I won't ruin the dress, Father. I know how worried you were about the expense!"

"I am not worried anymore, Daughter. You are ready for it." He looked at my mother who was right behind me. "Shall we go?"

I heaved a long sigh. "Do I really have to do this? I feel so strange dressed up like this. I don't even know how to walk in this thing! Can I please just stay home instead? Couldn't you tell them that I wasn't feeling well?"

My parents smiled at each other knowingly, as though they expected nothing less. "This is serious!" I declared with frustration. "The cousins are going to laugh at me when they see me! And I am probably going to trip on the stairs."

"You are going to be fine, Daughter," my mother intervened. "The cousins won't laugh. But if they do, it won't be because they think you look funny. I know it is difficult the first time, but you will soon discover how pleasurable it is to feel beautiful. This is your time, Daughter."

I wasn't going to get out of this. I knew that. But I was disappointed just the same.

"You better start moving towards the carriage now, little one," my father said. "At the rate you're going, it will take you the better part of the day to get there!"

My parents laughed. Forgetting any attempt at daintiness, I hiked up my dress and stomped my way towards the carriage. I arrived in no time at all.

*

We got to the festival in time to make the required entrance. Tents were erected at various points along the edges of the field, each one the station of a noble family. In honor of my recently declared womanhood, we were invited to join the king that year rather than erect our own.

My parents walked slowly through the field towards the royal station, their faces beaming with pride as they showcased their daughter as a woman for the first time. I had seen other girls paraded this way by their families over the years; more often than not, they enjoyed the attention. Some twirled in their new outfits or took a few elegant hops up the steps to their seat. Most seemed delighted by the looks they received, despite the fact that this included the hungry eyes of many young men. I, however, felt none of this. The procession had me twisting my fingers into painful knots, cutting off my circulation until the tips became blue and I was forced to release them, only to start all over again.

"Don't fiddle so much," my father whispered as we walked. "Try to enjoy the moment!"

I was incapable of looking up. I continued to twist my fingers instead. There were just too many eyes on me. I could feel the marriage calculators bearing down—women making inquiries about my potential for their sons, sons making inquiries about my potential for themselves. What part, exactly, was I meant to enjoy?

"Yasodhara, enough with the fingers!" my mother eventually commanded under her breath. "If you can't enjoy this, at the very least pretend. I will not be embarrassed in front of the entire community!"

I unclasped my hands and tried to do as she demanded, but the moment I raised my eyes, the heat of the stares pushed them back down. I did not fidget again, but kept my arms unnaturally rigid by my side. How I longed to reach my seat and be done with the spectacle.

I succeeded in reaching my floor cushion without any embarrassing mishaps. I climbed the golden steps without tripping, sat down without falling over and kept my legs appropriately covered throughout the process. By the time I had settled down, I was exhausted. The short walk from the carriage to my seat had drained me of every ounce of concentration I had.

Moments later, the drums announced the arrival of the royal carriage and I had to undo my carefully crafted seated position to stand up with everyone else. Flower petals rained over the field as the royal family made their way through the crowds. The prince followed the royal couple up the steps of the platform, all of them dressed in matching cream-colored silk, white jewels sparkling along their necklines and the edges of their robes. The crowd watched intently as the family took their positions on the stage and in the cosmic order of their lives. Trailing behind them and arriving just a bit out of step, was the Second Prince, Nanda. He was supposed to be walking together with them, but he kept missing his cue. He was distracted by the jewels sewed into his clothing and kept stopping to examine them in the glittering sunlight. A servant had to nudge him forward. When he finally stumbled onto the stage, Mahapajapati was exasperated.

Siddhattha, however, was perfect. I could not take my eyes off him. He was only twelve years old, just like me, but he looked like a man. He carried himself with comfortable dignity, not a hint of hesitation in his demeanor. Once he had taken his seat, I watched as his dark eyes scanned the area, looking for me on the podium as I knew he would. News of my transformation had slipped out of our home and into every other like water threading its way out of a broken vessel. Everyone knew that I had been changed and *he* knew I would be sharing the royal platform with him because of it.

But the prince was not expecting to find me as I was. When his eyes caught sight of me, they widened with surprise. He had never seen me dressed up that way before. He did not seem to have considered what my transformation would imply.

Or at least, what the transformation would mean to him.

I had become a woman and in that briefest of glances I understood that he understood what it meant. I dropped my eyes instinctively, embarrassed by all the questions raised in that fleeting moment that I did not want to face. Was he horrified? Did he think I looked ridiculous? Did he even care? I did not want to know the answer to any of those questions.

Especially the last one.

My fingers were tied in knots again, parts of my dress caught between them, wrinkling the perfect fabric. I could not decide if I should I look up or not. I was desperate to find out if he was looking at me or whether his attention had already pulled him elsewhere. I twisted as I agonized, not knowing what I should do. Eventually, the anticipation suffocated me and I had no choice but to raise my eyes.

I found him looking right at me, smiling the kind of smile that felt like the warmth of the sun after a long shadow. I exhaled.

"Stop fiddling, Ananda!" I turned to my left and saw Ananda and Devadatta in their family tent right beside us, one of them being reprimanded for attempting to squeeze his fingers into his shoes. Both brothers had been pushed into hard wooden sandals and Ananda was clearly miserable because of them, furiously scratching inside his sandals the way I kept scratching my forehead. Ananda was trying to look distinguished, but he just didn't have it in him. He was too sweet for such hard footwear. Devadatta, however, looked proud in his ridiculous attire. He sat on his seat as though he was the king himself and he sneered at his little brother with contempt. After yet another parental reprimand and a slap against the back of his head, Ananda abandoned his blistered toes and looked away with a heavy heart.

I felt so bad for him. I wanted to fight Devadatta for him, but there was nothing I could do from where I was. I caught Ananda's eye and gave him a sympathetic smile, which he appreciated.

I turned my attention to the entertainers who had just arrived on the field. A series of snake charmers were taking their places, settling into position in preparation for their performance. Each one was dressed in a different color: gold, red, green, purple. They wore large golden-hooped earrings and their turbans were attached with magnificent silver clasps. They opened their baskets in unison, pulled out their flutes and began to serenade the cobras out. Most of the cobras were up and swaying within minutes, but the boy in green who was closest to our tent was having some difficulty. His snake would not comply. It seemed to be asleep in its basket and would not rise on command. The poor boy was desperate to get it to wake up, but no amount of cajoling would get that cobra out of its nest. Devadatta started jeering at the young performer and soon others joined in. The poor boy was mortified.

I had no patience for Devadatta's arrogance. There was no reason to be so cruel. I shifted around in my seat as I wrestled with my annoyance. A few pebbles were pushing into my folded ankles and I swept them out from under me. If only there was some way to get back at him.

And then . . . an idea.

I picked up the little stones and stared at them. Most were jagged and rough, but one of them was soft and smooth. I moved it around between my fingers as I pondered the possibilities.

I leaned to the side and scrounged around, trying not to elicit any attention from those around me. *There must be a stick around here somewhere.* I kept patting the floor hoping to find what I was looking for, but nothing met my searching fingers. And then I remembered one of the decorative clips my mother had placed in my hair. I reached up and very carefully pulled it out. Thankfully, it was not holding anything in place. It was just for show and it was the perfect size. Flat and thin.

I tied a section of my silk wrap to one end of the clip, made a loop and tied another part of the silk to the other. I then set the stone on the inside edge of the cloth. I looked around to ensure no one was watching, and when the moment was right, I pulled back the cloth with one hand and pushed the clip forward with the other, aiming directly for Devadatta's insolent face.

The stone flew out of my hands with shocking speed and hit him right in the nose.

"Hey!" Devadatta screamed as he jumped to his feet. Everyone turned their attention towards him, wondering what had happened, but the evidence had disappeared as quickly as it had manifested.

"What's wrong with you?" his father hissed with embarrassment.

"Someone just threw something at me!" Devadatta complained as he rubbed his nose.

"You're imagining things! Stop bothering everybody and sit down!"

Devadatta was looking around with fury, searching for the culprit.

"I said, sit down!" his father threatened.

Devadatta obeyed, but he kept looking around with paranoid intensity. When his eyes reached me, I could not hide my grin. Or the impromptu sling in my lap.

"Was that *you*?" Devadatta mouthed the words across the tent to me.

I shrugged and opened my hands in a gesture of happy defeat.

"But ... how?" he demanded without speaking aloud, even more infuriated now.

My smile was as wide as the River Ganga.

*

I settled back into my seat with self-satisfaction and found both my parents staring at me incredulously.

"Are you upset?" I mumbled.

"Yes," was my mother's curt reply.

I dropped my head in shame. I never intended on getting into trouble and I certainly didn't want to upset my mother, particularly that day—of all days. Before I could make an attempt at some sort of an explanation for my behavior, my father leaned over and whispered, "That *was* a great shot though!"

I looked up at him and met his grin with my own. Apparently, Devadatta was not a particularly sympathetic victim.

"All right," my mother whispered. "That's enough. Thankfully no one saw you."

I glanced over at Siddhattha, wondering if he had seen my victorious intervention, but he was engaged in a conversation with his father. I was admittedly disappointed by that.

My mother took the clip out of my hand and undid the silk knots it was tied with. She winced as she reached over to place it back into my hair. Her back bothered her, but she refused to discuss it.

"I hope you are satisfied because that cannot happen again," she said.

"I know," I replied.

"You are on stage, Yasodhara. And you are a woman now. You must play the role you have been entrusted with. Understood?"

I nodded and straightened myself out.

"She really did get him, though, didn't she?" my father exclaimed proudly as he nudged her.

"Yes, she did," was my mother's reply. She was smiling despite herself.

*

After what seemed like an unending litany of festival performances, it was finally time for the grand finale when the field would be ritually plowed for the first time, marking the beginning of the season. The advantage of a long dress was that I could shift my legs around with some discretion, but even with those little stretches, I was sore with stillness. When I was finally allowed to move, I got to my feet with tremendous relief. My toes were tingling and my knees were aching, but I tried not to show it. I watched with everyone else as the king was summoned onto the field to take the first steps into the new season for us. He strode forward with his head held high, clearly relishing the moment. He wrapped the reins of the plow firmly around his broad hands.

He took his first steps and received the expected polite applause, but the king did not stop there. His strides got longer and he went further, and excitement began to mount. As the gray-haired king pulled the plow further and further, men began cheering while the ladies were swooning. He was only supposed to take a few steps, but he was eager to show off that day and there was nothing the subjects of Sakya loved more than to see their king in the fullness of his masculinity. By the time he reached the far end of the field, pandemonium had completely overtaken the crowd. Even the royal tent had gotten out of control and I was almost shoved off the platform by all the jostling. Everyone was carried away by the vision of their hero dominating the field.

Which meant that no one was paying attention to the prince.

For a rare and precious moment, Siddhattha was not at the forefront of public preoccupation. All his life, Siddhattha had been constrained, his every movement guarded and watched due to an astrological pronouncement that his father could not forget. As soon as he realized that everyone was preoccupied by his father's manly display, Siddhattha slipped out of the tent and into the woods on the other side of the field. I was just as preoccupied as everyone else, exultant as I was at finally being able to move my stiff limbs without reprimand.

By the time I turned to look for him, he was gone.

*

Siddhattha slipped into the forest behind the field and wandered slowly between the ancient trees. He moved through their realm cautiously, his fingers trailing across their bark, each step taken with care as he tested the forest depth. The light danced before his eyes, twinkling with transience, moving over the leaves and disappearing into blackness only to resurface again like sparkling fairies.

The air was soft and cool. The weight of the sun was lifted, but he wasn't cold. Insects chatted intermittently, creating a vibrant harmony of noises around him. There was so much life wrapped into the space between the trees, so much talking and humming, moving and living. Palace life bustled constantly, but it was nothing like this. The forest's movements were softer somehow. Less combative. And yet it promised something devastatingly dangerous at the same time . . .

Siddhattha listened for the guards or the anxious footsteps of panicked family members. He strained his ears, but the festival seemed miles away. Even if they had noticed his disappearance, where would they look? How could they find him when he was wrapped in the immensity of that shimmering green world?

A clearing lay up ahead. A soft blanket of grass was nestled under a delicate rose-apple tree. The tree reached higher than most, spreading its branches far and wide, creating an umbrella effect right over the empty spot at its feet. The tree's pink and white flowers were surrounded by bright green foliage, all of it dripping towards the floor like a cascading waterfall. It was the most beautiful tree Siddhattha had ever seen. And it seemed to be waiting just for him.

He sat down. Sunlight twinkled delicately all around him. He closed his eyes and breathed in the gentle fragrance of the rose-apples. He breathed out, silence deepening inside him. He felt like he was inside a dream, wandering inside his mind for the first time without anyone to interrupt. He was not sure where he was going, but he had taken one step and he wanted to take more. He suddenly wanted to wander inside his mind forever. The stillness felt like paradise.

But it was not meant to be. Not yet, anyhow. The guards were on their way.

Somehow, they had found him after all.

Surpanakha

When I was sixteen years old, a traveling theater group offered to perform a ten-day rendition of the *Ramayana* for the royal court. They had come all the way from the southern Tamil Kingdom and had been touring the countryside for many moons. We had been hearing rumors about them from traveling merchants and we were eager to see them for ourselves. When they finally arrived with their many horse-drawn carts filled with *Ramayana*-related treasures, the king was thrilled. He gave them access to one of his gardens and provided them with all the carpenters and tools they needed to create a stage worthy of the endeavor. When opening night finally arrived, the community flooded the palace compound, each one of us in our best attire, excited to savor the sensuous delights that only the stage could provide.

My parents and I were offered seats on the Royal Podium, just behind the king and his family. Piles of cushions were laid out for us—more than any of us could reasonably use. I shoved mine to the side and kneeled on the thick carpet with my legs tucked underneath. I straightened my back and craned my neck in anticipation, but the stage was a darkened landscape, shielding its mysteries from those of us desperate to see. I drummed my fingers impatiently against my knees.

"May I sit with you, Cousin?"

I jumped at the sound of Devadatta's voice. He was standing with regal formality by the empty spot beside me, dripping with some kind of noxious quality that I could not quite identify. I wanted to say no.

"Of course," I stammered instead.

"Lovely," he replied as he slithered onto his seat. I scooted to the side and bunched up my shoulders to become as small as possible, but he stretched out his body as though the podium belonged to him. When a servant arrived with a tray of drinks, he grabbed a cup for himself and waved the servant away before the rest of us had a say. I caught sight of Siddhattha, who was sitting directly in front of me, a gentle expression of understanding on his face.

"This is rather exciting, don't you think?" Devadatta asked in the hopes of directing my attention back to him.

"It is," I replied, my fingers fidgeting with a will of their own. "I wonder how long we will have to wait before it starts?" I looked at Siddhattha, but he was facing the front again.

"Well, if you feel restless, we can sneak away for a little walk together."

I recoiled instinctively, repulsed by his demeanor. He, however, was undeterred and only leaned in more. I was on the verge of jumping to my feet when a rush of dazzling light suddenly erupted out of the ground. A discreet moat of oil had been dug around the stage, so that when it was lit, the area was flooded with light in one quick burst. The flames licked at the air, causing everyone in the audience to gasp. I hadn't noticed until then how dark the sky had become. Now *we* were the ones in the shadows and the stage was like the sun.

An actor appeared dressed in simple blue cloth with a green sash tied around his waist. "Welcome Great Maharaja, King Suddhodana!" he thundered as the audience burst into applause. "It is our honor to present you with a piece of the *Ramayana*: the dramatic scene of Surpanakha!"

He took a theatrical bow, soaking up the applause with feigned humility. I clapped so hard, I almost broke one of the rings I was wearing.

"Of course, we would have loved to perform the entire story for you," he continued, "but as I am sure you all know, the *Ramayana* is much too elaborate for any of us to tell in one lifetime. One segment will have to suffice for our ten-day performance. We certainly hope, though," and here the actor took another deep bow, "that you will forgive our limitations. We know how cherished the *Ramayana* is in this kingdom. We will do our best to do it justice."

The king nodded graciously.

"As you all know, Lord Rama was supposed to be crowned king of Ayodhya, but due to a set of unfortunate circumstances, his father exiled him into the forest instead. Rama was joined by his beautiful wife Sita and his ever-loyal brother Lakshmana. Together, the three of them were forced out of the palace and into the wilderness for fourteen years.

"They had many adventures during that time, and it would take us fourteen years to tell them all. But the scene we will share with you is the moment when the terrible demoness Surpanakha makes her appearance. As I am sure you know, Surpanakha was a horrific creature, but when she discovered Rama in the forest, she fell madly in love. She tried to seduce Rama but she failed. Then she tried to seduce Lakshmana and that attempt failed too. Her fury at being rebuffed sets the rest of the *Ramayana* on its dramatic course. Indeed, without her, nothing else would have happened."

The actor paused to ensure his words had the desired effect. When he was certain no one was breathing, he put his palms together and bowed one last time. "It is her story that we now tell."

As he stepped away, the curtain lifted to reveal a beautifully produced stage. The wooden floor was transformed into a forest landscape, with every kind of greenery built into it. Birds chirped overhead and wild animals were roaring in the background just as a troupe of musicians walked in. The men were bare-chested, with their lower bodies wrapped in red cloth, trimmed with gold. They seated themselves in a corner, placed their magnificent drums carefully into position and began a rhythm that brought the sounds of ancient storytelling to life. Lute players soon followed, adding their sounds to the night air, and then singers joined, filling the garden with a beautiful high-pitched melody. The momentum was so carefully crafted, so hauntingly produced, that I did not feel time passing. I was carried elsewhere, to a time when time did not mean a thing.

And then Surpanakha walked onto the stage.

I gasped. She was not the terrible ogress I had grown up hearing about. She had changed her shape in the hopes of wooing the brothers and she was breathtakingly beautiful. She was wrapped in brilliant gold-colored silk and her long braid was punctuated by a whole bouquet of freshly cut flowers. She wore a glimmering crown and she was covered in jewelry that chimed with every step she took. Her most exquisite feature, though, were her eyes: they were painted with thick black lines that reached all the way to her temples.

Surpanakha took center stage and began to sing. Night after night, I watched enraptured as Surpanakha lived out her story. I had always hated her as a character. She was responsible for a war of epic proportions, the sister of the evil demon Ravana who abducted Sita and set the whole world on fire. But this troupe gave us a different version. Through their magic, she was becoming a tragic character instead. The Surpanakha I watched on stage was lonely and wanted to be loved. She tried to win Rama and Lakshmana, but they laughed at her, teased her, and even humiliated her. They toyed with her as they threw her back and forth between each other. I was horrified by their behavior and could feel others in the audience recoil with a similar aversion. Rama was supposed to be a great hero, a king who ruled with justice and truth. How could he have acted that way?

I thought people would raise their fists against this version of the story, but no one did. Night after night, the troupe transported us elsewhere, telling us the story from her point of view. Their rendition was so compelling, Surpanakha a character so sadly overlooked, that Rama had no choice but to take some of the blame. He was becoming a more complicated king in our collective imagination, while Surpanakha's voice was finally being heard.

"I'm back," Devadatta declared with self-satisfaction on the last night of the performance.

He slithered his way into the small space beside me without the slightest attempt at courtesy. I stared at him incredulously, sighed, and turned away. Surpanakha was in agony, having spent the previous evenings begging the men to love her, but they had treated her with cruel disdain. Tonight, she would make her final and most desperate plea to the men she hoped would love her. When the curtains were lifted, Surpanakha was on the ground with her hair disheveled. She then sang a song of torment that broke my heart.

Devadatta burst with laughter as she shed her tears. Without even thinking, I whacked him on the arm.

"Oh, come on, Yasodhara. You don't actually feel bad for her, do you?"

"Are you serious? Are you not paying attention?" I exclaimed, having taken the bait without realizing it. "Look at how sad she is!"

"She's a demon! Who cares?"

"*I* care! And so does everyone else in this audience, if you haven't noticed."

When Surpanakha could no longer accept the humiliation, she became enraged and raced to attack Sita. Lakshmana threw himself in between the two and before we had a chance to realize what was happening, he was hacking at her violently, slicing off her ears, nose, and breasts in a volcanic eruption of blood.

"Yes!" Devadatta cried out in victory, as everyone else clutched at their hearts.

Surpanakha wailed into the night as the curtain fell for the last time.

*

The ten days of performance had passed so quickly, I did not see the end coming. I wanted to watch for ten nights more. I could not believe how well the actors had performed, how mesmerizing the music had been, and how challenging their presentation. The story would never be the same for me.

When Surpanakha returned to Lanka, she told her brother Ravana of the terrible humiliation the brothers had inflicted on her. Out of revenge, he flew to the north and abducted Sita, which launched the war that is at the heart of the *Ramayana*. The speaker on the first night had been right: the *Ramayana* would never have been set in motion without her.

I could not go home that night. It would have been impossible to sleep. I slipped past the guards and made my way further into the royal garden, hoping no one would notice. I wanted to keep savoring the experience, to carefully record all the details in my mind so as to never forget any of it. I loved everything about those ten nights, with the exception of Devadatta's repulsive responses. But I would not focus on him and let him spoil what was one of the greatest experiences of my young life. I shoved him to the back of my mind and concentrated on Surpanakha and the devastating story of her loss.

I was so absorbed by my thoughts that I did not notice who was behind me until I felt a slight tap on my shoulder. I turned around and found myself face to snout with a tremendous white elephant. I jumped back in surprise. It took a moment before I realized that Siddhattha was seated on its back, his legs tucked behind the great beast's ears.

"Hello there, Cousin. I hope I didn't startle you."

"You certainly did," I replied. "Am I in trouble for being here?"

"I won't tell if you don't," was his mischievous answer. "Would you care to go for a little ride?"

"Do you mean up there?" I pointed. "You can't be serious! How do you expect me to get up?"

Siddhattha tapped the elephant twice and the great beast slowly lowered itself to its knees.

"Give me your hand," he said as he extended his own.

I looked around to make sure no one was watching. It would create such a scandal if anyone saw, but Siddhattha's eyes were twinkling and I could not resist. I tossed my sandals to the side, reached for his hand and climbed my way up the elephant's body, swinging around to sit behind him.

"You are going to have to hold on," he warned. "She really likes to sway!"

"Hold onto what?" I asked as the elephant got to her feet, throwing me into nauseating motion.

"Hold onto me!"

I grabbed his waist and squeezed my knees against the animal's back.

"Isn't there supposed to be a box for us to ride in? Why are we riding this way?" I called from behind him.

"I feel too far from the animal when I ride in one of those. I feel safer this way. You know what I mean?"

I felt myself sliding back and forth as the animal lumbered into motion.

"Not really . . ."

He laughed with delight.

We plodded along, moving from one garden through to the next via hidden pathways that connected the gardens to each other. Siddhattha knew his way around, guiding the elephant as we chatted. I never before realized how extensive the palace compound was. One could wander through the gardens forever. They were filled with flowers, lotus pools, waterfalls. And there were so many animals that I had never seen! Deer, monkeys, owls, swans. Gentle creatures everywhere. I even spotted a sloth hanging lazily in a tree!

As the sun was beginning to break through the sky, we came to the entrance of one garden I had heard about but never imagined I would see for myself: the legendary Peacock Garden. It was the king's private sanctuary—a garden that was exclusively reserved for members of the royal household. Siddhattha tapped the elephant twice behind the ear and the animal lowered herself to the ground.

"Shall we walk from here?" he asked as he hopped off.

I looked down. I didn't think I could hop quite as nimbly without breaking a limb. Climbing up the beast was one thing, but jumping down was much more intimidating. I looked at him with obvious concern.

"Don't worry. I will catch you."

"Are you sure about this?" The ground seemed very far.

"Trust me," he smiled.

I didn't think I could jump, so I tried to slide. It seemed to work at first, but within a few seconds, I lost control. I screeched and tumbled.

And landed right in his arms.

"Sorry," I mumbled with reddening embarrassment.

He did not respond, but just looked at me with that infuriating smile he always seemed to wear, so I pulled away and took a moment to smooth down my dress. I was rattled for a few reasons, but I could not admit to any of them.

"Come," he said. "I want to show you something."

He took my hand and led me into the privacy of the secret garden. We walked through dark passageways of breathtaking beauty that were wild and yet organized all at once. I had never seen anything like it before. There was something haunting about the space—like Surpanakha's song.

We reached the edge of the garden. It led us to a cliff that overlooked the entire valley. At the cliff's edge, there was a bench under an extraordinary asattha tree.

"This was my mother's tree," Siddhattha explained. "I wanted to show it to you."

I approached the tree and lay my palms against its trunk. It stretched high into the air with majestic grace. Its many layers seemed to enfold the secrets of the whole world inside them.

"It's magnificent," I whispered.

"My mother used to come here. She believed the Goddess was rooted here. In this very tree."

I circumambulated the tree as my offering, my fingers trailing the bark.

"I can see why," I said. "This is no ordinary tree. It is a tree that sees others. That invites you to see it."

"*Darshan*," he whispered. "That's what she always said."

I stopped circling and looked over the edge of the cliff. We were so high and could see so far. I took in a long breath of fresh, early morning air.

"We have a special tree like this at home, just in front of our house. I would love for you to see it one day."

But to this he did not reply.

The Choosing

Whispers were circulating. The prince was going to have to choose a bride and produce an heir of his own. He was already sixteen years old.

Of course, his age was not the real issue. No matter how much he spoiled his son, the king remained instinctively aware of his son's indifference to all things royal. The warnings he received when his son was born—the astrological pronouncements, the name the goddess had bestowed upon him, and his behavior in so many ways kept the king's stomach tied up in knots. Although the astrologers did say that there was a chance he would stay home and become a great king, deep down the alternative ate away at him. Siddhattha was simply not like other princes. He did not relish in the pleasures his station provided. Somehow, he always seemed apart, as though his heart belonged elsewhere.

Suddhodana missed Maya at times like these. What would she have said? Were the whispers something to listen to? Was it time for him to marry? He had a faint suspicion that she would never have forced their son into anything he did not want. Perhaps she would have made excuses for him, tried to convince him that their son was fine the way he was. That his sense of responsibility would emerge when the time was right.

But maybe not. Maya was not nearly as romantic as he was. She had been the practical one—much more than he had ever been. She was the embodiment of wisdom, whereas he was all soft compassion. He had been a much better version of himself when she had been around. Without her, he felt like he was half of who he used to be.

Maya would never have raised Siddhattha with such abandon; of that, he was certain. She would have been stern with their son in ways he simply could not be. She would have insisted he take up the burden of the throne from the day he took his first steps. Siddhattha would probably never have been so aloof about his role in their kingdom had she been there to raise him. What had he done to his son? The fear Suddhodana carried inside him was intolerable. He desperately wanted to raise a future king, but he did not know how to do it without her.

He certainly did not invite Mahapajapati to participate, although she was there. Always there. Watching, paying attention to dynamics he did not have the courage to see. The king never asked her what she thought or encouraged her to play her role. He sidestepped her each chance he had, accusing her of not being Maya when she should have been. Accusing her of not being the sister who died.

Members of the royal court were acutely aware of these personal dynamics in the king's household. The whispers grew louder as people began to worry about the kind of king this young man might turn out to be. Something needed to be done if Siddhattha was going to rule. Something needed to capture the prince's attention soon.

According to his very anxious ministers, marriage was the answer. They were convinced that the pleasures of marriage would open Siddhattha to the world. He would become more attached to his place and more concerned with the obligations of the throne. Marriage would anchor him to the seat he was supposed to take. Day and night, ministers hovered around the king, taking every opportunity to remind him that it was time the prince chose himself a bride. Eventually, the king had nowhere left to turn. The whispers were being hollered into his royal ears.

Convincing the prince to choose a bride, however, would not be simple. Everyone was aware of that. The prince was not an easy one to catch. The king and his ministers therefore hatched a plan that would entrap Siddhattha before he knew what hit him. They issued a proclamation across the land, requesting that all maidens of high birth present themselves to the royal bachelor seven days from thence with an offering. Although they did not explain the intention, it was obvious to everyone who heard it: if the prince was sufficiently nudged, he would make one of them his bride.

The trick, of course, was not to tell him about it until the very last minute. He otherwise risked packing his bags and disappearing (or disappearing without any bags at all) moments before the women arrived.

On the day of the Choosing, the ministers entered the prince's chambers to wake him with the news.

"Good morning, Your Highness!" Chief Minister announced gingerly as he pulled back the curtain surrounding the prince's ornate bed.

The prince sat up, feeling a bit disoriented by the sudden appearance of a retinue of gray-haired politicians in his bedroom.

"What are you doing here?" inquired the prince, as he rubbed the sleep out of his eyes.

"It is a very special day, Your Highness," explained Chief Minister, attempting to sound confident. The others were silent, but each one of them was staring at the prince intently, as though he was about to grow fur or change colors.

"What makes today special?" he asked, his curiosity—and suspicion—mounting.

"All the high-birth maidens of the Sakya Kingdom are arriving here today for your pleasure, Your Highness! They will await your presence in the Throne Room. They are bearing gifts in the hopes that one of them might please you."

The plan that was unclear a moment before was suddenly crystal clear to him. With not a little mischief, the prince asked, "Every maiden will be *here*? Just like that? They will all suddenly show up on the same day? At the same time with gifts?" he asked. "What an interesting coincidence, Chief Minister."

Chief Minister cleared his throat uncomfortably while the other ministers were suddenly looking elsewhere. No one dared look directly at the prince.

"Uh, well . . . Yes, Your Highness. Not quite a coincidence. Your sharp intellect is no match for us. They were invited a while ago . . . perhaps we forgot to mention it?"

The prince smiled.

"All right, Chief Minister. No need to worry. What should I be expecting?"

Chief Minister sighed appreciatively. "The ladies are here laden with gifts for you. As I am sure you have already surmised, your father hopes that one of them might please you sufficiently that you may make of her a bride."

The prince, still in his sleeping attire, pulled himself out of bed and tousled his long black locks lightly. "There is no way out of this, is there?" he asked.

"Unfortunately, Your Highness, there does not seem to be."

"Very well," he replied as a servant appeared by his side, prepared to dress him. "I assumed I would have to face something like this eventually. I will meet the maidens."

Relief spilled into the room and everyone applauded. The day would be a success (although Chief Minister would keep the prince under close watch just the same).

"We will leave you to your attendants. When you are dressed and ready, it will be our honor to escort you to the Throne Room." Chief Minister turned and was about to usher the others out when the prince cleared his throat.

"Just a moment, Chief Minister."

"Yes, Your Highness?" he replied, turning back around.

"I would like to make one adjustment to your plans, if you do not mind."

"Of course, Your Highness," Chief Minister replied automatically with a bow.

"I have no need for gifts," said the prince. "I have more than any human being could possibly want. I will not accept their offerings."

Chief Minister looked at his prince with a curious expression. "Not accept offerings, Your Highness?"

Siddhattha nodded silently.

"You realize, of course, that the community will be outraged. A future king must be willing to accept the gifts of his grateful community."

"I do realize that, Chief Minister. But if you expect me to participate in this production, these are my terms."

Stunned silence swallowed the room.

The prince continued, "I will, however, be very happy to *provide* the ladies with gifts instead. If you will bring up one of our jewel-filled caskets, I will distribute ornaments to the maidens who are taking the time and making the effort to present themselves here today."

Chief Minister looked at the young man standing before him, so determined and clear. The prince would not waver on this point. He was certain of it.

"There is no way out of this, is there, Your Highness?" Chief Minister asked with a knowing smile.

"Unfortunately, sir, there is not," replied the young prince with his eyes shining bright.

"As you will, Your Highness."

Chief Minister turned around and walked out of the room, still stunned but also slightly in awe. This young man was unlike any other he had ever known.

*

"You can't be serious!" I exclaimed. "I have to stand in line to present my face to the prince?! Do I look like some kind of prize?"

How could my parents ask me to participate in such an event? It was humiliating! To stand in front of the entire kingdom dressed up in clothes that turned walking into a complicated maneuver ... and all so that the prince could examine each one of us as though we were a pile of cooked foods prepared for his pleasure?

"Mother," I begged, "I really don't want to do this. Please don't make me go. This is embarrassing. I will do anything not to go!"

"I am sorry, little one, but a Royal Proclamation cannot be ignored. You have been summoned to the palace. You have to go."

How could the prince do such a thing? And how dare he do this to *me*? I secretly believed I meant more to him, and suddenly I was being lumped together with every other maiden in the Sakya Kingdom. My mother fussed around me, adjusting me in various ways, but I would not cooperate.

"Yasodhara, dear," my mother interrupted as she pinned the last of my wayward strands of hair, "don't you think the prince would notice if you decided *not* to go?"

"What?"

"The prince, dear," she explained as she continued her adjustments. "Don't you think he would notice if you *didn't* go?"

"Do you think he would?" the question out of my mouth before I could stop it.

She smiled and patted me on the head. From the moment I had heard about the proclamation, I had experienced a whole array of mixed emotions, but they were jumbled up in my mind and I had not taken the time to parcel them out. I thought the emotions were primarily of outrage, of righteous indignation, of insult.

But as I watched my mother hum to herself as she collected the hairpins and placed them back into their little treasure box, I realized what the leading concern had been all this time. I was not really concerned about the public scrutiny I was being asked to endure. I was concerned about something else entirely...

What if he chose someone else?

*

The trumpets blared as our family entered the room. We were, unfortunately, the last to arrive. I wound up fussing way more than was necessary once I had agreed to attend, and we arrived late as a result.

The room was bursting with beauty. Hundreds of young women stood ahead of me, each one more dazzling than the next, and each one drenched in a different perfume. When the wave of scents reached my nostrils, I thought I might be sick.

My parents were whisked away from me while I took my place at the end of what had become a very long line. We should have arrived earlier. I was upset with myself for that. I looked at the faces around me, shining with hopefulness. The prince was every maiden's fantasy. He was handsome and strong, confident and playful. And he was positioned to become the next king. Every young woman in that room knew how lucky she would be if she were chosen.

"Isn't this exciting?" the woman in front of me gushed. "Can you believe this? I can barely breathe I am so excited! I haven't slept in days! What do you think of my hair? I wasn't sure about the look but my mother insisted. Do you think it's too much?"

I stared at her in disbelief.

"You don't like it, do you? I *knew* I should have gone for something simpler! I don't think the prince likes too much adornment. I probably put on too much perfume too! Oh, this is terrible! How long do you think we will have to wait before he arrives?"

What a chatterbox.

I turned away, but this seemed to have no effect on her. She kept rambling about her outfit and her face, worrying that the kohl was getting smudged under her eyes, or wondering when we might be served something to drink. It was maddening.

"I am sure you will be the one chosen, so you can stop worrying," I said in a pathetic attempt to soothe her into silence.

Unfortunately, it did not work.

"Oh my! Do you really think so? What makes you say that? Have you heard anything? Is there a rumor? Oh, but how marvelous! Me? A queen? Just imagine all the clothes I would get to wear, and the jewels, and what a perfectly beautiful husband and—"

"Yes. You as the queen. *Perfect.* That would make me most happy for you," I blurted out angrily. She was making me crazy.

She finally stopped rambling and stared at me with disbelief. "But I don't understand," she said. "Don't *you* want to be queen too?"

"No I don't, if you really must know."

"Why wouldn't you want to be queen?" she asked, genuinely astonished.

"I just don't want to!" I said with the petulance of a little child. "And I don't need to explain it to *you!*"

I should not have allowed myself to get so incensed, but I could not seem to get my emotions under control. They were whirling around me with abandoned chaos. *Of course* I wanted to be queen. I would be crazy not to.

But then again, part of me was also telling the truth. Becoming queen was not a minor detail. It would involve changing every aspect of my life. Whatever freedom I had would be lost once the jeweled headdress was placed on my head. I would be exchanging the little bit of wistfulness a young woman was entitled to for a palace full of golden restraints. I was not entirely convinced that such a trade was worthwhile. Everyone knew how protective the king was.

I turned away from the chatterbox. The conversation was making me sad in ways I did not want to face. Maybe he *would* choose someone else. He was bound to with so many women ahead of me. And then I wouldn't have to be queen.

And then he would be married to someone else.

The royal prince's arrival was announced with conch shells blaring. He entered the room wearing his royal turban and draped in the most magnificent robes I had ever seen. They were dyed a golden orange color that shimmered as he moved towards the stage. I thought I was seeing the sun set against his shoulders. My mouth fell open but I closed it quickly before anyone noticed.

The prince stood in front of the Lion Throne, eager ministers on either side of him. A tremendous golden casket was brought to his side and the cover was removed. The maidens gasped as the glittering pile of treasure was revealed.

I then watched as one beautiful woman after the next was called to the stage. The prince greeted each one silently and delivered an ornament into her eager hands. He did not say a word to any of them. He smiled, bowed his head slightly, and bestowed a royal gift. It was the same procedure with every single one. The quiet routine seemed to take forever and I was not sure what any of it was supposed to mean.

As I inched my way closer, I noticed that the casket was emptying rather quickly. There were so many women! Perhaps they had not foreseen how many gifts he was going to have to offer? What would happen when it came to my turn? Would there be anything left for me?

Suddenly, I heard my name being called and a servant beckoned me towards the stage. My heart fluttered with palpitations and fresh drops of sweat raced their way down my back. My fingers were aching to fidget, but I knew better than to give in. I kept my arms by my side and held my breath as I approached the prince.

Siddhattha reached into the casket to bring out my gift only to discover, to my absolute mortification, that there were no jewels left. He had just given away the last of them to the chatterbox ahead of me! Standing before the entire kingdom with my head bowed and my empty hands raised, I was overwhelmed with humiliation. I did not know what to do. I just stood there, petrified.

"It seems the casket is empty," he said with his familiar smile.

"Apparently," I replied, trembling despite myself. "What should I do? Should I just go back?"

"Not just yet . . ." He waved away the scurrying servants who seemed frantic as they tried to solve the problem, and instead reached for his own necklace. He unclasped it and presented it to me with a grin. "I do still have this . . . May I?" he asked as he motioned for me to turn around.

He hadn't spoken to anyone else the entire morning, but here we were in an intimate exchange. And he was not giving me a random piece of jewelry from his coffers, but his very own necklace. I turned around and pulled my braid to the side, struggling with emotions I did not recognize. He placed the necklace around my neck and clasped it with his soft fingers. When he was done, I turned to look at him. He was the only person in the room. The only person in the ten-thousand universes.

No one was ushering me off the stage. We were simply standing there together, in a bubble of our own happiness, smiling at each other stupidly. Forgetting where I was, I reached for his right hand. He gave it to me, looking at me with warm curiosity. And then I did something I never imagined I had inside of me to do: I carefully removed his ring with the royal insignia. Before I placed it on my own finger, I looked up to be sure it was right.

And it was. He was smiling at me from ear to ear. He helped slide the ring onto my finger as the room burst into applause.

The Choosing was over. We had chosen each other.

The Peacock Garden

The doors to the Throne Room opened. My father stepped over the threshold and waited for the king to acknowledge him. He had been invited into that chamber many times before, but he could never quite get used to the splendor of it. The imposing architecture with arched ceilings, the glitter of inlaid precious stones, and layers of silken carpets left him mesmerized every time.

My father approached the king in the appropriate manner, bowing ceremoniously, touching his hands to the king's feet and bringing them back to his face.

"You wanted to see me, Maharaja?" he asked as he stood back up.

"Yes, my friend. I thought you might join me for a little stroll this morning."

"With pleasure, Your Highness."

My father had expected the summons after our public display of affection; he knew he would be invited to discuss our potential marriage and he was worried about it. He waited for the king to descend from his royal stage and the two men made their way out together. They meandered along opulent palace corridors, passing obsequious servants, each one of whom scraped to the floor at the sight of them, until they reached the outdoors and found themselves at the gate of the king's private garden.

They had been chatting lightly, but the threat of real conversation loomed. My poor father could feel the moment approaching. He lowered his gaze and pulled at the end of his scarf, twirling it around one of his fingers nervously.

"Dandapani, I asked you what you thought of all this?"

"What? Oh, I am sorry, Maharaja. What did you say?" my father mumbled.

"*The garden*, Dandapani. What do you think?"

My father looked up for the first time and realized where they were: the most private of the king's sanctuaries. The Peacock Garden. He took a step back and put his hand to his heart.

"Oh my … It is …" He could barely put the words together, so stunning was the space he suddenly found himself in. "Maharaja! It is magnificent," he finally managed to articulate. And then, the fated words, "It feels like Queen Maya."

The moment he said her name, he regretted it. No one ever mentioned the dead queen in the king's presence—not even her brother. My father immediately covered his mouth with a trembling hand.

"I am so sorry, Your Highness. I forgot myself . . . Her name escaped my lips before I could catch myself. I don't even know why . . ."

The king was quiet. A bead of sweat materialized over my father's brows. One never quite knew how the king would respond when Maya entered a conversation. My father barely breathed as his king took the time to process the name that had been unleashed between them.

After a moment of silence, the king resumed his stroll. "Thank you for saying that, Brother-in-Law. Thank you for saying her name."

Of all possible reactions, that was certainly not the one my father had anticipated.

"After Maya died," the king explained, "I was—as apparently everyone in the kingdom was aware—inconsolable. Mahapajapati probably suffered the most. I wasn't very kind to her when she was made queen in Maya's place. I am probably still not very kind to her, but I could not face a life without Maya. I never expected to love her as much as I did. We were so young when we began our lives together, but she was the right one. And the only one . . ."

The king turned towards my father, slightly embarrassed by his admission. "I suppose it sounds weak to admit such love for one's wife?"

"Nothing you say could sound weak, Your Highness," answered my father.

"You know, she used to say that we were like two wings of a dove . . . When she died, I felt crippled, like I had become half of who I used to be."

My father nodded with quiet understanding. The two men resumed their stroll. The trees drooped over and around each other, while the flowers grew wildly in all directions, seemingly chaotically, and yet somehow purposefully orchestrated at the same time.

"After Maya died," the king continued, "I spent a lot of time in this garden. It didn't look like this all those years ago. It was much more manicured then. But one day, I noticed a plant that Maya never liked. It seemed to be staring at me and suddenly I hated it. Before I knew what I was doing, I dropped to my knees and was ripping the plant right out of the ground. Soon, I was tearing the garden apart, cutting away at roots and moving plants around with wild abandon, my hands becoming filthy and scratched. The gardeners were furious with me. Not only was I ruining a perfectly well-tended garden, but I was taking their place, working at something that was not my station to do. But I couldn't stop myself. The earth was calling to me, almost yelling at me. I had to throw myself into it. I had no choice."

My father was surprised. They had never talked so openly before.

"Do you remember the *Ramayana* that was performed here a few months ago?" the king asked.

My father nodded. It was impossible to forget.

"Do you know the end of that story? What happens to Sita after Rama rescues her from the evil demon Ravana?"

"She and Rama eventually return to the kingdom of Ayodhya to reclaim it," my father replied.

"Yes, but the story does not end there. Rama's subjects worry about Sita's purity. She had been alone in Ravana's palace for a long time. To appease his community, Rama exiled her all over again, and so she returned to the wilderness, but this time she was alone without anyone to protect her."

"That's right. And she gave birth to twins in the forest, didn't she?"

"Yes. All by herself," said the king with unconcealed admiration.

"I had forgotten about that," my father admitted. "But what happens after that? Don't they all eventually reunite?"

"Some people believe so, but not according to one storyteller. I met him not long after Maya's death when I was out hunting. According to him, Sita never returned to the palace with her husband. She died in the forest instead."

"That is new," said my father.

"According to this storyteller, Sita had undergone many trials for the sake of her husband. When Rama was exiled into the forest by his stepmother, Sita went with him. When she was captured by the demon Ravana, Sita refused to let anyone save her until Rama arrived to ensure that he received the honor of saving her himself. When Rama suspected her of infidelity, Sita walked through fire to prove her innocence. When he was invited to return to the palace after that, Sita followed. And when the royal subjects began to suspect her of infidelity, her husband asked her to leave the palace all over again for the sake of the kingdom's harmony, and Sita did as she was asked.

"By then, Sita was pregnant with the twins, but she entered the forest all by herself without a word of complaint. When Rama found her again, years later still, he regretted having abandoned her and begged her to return with him. He suggested she walk through fire again, but this time in front of his entire kingdom."

The king took a breath. He felt tired just thinking about all the trials Sita had been forced to endure.

"And you know what she said?"

My father stared at the king.

"According to this storyteller, she said no."

She said *no*? In all his years, my father had never heard an ending quite like that.

"Maya and I used to argue about this story often." The king smiled at the memory. "She always took Sita's side and I always took Rama's. We never could agree about who was the better of the two. If only Maya had been around to hear this particular ending, she would have felt vindicated."

"But what happened when Sita said no? How did Rama react?" my father asked.

"The most extraordinary thing happened, Dandapani," answered the king. "Rama never had a chance to respond. Sita refused her husband and then called upon her mother, the Earth Goddess, and begged her to take her home. The Earth Goddess heard her, opened her mouth and swallowed her whole, bringing her back into the silence from whence she came."

My father stopped walking. "Maharaja, why are you telling me this story?"

"Because I wanted to say no to Maya's death the way Sita said no to Rama. I wanted to refuse my circumstances and disappear. That's why I kept returning to the garden. I think I was hoping the Earth Goddess would take me away."

My father was astonished. He had not realized until then how profound the king's sorrow had been.

The king picked up the pace and continued. "I tore this garden apart. I would wake up early in the morning and rip roots out with my bare hands, throwing myself into my pain with a vengeance. But gardening is mysterious work. My rage slowly subsided, the dark soil calming me with its open invitation. Soon, I found myself trying to work with the earth. I didn't want to destroy it anymore. I wasn't trying to pull the Earth Goddess out by force. I was ready to care for her instead.

"I spent hours after that trying to create a garden that matched what I envisioned, but I had sorely underestimated the process. One does not create a garden in a day or even in a year. Sixteen years have passed and I suspect it will take at least sixteen more to create the garden of my dreams. But I have learned something very special in the meanwhile: that a garden is whole and beautiful at every stage in its development. And yet, at the same time, a garden is never complete."

To be whole and yet never complete, my father repeated to himself, folding the words into his heart. He wanted to share them with my mother when he returned home. He suspected she would understand what the king meant ... perhaps more than he himself felt capable of.

"So eventually I gave in," the king continued. "I returned the tools to the gardeners and took back my place on the throne. I could not justify any more time away. The garden had given me the peace I had come to find."

The king filled his lungs with a deep breath, as though inhaling the garden into himself. "But I have not completely relinquished my role here," he added coyly. "Every morning, I meet with Chief Gardener and we examine the details of the landscape together. He does not touch a leaf without consulting with me first."

There was something transcendent about the king, despite his flawed humanity. It made the weight of the words my father needed to speak that much heavier.

"When you said her name aloud Dandapani, it was ... Perfect."

"Why, Maharaja?"

"At first, I didn't entirely understand what I was doing in this garden. I thought I was here to hammer out my pain, to tend to my own heart as I turned the soil in my hands. But there was more to it than that. This garden became my way of speaking to Maya. I filled every inch of this space with my songs to her. There is not a stitch of green that is not infused with my love for her. When you said her name, you said everything that this place is to me."

My father felt a flood of emotion. Maya was loved more than she probably ever realized.

"That is why I thanked you, Dandapani. Because you see her here, just as I do."

A brilliant peacock strutted towards them, his tail fanned wide open. The king laughed at his approach. "The peacocks here," he explained with more lightness in his voice now, "were brought here for her too. Maya used to tease me that I strutted like one. When I got too big for myself, she would chide me as only she could, telling me that I was acting like a proud peacock and asking me where I put my tail. I brought the peacocks here to keep myself in check since she is no longer here to do it herself."

To my father's surprise, the peacock actually extended his long neck towards the king, pushing himself forward. The king chuckled as he patted the peacock's little head. "Yes, yes, my dear blue friend," he said, "you are indeed magnificent. But I am still king and you are still just a bird. Don't get ahead of yourself." Both men laughed lightly at this remark.

The king spent the rest of the afternoon pointing out various plants to my father, explaining their history and the particular qualities of each one. He asked my father his opinion about the placement of various flowers, described the technicalities of fertilizer and sunlight, and caressed petals as though he was touching a lover's body. It was almost too intimate to share. Like the privacy of spontaneous poetry.

The edge of the garden gave way to a resplendent view that plummeted off the cliff and spilled onto vast expansiveness. A small bench was placed just before the drop, beneath a brilliant tree. The king invited my father to sit next to him as his equal. It was time for the conversation to change course.

"I suppose you were not surprised by my invitation today, Dandapani," the king asked.

"Indeed, I was not, Your Highness," replied my father, who became agitated all over again, and was suddenly desperate to pull at the end of his scarf.

"Our children have chosen each other. That much is clear, is it not?"

"They have," replied my father quietly. "Your son chose my daughter and she chose him in return."

"So it is settled then!" exclaimed the king as he jumped from his seat, apparently about to bounce back to the palace. "Our children will be married!"

"Umm . . . Your Highness?" my father mumbled.

The king stopped and looked back at my father, who remained anchored to the bench they had been sharing.

"What is it? Why are you still sitting there Dandapani? Let's announce the news to our wives and begin the preparations!"

The buoyant king lifted his face to the garden and called out, "Maya? Did you hear that? Our son is to be married!"

My father did not move.

"What is it, Dandapani? Why are you looking at me like that?"

My father stood up slowly. He looked up at the king and immediately looked down again.

"Come now, speak up! Are you worried about the dowry? We will work that out later. I am sure you have prepared an appropriate gift. I am not concerned in the least. What could possibly be wrong?"

"Your Highness," stuttered my father, "would you mind sitting down for a moment. There is something I would like to speak to you about. If . . . if I may?"

"Of course you may. We are family, now more than ever. What is it?" The king was baffled by my father's unusual behavior.

"Well . . . may I speak candidly?"

"Of course." The king sat back down and was now paying careful attention to his perturbed brother-in-law.

My father gathered his courage and lowered himself to the ground to speak from bended knees.

"You see, Your Highness, there have been some concerns ..." He took a deep breath. "About the training of your son. That is ... about his ... his lack of training ..." His voice trailed off.

The king rose from the bench before my father could finish his sentence and glared at Dandapani menacingly. My father's heart stopped beating, his head so low now, his nose was an inch from the ground.

"What in all the gods' names are you implying about my son?"

My father did not reply. He tried to stop breathing.

"My son is a GOD in human form!" he bellowed angrily. "What exactly are you suggesting about your future king?!"

The king's hand had traveled to the sword that was strapped across his shoulder, his fingers wrapping tightly around its hilt. "You might do better to remember yourself!" he declared to the terrified shell of a man kneeling at his feet. The king was perfectly within his right to slice off my father's head. Both men were aware of this fact.

But the king did not slice off my father's head. He looked down at the man who was his friend and relative, and then looked up at the garden that carried Maya's presence. A faint whisper seemed to be blowing through the trees.

Darling, it said. *Listen to him.*

Slowly, his grip relaxed and he let go of his sword. He took a few deep breaths and sat back down. "All right, Dandapani. I am listening."

My father remained frozen for a few more faltering heartbeats, waiting for any other incoming explosions. When none came, he knew it was time to say what needed to be said.

"Your Highness ..." my father mumbled with a trembling voice, "Siddhattha is a fine man. He is beautiful and strong, elegant and ... extremely intelligent." His courage slowly rebuilt itself with the compliments he paid the prince. "My daughter is fond of him and I have no doubt he would be an excellent match for her. But ... but since the queen's death ..."

The king's eyebrows shot up, but he restrained himself.

"Since her death, you have protected your son ... to the point that he has not received any formal training. He has never seen a battlefield and never gone to school. Although no one doubts his extraordinary abilities, without proper training ..."

My father looked up briefly to check on the king's composure. He was still listening, so my father closed with the statement he had been holding in his heart since the day of the Choosing. "It is a concern that I cannot hide if we are to discuss the possibility of marriage between our children." He bowed his head to the ground again and touched the king's feet with humility.

The king did not respond for a long time. He stared into the distance, a familiar sadness covering his face like a shadow, his wrinkles seeping into his eyes. Deep down, the king knew that Dandapani was right.

Eventually, King Suddhodana rose from his seat, his body weighing so much more than it had a few minutes before. He touched my father gently on the shoulder and said, "Come, my friend. It is time to return to the palace."

The Competition

The king could not accept my father's concerns. If any of his subjects doubted the prince's capacities, he had no choice but to prove them wrong. What kind of king would he be if he hadn't? It was his foremost obligation to present the Sakya Kingdom with a successor they could have confidence in. He could see no other way.

With my father's reluctant acceptance (and without my knowledge!), the king declared a public competition to be held at Sihadvara, the field where the legendary King Sihahanu defeated an army of militant invaders a generation earlier. Noblemen and princes from near and far were invited to participate. The winner would be granted me as their wife.

I spent the days leading up to the competition hiding in my home. To try to articulate how furious I was with the spectacle my life had become was impossible. I could not believe my father had agreed to such a humiliating ordeal.

"Yasodhara, everything will be all right," he tried to say as I ignored him into the next room. "Daughter, I promise that you will be fine!"

"You don't know that." I slammed another door against its frame.

On the morning of the dreaded event, my father came to find me in my room. I was sitting on my bed, trying to bead a necklace to help pass the time. The beads kept slipping out of my trembling fingers. It was not the best activity to have chosen given my aggravated state.

"May I speak with you?" he asked.

I turned my back to him. He walked in anyway and sat on my bed, just a hand's length away from me.

"Daughter, I know how upset you are. But most girls would be thrilled with all this attention. Don't you realize how valuable you have become to the kingdom? Every eligible man in the land will be fighting to have you as their wife. For most girls, this is a dream come true."

"I am not like 'most girls' and you know that!" I answered. "This is not my Dream-Come-True! This is not how I want my husband to be chosen!" Tears welled up in my eyes for the first time since the competition had been announced. I wiped my face on my arm, trying desperately not to cry but finding it impossible to resist.

My mother came into the room and sat on the other side of me. She put her hands on mine. Sobs traveled heavily through my body.

"Daughter," she finally said. "Tell me what is making you so upset."

I knew the answer but I did not want to admit it. I was so proud and stubborn in those days. It was agony to let my voice express the truths of my heart. I looked into her strong eyes, attempted to speak, but failed. My eyes filled with tears all over again.

"Can I ask you something?" she requested tenderly.

I nodded my head as I wiped my nose with the back of my hand.

"Are you afraid of who might win the competition? Is *that* what worries you most?"

"Of course that worries me, Mother!" I answered furiously, surprised by the intensity of my own response. "What if somebody terrible wins the competition? What if it's a prince from some faraway kingdom and I am forced to leave home forever? Even worse, what if Devadatta wins? Can you imagine that? He's been practicing archery since he was a child! He could easily win! And then what kind of a life would I be condemned to?" The fears fell out of my mouth and right onto the bed between us. They were the words I had been repeating to myself since the announcement was made.

"We want Siddhattha to win too," my father admitted quietly. "We don't want you to leave home. We have been praying for his success every day."

"And what if he doesn't win?" I pleaded. "What will happen to me then? We already chose each other! What will I do then?"

*

The competition would have two parts to it: archery and debate. It was going to be a long day. I took my place in our family tent, my parents placing themselves on either side of me. My eyes were red and swollen from all the crying I had done. I did not imagine I looked like much of a prize.

The royal tent was raised next to ours and between the two were Sihahanu Raja's bow and his bag of golden-tipped arrows, the weapons that Siddhattha's grandfather had used to save his kingdom from destruction.

Legend claims that when the battle was over and the field was covered with blood, Sihahanu Raja was overcome with regret. His responsibility was to his kingdom and its protection, which he fulfilled. But when the war was over, he looked at the corpses that covered the ground, the foreign ones intermingled with his own men, and he begged the gods to never have to go to war again. He then raised his bow high over his head and slammed it down with all the force of his lion-like frame. According to the storytellers, the Earth Goddess opened the ground and caught the bow in her hands. She planted it into her abdomen and wove her veins around it. No one had been able to uproot it since.

I stared at the upper half of the magical bow before me, imagining the hidden half covered with knitted roots, anchoring it under the earth. I could not imagine the kind of power Sihahanu Raja must have had to be able to sink his weapon with such force, the kind of commitment he embodied to have the gods respond to him so clearly. I wished I could find that kind of power within myself. The kind of power my mother told me I already had inside.

The subjects of Sakya trickled slowly onto the field. Colorful carpets were flicked open and spread over the soft grass. Women ladled steaming curries into ceramic bowls, grandmothers scolded undisciplined children who ran out too far or made too much noise, and men squatted in circles to discuss the intermingling threads of their lives. Every once in a while, someone would turn towards me and stare.

The prince arrived early, the edges of the field having only started to fill. He did not make an entrance or have himself announced in any way. He walked alone, approached Sihahanu Raja's bow with an offering of a simple flower garland, bowed, and then took his position across from the tent in which I sat. He carried nothing with him. No props or weapons of any kind. He stood unadorned, almost bare, wearing simple cotton clothing. Nothing to identify him as the prince of our kingdom or to declare that he was prepared to fight.

His composure sent me spiraling into doubt: did he not realize that the best of men would stand against him that day? That men with bigger arms and swifter aim would compete for me as their bride? Maybe he didn't even care? What if it did not matter to him who I married? What if he was prepared to choose someone else? The awful chatterbox who stood in line ahead of me during the Choosing flashed in my mind. She was so eager, so desperate to please. He had dozens of beautiful women fawning over him at every turn. The insecurities were tightening around my heart, strangling me right there on the podium for all to see.

The King of the Sakya Kingdom, seated just a few steps away from us in his own tent, gave the signal for the ceremony to commence. Drum-beaters immediately swarmed onto the field from every direction, marching briskly and in unison, each one clad in golden cloth tied around the waist. Their upper bodies were painted with streaks of red, creating an impression of pulsating muscles over the skin. When they reached the center of the field, they bowed with palms together, first to Sihahanu Raja's bow, then to the royal family, and last to us. They then swung their drums into place.

The beating started slowly. A few beats and then a stop, and then a few more beats. They were calling the games into existence, beating them into life. A few more beats. Silence. A few more. And then ... the rhythm was woken from their hands and catapulted onto the field. Beating and beating, the sounds became thunderous, moving swiftly like soldiers racing into battle. It created an exhilarating energy. I felt it pour into me, sink deep into my abdomen, as though the sounds sprang from a source older than time. Fatigue and tension were swept away as I felt invigorated for the first time in days.

Men from near and far strode onto the field, following the sounds of the drums that were calling them. They lined up beside the prince, one after another. There were men I recognized, such as Nanda, sweet Ananda, and Devadatta, but many others I had never seen before, dressed in strange costumes that suggested that they had come from far away. Each one of them bowed to us before turning away to face the field that promised to decide my life.

The drummers continued their pounding as the royal temple priest led a procession of attendants towards us. Each one of them carried a dark ceramic bowl filled with liquefied butter and a lit wick. The sun outshone the light produced by the butter lamps, but the smoke that rose from each dish created a wispy trail around them. The royal priest lifted his lamp high above him and waited for the drummers to pull their rhythm to a stop. When silence had settled, he raised his eyes to the sky and called upon the deities with a broad and powerful voice.

"Mahadevi, Mahadeva! Goddesses and gods from above and below! Bhumidevi and Abhayadevi! Sakka, Varuna and Agni! Durga and Rudra! We call upon you, upon the deities we know and the deities we have yet to know. May you bless these games with your shining presence and reveal the true victor at the end!"

He then closed his eyes and circled the lamp over his head, his attendants following his movements with their own lamps. They sang words that none of us could understand, chanting sounds that belonged to other realms. They then placed their bowls in a circle around Sihahanu Raja's bow, bowed with reverence to the memory of that great king and quietly walked away.

It was time for the archery competition to begin.

The royal captain of the king's army stepped forward, having been chosen to supervise and judge that portion of the games. He walked over to the series of targets that were set up in the field and examined each one carefully. They were all made of hay and wood and were placed at an incremental distance.

The last and furthest of the targets, however, was made of iron and was painted with brilliant colors. No one was expected to pierce that one; it was placed there symbolically to remind the contestants that human beings have limitations, no matter how powerful they may appear to be.

When he was satisfied with his inspection, the captain walked back to the center and announced the beginning of the competition. The crowd roared with excitement, shouts of jubilation filling the air. I, however, felt myself go numb again. The invigoration I had allowed myself to feel only moments earlier had dissipated as fear reclaimed its familiar hold. My life had been recklessly tossed to the gods of chance and there was nothing I could do about it. I could not save myself or determine the course of my own future. I had to sit back and watch as men played a game that held me captive.

"First contestant . . ." Royal Captain declared with a booming voice, "is Prince Viriya of Kosala!"

People all around gasped as the name "Kosala" rippled through the air. The Kingdom of Kosala was one of our arch-enemies! How dare they send an ambassador to fight for my hand? I looked over at the king who seemed just as surprised. Did our king not even know of his arrival?

I leaned forward, curious to see who this enemy would be. A large man stepped forward. He was draped in green silk and carried a bow decorated with green feathers at the top. His jaw jutted forward, making him look as though he was chewing something. I would have laughed if I was not so nervous.

Angry whispers wafted around, but the contestant moved through the commentary with a proud gait. If he was bothered by his antagonistic surroundings, he did not show it. He strode into the center of the field as if he owned it and immediately aimed at the first target. The arrow shot out of his hands faster than I thought possible and sank into the center with a quick burst. The Kosalan stepped on the line to face the second mark and it too landed perfectly. One could not deny the grace with which he moved, despite his protruding and masticating jaw. He hit each target easily, as though his movements required no effort at all. He went over to the third mark and hit it in the middle yet again, even though this one was significantly further than the previous two.

There were a few cheers from the audience, but I was furious. If he thought I was going to run off to Kosala with him, he was mad. I would kill myself before I ever let that happen! I sank into my seat as a chill laced itself around my spine.

"The next contestant is ..." thundered Royal Captain, "Nanda, son of Suddhodana Raja!"

Nanda's name produced a very different effect from the previous contestant. He had become famous for his looks, having been designated the most beautiful man in our kingdom. Women of all ages squealed as Handsome Nanda sauntered forward wearing an outfit of spectacular gold cloth. The upper material was pulled much too tightly around his chest and shoulders. How he hoped to move with his clothing stretched against him that way was beyond me. I was sure the material would rip apart as he reached for his arrows.

Women swooned as he moved towards the first target. One woman hollered, "You're the god of my loins, Nanda!" Another ran onto the field and threw her arms around his feet. Her family members rushed in to drag her away. She giggled and waved frantically all the way out. Queen Mahapajapati looked away with shame.

Nanda, however, was unabashedly pleased with these reactions. He flexed his muscles underneath his tight clothing, pumping his chest as he took his position. He lifted his bow and slowly placed the arrow alongside the string. Eventually, after what seemed like an eternity, Nanda released the arrow with a theatrical wave of his arm. It hit the mark well enough, but rather softly.

My father stifled a laugh. It was not a tremendous achievement by any standard, but cheers exploded from his female admirers. When he tried for the second mark, however, the arrow sailed far to the left of its intended target and landed in the mud. My father could not contain his laughter by then. "Quite a show he makes for such an effeminate outcome!" he declared as he smacked his knee.

I giggled, but my mother gave us both a stern look. "There is nothing *effeminate* about failure, Husband," my mother reprimanded. "The fact that he cannot shoot an arrow properly makes him a pathetic archer. It does not make him a woman!"

My father's face fell. He knew better than to say another word.

A few other contestants were called to the field after Nanda, but none of them managed to hit all three targets the way the Kosalan warrior had. Ananda, however, did a most unexpected thing when his turn was announced. I knew he could shoot relatively well. I expected him to at least succeed in the first and second round, but he failed on the first try. He lifted his bow, pulled the arrow alongside the string, and then let the arrow drop by his feet instead of releasing it for flight.

It was a strange demonstration, but Ananda's face was composed. Contented even. It was only much later that I learned that Ananda's loyalty was at the source of his display. He loved both the prince and me too much to come between us. He respected the Choosing, respected our having chosen each other. He would rather be embarrassed in public than try to separate us.

"Next contestant . . ." boomed Royal Captain, "is Devadatta of the Gotama clan!"

Devadatta stepped forward wearing a black silk outfit studded with glittering white gems. He walked with his head held high and his chest puffed out. He approached the first mark and placed his feet carefully on the line. He drew out an arrow and deliberately placed it alongside his pulled string. He aimed and then turned his head towards me as he released it. A sickening grin slid over his face as the arrow hit the mark.

I recoiled, my body folding into itself. He laughed at my reaction and then moved towards the next mark. He hit that one and the third perfectly. It was devastating. Frightening even. My mother put her hand on my shoulder for support.

Royal Captain stepped forward for the last time. "It is my honor to introduce the final contestant of the games!" He paused for dramatic effect and then declared, "Prince Siddhattha Gotama, son of Maharaja Suddhodana, King of the Sakyas! Successor to the Lion Throne!"

Tremendous cheers erupted from the sidelines. It was finally Siddhattha's turn and everyone was filled with hopeful anticipation. I watched the king and queen lean forward, trying to hide their angst. So much was at stake. For so many of us.

My own face must have been terribly contorted with worry. I could not muster the energy required to conceal my emotions. I had never seen Siddhattha with a bow and arrow. Was he any good? And what difference would it make even if he were? Two men had already won the archery competition— and two horrible men at that! A Kosalan and Devadatta! Even if he did succeed, what would happen? Would I be married to three men at once, two of whom terrified me? What were the contingency plans in the case of a tie? I could not breathe.

And then a new wave of fear collided with the others: *where was his bow?!* The prince had walked onto the field without a weapon.

I began to panic. I tried to articulate the problem to my mother but my throat had become painfully dry. The prince, however, seemed as steady as ever. With his empty hands by his side, he addressed his host.

"Royal Captain?"

"Yes," Royal Captain replied, a bit surprised by the interruption in protocol.

"Might I address the king?"

"Of course, Your Highness."

The prince turned to face his father and, with a strong, confident voice, asked, "Father, might I be granted permission to use the family bow?"

The king rose from his seat, unsure of how to respond. "Son," he mustered, "of which bow do you speak?"

"I would like to use my grandfather's bow to win my bride. I would like to use Sihahanu Raja's bow."

The king took a step back. He had not expected such a request. No one had.

"But Son, that bow has not moved since it was planted in the earth all those years ago. No one can move it now. It is being held by the Earth Goddess."

The king clapped for a servant and commanded, "Quick, get my son a bow and some arrows from the armory."

The prince shook his head. "No need, Father. If you grant me permission, I would like to use my grandfather's weapon instead."

The king stared at his son. "Of course you have my permission, Son, but . . ."

"Thank you Maharaja," was his quick reply.

The prince strode over to the entwined bow without another word. He clasped it with his right hand and pulled it out of the earth as easily as if he was pulling a flower out of a vase.

Sihahanu Raja's bow, the magical weapon that had been sealed into the earth with the power of a Lion King's vow, was released without the slightest resistance. The king's mouth was hanging open as he stared at the bow in his son's hands. The queen stood in her husband's shadow, marveling at the boy who had become a man.

The prince picked up the bag of golden-tipped arrows and slung it over his shoulder. He turned towards the field and hit all three targets before anyone had regained their composure. He then walked towards the fourth, the Iron Gate at the end of the field, pulled back the last of the arrows and shot with lightning speed. It sailed through the air, pierced through the iron wall and sank into the earth behind it.

*

I wanted to jump out of my seat and race into his arms! His performance was unbelievable—superhuman even! He retrieved the magical bow from the Goddess' closed hands, he hit every target perfectly, and he tore through the Iron Gate! How was any of that even possible?

The people were cheering wildly. The king and queen had forgotten their required decorum and were jumping up and down along with everyone else. Ministers of every persuasion raced onto the royal platform and clapped the king on the back with loud "hurrahs." Mahapajapati was swarmed by her own attendants, all of whom were congratulating her enthusiastically. The women chatted away excitedly with their high-pitched voices while she wiped away the tears that were lining her cheeks.

My father had jumped out of his seat as the final arrow made its way through the Iron Gate. His hands flew to his head and gripped his hair as he bellowed to my mother, "What an athlete, Pamita! Did you know he could do that?" My mother nodded but remained silent, her hand clutching at her heart.

The clamor went on for quite a while. It was the kind of excitement that heals; the community savored it like warm honey. My own exhilaration, however, petered out more quickly. There was one more event Siddhattha would have to win if we were to be wed. I was stunned by his natural abilities, I was beyond myself with pride, but I could not let myself celebrate until the games were complete. The debate-portion of the games remained and I had no idea how it would unfold. Siddhattha had never done any studies. How exactly was he planning on winning *that*?

Royal Captain walked through the sounds of celebration towards the royal tent and requested an audience with the king. As if on cue, the high priest materialized by his side, and together they were invited up the steps. The king waved his ministers away so that they could discuss the next round in privacy. After a few moments of secret consultation, the priest nodded, bowed to his lord and made his way back to the center of the field.

The drummers followed, beating their drums with a powerful sound, calling the people back to attention. When everyone had settled back into their seats, the priest announced the next phase in the proceedings.

"PEOPLE OF THE SAKYA KINGDOM!" he thundered. "It is now time for the second and last event in these games!"

The people burst with applause, exhilarated by their newfound pride. He waited for the noise to settle and then continued.

"It has been declared by our Royal Monarch, Suddhodana Maharaja of Sakya, that the three most successful archers will be invited to participate in the debate: the Prince of Kosala," (people booed), "Devadatta of the Gotama clan," (a few cheered), "and Prince Siddhattha, son of Suddhodana Maharaja, heir to the throne!" (the crowd went wild all over again).

"There will be two sets of questions," he continued. "The first will be focused on political tactics. The winner will be determined based on eloquence and strategic comprehension. The second set of questions will have to do with heavenly matters." The priest paused for effect, and then threw his arms into the air and bellowed, "May the best man win!"

People launched themselves off their cushions and rugs with another round of enthusiastic applause. Everyone was so excited by the prospect of their prince winning glory for them. It had become the event of the century. A story that would be told for generations to come.

The three contestants who had stepped forward when their names were called all bowed to the priest and then listened as he outlined the instructions. Devadatta kept his malevolent eyes on Siddhattha the whole time. The Kosalan, meanwhile, looked baffled, as though he did not really understand what was going on, his eyes darting left and right like an animal lost in the woods. The prince remained as centered as ever. He kept his eyes on the ground when he bowed, and he nodded at the priest when he stood back up. Neither one of his opponents seemed to concern him at all.

The problem with the debate segment was that it was difficult to follow from a distance. Unlike archery, which was visually spectacular and could be appreciated from almost any point on the field, debate was a discussion held in a small circle, most of which no one could hear. Keeping the audience engaged promised to be a challenge.

The priest placed himself at the center of the circle and launched the first of his questions at the contestants. They were instructed to keep their seated positions and answer him without rising. For most members of the audience, body language was the only means by which they might interpret what was going on.

One contestant was especially transparent in this regard. The Kosalan remained still and silent while the others immersed themselves in the debate. The Kosalan stared at the others but never contributed. Eventually, the priest called for a break in the discussion and walked towards the royal tent. He spoke quietly to the king. Everyone waited, wondering what was going on.

The priest nodded as the king provided him with instructions. He then stepped forward and addressed the crowd.

"People of the Sakya Kingdom," he cried out.

People had begun to distract themselves with their own conversations, not being able to follow the one at the center of the field. He cleared his throat and tried again.

"PEOPLE OF THE SAKYA KINGDOM!" he thundered at the top of his voice. This time, people looked up.

"Our guest, the Prince of Kosala, does not speak our language. Can anyone here serve as interpreter so that he may continue participating?"

I couldn't believe it. I had never thought that could be a problem, but obviously he did not speak our language! Why would he? I held my breath, hoping the language barrier might in fact disqualify him.

The priest waited a few moments and then asked the crowd a second time, "People of Sakya! Does anyone speak Kosalan? We would like to offer our guest the opportunity to continue as a contestant."

The Kosalan stood up and looked at the crowds that were looking at him. There was a pleading expression on his strange face.

A third and last time, the priest asked the crowd for help, but no one responded or came forward. How could he have come here without thinking of bringing an interpreter? He was obviously a skilled archer, but not the brightest tactician.

When sufficient time had passed, the king nodded. The priest spoke again.

"Because our guest cannot participate in the debate, we have no choice but to declare forfeit on his behalf."

He then turned to the foreign prince and said, "Prince Viriya of Kosala, your participation in these games has come to its conclusion." A junior temple priest escorted him off the field. The Kosalan's jaw chewed absently at the space inside his mouth as he walked away.

"There are now only two contestants left," the priest announced. "The debate will be between Prince Siddhattha and Devadatta." He then invited the crowd to approach the circle so that everyone might bear witness.

The priest picked up the thread that had begun earlier and asked the two contestants the following question: "You are interested in attacking a neighboring kingdom that is rich in resources. What steps would you take in order to accomplish this?"

Devadatta was the first to jump in. "That is simple, Brahmin. I would begin by investigating the kinds of artillery and manpower at that kingdom's disposal and I would ensure that my own army was stronger."

"How would you accomplish that?" asked the priest.

"I would send spies into their territory to investigate. Once I had all the information I needed, I would put together an army greater than theirs and I would attack when they least expected it." Devadatta spoke with nauseating smugness.

"And what if your own army was not as powerful as theirs? What would you do then?" asked the priest.

"I would put all my resources into developing my own army to match theirs. The resources I would gain access to by invading their territory would soon compensate for the cost."

I had to admit that his answer made sense. It was logical and it would probably work. If one wanted to attack a neighboring kingdom, how else could it be done?

"Prince Siddhattha, what is your response to this question?"

"I concede that Devadatta's first response is correct. If I was king and I was interested in attacking a neighboring territory rich in resources, I would begin by sending spies to investigate on my behalf."

A frightened hush had fallen over the audience. Had the prince really conceded Devadatta's point? I looked over at the king and saw a shadow of concern pass over his face.

"But . . ." he continued, "I would not send spies to investigate their manpower. On this point, I must respectfully disagree with my fellow contestant."

The priest was as surprised as the rest of us. "What exactly would your spies be investigating, Your Highness?"

"I would ask my spies to investigate something else entirely. I would ask them to find out if the ruling body of this kingdom, together with its army officials and soldiers, holds regular and frequent assemblies. If they do hold such assemblies, I would ask them to find out if their assemblies are held in harmony and conclude in harmony. I would ask them to find out if this community respects its elders, respects its own ancient traditions, if the men in this community are good to their wives and daughters, if they do not compel them against their wills, and if provisions are made for their teachers."

This was a most unexpected response.

"What would be gained from such an inquiry, Your Highness?" the priest asked.

"What would be gained, Brahmin, is a clearer sense of their abilities. If the answer to all of these questions is yes, then I would in fact *not* invade their territory. A community that does all of these things—that holds regular and frequent assemblies and holds them in harmony, that respects its elders, its traditions, its women, and its teachers—a community that does all of that cannot be easily conquered by an invading army. Any attempt at attacking such a community would fail, or it would cost my own kingdom more than it was worth. I would therefore not go forward with the attack."

Devadatta raged his way back into the debate. "You are such a coward, Cousin! *Of course* a kingdom like that can be properly invaded. You just need the right kind of army and enough weaponry! It doesn't matter how *harmonious* their assemblies are! You just need the power!"

Siddhattha smiled softly. "You are not the only warrior who thinks this way. But no amount of firepower can overtake a community that is held together by such strong bonds. If an investigation led to such a conclusion, I would not invade. It is up to our esteemed referee to decide which of our answers is most correct."

*

The priest stepped forward. "Let us move on to the second half of the debate. We turn now to heavenly matters."

The discussion took off immediately. I was eager to hear what they were saying, but I was feeling dizzy. The competition seemed to be on the verge of concluding and I was exhausted. I had not eaten properly in days and hunger suddenly announced itself ferociously. I did not want to get up and miss the concluding segment, so I reached for the plate of deep-fried onion balls that had been circulating and stuffed a few in. I then leaned forward again and tried to catch what was being said.

"Can you define Brahman for me please?" the priest asked.

Devadatta answered with a quiver of desperation in his voice, "Everyone knows what Brahman is!"

"But what is it exactly?" prodded the priest.

"I was trained by the greatest gurus in the land. I studied with the most famous teachers and spent time with them in forests, in caves, and in our family study hall. I know the answer to this question because I have learned it from them. Brahman is Ultimate Reality!" he declared with his head held unnaturally high.

"You have been taught well, Devadatta. Yes, Brahman is Ultimate Reality. This is a good definition. But what exactly *is* Ultimate Reality? Can you explain it for us?"

Devadatta pulled himself up straighter and continued his monologue. "Ultimate Reality is everything and everyone. It is the Self inside each one of us, and it is everything around us as well. This is what I have been taught by the gurus and the mahagurus who have trained me in the proper way."

Siddhattha remained silent. He was listening, but he was not jumping in. He seemed to be waiting for something.

"Very good, Devadatta," said the priest with a slightly patronizing tone. "The Self and Brahman are indeed one and the same. But how do we know this to be true? Can you demonstrate the relationship between the two?"

Devadatta looked baffled.

"What do you mean *demonstrate*? How can this be demonstrated? We know this is true because our teachers have taught it to us in this way. This is the wisdom of our ancestors. That is why it is true. Anyone who has been properly trained knows the truth of what I say."

Although Devadatta spoke with haughty disdain, his brewing discomfort was obvious. The priest turned to the prince. "Your Highness, would you like to answer these questions? What is Brahman and how can we know it?"

The prince let the question sit between them for a moment and only when he had his thoughts collected did he answer.

"Devadatta is, once again, correct. My fellow contestant has defined Brahman the way our teachers have—as the Ultimate Reality, as Truth, as Everything. It is what is inside of us as much as what is outside. Indeed, the distinction between 'inside' and 'outside' is an illusion, for it is all Brahman. Distinctions are illusions of the mind."

Siddhattha had begun by acknowledging Devadatta's answer, but it was obvious that more was coming. Devadatta pounced preemptively.

"How dare you talk of teachers, Siddhattha? You never studied a day in your life!"

"You are again correct. I have never studied under a teacher the way you have. I have not had the privilege of spending all the time you have spent listening to others and learning the truth as they see it. You have been trained and I have not been trained."

Devadatta never expected the prince to openly admit to his lack of training— and this without the slightest element of shame. Before he could respond, the prince continued.

"I don't think, however, that we are here to discuss our qualifications. We are here to discuss Brahman. The question posed by our illustrious priest was, how can we know Brahman? Am I correct?"

"You are indeed, Your Highness. How can we know Truth and its pervasive nature? Can you demonstrate it for us?"

"I can indeed, Brahmin. Would someone be so kind as to bring me a cup of water and a plate with some salt?"

It was an unusual request, but the priest clapped his hands and had the materials summoned. A young boy soon scuttled over holding a tray with the requested ingredients.

Siddhattha lay the tray down in front of him and presented the cup of water to Devadatta. Devadatta was unsure how to respond, but he eventually reached out and took the cup.

"Devadatta, would you mind taking a sip of this water for me and telling me how it tastes?"

"All right . . ." he mumbled, clearly not enjoying being used as a puppet in his opponent's performance.

"What does the water taste like?"

"It tastes like water," he answered.

"Does it taste salty?"

"No. It tastes like ordinary water. I already told you that!" Devadatta barked.

"Now then," the prince continued, "would you mind pouring this plate of salt into the water for me?"

Devadatta did as he was asked.

"Would you now taste the water again?"

Devadatta raised his eyebrows at this request. "Why should I do that? It will taste terrible! Are you trying to poison me?"

"I am not trying to hurt you, Devadatta. I am illustrating a point. Would you do me the honor of tasting the water please?"

Devadatta took a small sip of the water and spit it out dramatically. "This water tastes like salt!"

The prince smiled. "Yes, the water now tastes like salt because salt has been poured into it. Would you now please take the salt *out* of the water?"

"Excuse me?" said Devadatta. "How do you expect me to take the salt out of the water?"

"Well, is the salt in the water?" asked Siddhattha.

"Yes."

"How do you know?"

"I could taste it!" replied Devadatta.

"So you know there is salt in the water, but you cannot separate the water from the salt?"

"Obviously!"

"Just so, dear opponent of mine. Brahman is in all things and it cannot be separated out. Truth is everywhere, in everything alive and everything that lacks life. It is in the rocks and trees, in the air, in the earth, and it is in you and me. It is *in* everything, because it *is* Everything.

"Just as the salt cannot be pulled out of the water, so Brahman cannot be pulled out of anything around us and shown as a separate entity."

Devadatta was stunned, but he recovered quickly. "But you still did not answer Brahmin's question! You have answered the opposite in fact, because he asked you to demonstrate Brahman and all you did was demonstrate that it cannot be demonstrated! How can that be right?"

"But I did demonstrate it, Cousin. The demonstration is in the taste. You can taste Truth, and that is how you know it is there. That is my answer."

Wearing the Red Line

The festivities went on for days. Celebrations took place at my parents' home, in the palace, and they covered the ground in all the spaces in between. By the time the wedding was over, hundreds of meals had been circulated for hundreds of guests over a period of many days. Ritual blessings too many to count had been poured over both of our heads.

It was a time of dizzying sensuality. Layers of color swirled around me, voices rang like bells around my ears, and the variety of succulent dishes never seemed to end. But I don't think I ate a bite the entire time—the knot of nerves in my stomach made digestion an unlikely enterprise. Combined with the line-up of aunties taking turns to squeeze my face like a ripe melon, appetite was simply impossible to conjure.

The sacrificial fire was the wedding's ceremonial centerpiece. The head priest had it built in the palace courtyard and the entire community was invited to bear witness on the last day. When the ritual fire was ready, it would have the power to bind two people together for life. I would be asked to circle it with my husband's name on my lips. After that, I would be his wife.

The priest patiently poured his ancient songs into the conflagration. His hands moved ingredients around while he sang, rotating magical elements and flinging them into the fire at various intervals like a master chef stirring a pot of prayers together. He chanted and swayed for what seemed like hours in front of the flames. So much butter had been poured into the fire that the flames were turning black.

"Close your eyes, Daughter," my mother whispered. "You are going to smudge your make-up."

I couldn't look away. I felt like I was being reborn in that moment, the priest's moving hands forging me into a new being. I wanted to see.

"Daughter," my mother insisted as she adjusted my hair, "watch from inside your mind."

I closed my eyes and let myself slide into mental quiet. The sounds of the crackling fire merged with the priest's voice. I felt myself disappear.

Soon a finger was tapping me on the shoulder. The priest had left his seat and had materialized right beside me.

"The fire is ready for you, Sri Yasodhara."

He had startled me. "Right now?"

He nodded.

Anxiety flapped its wings. I turned to my mother, hoping she could save me somehow, but she was caught in her own emotions. She pulled out a small make-up box, motioned for me to lower my head and added one last layer of red dye into the parting in my hair. It was the red line that was the symbol of the marriage to come.

"You are a beautiful bride, Daughter," she whispered. "I am so proud of you." She then removed her Durga pendant and placed it around my neck.

"What are you doing?" I asked, startled by the unexpected gift. "This is your favorite!"

"And now it belongs to you," she answered quietly.

"But why?"

"You are leaving your home and joining another. The Goddess will take care of you in my place."

"But you will still be my mother, won't you? Why does she have to take your place?" I asked, the fear of separation mounting rapidly.

"This is the way of things. You know that."

I did know that, but I wouldn't be that far away. I would still be able to visit from time to time . . . wouldn't I?

"What are you saying, Mother?"

Her eyes filled with tears. "In time, you will understand. Keep the Goddess close to you. She will make sure you never forget who you really are."

She tucked the pendant under my clothing and adjusted my appearance one last time. I was rooted to my spot, despite the priest's hovering. I grabbed my mother's hand and clung to her. I did not want to let go.

"Do you remember the instructions I gave you, Sri Yasodhara?" the priest asked as he gently encouraged me away.

I felt her hand slip out of mine.

"Sri Yasodhara," he repeated, "do you remember?"

I looked up and realized that everyone was watching. I nodded.

"Keep the fire to your right side," he counseled.

The priest walked back to his seat, leaving me stranded before a fire that promised to rebirth me. I looked back at my mother who seemed to be receding into the background. My old life was fading away.

I looked through the fire and caught flickers of Siddhattha on the other side. He was watching me intently, waiting for me to take the first step. This was to marry *him*, I reminded myself. I reached for the Durga pendant and held it tight. I finally lifted my right foot just as the priest lifted his mantras out of the air and broke out of the circle of doubt. I was not going to remain stranded in the realm of the in-between.

I circled the flames with my painted feet, my jewelry chiming like an orchestra that accompanied the priest's voice. I circumambulated the fire with my head lowered, the string of pearls that connected my nose ring to my right earring swaying softly against my cheek. I concentrated on the face of my beloved the way I was instructed to, bringing his name with me with every step.

"Siddhattha," I whispered quietly with my eyes half-closed.

I was woken from my reverie by the sound of footsteps behind me. I turned around to find Siddhattha approaching.

"What are you doing?" I whispered as he joined me in my ritual circumambulation. "You aren't supposed to be here."

"I know."

"Then what are you *doing*? You are supposed to be watching from your seat over there!"

Siddhattha smiled.

"We chose each other, Yasodhara. So we circle the flames together," he explained as though it was the most natural thing in the world.

He would not say another word. He just continued following the pace I had set, circling the sacred fire by my side. I could feel the talk beginning to form around us already, gossip queens spinning yarns of words about our scandalous behavior. They would be *tsk tsking* with disapproval and nodding their heads. And of course, *I* would be the one blamed for it. The woman always is.

I did not dare look up; I could not imagine meeting the looks that were staring down on both of us. I stared at my feet instead, watching the little anklet bells swing. The priest must have been puzzled by Siddhattha's behavior, but he did not skip a beat. His lilting sounds kept on pulsating as we pursued our pilgrimage around the sacred fire together. By the time the priest had concluded the ritual, the prince and I had become one.

*

Little was expected of Siddhattha and me after we married. We were free to spend our days enjoying the luxuries our station provided. For the first few months, Siddhattha and I filled our time with each other, learning who the other was with deepest intimacy. We hibernated in the royal apartments for as long as we could stand, and then charged into the gardens with giddy enthusiasm to stretch out our lazy limbs. We spent hours exploring the elaborate network of passageways that connected one garden with the next. Sometimes we played hunting games in the palace, searching the corridors for secret rooms and buried treasure. When we got bored, we ventured into the great palace kitchen and scavenged for sweets. We even squatted in the corner the way the staff often did, and sipped tea out of clay cups, listening to the gossip that was ladled into the room with regular abundance.

It was not a busy life by any standard, but we were happy. The only strange thing was that we never seemed to go very far. The palace compound outlined the limits of my new world. Every once in a while, I wandered over to the palace gates and looked at the territory on the other side. The paths I used to take—paths that were so familiar to me after years of racing over them—peeked out at me through the bars. For reasons I could not understand, I was meant to stay inside.

I decided to ask the king about it after the morning meal one day. He was supposed to meet with two householders who had been arguing over the proprietary rights of a particular fig tree, but their appearance at the royal court had been postponed, leaving the king with some spare time. Apparently, the argument had boiled over the night before and one of the householders had smashed a pot over the other one's head. The negotiations would have to wait for a full recovery.

I inched over discreetly. "May I ask you a question, Maharaja?" I asked with a demure voice. Mahapajapati and Siddhattha were in the midst of a fiery legal debate over land rights and fruit trees, while Nanda was intently focused on the peas in his plate, carefully examining each one for reasons I could not fathom.

"Of course, Daughter. What can I do for you?"

"Well ..." I had not prepared my question and I certainly could not ask it directly. I looked for some way around. "You know, my mother and I used to love shopping at the market in town. I haven't been in ages. I would love to go with the prince and look at what the traveling merchants have brought in. Do you think we could go during the half-moon festival?"

The king's face changed instantly. He had smiled affectionately when I first approached, but as soon as he heard my question, his face darkened.

"That is unfortunately impossible, Daughter."

"Why?"

"That is none of your concern."

I should have walked away at that point. I was supposed to accept the world the king had created for me, but it made no sense. Why couldn't we leave? Was I really expected to circle the palace compound for the rest of my life?

"Your Highness, I don't understand. Please tell me why."

Mahapajapati and Siddhattha stopped arguing. Nanda, however, was still enthralled by the peas on his plate. *Was he counting them?*

"Because that is the way things have to be. There is nothing more you need to understand." He got up from the table and walked off without another word.

I turned to the others and stared at them with a look of incredulity. Siddhattha excused himself and followed his father into the next room.

"Mother-in-Law, what is going on?" I asked desperately.

She called the servant over for a cup of warm ginger milk.

"Did your parents not explain any of this to you before you were married?" she asked while her cup was being filled.

The wedding had taken place a few months earlier. I tried to remember any conversation that might have explained my current situation, but I could not think of anything.

"They told me what to expect as a princess I suppose. My mother reminded me many times about the obligations I would have to carry out, but ... no. Nothing like this."

"I see," she said as she waved the servant away. "They never said anything about Siddhattha's birth?"

"What does his birth have to do with this?" I asked, genuinely confused.

Nanda looked up from his plate and stared at me. "Do you mean that you have no idea? You married him and you don't even know?"

I had forgotten he was there.

"Go back to your peas!" I replied defensively.

"Fine by me," he answered. He picked up his plate and walked out. Servants rushed to follow him, apparently prepared to catch any peas that might slide off his plate.

"What's with the peas?" I asked, as the door closed behind him.

She shrugged. "Someone told him they would improve his virility. He has been preoccupied by them ever since."

I laughed, despite myself.

"Mother-in-Law," I said, returning to the topic, "What don't I know?"

Mahapajapati and I spent the morning sitting in the courtyard together. She told me the stories that surrounded my husband's birth, stories of prophecies

and predictions, about the risk of his leaving home even though he was supposed
to stay, and the weight of his name and what it might portend. She didn't tell me
the extent to which the king had shielded his son's reality, but enough for me to
begin to understand.

"I knew the king was protective, but I thought it was just because he was a
prince. That all princes were raised that way. I never realized that this had to do
with Siddhattha's birth chart. How could I have not known that?"

"I suppose people have been protecting you too, not wanting to upset you
with all of this."

"But why wouldn't my parents tell me? Why didn't my mother explain this to
me before I married?"

"Probably for the same reason," she said.

My mother never protected me from the truth. It was not like her to leave
such important information out. And yet ... would I really have entered my
marriage as happily if I had known? I thought back to our conversation by the
sacrificial fire, just before we were wed. Pieces were falling into place.

"Is this why we always played here as children? Why he never came to us?"
I asked.

She nodded. I had never really wondered about his perpetual presence in the
compound. It had always just been a fact of the world I lived in: he was here and
we came to join him. I never considered the possibility that he was forbidden
from leaving.

"Does this mean that Siddhattha has never gone beyond the palace gates? Not
once since he was born?"

The queen shook her head. "Siddhattha has only ever known what is within
these palace walls. His father does not want to take unnecessary risks. The prince
must become king."

"But *obviously* Siddhattha will become king! The prophecies have already
been proved wrong because he married me. He didn't leave, so the king does not
need to worry anymore. Siddhattha is bound to the world because he is bound to
me ... Right?"

Mahapajapati swirled the milk inside her cup. She did not answer.

*

It is surprising how quickly we can adapt to new situations. The king had dictated
the limits of my new life and I learned to accept them. After all, I had not joined
the royal family in the hopes of pursuing personal whims and desires. I had
entered the royal household aware that there would be responsibilities to

shoulder—to the subjects of the Sakya Kingdom, to the royal family, and most importantly, to my beloved husband. If he was bound to the palace walls, I was bound with him. There was no other place I wanted to be.

There was, however, one responsibility I seemed incapable of fulfilling: no matter what I did, I could not conceive a child. My womb was empty for many years.

At first, I could accept not being pregnant. After all, not everyone becomes pregnant in their first year. The midwife was not worried and neither was I. But soon the time began to feel long. A second year passed and then a third. The subjects of our kingdom began to talk. I was failing in my most sacred of obligations. The throne required an heir and I was not providing.

"Please don't worry so much," Siddhattha tried to reassure me.

"But I have to worry, Husband! It is the reason you married me and I am failing!"

He sighed. We had gone over this so many times, but I would not relent. "It *isn't* the reason I married you. You should know that by now."

I looked away with shame. He loved me with such tenderness. He should have been arranging for a second wife as everyone insisted, but he refused. He would not even visit the courtesans in the Women's Quarters. Hundreds of lavishly adorned women, each one trained in the sixty-four arts of love, lazed about idly in a discreet section of the palace compound, but he never paid them any attention. I could only imagine how bored they had all become.

When a fourth year passed, I became desperate. I sought out other midwives and healers, plant peddlers and priests. I tried anything I could get my hands on in the hopes that something might eventually work. Some of the potions made me sick. I turned my bed to face the sunrise. I hung blessings in my window. I even had scrapings from Lumbinidevi's tree delivered and placed in auspicious positions around my room. I tried it all, but when my fifth year remained as barren as all the years before, I lost hope. Although everything else was seemingly flawless, my body remained a desert landscape.

My mother-in-law kept trying to talk to me, but the more time passed, the further I pulled away. I could not face her with my failure. I was convinced she was disappointed, even if she never said she was.

"Where is the princess?" I heard her say outside my door one morning.

"She is in her room, Maharani," my maidservant replied.

"Ask her to come out, please."

Neelima shuffled her feet, not quite sure how to avoid refusing the queen while remaining faithful to me.

"Is something wrong?" she asked.

"I beg your forgiveness, Maharani. The princess has asked to be left alone."

And then I heard it. The reprimand on the other side of the door. The question I was certain she was asking herself that she did not want to say out loud: *is she not pregnant yet?*

"Let me inside, Servant."

Poor Neelima had no choice. She pushed open the door and let my mother-in-law in. And there she found me, sitting on a pile of old cloths, waiting for the Bleeding to subside.

"You are bleeding again?" she asked.

I looked down. "My apologies, Maharani."

She sighed. I expected her to turn away from me, but instead she walked right in.

"Wha . . . what are you doing?" I asked, terribly embarrassed to be in the midst of my Bleeding in front of her. I could not get up to greet her.

"You may go now," she ordered Neelima, who was standing by the door with her mouth hanging open. When Neelima did not respond, the queen closed the door for her and sealed us in.

She sat down beside me and gave me a long hard look. "You still aren't pregnant?"

"Obviously not," I replied, a bit more harshly than I had planned.

"And you are upset about that."

"Obviously . . ." I lowered my eyes and played with my fingers.

"You know, I waited a long time to become pregnant too."

Cautiously, I raised my eyes. She took a deep breath, as though she had spent a long time feeling exasperated with me. "Your silence has been going on for far too long, Daughter. You are suffering, but you are too proud to talk to me about it. Instead, you have risked your health trying magical potions that are more likely to kill you than do much else."

I knew I deserved the reprimand, but I remained silent.

"The palace is a lonely place, Daughter," she added more softly. "You should let me take care of you."

My hardened defenses finally began to crack at the sound of those words. She was a much better person than I ever allowed myself to see.

"Do you miss your mother? Women often do in times like this."

Perhaps it was because of the Bleeding, but the moment she mentioned my mother, the tears welled.

"I miss her very much."

Despite our customs of keeping those who are in their Bleeding apart, Mahapajapati reached out and took me into her arms.

"She isn't well, you know," I said between swollen heartbeats. "She can't leave her house anymore and I am not allowed to leave the palace, so I don't get to see her at all . . ."

I had not confessed that hurt to anyone. My mother's back had gotten very bad and it had become difficult for her to walk. She used to come with my father to see me, but the past few years had changed her. Most days, she was confined to her bed. The palace had become too long a journey for her to make.

"And now I can't even get pregnant," I sobbed. "It's been *years* and nothing has happened! What's wrong with me?"

Mahapajapati held me close for a long time, waiting for the sadness to run its course.

"I remember feeling the same way when it was me," she said consolingly. "And my sister did too. Poor Maya only became pregnant at the very end of her life. Women in our family seem to be cursed with this difficulty. We were never like other women who can produce half a dozen males in as many years. I have only had one child and Maya did too. And it took each of us a long time."

I knew that both Siddhattha and Nanda were the only children from their mothers, and yet I never made the emotional connection for myself. I had somehow convinced myself that I was the only woman in the ten-thousand worlds to have had difficulty becoming pregnant.

"I am sorry, Mother-in-Law," I whispered, embarrassed for the first time.

"What for?"

"For not confiding in you. I don't know why I didn't think that you would understand. I thought you were angry with me for being childless."

"You did not think beyond your own self, Yasodhara. That is not wise."

I looked down, ashamed of myself for having overlooked her. "Do you think I will ever produce a child?" I asked, hoping she could provide me with some relief.

"No one can know that," she replied. She was not prepared to make me feel better with false assurances or sweetened hopes, even though I would have accepted them gladly.

"But worrying about it won't help," she said as she patted my hands. "No more crying."

Soil and Suffering

One morning, Siddhattha and I decided to go for a walk. It was a beautiful autumn day, the air crisp and fresh after a torrential monsoon season. It was a perfect morning to wander through the Flower Garden, one of our favorite destinations.

We slipped into the quiet with familiarity. The gardeners moved away as we approached, providing us with the privacy we craved without our having to ask for it. Within moments, we were engulfed by giant flowers of every variety.

"Look at the size of this one, Husband!" I exclaimed. "It must be as big as my head!"

Siddhattha smiled at my exuberance and pretended to measure my head against it. "Just about the same size actually!" he replied. "Which is amazing, given how big your head can be!"

"Hey!" I said, pretending to be angry. I poked him in the chest with my bejeweled finger, and added, "I am not the only one with a big head here, my dear Raja-To-Be. In fact, I think your head might be even bigger than this one! Maybe we should pluck it off its bush and frame it just for you?"

I aimed for the flower theatrically, as though I was about to tear it away from its life force. Siddhattha jumped. "No, Yasodhara! Don't do that!"

I paused in mid-gesture, surprised by his reaction. He rarely jumped that way. I was usually the one to burst with emotion.

A moment later, he mumbled an explanation, "It's just that ... it would be a crime to hurt a flower like that."

I lowered my hand. "I am sorry ... I didn't mean to cause you grief, Husband. I was only teasing."

"Oh ... Of course, darling. I am not sure what came over me," he said, scratching his forehead.

"Why don't we keep walking?"

"Good idea." He reached for my hand and held onto it for a moment, as though he was trying to steady himself.

We soon found ourselves on the outer edge of the garden. The wild forest created a natural boundary, announcing the limits of the king's palatial compound. We were forbidden from going further.

"You know, Husband . . ." I said tentatively, letting my voice trail for a moment, "I think today is an important tilling day for many families. The guards are few in number."

He smiled at me, his twinkle having returned in spades. "You're right. It *is* a perfect day for tilling the fields." He looked around and added, "Where *are* the guards? Do you see any?"

I looked around too, but we were alone, unwatched, for the first time in ages. The excitement built up inside of me with a rush. "Oh Husband! Let's go before someone sees us!"

"With pleasure!" he said with all of his splendid charm. Apparently, he did not mind running from his shackles either. He took my hand to help me over the bushes that separated the manicured world from the wilderness.

The hush that surrounded us as the curtain of trees dropped behind us was instant. My skin tingled with anticipation, the air wrapping itself around me with vibrant energy. For a few moments, neither of us was capable of speaking. I kept listening for the guards, wondering if they were onto us. No one seemed to be around.

"Husband, let's keep walking forever!" I said, jumping gleefully like a grasshopper and clapping my hands. "What do you think? What if we never went back? We could live in the forest the way Rama and Sita did! When he was exiled from his kingdom, they managed to live in the forest together for many years, didn't they? Let's never go back! What do you think?"

How I had missed my freedom!

"What do you say, Husband? Shall we follow in Rama and Sita's footsteps and run away for a few years?" I was jumping up and down now like a child begging for a sweet. He, however, was standing quite still as he stared into the wilderness ahead.

"You certainly loved climbing trees when we were little, Yasodhara. I will grant you that," he responded.

Then he turned toward me. "But do you really think you could survive on nuts and fruits at this point in your life? Wouldn't you miss all the delicacies Cook makes for you? And what about the monsoon without a proper roof over your head? Are you really sure you are up to a life of forest-dwelling?"

That was not the response I had anticipated. He was supposed to join me in my fantasy, not challenge it with reality. I placed a hand on my jutting hip and scowled.

"Why would you say such things?" I demanded. "First of all, I could manage very well without Cook preparing my meals, if you really want to know! And second, why are you being so serious?"

"Ohhhh! I didn't realize that this was a play." His face was transformed by a wide grin, and then he said, "Right, then. Here goes: Yes, Wife. Let's run away and live in the forest and climb trees all day!"

He then cocked his head to the side and asked, "Is that better?"

"You are infuriating!" I responded as I swatted his arm. I turned away from him and stomped ahead, pretending to be much angrier than I was. I could feel him enjoying my tantrum, but I kept walking (making sure to sway my hips in the process . . .).

I had not taken more than two steps when I felt his strong arms wrap tightly around me. I screeched—so unaccustomed was I to any real contact between us outdoors, but thrilled by the surprise. I turned to face him and nuzzled my forehead into his broad chest.

*

The privacy of the green forest enveloped us. We had no idea that just ahead, the landscape gave way to a series of farmers' fields. The sounds of humanity caught us off guard. Farmers were singing as they tilled the land.

We pulled back from each other and slipped into the shadows, not sure if anyone had seen us. I was breathless, trying to quiet my heart that was pounding wildly in my chest. I peeked around the corner at the farmer who was closest to us. He was coaxing his water buffalos across the earth.

"I don't think he saw us, Husband. Do you?"

"No, I don't think he did," he answered.

"What do we do now?"

He did not answer right away. He was watching the farmer closest to us intently.

"Darling, do you think we could take a moment to watch him work? Would you mind?" he asked. "I have never had the opportunity to watch this kind of thing before. Have you ever been so close to a farmer's field?"

My shoulders dropped with disappointment. He wanted to watch someone *farm*?

"Of course, Husband." I said. "We can sit over there, under that tree."

He knew me all too well. He knew that I was sacrificing a savored moment of retreat for something unbearably ordinary.

"You *have* seen farmers work before, haven't you?" he asked, gazing at me with his dark brown eyes. I looked down at my fingers, more aware than I had ever been of his restricted upbringing.

"Well . . ." I said. "Not really. I mean . . . not often. Well, what I mean is, I never plowed a field myself or anything. I don't really know *that* much about it."

He smiled, aware that I was trying to protect him. "Of course you have, Wife. Please don't hide yourself from me. You must have seen farmers work many times during your childhood. It is only natural."

Siddhattha's upbringing had managed to completely exclude him from the world the rest of us lived in.

"Let's take a seat over there. You can watch them work without being seen. Watch as long as you want."

I led him to the spot under the shade of a neem tree and then watched him as he watched the farmer pursue the most ordinary activity in the world. He watched the way the plow cut into the earth, studied the beasts as they pulled the heavy weight they were harnessed to with the strength of their bodies, examined the men as they slaved. At one point, he seemed on the verge of running out onto the field to ask the farmer if he could try the work himself.

The farmer was slowing down. He was coming closer to us as his work neared the edge of the field. We were now able to see his labor from very close. Siddhattha leaned forward, keen to catch every detail.

The water buffalos were straining their necks, their curved horns moving this way and that as they yanked at the plow. They were exhausted, fighting their enslavement with every step they took. Perhaps they understood that their work was nearly completed and they were quitting in anticipation. The farmer was not singing anymore.

He kept coaxing them forward, pulling at the rope that was attached to the rings in their great, flaring nostrils, which seemed to upset them even more. They eventually dug in their hooves and refused to take another step. The farmer pulled out his whip and cracked it against their thick, leathery hides.

The sound made Siddhattha jump. He pulled backwards instinctively, as though the whip was thrashing against his own skin. The whip cracked a second time and then a third, and each time, Siddhattha reacted with visceral emotion. He gripped his knees, as though he was in pain, as though *he* was the water buffalo attached to the plow. I wanted to say something to him, to console him or explain the realities of farming to him, but the farmer was too close to us at that point and we risked being discovered.

The farmer was truly frustrated now. There was so little of the field left to plow and he obviously wanted to get the work done, but even with the whip, the water buffalos refused to move. The farmer, who was himself dripping with sweat and seemed just as exhausted, eventually relinquished. He undid the harness to set the animals free, leaving the plow behind for another day.

"Well, Husband? Shall we get back to the palace grounds now?" I said as I stood up. I was trying to sound chipper, hoping to lift the mood that seemed to have covered him like an ominous fog.

Siddhattha did not respond. He was still staring at the space where the water buffalos once stood.

"Husband?"

He cleared his throat. "I'm sorry, darling. I know I have asked so much of you already, but . . ." he looked over at the field apprehensively. "Would you mind if I took a closer look now that everyone has gone? I have never really seen a plow from up close before. I would also like to see what the soil looks like after it has been tilled. Do you mind?"

He wanted to stay *longer*? We had already been there for such a long time . . .

"Of course."

Without another word, Siddhattha crept towards the plow. He kneeled in the soil and began to study the equipment. He examined the wood, put his fingers into the moist earth they had been tilling and picked up the remains of the rope that had been harnessed to the animals' nostril-rings. He caressed the rope, his eyes far away. Eventually, he sat down, right by the edge of the gash in the earth. He crossed his legs and closed his eyes, the rope cradled in his arms.

Only as the sun was dipping into darkness did Siddhattha open his eyes again. He got to his feet and headed back towards me. I watched him, stunned first by his departure from me, and then by his return. I felt like he had traveled a tremendous distance in the time he had sat by the plow.

I felt left behind.

"Are you all right?" I asked.

He did not answer. He took my hand into his and started the journey home, absorbed by his own silence. I focused on him as he moved through his mind, not letting me in. The loneliness was overwhelming.

"Will you say something?" I pleaded. "What happened to you while you were sitting out there?"

He kept walking, holding onto me tightly. "I will tell you everything, but I want to get you back to the palace first. It's getting dark."

I took my eyes off him and looked around. The trees that had seemed so majestic earlier now seemed to be looming over us, as though they were listening, watching our every move. A chill slipped into my veins. Terrible stories had been told about the forest at night. There were predatory animals and unpredictable insects that could make you sick with the slightest nibble of your skin. Forests were also the haunts of ghosts and wicked deities that took pleasure in putting obstacles on your path. Although I had claimed to be capable of living as a forest-dweller, now that the sun had set, the forest was the last place in the world I wanted to be.

"Yes, we should get home ..." I muttered as the deepening darkness folded over me. Siddhattha wrapped his arm around my trembling shoulders.

"Tell me what happened while we walk," I said. "It will help."

He moved a branch gently to the side so that I could pass. "Well, I think a realization is what happened," he began thoughtfully. "I realized that the world is alive. That everything is alive."

"What do you mean, *everything*?" I asked as an owl hooted in the tree above us.

"I mean *everything*. I watched that farmer and I could see his aliveness as I have never seen it before. He was alive the way the smallest of insects is alive, or the most powerful of work animals."

"But of course the farmer is alive," I replied. "I don't understand what you are saying." I held onto his arm as I stepped around a boulder.

"Think about what the teachers have always said: that there is a hierarchy of people in the world. Brahmins and royal families are at the top, and peasants fall near the bottom, right?"

I tripped on a protruding root and he caught me. "Careful," he urged softly.

"Say what you said again?"

"Each family is placed somewhere along the hierarchy of value," he repeated. "Priests and royal families are at the top and peasants, like that farmer, are further down. Isn't that what we have always been told?"

"Of course. What of it?" I asked, confused by the direction of the conversation. A thicket blocked our path and Siddhattha pulled it apart so that I could step through, but I still got scratched. I did not remember the path being so difficult on the way in.

"Well, I thought this meant that peasants were somehow different from royals," he continued, unruffled by the complicated terrain. "That peasants had a different kind of life somehow. I can't explain it, but it always seemed that way to me."

"All right. So?"

"Well, it became clear to me that peasants are *not* different from us. They have the same life coursing inside of them as we do. This is what the sages mean when they tell us that everything is Ultimate Reality. I really understand what that means now."

"Didn't you say something about this at the competition before we were married?" I asked, trying to keep up with him.

"I did, but I don't think I fully understood what I was arguing about until this moment. I think I can *taste* it now," he answered with a smile in his voice.

When I didn't respond, he continued.

"The farmer and I are the same in ways I never appreciated before. Never realized was true. The farmer felt like my brother. I have never felt that way about a farmer before ..." He paused for a moment and then said, "Of course, I never had much interaction with farmers before either."

He walked quietly for a while after that. I looked up at him for the first time since we began our walk home and realized how selfish I was being. I wasn't really listening to him. I was allowing myself to be overtaken by anxiety instead.

"Keep talking," I said. "I am listening."

"Well ..." he continued. "When I realized that the farmer could be my brother—*was* my brother in fact—something cracked inside of me."

"What do you mean?"

"I mean ... my heart saw his suffering and his fellow humanity all at once. It was an overwhelming emotion, as though an earthquake had broken something open."

A deep quiet descended over me. I was listening intently to every word he was saying now.

"I kept staring at the farmer's skin. It was darkened by the sun, as though he had spent many days working under its glare. And it was rough in so many places, calloused like a tree root. His hands were like leather, not very different from the water buffalos' hide. And he was sweating so much. His clothing was soaked with his labor. Every inch of his body spoke of suffering. I don't think I have ever seen anything like that before."

I had not noticed any of these details, or at least had not given them any consideration. He was just another farmer. They all looked the same to me, but Siddhattha had seen him.

"It wasn't just the farmer though. It was the water buffalos too. They are such mighty animals, and yet they seemed so tired. How much had they been forced to endure? And what about those nose rings? I kept imagining how their nostrils were pierced, what kind of tools must have been used. Can you imagine being pulled around by a nose ring?"

I touched my own nose ring instinctively. I had never thought of that.

"When the farmer cracked the whip, I thought my heart would stop! I could not imagine the kind of suffering that would lead a man to whip a fellow creature.

I could not imagine what it would feel like to *be* whipped either! Those poor animals . . . I saw their suffering too.

"And then when I approached the earth after they left and I examined the soil they had been preparing, I found it littered with tiny creatures that had been cut into pieces by the plow. There they lay, inside the earth as though piled inside a funeral mound, destroyed by the tools that bring food to our table."

A shiver ran down my spine. I was not sure why, but I was becoming tangibly afraid of what he was saying. As though his realizations meant something important . . . dangerous even.

Mahapajapati's words from years before rang in my ears: there were prophecies made at his birth that he would leave . . . I clutched the Durga pendant I wore around my neck and made a silent prayer.

"Yasodhara, what are you thinking about?" he asked, aware of the change in me.

"I am not sure, Husband," I replied slowly, letting the pendant go. "Can you explain your experience in a different way?"

"But isn't it obvious? All of those creatures—the tiny insects, the beasts, the farmer . . . every one of them was suffering. And every one of them—even the insects—felt like my brothers. They *are* my brothers, Yasodhara! And they suffer. They even die just so that we can eat."

"I see . . ." I answered, my head spinning. "Everyone suffers. That's true . . ."

"But?" he stopped and turned towards me. "What are you not saying?"

"Well . . . you are right of course. All creatures suffer. And in some way, we are surely all connected. All *brothers*, as you say. But . . . but how else could it be? There is no alternative to suffering, Husband. We live, we die, and we suffer in between. That's the natural way of things. What else can there be?"

His eyes grew wide with surprise. "No alternative?" he asked.

I wondered if I was supposed to soften my view for his benefit, but I could not imagine lying to him.

"No, I don't think there is. When a woman gives birth, she suffers. When a farmer tills the land, he experiences hardship. When we eat animals, it is death that we are ingesting. How else can life be?"

It was the only thing I knew how to say, the only truth I had inside of me. But the look on his face was not what I hoped for. My answer troubled him.

"What's wrong, Husband? Have I upset you? I didn't mean to. I just don't know what else to say."

He did not answer.

"Husband?"

But he would not speak. In fact, he did not speak again for the rest of the way home.

We reached the edge of the palace boundary and crossed the bushes into the Flower Garden. He did not take my hand to help me cross over this time and he did not ask me if I was all right. He did not say a word. He just kept walking, locked inside the world he carried in his mind.

A world I was once again forbidden from entering.

12

News

Years later.

My maidservant was sweeping my chambers as I worked through my bead collection. I had dozens of beads of every color and variety—beads made of precious jewels, others made of glass, and all kinds of wooden beads that had been carved by famous artisans. My favorites, though, were those Siddhattha had carved himself.

I was examining a sandalwood bead he had given me recently. It was the strangest bead he had ever made—a wooden bead carved into the shape of a tree. There was something mysterious about it—about carving a piece of wood into the shape of a tree.

I placed it on the bed in front of me and wondered what I could do with it. I wanted to wear it, but its leaves spread out too wide to be strung on a necklace. Perhaps I would paint it.

"Maidservant, do you remember that painting kit I received a while ago from the Kashmiri delegation. Where did I put it?"

Before she could answer, I had hopped off the bed and was rummaging through the art-chest on the other side of the room. "I don't see it in here ..." I said as I pulled materials out. "Do you remember the kit I am talking about?" I lifted my head up and a wave of dizziness sent me spiraling to the floor.

"Your Highness!" she cried out as she ran to my side. "Are you all right?"

I shook my head, a little surprised by the fall. "Goodness! I don't know what just came over me."

She tried to help me up, but I refused. "Please don't fuss. I am fine."

I pulled myself up and sat down on the edge of the art-chest, grabbing at the sides to keep myself steady. She eyed me carefully, but did not say more. She returned to her sweeping.

"I think the painting kit may still be in the Gift Room. Shall I fetch it for you?" she offered.

"Yes, that would be helpful."

"Right away." She put down the broom and scuttled out. She was probably alerting others about the mishap, but I tried not to think about it. The palace could be so small at times.

As soon as the door closed, I made my way back to the bed and allowed myself to sink into it. It wasn't the first time I was overcome by dizziness. Something was wrong.

I picked up the carved wooden tree and looked at it again. What was he thinking when he chose to make it, I wondered. What was he trying to say? Before I even realized how tired I was, I drifted off to sleep with the tree in my hand and slipped into a dream . . .

Siddhattha and I were in a distant land in a distant time. He was the prince of a great kingdom and I was his bride. We had two children and everything felt perfectly pleasant.

But then the kingdom's people rioted and there were fists in the air, demanding that the prince be deposed. They did not want him to inherit the throne. The prince went to see his father with the hope that he would protect him, but to my astonishment, the king refused. The prince could not take the throne. He had to go. He could not be trusted with the kingdom anymore.

The prince had been practicing generosity to an alarming degree. He had made a vow that he would give whatever anyone asked for. Not a safe vow for a royal to make. He began with small things—a few gifts here and there—but soon people realized that he never said no, and larger requests were being made.

"Please, Your Highness, I need more gold for my daughter's dowry."

"Of course," he replied as he pushed a pile of gold towards his requestor.

"Please, Your Highness. I require more land."

"Of course," he replied as he drew up documents in the petitioner's name.

If the king had not put a stop to it, he would have given the entire kingdom away. He had to be deposed. There was no other way.

"I am sorry, Son. But the vow you have taken has put the entire kingdom in jeopardy. You cannot have a prince's power and give it all away."

"I understand," he replied.

I could have let him go without me. I could see that option in the dream. It was not I who had made the vow. My children and I could have stayed in the palace. He was the only one who needed to go, but I was his wife and could not let him go alone. So I packed my bags and followed him into exile with the children. We moved to the forest together as a family.

It was an adjustment at first. No more servants, no comforts of any kind. We had to build a home out of branches and leaves. We had to pick fruit and nuts for food. It was so far from the world I had known, but I did not complain. I was a loyal wife and I stood by my husband. He was a great soul and his determination to practice generosity was inspiring. I accepted our new circumstances and we found our happiness again, settling into our new forest-dwelling routine.

But then one day, while I was out picking fruits, the earth shook with pain and I knew something had gone terribly wrong. I dropped my basket and raced home in a panic. I found my husband sitting quietly in our hut, staring at the forest floor.

"Husband! What happened? I felt the earth cry out in pain!"

He did not respond.

"Husband, what's going on?" I pleaded desperately.

Silence.

"Husband!" I shrieked. "Why aren't you answering me?! And where are the children?"

He remained still as a statue, as though he was not even there.

I raced around, calling the children's names, looking in every place I could think of that they might be in. My heart was pounding with terror. Where were the children?!

I ran back to my husband and shook him by the shoulders. "Husband!" I yelled. "Stop staring at the floor and tell me where our children are!!!"

My husband slowly lifted his face, tears streaming. "The children are gone."

My mouth dropped open. "What do you mean, gone?"

"A man came while you were out. He needed slaves to help his wife with her chores. He asked for the children. I had no choice but to give the children to him."

Time stopped.

"Husband, what are you talking about?"

My husband looked up at me with heart-breaking despair. "My vow . . ." his voice trailed away in pain.

I dropped to my knees in front of him. "What about your vow?" I asked in a barely audible voice. He could not possibly be saying what I thought he was saying . . .

"My vow. The man asked for our children. He needed slaves. I had no choice but to give what he asked for . . ."

"NOOOO!!!!!!!!!!" I screamed as I pounded him with my fists. "NOOOO!!!!!!!!!!"

"Princess! Wake up! Wake up!"

Neelima was standing over me, shaking me by the shoulders. I opened my eyes with what must have been a wild look. I was drenched with sweat.

"Where am I? What happened?"

"You are fine, Your Highness. You are safe in your room. You were having a bad dream."

I wiped the sweat from my forehead and slowly pulled myself up, but the dizziness reclaimed me and I fell back against the pillows.

"I am going to call the healer," she said. "You don't look well."

"No." I refused.

Neelima looked even more concerned by that, but she knew not to argue with me. She nodded and bent down to pick up the scattered painting materials she had dropped on the floor. One of the bottles had shattered. A puddle of red paint was seeping along the marble tiles.

"I am so sorry for the mess. I will go get a bucket to clean this up."

She bowed and slipped out of the room. I stared at the growing puddle on the floor. It seemed to be pulsating with life, moving across the tiles, spreading like a blood-red vine. All of a sudden, I bolted up as the force of clear understanding struck me.

I was pregnant.

*

I calculated and recalculated the weeks on my fingers. I had stopped paying attention to my body's cycles years ago. It did not seem relevant anymore, so I had to work hard to retrace the time. I went over the details repeatedly and I kept finding myself at the same point: it had been almost three moons since I last entered the Bleeding Time.

We had waited twelve years. *Twelve* years.

I had to tell Siddhattha . . .

But how? Hope had been cancelled for both of us long ago. We had grown used to childlessness. It wasn't even much of a discussion anymore. The entire kingdom seemed to have settled into an empty apathy on the subject. I was not going to produce an heir and the prince refused to take a second wife. The conversation had been extinguished. What was I supposed to do now?

Neelima was silently mopping up the spill of blood-red paint. I stepped around her and walked over to the window.

What about the dream?

I wrapped my arms protectively around my belly. The dream was not of an ordinary making. It felt like it had been delivered from another realm, and it was warning me about something. Warning me about *him*.

I paced the length of my room as I replayed the story in my head, the bangles on my wrists striking each other as I moved briskly from one end to the other. In the dream, I had left the palace for him. I brought my children with me and followed him into a life of hardship. I was loyal every step of the way—the perfect wife. And the moment I turned my head, *he gave our children away*?

It was just a dream, I muttered to myself as I sat down. It was nothing more than that. It never happened. Siddhattha would never do anything like that.

But it was so real! I stood up and started pacing again. I could not shake the feeling that he *had* done that. He *did* give our children away! And what else would he have been prepared to give after that? Would he have given *me* away next? Sita went to the forest *with* Lord Rama and they stayed there together. When she was captured by the demon Ravana, he moved heaven and earth to find her. He never gave her away. How could Siddhattha give his family up that way?

But . . .

I stopped pacing.

Rama *did* give Sita away in the end. When he was called out of exile, he returned with her to the palace. But when rumors began circulating about her, he asked her to leave. He gave her away, even though he knew she was innocent. She returned to the forest all by herself. He chose his kingdom over his wife. And Siddhattha chose his practice of generosity over us. It had happened before.

It could happen again.

My arms stayed fixed around my belly. I was suddenly mortally afraid. I could not tell Siddhattha about this pregnancy.

There was a knock at the door.

"I will get it," my maidservant said. I had forgotten she was there.

She opened the door and let my husband right in.

"Where have you been? The midday meal has come and gone and you never joined us. Is everything all right?" he asked.

Concern was etched all over his beautiful face. All at once, my heart melted. How could I have imagined all of those terrible things about him? I did not know what had come over me.

"Oh, Husband!" I cried out as I threw my arms around his neck. "I am so sorry I doubted you!"

"Are you all right, Yasodhara?" he asked.

I wiped my cheeks with the backs of my hands. "Yes," I sniffled with a smile. "I am perfectly all right."

He looked at me with some uncertainty, but then did the strangest thing. I thought he would ask me what had made me cry that way or what I meant when I said that I had doubted him, but he didn't do that at all.

Instead, he patted me on the shoulder and said, "Right. Well, I am glad you are well. I have some things to do with Chariot Driver. I will be back later to check on you."

And without another word, he turned on his heels and walked out the door.

The First Sights

"Let's go, Channa," Siddhattha commanded his Chariot Driver as he swept past him.

"Where are we going, Your Highness?"

"We are going *out*! That is where we are going! Out of the palace compound. *Out!*"

"Umm . . . What exactly do you mean by 'out,' Your Highness?"

"My father is on a tour of the countryside," Siddhattha explained as he swooshed through the corridors, "the ministers are celebrating the arrival of Chief Minister's grandson, and the guards have retired for a game of dice. *So we are going out!*"

Channa felt certain that his role was to dissuade the prince at this point, but he had no time to argue. Siddhattha was charging through the palace as though his legs were on fire and he had to race to keep up with him. He knew he was forbidden from escorting the prince out of his prison, but how exactly was he supposed to stop him? He ran behind him, mumbling to himself with disorientation. Were they really going out? *Now?*

"Get the horses, Chariot Driver. We don't have a moment to spare! I want to ride my own steed and I want to ride fast!"

Channa took off towards the royal stables, his hands shaking and his heart palpitating. He was disobeying a royal command, but he was being forced to follow another command in order to do so! What was he supposed to do? One royal commanded one thing and another royal commanded another! It was crushingly unfair for these men to shove him in the middle of their father-son dispute, especially since he was the one who would probably end up paying the price.

Channa slowed down as he approached the stables. The rich smell of hay met him at the entrance, soothing him like an old friend. Horses were so much safer than the unpredictable ways of men. He could speak with horses, communicate truthfully without the burden of having to forage through an infinitely complicated tapestry of obscure intentions. He always breathed more easily when they were close at hand.

Channa grabbed a handful of hay as he walked over to Kanthaka, the prince's royal steed, and offered it to him. His hands were trembling. He reached up and caressed the luxurious white mane to help calm himself down.

I could be executed for this, he thought to himself. *Executed.* My head could be chopped off like a coconut from a branch. It was no minor offense to disobey the king—particularly on this subject. The king was famously protective of his son and remained petrified of potential abandonment, despite the fact that the prince had become a man a long time ago, despite all the ways the prince had proved his loyalty to his station, despite how seriously he had taken his responsibilities as heir to the throne. But there was no talking to the king about this. He was obsessed with his son remaining close to home.

Channa stroked Kanthaka contemplatively as he recalled all the ways this unfortunate reality had unfolded over the years. He had grown increasingly concerned about it, but like everyone else in the palace, he was not welcome to comment. Siddhattha was an exceptional young man. Why couldn't the king see that? And why couldn't he see how much pain he was causing his son by stifling him in this way? The prince was starved for real life, starved for the world his subjects lived in, but it was forever denied him. The palace was nothing more than a gilded cage and Siddhattha was suffocating in it.

Kanthaka stamped his hooves abruptly and yanked his head out of Channa's reach.

"My goodness, Great One!" Channa chuckled. "You have not changed, have you? You never could stand being cooped up in here!"

Channa thought back to the days when Kanthaka had first arrived at the stables. He had never been so challenged by a horse before. He had spent weeks trying to break him into submission, but without a glimmer of success. Kanthaka would not be told what to do. He was built to run free and he rejected confinement with ferocity. Eventually, captivity began to seem like a tragedy. Channa's attempts to break him grew less enthusiastic by the day. He was on the verge of asking the king for permission to return the horse to the wild when the prince arrived at the stable doors.

"Your Highness!" exclaimed the young Chariot Driver, as he hastened to adjust his appearance. "What a delightful surprise. How can I be of service to you?" He bowed low to the ground, touching the prince's feet with one hand while tugging his disheveled clothes into place with the other.

"I heard about a wild horse, Chariot Driver. May I see him?"

"It would be my honor, Your Highness, but I am afraid he is not ready yet."

"That does not worry me. I would still like to see him."

"Your Highness, I could not live with myself if any harm came to you," Channa replied. *And I don't think the king could live with me either* . . .

"You need not worry, Chariot Driver, although I appreciate the concern." He looked down at the stooped servant and added kindly, "Please rise, Chariot Driver. There is no need for formality here." Channa lifted himself off the ground and looked up at the face of the prince he had only seen from a distance until then.

"What is your name, Chariot Driver?" asked the prince.

"Channa, Your Highness," he answered with some discomfort. He had never been asked his name by a royal before.

"That's a nice name. It means 'covered,' doesn't it? You must be a source of protection to those around you."

"Thank you, Your Highness."

Siddhattha put his hand on Channa's arm. "Channa, bring me to see this horse I have heard about."

He was supposed to refuse.

"This way, Your Highness," he found himself saying instead, "but please be careful."

Channa walked the prince over to Kanthaka's stall. Usually, whenever anyone approached, Kanthaka kicked against the door and bucked wildly. Channa braced himself for the violence he was expecting, but to his surprise, nothing happened. He could hear the beast breathing and his hooves shuffling, but for some reason, Kanthaka did not threaten to tear the building apart.

Intrigued, Channa approached the opening in the door very carefully and peeked inside. He expected to be catapulted across the room with a violent kick to the door between them, but again—nothing happened. Gaining confidence, he stretched his neck and let himself look fully inside the forbidden stall, hoping against hope that he would not be beheaded in the process.

What he saw stunned him: the horse was neither unconscious nor sick (which was what he was beginning to wonder). Kanthaka was standing perfectly erect, looking straight ahead. It was as though he was waiting for something. Waiting for him to open the door.

"This is most unusual, Your Highness," he said as he pulled himself back from the opening. "I have never seen Kanthaka so calm."

Siddhattha was breathing quietly, waiting, much like the horse. "Open the door, Chariot Driver."

Channa did as he was asked. He slid the door open very slowly, moving it one finger's breadth at a time, checking regularly to ensure that Kanthaka remained as calm as he seemed. When no sudden moves threatened, he finally allowed himself to pull the door completely open. Kanthaka stood gracefully to attention, his body shimmering a brilliant white.

Channa had rarely had the privilege of appreciating the animal's full stature. Kanthaka fought him each time he approached. But for the first time, Channa could really look at the horse in all his splendor. Kanthaka's eyes glittered with power; his muscular body seemed to have been carved by the gods. He was at least two hands taller than any horse Channa had ever known, his long white legs reaching for the heavens. His mane like liquid silver.

Channa realized that the horse was not standing that way for his benefit. The horse seemed, in fact, to be looking right past him, waiting for the one behind him. Channa stepped to the side.

The prince and the horse looked at each other for a long time. And then, very softly, Siddhattha took a step forward and reached out his hand. Kanthaka did not even bristle. He stayed exactly where he was and when Siddhattha's hand was fully extended towards him, Kanthaka reached with his neck and smelled him like an old friend.

Siddhattha stroked Kanthaka's mane, with Kanthaka's great head soon nestled in the nook of his arm. Channa's heart melted as he watched these two beings get to know each other for the first time. A meeting of giants.

"Chariot Driver!"

The prince!

Channa had been daydreaming and the sound of the prince's voice snapped him back into the present with devastating power. *Lord Vishnu, protect me from my own incompetence!* he exclaimed to himself in a panic.

"Chariot Driver! Where are you? What are you doing?"

Channa ran to the stable entrance and poked his head out. "My most sincere apologies, Master. The horses are almost ready. Please give me just one moment and I will come out with them."

He ran back into the stables and quickly flicked Kanthaka's golden bridle off the wall. He had him prepared and saddled in seconds and led him out the door. The prince mounted his steed and was already galloping into the future before Channa had even saddled his own. Siddhattha could not wait another moment to charge into freedom.

And Kanthaka was just the horse to carry him there.

*

I was pacing again. Siddhattha had left before I had a chance to say a word. The dream was haunting me. I kept trying to set it aside, but it was impossible. He gave our children away in the dream and now he had walked away from me before I had a chance to tell him about the pregnancy. What would his reaction be after I gave birth?

"Neelima!"

"Yes, Your Highness," she replied almost immediately from behind the door.

"Go get the prince. He went somewhere with Chariot Driver, so he might be at the stables. I must speak with him right away."

"Of course, Your Highness," she replied with a quick touch to my feet. "Right away." She scurried out of the room and closed the door behind her.

If he was planning on giving us away, I wanted to know. I *needed* to know. I would not be abandoned without warning.

I paced impatiently. He was never very far given the reality of his imprisonment, so I did not anticipate waiting long, but time seemed to pass slowly. Neelima had not returned. Had she gotten distracted along the way? That wasn't like her. I was not prepared to storm through the palace corridors myself; it would have been unseemly and the servants would have talked. By the time she returned, my fear had built up an alarming momentum.

"What took you so long?" I demanded. "I have been waiting forever!"

Neelima kept her head lowered, accepting my admonishment without complaint.

"Wait … why isn't he with you?" I asked once I realized she had returned alone. "Neelima, where is the prince?"

She kept her head down. She did not know how to say the words.

"Maidservant, where is he?" I asked again, feeling the panic rise like bile.

She took a deep breath. "He is not in the palace compound, Your Highness. We looked everywhere."

*

They rode together for a long time, hours passing without a break in rhythm. Siddhattha was mesmerized by the long stretch of road tumbling under his horse's hooves. He wanted to ride forever.

Channa could appreciate the charm of the experience, but all he could think about was the distance they were covering and how long it would take for them to get back. When was the king scheduled to return? Would he be back from his tour before them? If so, he was a dead man. He kept looking over his shoulder, wondering when they could steer themselves back home, although it was probably too late to make a difference anymore.

Eventually, Siddhattha slowed the pace. The horses were exhausted and needed rest. They dismounted by a bubbling stream. Channa let his body drop to the ground with a thud. He was grateful not to be moving anymore.

The two men lay on their backs and watched the clouds drift over them while the horses grazed by their side. It was such a perfect moment that Channa was tempted to forget palace politics for a while. He did his best to ignore the anxious tugging at the back of his mind and allowed himself to rest dreamily alongside the prince, as though there was no other place in the world they were supposed to be.

How could the king strip his son of experiences like this? he asked himself. This was the best part of life, the best part of being a man, and the king had systematically denied his son all of it. What was so wrong with spending a few hours away? If only the king extended the leash a bit, the prince could be happy.

Just as Channa was beginning to convince himself that he had done the right thing by accompanying the prince on this journey, a shuffling noise caught his attention. He bolted upright, all of his protective instincts returning in a rush of emotion. Who was there? He could not see anything, but he heard the sound again. He jumped to his feet, his hand swiftly by his shoulder strap, prepared to pull out his knife if anyone came within a few steps of the prince. Siddhattha stood up as well, but he did not have the same panicked expression in his eyes. He was watching with curiosity instead.

"What do you think that noise was?" Channa asked as he scanned the area.

"I am not sure," said the prince, "but I did hear something. Somebody must be here."

"Do you think we've been found out?"

Siddhattha did not answer. He was staring straight ahead with studied attention. On the other side of the stream stood a circle of tall trees—the doorway to a forest that probably extended for miles.

"What is it, Prince? What do you see? Is there movement ahead?" Channa drew out his weapon and was ready to pounce.

"Put your knife down, Channa. I don't think it's necessary."

A very old man appeared out of the clearing between the trees. He seemed oblivious to the two men watching him. Although they thought that they were alone, this man seemed to come out of nowhere, was on his way to somewhere, and did not seem remotely bothered by the possibility of others watching him. He was paying close attention to each step his old, broken body was trying to take. He was very, very old. The oldest man Siddhattha had ever seen. His withered walking stick seemed as brittle as the bones must have been in his body.

Channa immediately relaxed. *Ha*, he thought to himself. *Just an old man. Nothing for us to worry about.*

Siddhattha, however, had a very different response.

"Chariot Driver," whispered Siddhattha, as the old man's long walk by the stream continued with unbearable deliberation, "have you ever seen anybody like him before? What's wrong with him?"

"What do you mean, Prince? I don't understand your question."

"I mean . . . well, look at him. Look at his body. Have you ever seen anything like that before?"

Channa turned to him, somewhat puzzled. "But Your Highness, that is simply the effects of old age. There is nothing unusual otherwise—at least that I can see. He is just old."

"But I have never seen anyone *that* old before, Channa. Have you?"

Channa began to understand the problem, but before he had a chance to reply, the prince was already putting it together in his own mind.

"Why haven't I ever seen anyone that old before?" he asked with sudden alarm. "I have seen my father grow older with time, of course, but I have never seen old age like that! Why haven't I seen that before?" The prince had become agitated as he watched the man move slowly across the field.

Channa wanted to answer him truthfully. He wanted to tell him that the king had made sure that his son would never see the effects of old age. That the very elderly had been systematically kept away from him. That there was an astrological reading at his birth that warned the king of his son's future. That more than anything else, the king remained terrified that if he encountered suffering, his son would run away.

There was so much Channa longed to tell him. They were far from the palace, from the eavesdroppers and the gossipmongers and the politics that had no end. If ever there was a time to tell him the truth, this was it. They were safe here. Channa looked up at his master—at the man he loved in friendship despite the difference in their stations—and his shoulders dropped with pathetic resignation. How could he tell him all of those things? They were not his truths to tell. It was bad enough that he had helped him escape the restricted area. Telling him the truth would be more than he could feel responsible for.

Channa's eyes followed the old man whose every step was measured. Siddhattha broke the silence.

"Chariot Driver," he whispered quietly.

"Yes, Your Highness."

"I know you will find this question . . . naïve, but I simply must ask it."

"What do you want to ask, Your Highness?" Channa's compassionate loyalty to the man he was standing next to growing deeper.

"Well . . . I am wondering: Old Age like that . . . will it . . . could I . . . ?" He did not seem able to complete his sentence, but Channa understood what he wanted to know.

"Yes, Your Highness. If you are fortunate enough to live that long, Old Age like that will happen to you one day too."

*

"You see!" exclaimed the first of the Four Great Gods as he watched the scene below unfold. "I told you it was time! This is what we've been waiting for!"

The Four Great Gods had been sitting on a cloud for what seemed like eternity, waiting for the moment when the prince would finally be ready to engage with the Four Sights. They were not permitted to intervene until they were certain the time was ripe. They had been waiting patiently for years. They had taken their position as guardians even before the prince was born. They watched him sail into his mother's womb and followed him carefully from gestation onwards, but twenty-nine years was longer than they had expected to wait. They were itching to get the story moving.

"I told you he was ready! Did you see how he reacted to that? This is it!" The God of the Eastern Direction declared triumphantly.

The other three gods were still leaning over the edge of the cloud on their large round bellies, each one of them studying the scene from their own direction.

"Well?!" demanded the God of the Eastern Direction impatiently. "What do you think? Shall we go ahead with the rest now?"

The God of the Northern Direction was the first to lift himself up. "I do think you are right, Brother. He had a strong reaction to Old Age. It may indeed be time for us to do our part in this story."

The God of the Southern Direction pulled himself up too and seemed to agree, but the God of the West was still dangling his head over the edge of the cloud.

"Brother of the West, what do you think?" asked the God of the East. "Is something else happening down there? What are you watching?"

The God of the West did not respond.

"Brother? What are you doing?"

Still no response. The other three gods looked at each other with uncertainty, but then one of them cracked a smile and they all broke out into great fits of laughter. One of them slapped the God of the West on the shoulder hard to wake him up. The God of the West jumped, yelping with surprise at having been swatted in the midst of a much-cherished nap. He flipped himself over quickly and found his brothers clutching their bellies as they laughed at him. If the cloud had been hard enough to bang, they would have been banging their fists in laughter too.

"That wasn't nice!" he complained as he rubbed the edge of his shoulder. "You didn't need to hit me that hard!"

"Well then don't fall asleep when you're on duty!" responded one of the others, still laughing heartily at what had become a family tradition.

"We've been on duty for twenty-nine years!" he complained again.

"Well, while you were sleeping, you missed the moment we've been waiting for, for twenty-nine years," explained another. "The prince is ready. We just sent him Old Age and it worked. It's time to do the rest!"

The God of the West dropped his mouth open with surprise. "Now?"

"Yes, now!" they all replied with great big smiles.

"Wow . . ." he whispered quietly, as he rubbed his sore shoulder.

"Shall we get going?" the God of the Eastern Direction asked gleefully. "We have work to do!"

*

The two men were about to mount their horses for the return trip home when another strange noise caught their attention.

"What was that?" Channa asked immediately.

The old man had disappeared into the woods a while ago and they were sure they were alone again. It had been a strange apparition that neither of them could explain, but it was over and it was time to return to the palace. The sound of more movement in what was supposed to be a deserted area unnerved Channa.

"Could it be the old man again? Did he come back?" Siddhattha wondered.

"Who knows? I still don't understand where he disappeared to. And where did he come from? What kind of a family lets an old man walk around by himself like that, anyway?"

"Maybe there is a village not too far away."

"Perhaps, but it still doesn't explain his sudden disappearance," Channa said, almost to himself.

And then the forest rustled again.

"Something is out there, Prince," Channa whispered. "I don't think it is safe to remain here. We should go."

"I am sure it isn't anything to worry about. It might just be a snake or a small animal caught in the thicket."

"Still, Your Highness, we should go . . ."

And then, another man appeared—he stood in the very same clearing among the trees that produced the old man before. He too was walking very slowly.

"Who is that?" whispered the prince with curiosity.

"How should I know?"

Siddhattha's eyebrows lifted at the informality of the response, but Channa did not notice.

The man walked along the same path as the previous old man, but there was something different about this one. As he came into view, the two men realized that he was covered with skin lesions and dark boils. He was almost purple in color and there was liquid seeping out of some of the bigger bubbles protruding from his flesh. His face was ravaged with pockmarks.

"Lord Vishnu, protect us!" Channa exclaimed with shock. "Step back, Your Highness! That man is dangerously ill. You must not get within breathing distance of him!"

Channa quickly pulled the prince behind a tree and held onto him protectively. *This is terrible*, he thought to himself with panic. *If the prince becomes sick, I will never forgive myself. This is a disaster! Why didn't we leave before?*

The prince was lost in his own thoughts too. Just as with the previous visitor, this scene was also entirely new to Siddhattha. He had never seen a body wasted by illness this way. His mind reeled with questions while his heart felt as though it would crack with pain.

"Channa," whispered the prince to his companion.

Channa did not answer. He was staring with desperation at the man walking by them.

"Channa!" he repeated.

Channa turned to his ward. "Yes, Your Highness?"

"What is wrong with that man? Why does he look like that? Do you know what that is?"

And there it was again.

That same look of concern and confusion Channa had seen on the prince's face only moments earlier when the first man had passed them by. His own fears washed away and he looked at the prince with renewed awareness. While he was wrapped up in personal anxiety, the prince was working furiously to understand the reality passing in front of him. The prince did not know what he was looking at. The king had shielded Sickness from his son too.

"That . . . I am afraid, Your Highness, is Sickness. That man is very ill. He is not long for this world. He has the Skin Disease. It eats away at the body very slowly, until it destroys it completely."

"Why have I never seen anything like that before? I have never seen a body so devastated. I did not even know it was possible to look like that! And why do you know about this and it is so foreign to me? What have I been missing?"

Channa wanted so much to answer him. He wanted to tell him about everything that had been kept from him, but he knew better than to answer those questions now. He put his hand on the prince's shoulder instead.

"They say that the Skin Disease is very painful, Your Highness. They say it burns."

"Is it common? Do many people face illness like that?"

"Yes, it is very common. Many people from my village died from the disease when I was younger. It is why I left home all those years ago. It is what brought me to your service."

Siddhattha looked at his friend with compassion. "I am sorry, Channa. I did not know."

"Please don't apologize, Your Highness. It happens. It is part of life. People become sick. There is nothing we can do about that."

"I just wish I had known . . ." Siddhattha's voice trailed off. "It seems so painful. His face contorts with each step he takes. Did you notice that?"

The expression of sickness was all too familiar to Channa. He did not need to watch the man's face to recognize the agony it produced.

"We must help him cross to wherever he is going!" the prince suddenly exclaimed as he made to move from behind the tree. "We can't just stand here and watch him suffer like that!"

"No!" yelled Channa as he pulled him back. "You must not approach that man! It is too dangerous, Your Highness. Please stay away!" There was nothing Channa hated more than the Skin Disease. And there was no one he felt more protective of than the prince.

Although Siddhattha was shocked at being refused with such adamancy, he recovered quickly. "No, Channa. I cannot stand here uselessly while a man hobbles by in so much pain. I must help him."

Siddhattha turned around and was about to race over to the man they had been watching when . . .

The man with the Skin Disease had disappeared.

*

Channa could see the effects the recent events were having on the prince and he was worried about where they might lead. It was definitely time to go.

"Your Highness, please let us go home now. The king might have already returned from his tour."

Siddhattha was quiet. He was processing the sights of Old Age and Sickness in his mind with concentration.

"Your Highness, please mount your horse. We must get back." Channa had one hand on Kanthaka's saddle and offered the other to the prince in the hopes that he would take it. Slowly, almost absent-mindedly, the prince lifted himself onto his brilliant-white steed. Channa breathed a sigh of relief. Finally, they would be going home.

Channa was preparing to mount his own horse when a disturbance caught his attention. It sounded like a quiet rumbling beneath the ground at first, but the noise grew louder and soon it was like a stampede heading towards them! Channa broke out of his paralysis, threw himself onto his horse, and grabbed the reins of Kanthaka beside him. There were strange moaning sounds all around them now. "I know what this is!" Channa cried. "This is an enchanted forest! Black magic! We must run!" He kicked his horse and pulled Kanthaka with him into a run.

Siddhattha was thrown by the suddenness of movement.

"Whoa!" he cried as Kanthaka was being dragged away. "Whoa, Kanthaka! Stop!" The prince managed to regain control of the reins and pulled himself to a halt. "Chariot Driver!! What is going on with you? What are you doing?" he demanded with frustration.

"Your Highness, those noises . . . Something terrible is coming! We must go. Please, Your Highness. We have landed in an enchanted area and we must escape. Please let us leave!"

Siddhattha studied his companion carefully and considered the possibility he was raising. The area did indeed seem to be enchanted. How else to explain the strange apparitions? And yet . . . he felt pulled to go back and look again. Something else was coming and he felt certain he was meant to see it.

"You may be right, my friend," he answered. "We may indeed have fallen into the trap of a magical ring, but not all magic is black, Channa. Sometimes enchantments are gifts delivered from above."

Channa's shoulders dropped. The prince was right, of course. Enchantments were not always evil. But they were always dangerous. That much he knew was true. Enchantments changed us. They dangled new realities in front of our eyes and transformed the way we see the world.

"Channa, I am supposed to see this. I am certain of it. These enchantments are for me. You must let me go."

Channa could not argue with him. They had been called to this place for a reason and the prince needed to complete the experience. He could not stop the prince from seeing whatever it was that was about to emerge from the magical circle of trees.

Siddhattha watched as Channa worked through the situation in his mind.

"Channa," whispered the prince, "let go of the reins."

Channa let go.

The two men trotted quietly back towards the area and what they saw took them both by surprise. This time, it was not one man or even two. This time, an entire community was pouring out of the clearing, everyone dressed in white, surrounding a bier that a few of them were carrying on their shoulders. A low, steady moaning accompanied their rhythmic movements.

The prince dismounted from his horse and took a few steps forward to get a better view. The little stream was all that separated him from this newest of apparitions.

"Tell me what this is, Channa. What am I looking at this time?"

"This is a funeral, Your Highness," Channa explained quietly. "This is Death."

The procession kept moving, the bier now directly in their view. A man's body was lying on top of the wooden stretcher. He was tightly wrapped in a white shroud, as though cocooned. His face was uncovered and his head was shaved. Bright orange flowers were scattered all over him.

"That is Death," the prince said to himself as he stared at the corpse. "I have never seen death before, Chariot Driver."

"No, Your Highness." Death had been shielded from the prince too.

"And that will happen to me too one day, I suppose . . ."

"Yes, Your Highness. That much is guaranteed."

"Death . . ." he whispered to himself.

And with that, the procession was gone.

*

The Four Great Gods were quiet as they bore witness to the scene they had just orchestrated below. It was a profound experience for all of them.

"I suppose it was the right time, then . . . right, Brothers?" asked the God of the Northern Direction.

"It was," replied the God of the East.

"His response to suffering was unlike any response I have known. It is changing him, isn't it?" asked the God of the West.

"It is."

They sat for a long time on their floating clouds, pondering the events that would have an effect on the entire cosmos. The God of the Eastern Direction eventually spoke again.

"I think we should wait before we deliver the last of the Sights. I think he needs some time before we complete our intervention."

The other three nodded in agreement. It had been a big day for everyone. A bit of rest before the unveiling of the last Sight was a good idea for all.

14

The Fight

Siddhattha returned to the palace without stopping by my chambers. I heard him as he passed through the hallway. I whipped my door open with fury.

"Where have you been?" I demanded as I chased after him. "We've been looking all over for you!"

I had never spoken to him that way before, but my emotions were boiling over and there was no stopping them. At first, I had refused to believe that he was gone and spent hours tearing through the palace looking for him myself. I even checked the Women's Quarters—for which I resented him bitterly. The moment the courtesans recognized me, they lifted their heads like venomous serpents and I think I even heard one of them hiss at me! Nothing was more humiliating than to have to ask them where my husband had gone!

"Please, Wife, I have a lot on my mind," was all he said in response. He was striding through the corridor towards his room as though I wasn't even there.

"Husband, tell me where you went! Tell me something! Please!" I could not believe he was ignoring me. I was so angry, and at the same time I was terrified. I thought I had lost him. Now that he had returned, I found myself even more afraid. I could not let him walk away.

"Siddhattha," I cried, "please stop. Tell me where you've been!"

He stopped and turned to look at me, although I was not sure he was actually seeing me.

"Yasodhara, there is no need to worry. I am here, safe and sound. You can see that with your own eyes. Now please let me *be*!"

Before I could answer, he was moving again, down the dark corridor towards his room. I felt as though I had been waved away by imperial command. I stopped chasing and watched as he moved onwards without me.

Servants suddenly materialized all along the corridor. It was time to light the oil lamps, and they had been waiting for the prince and I to finish our argument. They slipped around me like muted acrobats, none of them daring to look in my direction as they lifted themselves onto bamboo poles and catapulted themselves from one lamp to the next. In moments, the hallway was glittering with light. The marble floor looked like a pool of black water, tempting me to drown.

I had never felt so far from my beloved as I did in that moment. He was moving away from me, leaving me, but he would not say why. I stood all alone in a sea of shame, exiled without explanation.

And what about my news? My hand covered my belly instinctively.

I considered retiring to my chambers, but ... No! This wasn't right! I had news to tell him! Important news! Fury returned like an old friend, fueling me towards his room. I marched right up to his door and without knocking, without even the semblance of an invitation, threw open the door and stormed inside.

Siddhattha was sitting on the edge of his bed, holding something in his hands. He jumped at my intrusion.

"Why are you ignoring me?" I demanded angrily with my hands on my hips, bangles clattering. "Why won't you tell me where you've been?"

He didn't answer. He just stared at me and looked down at the thing he was holding. It looked like some kind of rope.

"Husband," I repeated. "Why won't you talk to me? Where have you been?" I always resorted to repeating myself when I was unnerved.

"I don't want to talk right now, Wife. I am not ignoring you. I asked you to leave me alone for a while."

"But *why*?" I asked. "I don't understand!" I felt my anger turning into tears at the edge of my voice.

He slumped into himself.

I took a deep breath and walked over to the edge of the bed. "What happened?" I asked, this time with concern. "I have never seen you like this."

"I ... I don't know. I have a lot to think about right now. I wish I could tell you what happened, but I don't have the words yet. I need some time. Can you please give me a bit of time?"

How could I refuse a pained request like that?

"Of course, Husband ... but ... could you just tell me where you've been?"

"Not yet, Yasodhara. Please leave me alone."

I had no recourse left. I had to do as he asked. I got up and reached for the door when I remembered something.

"Um ... Husband?"

"Yes?"

"What is that?" I pointed at the object he was holding.

He quickly covered the rope with his hands. "It's nothing."

"Is that . . .? Is that what I think it is?" I asked.

"It is not your place to ask me what I have in my hands, Wife! Now leave me alone!" he answered angrily.

"That's the rope from the water buffalos, isn't it? The rope that bound the buffalos to the plow? The one we saw all those years ago when we slipped out of the palace compound? You took it?"

"How many times do I have to ask you to leave me alone, Wife? I need time to think!"

"Not until you explain that rope to me! Why would you take it?" We had tumbled into our argument all over again. I could feel Durga banging against my chest under my clothes as I moved, but I ignored her.

"I don't know why. It meant something to me and I kept it. Are you satisfied?"

"No. I am not satisfied! What does it mean?"

"I don't know what it means! I don't know what anything means anymore. I don't know what I am even doing in this palace, what I am doing wearing these clothes, going through empty rituals and sitting through meals that take forever! What am I *doing* here?"

His sudden outburst took me by surprise. I looked at his riding outfit and could not understand the problem.

"What are you talking about? What's wrong with your clothes? And those *empty rituals* as you call them make up the fabric of our lives. How can you talk that way?"

"This life doesn't make sense to me anymore, Yasodhara! I don't understand what I'm doing in it! It's the only life I have ever known and most of it has been a lie! *You* lived a life outside these walls as a child. Don't you remember? What exactly do you like about this life we're living? Don't you ever want to leave?"

He was scaring me.

"No. I don't want to leave. I chose this life to be with *you*. You are trampling on everything we've built!"

"But that's the thing! We haven't built anything! This entire life is a lie!"

"What in all the gods' names are you talking about, Husband? What *lie*?"

He seemed to be on the verge of answering, but then held his tongue. He returned his attention to the rope that he was kneading between his fingers.

The silence was unbearable. It frightened me too much to sustain.

"Answer me! What lie are you talking about?" I demanded of my tortured husband.

Siddhattha sat before me, drained of energy. He took a deep breath and then spoke words that pierced my heart like a sharp blade.

"You know very well what lie I am talking about, Wife. It is the lie you adopted the day you married me."

I felt myself stumble in my own mind.

"What ...?"

Siddhattha stood up to face me. "It is the lie of this entire life, Yasodhara. Of the rules keeping us both shackled to this cage. It's the lie of pretty things and surface happiness. It's the lie we have both been wrapping around ourselves for years. I cannot live a life of lies like this anymore!"

I could hear muffled sounds outside the door. I hadn't closed it properly when I threw myself into the argument. Servants had congregated on the other side and were listening to every word.

"I don't understand ..." I stammered. "I haven't been lying, Siddhattha. Nothing about this life is a lie to me ..."

"But it isn't real."

"Why?" I demanded. "Because we have to stay inside the palace walls? Is that it? Just because we are not free to roam the kingdom? That doesn't make our lives a lie! It's the price we've been asked to pay for the responsibility of our stations! It isn't a *lie*!"

"But it *is* a lie! What we look at, what we eat and talk about—everything is controlled! We aren't free!"

"What is controlled according to you? I don't understand!"

"Yasodhara, when was the last time you saw Old Age? Can you tell me that? When was the last time you went to a funeral or saw the effects of illness on a human body? Tell me!"

"Well ... I don't know. What difference does it make? Why are you asking me that?"

"Yasodhara, I have never seen Old Age. Don't you find that strange? Until today, I had never seen what Old Age really does to the body. I have lived in this palace compound my entire life, and yet somehow—despite all the people in it—I have never seen anyone reach a very Old Age!"

"That can't be true. I am sure we have seen somebody age here ... It's not possible. Somebody ..."

"Nobody, Yasodhara! Nobody! I have never seen it here! Don't you find that strange? You saw Old Age before you came to the palace, but since you married me, you have never seen a really old person!"

"Of course I have! I just can't think of anyone right now. You're confusing me, but if I had time to think about it, I am sure I could think of someone ..." I began to twist my fingers into knots. "And in any case, what are you implying? Are you suggesting that some kind of magic is stopping people from growing old here? I know I have grown older! And so have you! We are growing older every day. So what are you trying to say?"

My head was spinning with the force of this argument. I was trying to hold on, to keep my balance, but I could not understand what any of this meant. We had never fought before—not like this. And the things he was saying . . .

"Yasodhara, I am telling you. Nobody has ever reached Old Age inside these walls. And I don't think magic is the reason. I think Old Age has been kept from me."

"Nonsense!" I blurted out.

But as soon as he had said the words, I knew that they were true. I thought back again to the conversation I had had with the queen when she explained the predictions that were made after Siddhattha's birth. When she explained why the king had become so protective of his son. Had the king gone so far as to exclude the elderly from ever showing their faces? That was madness. It couldn't be.

"You know I'm right, don't you?" he asked more gently now. "I have been kept from seeing the world as it is, haven't I?"

My legs were giving way. I reached for the bed and lowered myself down. The thought of my mother came flooding towards me. I hadn't seen her in years . . . *Was this why?*

"Yasodhara, this world we live in—none of it has been true. My father has kept his hand over my eyes, shielding me from everything."

Tears began to run down my face. My world was coming to an end. How had I allowed myself to become so accustomed to a world that made no sense?

"Yasodhara, I cannot live this life anymore. I need to find answers to the questions I have. I don't know how or where I will go, but . . ."

"But what?" I asked in a small voice.

"But I can't stay here anymore," he finally said.

He was going to leave. Just as the predictions said he would. I wanted to crawl into a corner of the room and disappear.

But a moment later, I screamed with the hurt of betrayal instead. "No! You can't do that to me!"

"I have to . . ." he answered quietly.

"But you have no right! Not now! Not when I'm pregnant!"

My hand flew to my mouth the moment the fateful words escaped. The rope slipped out of his hands and fell to the floor.

"Wha . . . what did you just say?"

I looked down, furious with myself for blurting out my news that way.

"Did you say that you are pregnant? *Now?*"

I nodded.

"Are you certain?"

I nodded again.

He looked at me for a long time; I could not even begin to imagine what he was thinking. Was he going to leave me right there and then? Was he going to wave me away?

Siddhattha did not do either of those things. Instead, he looked at me with his eyes wide open and then did the one thing I had failed to expect: he smiled.

"You are pregnant, Wife?" he said, with beautiful tenderness.

I nodded.

"You're pregnant," he repeated. "How long have we waited for this?"

"Twelve years," I replied. The numbers were engraved in my heart, each year a painful marker along the way.

"Yasodhara!" he cried as he grabbed me into his arms.

"I am so sorry I fought with you, Husband. I am so sorry! I forgot myself," I sobbed.

"There is no need for apologies, Yasodhara. You are my wife and my beloved. Apologies are not needed between us."

I leaned on him and allowed all my emotions to melt into our embrace. He was finally holding me and I was relieved, and yet . . .

"Are you really going to leave me, Husband?" I whispered with a cracked voice.

He did not answer.

"Will you?" I repeated.

"I don't know . . ."

15

In the Arms of a Tree

My pregnancy was far from the romantic pilgrimage I had envisioned. It was difficult. Painful even. And it was shrouded by the devastating awareness that my husband was on the verge of leaving me.

I spent most of my time in my room. I held my belly and stared out the window. My husband came often to visit and I could see that he was just as scared as I was. He didn't know what to do with himself and I didn't either. Sometimes we went for walks together. Most of the time, though, he came simply to sit next to me.

One morning, there was a knock at the door. The two of us had been sitting together since the break of dawn. We had both missed the morning meal and neither of us had noticed.

Siddhattha went to the door. Neelima was on the other side.

"What is it, Maidservant?"

She spoke in a hushed voice. "His majesty and the queen are on their way, Your Highness."

He had no interest in palace politics anymore and he was even less interested in seeing his father. He had been avoiding the king for months.

"Tell him I am occupied. I will attend to matters of the throne later this afternoon."

"I wish I could Your Highness, but I must warn you that he is determined . . ."

Siddhattha was on the verge of shutting the world out again when the king's voice was heard booming along the corridors.

"Son!" he bellowed as he rushed forward. "Don't close that door!"

Seconds later, the king's huge hands were up against the doorframe, pushing his way inside. Mahapajapati was right behind him.

I jumped at their arrival and quickly grabbed a shawl to throw over my morning dress. I wrapped it tightly around myself and tried to fold my hair into place. How embarrassing to have the king in my private room without even a moment to prepare! My round belly peeked out from between my protective arms.

"Daughter, apologies for this intrusion, but I will not be made to wait another instant!" the king declared as he barged in. The king was in a mood to fight, and apparently, the chosen arena was going to be within a few feet of my personal bed.

I pulled the shawl in closer, hoping it covered me sufficiently. I wanted to call my maidservant to my side to have her help me adjust myself, but Neelima had disappeared the moment the king crashed through the door.

"Father, I am not available at this moment. My wife requires my attention. Our discussion can wait."

The king's eyes burned. "This will NOT wait, Siddhattha! There is no later time! You have been avoiding me for long enough. We will speak now!"

The force with which he responded was more than I could bear. I looked away in shame, devastated by the sight of my husband reprimanded in front of me.

Siddhattha's feet were firmly planted. "Father, we will discuss matters of the throne in due time. I am here with my wife. Kindly leave these chambers and allow me to attend to her."

The king was reeling now, almost to the point of hysteria. "*Attend* to her? *Attend* to your wife instead of speaking with *me*? Are you mad, Siddhattha? Your wife has more than enough women around her, *attending* to her in whatever way she needs. A prince's place is not in a woman's chambers! A prince's place is by the throne!"

The queen stepped out of the shadows at this point and put her hand on her husband's arm. A delicate invasion of his anger. Her presence brought his temperature down to a less ferocious level.

"We must talk about matters of state, Son. Why are you avoiding your obligations? I didn't raise you this way. You were raised to become a king."

Now it was Siddhattha's turn to respond angrily. "Forgive me, Father, but I don't feel like I've been raised for anything at all! I received no training, never rode into battle or even toured the countryside to examine the limits of this kingdom! How exactly do you imagine you *raised* me? What kind of a king do you suppose I have been raised to be?"

The king blanched. Siddhattha had never lifted his voice against his father, let alone accused him of anything.

The king had been guarding himself from hearing those words since the day of the astrological reading. He was utterly unprepared to hear them now. His rage slipped out of his hands like grains of sand.

"Son ..." he stammered with pained confusion. "What are you saying? I have given you everything you could ever want in this life! How could you accuse me this way?"

Siddhattha's shoulders eased and he stepped towards his father.

"I know you have given me everything. I could never repay you for all that you have done for me, but you have protected me far longer than has been necessary. I have not seen much of the world these past few years. These walls have shut me out of everything. I haven't even studied or been trained in any skill."

"But ... you didn't need to, Son! Everyone knows that! Your performance at the competition was proof to the whole world! I didn't need to give you anything that you didn't already possess."

"Even if that were true, Father," replied Siddhattha, "there is *more* to know. There is more to understand." Siddhattha locked eyes with his father and added carefully, "Isn't that true? There *is* a lot more to learn, is there not?"

"I ... I am not sure I know what you mean, Son ..." mumbled the king shiftily as he looked away.

Siddhattha looked at his father quietly, and then turned towards me.

"Father, it is neither the time nor the place for this conversation. Let's leave this to later. My wife needs her rest."

The king looked at me as though remembering me for the first time. I tightened the shawl around me and stared down at my unpainted feet with no small measure of embarrassment. It was as though he had only now realized how undressed I was.

"You are right, of course, Son. My apologies, Daughter," he muttered in my direction. "Come, Mahapajapati."

The two of them walked out of the room, the king looking older than when he had come in.

*

I watched my husband as he closed the door, exhaling as I leaned against my bed. "You are going to have to talk to him, Husband. He's in pain."

"I know," he answered.

I felt a kick in my belly and reacted with a small cry. My husband was by my side as quickly as a bolt of lightning. "What is it, darling? Are you ill?"

I leaned into the pillows he was already piling up behind my head and smiled. "No. I am not ill. The little one kicked."

"He kicked?"

I took his hand and placed it on the spot where I had felt the foot. I shifted around in my seat until I felt the kick land against the inside of my abdomen again. Siddhattha jumped in surprise.

"I felt it!" he exclaimed joyfully. "I felt it! He kicked! Did you feel that?"

To see my husband excited that way was like a cool rain shower after a hot day. He was happy and he was touching me affectionately as he had not done in a long time. He was touching *us*. I smiled with contentment as he marveled at the experience of feeling his child's life inside me.

"There it is again!" he cried with wonder. If I hadn't known better, I would have thought that the baby was just as happy as I was to receive his father's attention.

"I can't believe how strong he is, Wife! He is going to come out of there with arms as big as Bhima's!"

"And what makes you so sure it's a boy? It could just as easily be a girl, you know."

"No, no. This is a boy. I can feel it. This is my *son!*" he said with pride. The twinkle returned to his eyes in a way I hadn't seen in ages. "After all, a girl could never kick *that* hard . . ."

I swatted his shoulder with pretended insult, but I was thrilled to be teased again. He pulled me into his arms and held me tight with love. For a brief moment, it felt like nothing had changed between us and we were together as we used to be.

He held me for a long time. At first, it was an embrace brimming with the freshness of joy, but slowly it changed, and soon I could feel that he was holding me in sadness. He was holding me as though he was preparing to let go.

"Husband . . .?" I whispered, my lips touching his ear.

"Yes?"

I mulled the words in my mind over and over again, unsure of whether to say them aloud or to avoid the conversation altogether. We had not talked about the possibility of his departure since our fight all those months ago, but it floated around us everywhere we went. If I said something, would it turn the possibility into a reality? If I never called the words by their names, would they fade?

I turned the syllables around in my mouth, wishing myself to say them, willing myself to stop, so terrified of everything and yet desperate to speak the words at the same time.

Siddhattha could feel my torment. He finally pulled back and said, "What is it, Yasodhara?"

I stared at my belly that was hovering between us, connecting us in an entirely new way.

"Take me with you."

*

My husband spent the next few weeks pacing outside my chambers. I had shattered something between us with my request. I could hear the sound of the rift in the shape of his footsteps outside my door. I did not dare go out to meet him and he did not come inside. Loneliness echoed against my growing womb.

Much worse was the day I heard nothing at all. One morning, I woke up to find stillness on the other side. I placed my ear against the door, hoping to hear some evidence of his presence, but there was only silence. I opened the door just a crack and found an empty hallway staring back at me.

Siddhattha needed to get away. I realize now that a part of him was consumed with me, consumed with *us*, which made it difficult for him to breathe at times. He needed room to think. So one morning he got up and instead of walking towards me, he chose to go elsewhere instead. He headed for his mother's garden. The Peacock Garden. The only other place of refuge he had.

The moon was still hanging in the sky, sharing the heavens with the rising sun. The birds were just beginning to wake up, small chirps interrupting the silence intermittently. Blossoming flowers filled the air with perfume. A peacock was pecking at something in the grass, his long tail folded and trailing behind him. Siddhattha stopped to watch him for a moment. He marveled at the fact that, when they weren't fanning out their tails with extravagant pride, peacocks seemed so diminished. As though they were just another kind of bird and not something special to look at.

Siddhattha wandered towards the cliff edge of the garden and took a seat beneath his mother's tree. He stared out at the expanse of his kingdom, watching the colors of the landscape slowly come to life as the sun extended its reach. The kingdom stretched out for as far as the eye could see. All of it was supposed to be his to inherit.

He thought back to the water buffalos pulling the plow, harnessed by a rope attached to a ring in their nostrils. He remembered the farmer, his face wrinkled and burned by the sun, his hands as calloused as animal hide, and the tiny creatures whose bodies lay littered in the earth under the plow.

Everyone suffers, he repeated to himself for the hundred-and-eighth time. Everyone in his kingdom knows pain. His son would know pain the moment he emerged from his mother's womb. How would he solve it, he wondered. He had no answer to the problem of suffering. He had no way to make all that pain go away. A few royal edicts and a fatherly pat on the head would never be enough in the face of Old Age, Sickness and Death. Even if he administered his kingdom with the most precise interpretation of justice, even if he was the best father in the history of the ten-thousand worlds, suffering would still prevail. His subjects would still grow old, become sick, and die. His son would not live forever. He could not solve the problem of suffering. He could only hope to curtail it. And curtailing it was not enough.

A piece of red silk slipped off one of the branches above him and fluttered delicately onto his lap. It was bright red with a gold trim. Maya had come to this tree often to worship it and ask for its blessings; others had continued the tradition after her death. Siddhattha looked up and saw that the tree was covered with a fresh collection of silk strips. Large pieces had been wrapped around its trunk and smaller pieces hung on the branches and were stuffed into the tree's nooks. The tree looked as though it had been dressed for celebration.

And then he noticed something else: a mask attached to the trunk on the other side of the tree. Siddhattha got up to look at it more carefully.

The mask was not made of fancy materials, but it was elaborate all the same. Someone had taken great care in making it. It was the face of a woman, surrounded by gold and silver filaments and decked with beaded jewelry and shiny peacock feathers. The tree's bark stared at him through the holes where the eyes were supposed to be. Siddhattha took a step back and realized what the mask was meant to do: the tree was provided with a face through that mask. The mask brought the Goddess of the Tree to life.

Siddhattha put his hand to his heart as tears slipped out of his eyes like tiny crystals. He looked at the Goddess who seemed to be looking back at him. It was the Goddess his mother had worshiped. The mother he never knew.

"Mother," he whispered. "Are you here?"

The tree did not answer. She looked at him through the eyes of her mask.

"What am I supposed to do, Mother? How can I leave all of my responsibilities behind? How can I walk away from my wife and child? And Father? And the kingdom?" He did not know who he was speaking to. Was it to the Goddess? The tree? His mother? Was there a difference? He was not sure, but it did not seem to matter. The Mother was standing before him in all her glory. It was to Her that he spoke, whoever She was.

Siddhattha took a step towards Her and placed his hands on Her bark. He let the rough texture fill his palms. "Tell me what to do, Mother," he pleaded. "Must I really go? Is there no other way?"

The tree did not say a word. She remained where She was, watching him through Her magical eyes, the gold and silver filaments quivering lightly in the wind. He would have to answer those questions himself, he realized. He took a seat at the foot of the tree and pulled his legs up against his chest as he contemplated the questions he feared the answers to.

Time slipped past him without his noticing. The sun rose to its zenith in the sky and started to burn him with its gaze, but still he sat, lost in his question. Eventually, he looked up at the tree with the eyes of a pleading son. The tree folded Her branches around him and circled him with Her love. Although She could not give him the assurance he was looking for, She could hold him in her arms.

*

The Gods of the Four Directions were sitting on the edge of the clouds above, watching the scene below them with great intensity.

"This is it, isn't it Brothers?" asked the God of the Western Direction.

They all took a deep breath as they contemplated the situation below.

"I believe it is," replied the God of the East. "He is asking the questions. He is preparing himself to leave, but he cannot imagine how. It is time we complete this task."

None of the Gods made a move. They had been waiting for this moment for many years. It felt strange to be facing it now that it had arrived. What would they do with themselves after it was done?

"I am going to miss watching over him, you know," said the God of the South with a sigh. "I feel as though he has become our very own. We have watched him grow up into such a splendid young man." He wiped away a tear that was forming at the corner of his eye.

"I know what you mean," said the God of the West. "I have become terribly fond of him too. What will we do once we've given him the last of the Sights?"

They all sighed together in response. The Four Great Gods slumped into their cloud-cushioned seats and cupped their chins into their hands at the same time. They stared at the tree below who was holding him in Her arms. They were not the only ones who would miss him.

"Well?" said the God of the East in an attempt to break the spell of emotion that had taken them all captive. "We are not allowed to wallow here forever. The well-being of the universe depends on this moment."

The three others glanced at their elder brother, but they remained where they were, their eyes returning to the scene below them nostalgically.

"Brothers, I know this is difficult, but it is our role in this story," urged the God of the East.

They did not move, unable to bring themselves to accept what he was saying.

"We have no choice," he added with a reasonable tone. "You all know that."

"But there must be some other way, Brother," pleaded the God of the West. "After all, we can't be absolutely sure this is the time, can we? What if we're wrong? Maybe we should wait just a little while longer. Just to be sure."

"Brothers," the God of the East said with gentle impatience, "you know as well as I do that this is the right time."

"But what if . . ."

"No" he finally declared authoritatively. "The time has come."

The discussion was closed. They could not stall or change the story in any way. Siddhattha was ready to leave and he required the last Sight in order to imagine how it could be done. Their personal sentiments were irrelevant in the greater scheme of things.

"Very well," the three others grumbled together as they pulled themselves up. It was time to unleash the mysterious process of the last Sight. The universe was waiting.

*

The prince was still sitting in the Mother's embrace as evening began its descent into the sky. The Peacock Garden had become unusually still. Even the birds nestled in the tree's branches overhead were quiet now. They had been chirping throughout the day, but the evening breeze—which normally brought their chatter to a crescendo—had soothed them into dreamy silence.

A rustling sound caught Siddhattha's attention. No one had bothered him all day. The servants had surely discovered his hideout hours ago, but they had left him alone. Who was coming towards him? Another strutting peacock?

The rustle grew louder and Siddhattha leaned forward to see what it was. The tree resisted him, as though She did not want him to see. Her branches closed in, but Siddhattha barely noticed. He was transfixed by the sound he could hear approaching.

All of a sudden, as though a veil lifted right before his eyes, he saw what it was: it was not a peacock. It was a man. A man Siddhattha had never seen before.

The man was wearing dirt-orange robes and walked with a calm, steady gait.
Step.
Step.
Step.
The man was walking, but he remained where he was at the same time. No matter how many steps he took, he was also still, as though time and space were an illusion he had managed to manipulate. The Man in the Orange Robes was walking, but he was not approaching.

Siddhattha's attention gravitated to the Man's bare feet. To the texture of his skin and the strength of his movement. Siddhattha had never walked barefoot on the earth that way; he never left the limits of the smooth palace floors without the protection of elaborate sandals. He was not even sure he could manage walking barefoot if he tried. The bottoms of his feet were as soft as a baby's cheek. Every evening, servants massaged them with perfumed oil before he went to bed. He could not imagine what it would be like to walk the earth without anything shielding him from its texture.

The Man in the Orange Robes had very different feet. The skin was coarse and thick like a pad of leather, and it was as dark as the earth it walked upon. Each toe reached outwards like a wide-open hand, every muscle engaged. He looked down at his own feet and realized that his toes seemed cushioned by comparison. He had never realized before how delicate his body had become. *What must it be like to have such strength in one's footsteps*, he wondered.

Even more spellbinding was the *way* the Man walked. Each step he took was taken with quiet deliberation. He had the most powerful feet Siddhattha had ever seen, but he did not use them to pound the earth. On the contrary, he seemed to walk . . . almost lovingly, as though he was reaching out to meet the earth. It was like watching poetry come alive. Or a river take the shape of a man.

Siddhattha's eyes lifted and he looked at the whole of the man walking before him. The Man in the Orange Robes exuded something timeless. As though he was the earth's beating heart. Siddhattha felt himself fall in love. Not in a sensual way, but in a way that transcended the senses. He felt the kind of love that gave him a sense of who he wanted to be.

How extraordinary, he thought to himself as he looked into the distance contemplatively. *I have been surrounded by beauty all my life, but I never really knew what beauty looked like until now.*

When he returned his gaze to the Man in the Orange Robes, he found the man looking right at him. *I will follow the road you have shown me*, Siddhattha said to him with his mind. *The love I see in you . . . that is the love I vow to become.*

The two men—one of whom may have been a figment of the other's imagination—bowed their heads to each other in mutual recognition. And then, just as suddenly as he manifested into Siddhattha's life, the Man in the Orange Robes faded away.

The tree was still holding him in Her arms, but it was time for Siddhattha to be set free. He stepped out of Her embrace with the clarity of purpose he had been searching for. He had come to his Mother's garden to find answers to his questions and the answers had arrived. He would leave his father's palace. He would leave the kingdom and his family. He would walk away from everyone until he had burned down every obstacle inside his mind and love was all that remained.

He turned to the tree and bowed to Her with solemnity.

"I must go now, Mother. It is time."

Had he looked back, he would have seen a stream of leaves falling to the ground like tears.

Departure

Neelima was braiding my hair as I stared absently at the wall in front of me. Siddhattha had been gone a long time. Darkness was overtaking my thoughts like a lengthening shadow over a landscape.

I patiently submitted to the hair placement ritual I had endured every day since my arrival in the palace. I did not mind it so much when Neelima was the one to do it. She was capable of pulling all of my wild strands into place gently. She moved her fingers through my hair without yanking and the end result never felt like my forehead was being pinched.

I had, in fact, grown to enjoy the ritual. Neelima had become a confidante and we often used the time to talk with relative freedom. Friendship was in short supply as a member of the royal family and I had grown increasingly appreciative of the little bit of intimacy the two of us were permitted to share. While she wove my hair, we talked about all sorts of things together, from the daily details of my pregnancy and the nursery that was under construction, to royal scandals and the gossip that pooled out of the servants' quarters. What more did I have to attend to anyway?

On that day, however, I was silent. I could only stare into space as she plaited my hair for the benefit of a man who we both knew was no longer looking at me. I climbed inside myself and blew out the candle.

Neelima took her time, touching my hair in ways that reminded me of my mother. If I had had the energy, I would have offered a word of gratitude, but I could not. She was bringing the procedure to its conclusion, decorating the braids with little jasmine flowers, when the first birth pangs threw themselves against my insides.

"What is it, Your Highness?" Neelima asked with alarm as I suddenly doubled over with a cry.

"Your Highness, what is it? Is it time?"

I could not produce another sound. I was clenching my teeth.

Neelima should have run for help, but she did not want to leave me in the first throes of labor. She stared at me with concern, her arm wrapped around my shoulder as she tried to catch the pain.

"Great Goddess, help me!" I cried as another wave threw me to the floor. Neelima gasped as the white flowers she had been holding fell out of her hands and floated to the ground beside me. I watched them fall, focusing on them as though there was nothing else in the room. They were so small.

*

I moved in and out of consciousness for a long time. Whenever I managed to peel my eyes open, I found myself surrounded by unfamiliar faces. Women entered and left my room without even waiting to be announced. Sometimes they forgot to close the door and I would open my eyes only to find the door left wide open like a naked wound. Over and over, I begged whoever was closest to me to shut the door. I could not believe I had to ask for that myself. I was so exposed, but that seemed to be of little consequence. Other realities had taken precedence. Realities no one bothered to explain.

The silk sheets on my bed were stripped from underneath me without a word of apology. An old linen sheet was shoved in as its replacement. I watched a series of maids carrying armloads of straw into my room that they piled at the foot of the bed. Strangers' hands were pushing some of it into a bundle between my legs.

There was so much fuss, so many chaotic noises. Everyone had something to take care of. Despite the many bodies surrounding me, though, no one had thought to explain anything to me, to tell me what was happening. I could feel roving hands moving around me, shoving me, adjusting me, and voices talking about me. But no one was talking *to* me. I was at the center of everyone's attention and I was forgotten at the same time.

I was scared. From the moment my pregnancy was announced, it was as though birth stories were the only ones anyone told. And most of them were terrifying. Women dying after they gave birth. Women giving birth to dead babies. Babies dying at birth or born so deformed one wished they had. There was no end to the stories women told and for some reason they seemed to relish telling them whenever I was around. As though my round belly reminded them of the stories that had been stuffed into the cupboards of their own memories and they were excited to finally have an occasion to bring them out. Like old soldiers around a campfire, these were the wars women fought. Proud of their victories, the survivors paraded their invisible scars around like gruesome trophies.

Despite what they may have thought, I did not need their stories to feel afraid. I had my own share of fears already, built upon family histories of loss that had haunted me from the moment womanhood leaked down my thighs. No household was free of these things. The Goddess of Childbirth was a dangerous creature to entertain. She took as often as she gave. My mother had her stories, as did so many of my aunts and cousins. I had watched Chief Minister's wife and her newborn baby die right in front of me. And my husband's mother died soon after she gave birth to him—a loss that continued to echo as one of the kingdom's greatest tragedies. Women's lives came and went on the hearth governed by the Goddess of Childbirth. To not be afraid was to not understand.

But I was afraid of more than this. I was afraid of life without my husband. I was afraid of where he might go and I was afraid that he was going to leave me behind. I was afraid of living in the palace without him. I was afraid of loneliness and I was afraid of disappearance.

I didn't want any of this. I didn't want to give birth or even to live. If he was going to leave me, I was no better than a widow. Who would love me after he left? What would become of me without him?

A sharp pain shocked me back into the moment. I lifted my head to try to see what was going on. Would anybody talk to me? Another knife grabbed me and twisted my insides. I arched my back and screamed.

A soft hand helped me settle back onto the pillow and mopped my forehead. I squinted through the wetness that was covering my eyelids until I made out the features of kindness looking down at me.

"Be patient, Daughter," Mahapajapati whispered into my ear. "Everything will be all right."

Her presence was quiet. As though the storms of the world did not touch her. I reached out to cling to her. I wanted to pull myself onto her shore, but pain assaulted me before I even had a chance to try.

I screamed and twisted my body angrily. I lifted my head and looked down towards the edge of the bed in the hopes that some kind of answer was awaiting me there, but all I could see was blood. Blood was everywhere, all over my legs, all over the bed, and all over the women who were attending to me.

Terror covered my mouth with suffocating intensity. I felt the moist hand of death hovering over me, threatening to strangle me. I had convinced myself that loneliness was worse than death, but now that death was so near, I realized what a lie that had been. I didn't want to die! I wanted my life back! I wanted my baby! Where was my baby? Why wouldn't anyone explain anything to me?

"Lumbinidevi!" I yelled to the Goddess of Childbirth. "Please don't take me!" The picture of my own blood swirled around me. "Hariti! Shashti! Save me! Save my baby!"

The midwife finally came into view. I was delirious again, my head thrashing from side to side. I was certain death was about to strike. The midwife came to the other side of the bed and grabbed my arms with her strong hands, binding me and creating a limit against which I could fight the panicked pain.

"Princess, you are in danger," she warned when she felt I was quiet enough to hear. "The Goddess is close, but she is not friendly. I need you to concentrate. I need you to put your fear away."

"Am I dying?"

"It has not been decided yet," she answered.

"Where is my baby?"

"Still inside you. The heart is beating, but it won't survive much longer this way. You are losing too much blood. I will have to get the baby out myself."

I looked at her with confusion. What did that mean? How could she get the baby herself?

"I will put my hands inside of you, Princess," she explained without my having had to ask, "and I will pull the baby out. It will hurt more than anything you have felt so far. I need you to be brave. Do you understand?"

I made an almost imperceptible nod, my face having turned as white as the sheet I was lying on.

Before any more words could be spoken, the midwife stepped around me and plunged her arms into my body with more violence than anything I had ever known. I thought I was being torn apart.

*

"Father, might we speak?"

The king was seated on the Lion Throne, studying ledgers that had been presented to him by Chief Minister. He raised his eyebrows at the sound of his son's voice, but he did not look up.

"You will have to wait," he responded curtly. "I promised a response would be delivered today."

Siddhattha bowed and took a step back. He was prepared to wait.

Chief Minister watched the prince recede into the shadows. He had grown into such a quiet young man, Chief Minister thought to himself. He remembered playing with the prince as a child, letting him ride on his back as he galloped him into mock battle. How many years had passed since those days? He touched his own face and felt the wrinkles that had formed around his eyes. He was an old man now, Chief Minister realized. He had aged.

"There is no urgency, Your Highness," Chief Minister said. "This can wait until a later time."

"No, it cannot wait, Chief Minister," declared the king with a threatening undercurrent. "When a king makes a promise, the God Realm pays attention. It is my obligation to consider this now."

Chief Minister knew perfectly well that the king's sudden passion was not directed at him. He looked back at the prince, who remained perfectly still by the door.

"Explain the problem to me one more time, Chief Minister," the king requested, almost as though he wanted to extend the amount of time he made his son wait for him. If the prince refused to take care of his obligations, the king would be sure to perform those obligations for him. And he would force him to watch.

"Certainly, Maharaja," Chief Minister replied, hiding his own discomfort. He stepped forward and began to outline—with a tone that was well rehearsed by now—the nature of the negotiations.

"The Licchavis have offered to sell us some of their horses at a much better rate than we have been paying. Unfortunately, they request payment in gold. Your Highness must decide if he is willing to part with the amount of gold required in order to make this purchase."

"How much gold?" the king asked.

"Enough to make a sizable dent in the royal coffers, Your Highness. The numbers are there before you on the ledgers I have prepared."

The king looked at the ledgers one more time and then leaned back against his golden throne, the lion's growling mouth covering him like an umbrella. He sighed audibly and closed his eyes, as though he was imagining what his pile of gold would look like after such an expense.

"I am not prepared to release that much gold," he decided as he opened his eyes. "Go back to them with a counter-offer. Tell them that we are prepared to provide a portion of the payment in gold, but not all of it. Some of it will have to be made in trade. There must be something we have—other than gold—that they want. Bring them a bale of our finest silk and see if that captures their attention."

"Very good, Your Highness," Chief Minister replied. He bowed, collected his things, and made his way out of the Throne Room. Just before the door closed behind him, however, he stopped beside Siddhattha.

"Courage, my Prince," he whispered with affection.

Siddhattha nodded with gratitude. Both men understood the weight of what lay ahead.

*

Siddhattha waited to be acknowledged, but the king acted as though he had forgotten he was there. He preoccupied himself with the remaining ledgers.

Eventually, Siddhattha cleared his throat.

"Father?" he said. "May we speak now?"

The king looked up. "What is it?"

"I would like to resume our conversation."

The king looked at his son for a few moments, but instead of answering, he got up from his throne and walked towards the window.

"Father, may we please talk?" Siddhattha asked again.

"About what?" the king replied, his back turned against his son.

"I would like to leave, Father. I ask for your blessing before I go."

Suddhodana wheeled around like a tornado.

"What did you just say?" he bellowed as he stormed towards him.

Siddhattha did not back down. He had expected something like this. He took a few deep breaths before he replied.

"Father, I have given this a lot of thought. I no longer believe my place is on the throne. I have to leave."

The king's face turned purple with rage. "How dare you?!" he exclaimed with a seething voice, his body looming.

Siddhattha knew that he was betraying everything his father stood for. This was not what Siddhattha wanted. He did not want to cause anyone pain, and yet here he was, about to create misery all around himself. He dropped his head in shame.

"Father," Siddhattha whispered with a son's longing. "Please don't be so angry. Listen to what I have to say." He looked up at his father whose fury was seeping all around them like a lake of bubbling lava. "Please?"

Before the king had a chance to hurtle another wave of anger at his son, the doors of the Throne Room were flung open without ceremony. Neelima flew into the room looking panicked and sweating, her hands smeared with blood.

Both men were stunned by her arrival. Siddhattha stared at the splatters of blood she was covered with and the look of fear she was wearing on her face.

"Maidservant?" he asked her as he approached. "What happened?"

She could not find the words. She never expected to be the one to have to announce anything like this to the royal family. Least of all in the Throne Room. She fell to her knees, trembling all over.

"Maidservant," Siddhattha repeated, "there is no need to be afraid. Stand up and tell us what's going on."

She blubbered something incomprehensible and broke down in tears. Siddhattha realized that he would have to command her to respond or she would just keep falling apart.

"Answer my question, Maidservant!" the prince ordered with his royal voice.

The royal voice worked.

"Your Highness ..." she muttered painfully as she tried to get back onto her feet. "It's the princess. Labor has begun ..."

Siddhattha stood before the broken maidservant, spellbound. Screams came rushing down the hallway and tackled them all with brutal force.

"Is that her?" he asked. "Why is she screaming like that?" Another scream followed, piercing through them all. "What are you not telling me?" he demanded.

The sobbing resumed, tension spilling out of her more quickly than she could control.

"Neelima!" he cried.

The sound of her name brought her back to her senses. "It's not going well, Your Highness. I don't know what's happening, but there is a lot of blood. There's so much blood, Your Highness! And she keeps screaming!" she collapsed onto the floor again and sobbed with exhaustion.

Siddhattha turned to his father with a look of shock. He had been so focused on the question of his own departure that he had overlooked the immediate present. Women gave birth all the time. It wasn't supposed to be like this.

He turned back to my maidservant and asked the question that was on everyone's mind.

"Is she dying?" he asked.

"I don't know."

Neelima remained on the floor, fallen and frightened, while the two men stared into nothingness as the news slowly trickled its way into their minds. Siddhattha had never considered the possibility that I might not survive the birth. He had been so focused on the difficulty of having to leave me that he had never considered the possibility that I might leave him first.

"Neelima," he said quietly, using her name for the second time, "return to your mistress and take care of her. But come back regularly with news. Is that clear?"

She nodded and wiped her sniveling nose on the back of her hand. The prince helped her to her feet and sent her on her way. He then looked up at his father with life's great questions pouring out of his eyes. The king looked back at him, without the answers.

The anger was gone.

*

The two men sat together in silence. Countless cups of steaming milk had come and gone, but the story of my delivery had not reached a conclusion. The hours bled into each other with unhurried agony. They waited. And they sipped. The whole kingdom seemed to be sitting on a precipice.

Eventually, the king spoke.

"I don't understand why you want to leave, Son. What has made you so unhappy here?"

"It isn't that I am unhappy, Father."

"So why do you want to leave? You have everything you could ever want."

"I am not leaving for anything like that, Father. You know that."

"So you *are* leaving then? The decision has already been taken? Regardless of what I say?" The king's frustration did not take long to resurface.

"Yes, Father. I am leaving."

"But why?" he insisted.

Siddhattha turned the words around in his mind before he spoke them aloud. These were not easy things to say.

"Father, it has nothing to do with worldly desire. Or even with family. Or with station. I am leaving to find something else entirely."

"What else is there?" he asked, genuinely baffled.

"Well ..." Siddhattha began, "to be truthful, I am looking for the answer to pain. The answer to suffering that I cannot seem to find as long as I remain here."

The king looked at the door, as though waiting for it to burst open again. "Life *is* pain," was all he could reply.

"But that's the problem, Father. I don't think it needs to be. The pain we all face, the suffering that is at the source of so many of our experiences ... there must be an alternative to it. It cannot be the only version of truth out there."

"You sound like an idealist," the king mumbled in response.

"Perhaps," Siddhattha replied quietly. It was his turn to stare at the door.

The king could see the river of tender emotion that ran through his son. Siddhattha was not leaving out of indifference. That much he could see. He was leaving to find an answer. But an answer to life's difficulty? That was madness. Life *was* difficult. There was no answer to find. What exactly did he expect?

"Siddhattha, this makes no sense! Think of your wife's screams! Think of how she is braving her pain! Are you going to abandon her? Abandon the child that she is destroying herself to bring into the world for you? How can you possibly consider leaving at a time like this? I don't understand you!"

"I know."

"It is not enough just *to know*! If you know, then don't leave! You are going to break her heart!"

"I know that too, Father."

"Then why?!" he demanded passionately.

Siddhattha could not answer.

"I know you love your wife, Son. There is no shame in that."

Siddhattha looked down at his hands.

"Son, I lost your mother on a day like this. She gave birth to you and then she disappeared out of my life forever. I remarried, as was required, making Mahapajapati my queen, and I have had hundreds of courtesans at my disposal, but no one has come close to the wife I lost. I still miss her—all these years later."

Siddhattha was surprised by this admission. They never spoke of her.

"I miss her too, Father, and I never even knew her."

"There are few great women in this world, Siddhattha, and I believe we have both had the rare privilege of being married to one. Yasodhara is not like other women. You cannot throw her away to chase some fantasy. You will never find another like her. Just as I never found anyone to replace Maya."

"I am not looking to replace her. Yasodhara cannot be replaced. Yasodhara and I have been together for lifetimes ..." Siddhattha's voice cracked, but he braved the sadness and continued. "Father, where I am going, no one can follow me. Not even her."

He looked out the window and added, "For now, her place is here. And my place is to go."

*

Mahapajapati entered the room with a dignified gait. The terror that had launched Neelima through the doors had nothing to do with the demeanor the queen embodied now. She carried herself with stately authority. She walked right past her own husband and addressed my husband instead.

"Son," she said, "your wife has been through a terrible ordeal and she is very weak. She has lost a lot of blood, but the midwife believes she will survive."

Siddhattha exhaled.

"She is calm now," she explained. "But she will need much rest."

"What about ...?" the king began, but his wife cut him off in the most uncharacteristic of maneuvers. She maintained her focus on Siddhattha. "You have a healthy little boy, Siddhattha. You have a son."

Siddhattha lowered himself onto the couch as the tension he had been carrying for months drained out of him. Tears rolled down his face with an incomprehensible combination of joy and sadness. His wife was safe. His son was born.

He was free to go.

He reached for her hands and held them tightly in his own. "You have been a kind mother to me. I will never be able to repay my debt to you for all that you have done."

She touched his face with the tip of one of her fingers. The king watched an interaction he felt he was being consciously excluded from, but before he managed to regain his composure, she had walked away, the door closing softly behind her.

"Did she ignore me just now?" the king muttered to himself.

"Sorry, Father?"

"Mahapajapati. Did she ignore me?" he asked again, genuinely concerned.

"I don't know," Siddhattha answered from somewhere far away.

"You don't think she overheard our conversation, do you? When we were discussing your mother?"

Siddhattha looked up at his father who suddenly seemed like a lost little boy to him. Had she overheard their conversation? And if she had, would it really have been news to her? Hadn't he always treated his wife as a replacement?

Siddhattha shook his head. This was not the time to be discussing his father's relationships. He was still repeating to himself the words Mahapajapati had said. That his wife was going to be all right. That she was safe again. And that he had a son. His very own son! Siddhattha put his hand to his heart as it swelled with pride.

He had a son.

After all that pain, all those screams and all that blood, they had made it to the other shore. He pictured my face in his mind and he covered it with his love.

He looked up again at his father who seemed to be muttering something to himself about his wife. Siddhattha walked over to him and put his hand on his father's shoulder.

"Father, do you realize that I have a son? You're a grandfather."

"What?"

"Father, I have a son," he repeated with a smile. "You're a grandfather and I am a father. And Yasodhara survived!"

The king finally came back to himself. He took the words in slowly until a smile filled his broad face. "You have a son?" he asked, suddenly beaming. "In the name of all the gods in heaven, you have a son!"

The king pulled the prince into his arms and hugged him with all the ferocious love he had inside of him. The two men held onto each other tightly.

"You cannot go now. You have to stay to care for your son! At least until he is ready to take the throne!"

Siddhattha sighed as he gently pulled himself away.

"Father, you must understand . . . this does not change anything."

"How can you say that?" he stuttered. "What about your son? And the throne? Who will take the throne? Your son will not be ready for years!"

"You have Nanda. Why not him?"

The king laughed bitterly. "Nanda? You can't be serious! You know as well as I do that he would make a terrible king! He is more interested in his own looks than anything else. The kingdom would crumble under his leadership! He would fill the halls with beautiful courtesans and full-length mirrors!"

"Nanda has more goodness inside of him than that. The problem is that you have never expected anything from him. But if he is given the chance, I am certain he will prove that he has more to offer than what we've seen so far."

"Well, that's not a chance I am willing to take. The throne is not a game of dice, Son!"

"No, I agree. The throne is a station that deserves the highest attention. The gods would not look kindly on a random decision," Siddhattha replied authoritatively—like the prince he was supposed to be.

"There will be arguments over the throne if you leave," the king warned. "It will be chaos. Devadatta will be the first in line and others will follow."

Siddhattha could not argue with that. He knew it was true.

"You must see your obligations, Son," the king argued. "You cannot leave the kingdom this way. The throne belongs to you. I am an old man now. I have to turn it over to someone else. You have to take your place in the order of things."

Siddhattha looked at the Lion Throne that seemed to be staring back at him. It glittered in the evening light, jewels twinkling with enticement. That golden throne had been part of his mental repertoire for as long as he could remember. It had beckoned him, taunted him, welcomed him.

But he did not welcome it in return. The throne he was meant to sit on was made of leaves and birch bark.

"Son," his father continued. "Think of what the sages have always taught us. That there is a time for everything. There is a time for worldly things and there is a time to retire from them. It is *my* time to walk away, Son, not yours. It is my time to retreat into a life of contemplation. But you are young. The world of the senses is strong for you. Young men are not fit for renunciation. You should be taking the throne so that *I* can walk away from it. You have no right to reverse our roles this way."

It was the most reasonable argument his father had made so far. And it was true.

"Father, you are right. It *should* be your time to walk away. But that does not change the fact that it is my time too. Nothing can change that. I feel the call to leave and I must obey. It is a greater obligation even than the throne. Even than my wife and son. Forcing me to stay here would be like forcing a man to stay inside a burning house. This world is burning, Father; you cannot ask me to stay when I can see the flames."

"But it's wrong Siddhattha! You must see that!"

The prince considered the statement seriously. It was precisely what he had been wrestling with for a very long time.

"You may be right, Father, but if I stay, that would be wrong too."

"But . . . but what about the throne?" the king asked with desperation.

"The throne will find its king in due time. It always does," Siddhattha replied with soft confidence.

The king looked around the room, hoping that the solution to his problem was still within his reach.

"Is there really no way to convince you to stay? Is there absolutely nothing I can offer?"

Siddhattha wondered. Was there any way for him to stay? Could the quest be done from inside the palace walls?

"There is," he finally admitted.

The king threw himself at his son eagerly. "Anything! Tell me and it is yours! What can I do to ensure that you stay?"

Siddhattha thought back to his time in the woods with Channa, to the Sights he had seen that had set him on this course. To the realities of the world that he had failed to recognize until then.

"You would have to guarantee four things, Father, and I would stay."

"Anything, Son! Tell me!"

"You would have to guarantee that I would never grow old, that I would never become sick, that I would never die, and that my fortune would remain as it is right now. If you can guarantee these four things for me, Father, then I will stay."

The king took a step back, dismay overtaking him.

"No one can guarantee such things. You know I could never promise you any of that."

"Then let me go, Father. There is no other way."

Sadness

Protective chants drifted into my room on clouds of incense accompanied by a voice I did not recognize. The royal priest had retired to the forest and I assumed the new priest was the one outside my door. He didn't have Brahmin's self-confidence, which diminished the magical quality he was supposed to be conjuring. Each time the door opened, I caught sight of the burning butter lamp he was waving in circles around himself. The pollution of afterbirth was obviously bothering him, but I could not be bothered enough to care.

"Your evening meal, Princess," Neelima announced as she walked past the ritual into my room with a tray. "Cook has prepared rice and some lentil soup for you. There's also sweet milk with turmeric and a few of the cardamom desserts you like so much."

She put the tray down on the bedside table with a hopeful air, but I turned away.

"You must eat, Princess. Everyone is worried about you."

I kept my head turned and spoke into the pillow. "I'm not hungry. Please leave me alone."

"What if I brought you some yogurt then? The buffalos were milked yesterday and I am sure Cook has already made some with it. Yogurt is healing, especially after what you've been through. Would you eat that at least?"

I turned to face her with rising frustration. From the moment I became pregnant, food was all anyone seemed to approach me with. Everywhere I turned, platters were presented to me with shining enthusiasm. I stared at the tray beside my bed and wanted to throw it against the wall.

"Where's my husband?" I asked instead.

Neelima stared at me, dumbstruck.

"My husband, Maidservant. Where is he? Where is the prince?"

She hadn't seen it coming, despite the fact that she knew it would. It was only a matter of time before that question would have to be answered. She picked up the tray and brought it towards me again as the only reasonable response she could think of.

"Have you even looked at these beautiful sweets? You must eat them. I think Cook will throw himself into the cooking fire if I return with them on your tray again! He can't take any more rejection from you!"

"Enough with the food, Neelima!" I replied impatiently. "Tell me the truth. *Where is my husband?*"

Neelima set the tray back onto the table very carefully. She was doing everything she could to control her trembling. I knew it was unfair of me, but I needed to hear the words spoken aloud.

"Tell me."

Neelima dropped to her knees and lowered her head.

"He is gone, Your Highness. Prince Siddhattha is gone."

*

I always prided myself on being strong. I might have had a temper, but I managed despite it. I could make my way across any hurdle like a well-trained athlete. I never knew myself in any other way. Until, that is, I found myself alone in my room, nursing a newborn while I stared at the door.

Siddhattha and I had been together for such a long time. Our togetherness had always seemed timeless to me, as though it had been threaded from past lives into this one. We were not just husband and wife. We were everything to each other.

Or at least, he was everything to me ...

I could not understand why he walked away, so I stared at the door, day after day, wondering if it would ever open again. I lay on my bed, my baby beside me, utterly oblivious to his little cries.

Sometimes a servant would come barreling into the room to grab the baby who had been screaming without my noticing. It was only when I felt stronger arms take him from my own limp ones that I would realize what was happening, but by then it was too late. The child was being shuttled into another room, into someone else's care, and I was left to myself to stare at a door that would never open for him again.

My mother was the one to wake me from my slumber. I had not seen her in many years, but when she heard about the faraway look in my eyes, she knew what it meant and she lifted herself out of bed to see me one last time.

No one stopped her. Old Age was no longer something to fear because the prince had escaped despite every effort made to the contrary. The guards let their weapons clatter to the ground as she hobbled by.

"Princess," Neelima whispered as she peeked her head inside. "There is a special visitor here to see you."

I stared past her at the door I hated.

"Princess, I am going to bring them in. Is that all right?"

"I don't want to see anyone," was my answer. "Tell them to go away." I turned my back, expecting my wishes to be obeyed. The baby was not in the bed with me. I didn't know where he was.

The door opened with a slight creaking sound and I could hear the priest's voice slipping inside. He was repeating the chants he had been singing for days as though he was trapped in a mindless cycle. Over and over again, he sang the songs that were supposed to purify the air of all the mess I had made. I shut my eyes and tried to block him out.

Slow, uneven footsteps approached. They were not Neelima's. I kept my back turned, hoping whoever it was would go away. I stared at the floor because it was there.

The person pulled up a bench and sat down by my bed. Nothing was said, but I suddenly knew who it was. I could feel her presence, feel her love covering me like a soft blanket. Without a word, she reached out and began to caress my hair, her fingers trailing along the uncombed strands with familiar movement. I clenched at first—the intimacy surprising me—but she did not pull away. She just kept going, moving her hands through my hair, caressing the only part of me available to her.

I don't know how long she sat there with me. It must have been a long time. I didn't turn around. I just let myself be touched by her until I fell asleep. Although I had been lying in bed for weeks, it was the first time I really met my rest.

*

I was finally sitting up. My back was propped up by colorful silken pillows, a cup of warm fermented barley milk in my hand. But I was still staring at the door.

"Daughter," my mother said. "Tell me what happened."

I looked up at her briefly. The change produced by time was difficult to absorb. Her face was sinking into itself. Her back looked like a broken instrument, barely capable of holding her up.

"You know what happened, Mother. There's no point talking about it." I returned my gaze to the door. "Everyone in the kingdom knows."

She didn't respond right away. She was grateful that I was sitting up and that I was speaking—regardless of how curt my tone was. An improvement only a mother could love.

She leaned over very slowly and placed her withered hands over mine. "I am very sorry he left, Daughter. Whatever the reason was, I know it was not your fault."

Tears welled up instantly and began to drip out of my eyes, one at a time, each one its own puddle. She knew how to pierce through the tangled iron web that had become my protection.

"Daughter, you do understand that, right? That he didn't leave because of you?"

The pain morphed into anger almost instantly. "Well, he didn't *stay* because of me either, now did he?" I exclaimed violently, finally allowing myself to express what I was holding inside. "He left me, Mother! I am a disgrace now! And everyone knows! Everyone in the entire kingdom! He made me a *widow*!" I launched my cup against the door I had spent so much time staring at and watched it explode into a thousand little pieces. "How could he do that to me?" I screamed.

I turned to my mattress and sobbed like a child, my arms covering my head as I heaved with pain. "How could he do that?" I repeated over and over again.

"It's all right, sweetheart," she said quietly. "Let it out." She stroked my hair as I cried into the pillows and stained them with my salty tears.

After a while, she tried again.

"Daughter, do you know why he left?"

She was not going to let me wallow. I hadn't seen her in years, but the moment she appeared, she reclaimed her place in my life as though no time had passed at all. She was going to pull me into a conversation whether I liked it or not.

"I think there are enough gossipmongers in the palace who would be more than happy to provide you with a story. Why not ask them?"

"I do not want to ask anyone else. I have come here to ask you." She looked at me with her sharp, unrelenting eyes. "Why did he leave?"

I shrugged with fury. "How would I know? He left. Isn't that enough?"

"Daughter, I understand your anger, but please remember yourself," she said as she patted my hand. "Now answer me. Why do you think he left?"

"You are assuming he would confide something like that to me, Mother, but clearly I was irrelevant to him. Just another woman abandoned by her husband." The words were spitting from between my locked teeth.

My mother looked at me carefully. I saw a veil of frustration hover over her tired face, but it was quickly replaced by something else. Something I could not read. She adjusted herself slowly in her seat, as though trying to keep the falling pieces of her body together just a little while longer.

"Daughter, what I am about to tell you is extremely important, so please sit up properly and listen."

The time had come. The moment of truth which she alone could speak.

"The feelings you are having, the anger, the grief, and ..." she paused for a moment, trying to find the right words. "And ... the way you have turned away from your son ..."

My head snapped towards her in surprise.

She kept her eyes trained on me like a hawk and continued. "All of these feelings, Daughter ... They have a name."

That was the last thing I expected to hear. I thought she was going to tear into me for being the most horrible mother in the many thousand worlds. I was waiting for it. After all, deep down inside, I knew that I was. That I was the cruelest and most selfish mother ever to be born. *Obviously* Siddhattha left me ...

"Yasodhara," she continued softly, "these feelings that you are drowning in—they have been felt by others before you. That is why they have a name."

I peered over at her. The hatred moved aside as curiosity crept in.

"A name?" I asked.

"Yes, Daughter. They are known as the Great Sadness. It has happened to others and it is happening to you right now. It sometimes happens to new mothers after they give birth. When the Great Sadness arrives, even one's own child is not enough. New mothers turn from their babies and they turn from themselves. There is too much pain for love to find its place."

"But how can others have felt this, Mother? How many others have been abandoned by their husbands the moment they delivered? How many have had this done to them with an entire kingdom as their audience? There cannot be a name for that!"

"No, you are right. What you are facing is particular. Few have had to face what you are being called to go through in such a public way. But the difference is only in the detail. The storyline is always the same."

"*Detail*? My husband leaving me while everyone whispers about it is just *detail*?" The anger flew out of me like lightning.

"Yes, dear," she said quietly. "Detail."

"How can you say that?"

"I don't mean that your situation is not painful. What I mean is that the Great Sadness forms out of reasons that are different for each of us. The point is not *why* it arises. The point right now is that it does."

This flustered me. "So all you're saying is that I am sad, just as others have been before. I don't understand how this is important information."

"Because, Daughter, the Great Sadness arises at a dangerous time. It is a sadness that engulfs a woman when she is needed most. If you are not careful, it will destroy you. It will destroy your baby too."

She looked over at me with studied attention. She was speaking truth. I could hear it, but I didn't know what to do with it.

"Daughter," she continued tenderly, "you have been torn open in so many ways. Your body was ripped open when you delivered and your heart was ripped apart when you realized that he left. Your pain is deep and it is frightening you. But you must not allow yourself to stay this way. You must heal yourself. You must close what has been opened and it must be done carefully. Otherwise, you risk becoming a tapestry of scars."

"A . . . tapestry of scars?" I repeated quietly. "That sounds terrible. I don't want that." Tears were falling.

She smiled at me for the first time, her eyes sinking into the folds of her skin. "Of course not, Daughter. Nobody does." She moved some of my wild hair from my face. "Which is why you must heal. You must stitch yourself back together again. You cannot allow yourself to wallow in rage."

"But how?" I felt so bewildered. So far out of my own familiar terrain.

"One stitch at a time, little one."

I took a deep breath and leaned back into the pillows behind me.

With one finger, she turned my face towards her and added, "It begins by letting your son back into your arms."

Tapestries

My mother died not long after that visit. Although her wisdom was not lost on me and her words reverberated constantly inside the shell that had become my mind, the sadness was destined to grow wider and the loneliness tunnel deeper before I began to find my way out.

I oscillated between rage and depression as though they were two sides of the same coin. I could drift for days on my bed without speaking, staring at a door that remained closed against me, when all of a sudden, rage would erupt like a volcano and everything within reach went flying across the room as I screamed. It was a time of devastating suffering. I hated the gods for my mother's death. I hated *him* for his abandonment. And I resented my son, who wanted from me when I had nothing to give. Hatred swirled, poisoned me into an ugliness I did not know I could become. I was certain I was scaring everyone in the palace with the look in my eyes, spreading suffering around me like a contagious disease, but there was nothing I could do about it, even if I was.

But the truth was that my abandoned state did not cause as much turmoil as I thought it had. I thought I was the only one to have been shredded into pieces, the only one he abandoned when he left. But had I looked beyond myself, even for just a moment, I would have realized that everyone was affected by his departure. He hurt us all when he walked away.

Even the gods in charge of palace life, the gods of love and desire and of worldly things, sobbed in anguish when they realized he had escaped their clutches. Sometimes I caught sight of their twisted faces in the clouds. It rained for weeks over the palace compound after his departure. The gods were releasing monsoon-like tears all over us with their pain.

Heal yourself, she had said. Hold your son.

That was not an easy request. The tapestry of scars was already starting to cover me with its monstrosity. I repeated her words to myself over and over again, hoping that they would create a kind of magical effect.

I dragged myself to the nursery whenever her words pushed up against my skull. I would peel myself off the bed and walk to his room like a ghost in a trance and stand before that closed door. I would stare at it, just as I would stare at the door in my own room. I would stare and stare, but I would not go in. Closed doors had become a symbol of everything I felt myself becoming. I had no idea how to open them. No idea what else could be done with them. Eventually, I would abandon the thought of challenging them. I would slide down the wall and curl up into a little ball. I didn't know how to go in. I didn't know how to do anything.

*

One morning, I woke up in a fierce mood. It was not going to be a day of lethargy. It was going to be one of rage. I stormed into the stables with my hair in disarray and my clothes trailing behind me with madness.

"CHARIOT DRIVER!" I bellowed like a peasant as I yanked open the stable doors. "Where are you?!"

I stormed through the stables with abandon. My mother would have been horrified had she lived to see me in that state.

"Chariot Driver!" I repeated as I banged my way through the corridors. I launched everything on my path to the side like a wild bull, stampeding forward. I kicked closed doors open and relished the sound they made as they wacked against their frames. Closed doors were not going to assault me with their stillness today!

"Chariot Driver!" I screamed again.

I heard a shuffling sound behind me and whirled in its direction. Chariot Driver was rushing towards me, a panicked look in his eyes.

"I was calling you, Chariot Driver! What took you so long?"

Channa fell to his knees and put the crown of his head to the floor. "My deepest apologies, Princess. I was doing some work in the field behind the stables." He was trembling all over. And he was so thin.

"What can I do for you, Your Highness?" he asked, with his head still lowered. It was the appropriate posture for a servant to use when addressing royalty, but I felt that something else was keeping his eyes to the ground. That he could not face me for reasons other than what social hierarchy dictated.

"I was calling you! Didn't you hear me?" I demanded.

Channa choked back a muffled sound.

"Stand up, Chariot Driver." He hesitated, but eventually he pulled himself back to standing position. His head was still curled towards his feet.

"Look at me."

He lifted his face. What had happened to him? I knew the answer, but I was not prepared to face it. I had more pressing questions to ask.

"Where is he?" I whispered.

I expected him to feign ignorance, to ask me who I was referring to, but Channa had more integrity than that. We both knew perfectly well who this was about and neither of us was built to ignore it.

"He is gone, Your Majesty," he replied almost inaudibly.

"Of course he's gone!" I raged. "Everyone knows that! But where did he go? You were the last one to see him! *You* led him out of the palace compound! You know where he went! I order you to tell me where he is!"

I hated myself that way. I had never had so little composure. So little control over my own emotions. I was completely beyond my own power, flailing with hysteria.

"I ... I promise you, Your Highness. I don't know where he is," Channa sniveled.

"Well you must know something! How did he leave here? How did he get past the guards? Why didn't anyone notice the two of you escaping? Tell me!"

Channa was collapsing into himself. "I promise you, Your Highness," he cried, "I don't know. I don't know how we got out and I don't know where he is. I don't know anything."

"Liar!" I screamed. "You have to know! Tell me what you know!" I was sobbing with frustration. I thought the earth was going to crack under the pressure of my rage.

"But I don't, Your Highness. It all happened so fast!" he pleaded. "One minute, life was routine, and the next he was pulling me aside and begging me to take him away. I didn't know what I was supposed to do!"

"What were you *supposed* to do?" I cried. "You were *supposed* to say no! You were supposed to tell him that he had a wife and a son and that he was *supposed* to stay with us! You were *supposed* to say no!" I wanted to smash all of my anger against his broken body, beating him until there was nothing left of either of us. I hit his chest with my fists as I cried. Channa did not resist.

Eventually, my energy buckled and I fell into the dust. "You were supposed to tell him not to go because of *me*," I whimpered pathetically. "How could you let him run away?"

Channa lowered himself to the ground beside me. "Your Highness," he said quietly, "I begged him not to go. I spoke of you and of his newborn son many times. I reminded him of your loveliness, of your gentle compassion, of how strong your love is for each other. I begged him not to go, but his resolve was unshakable. No matter what I said, I could not change his mind. He was leaving and there was nothing I could do to stop him.

"When my words failed to convince him," he continued, "I hoped the guards would be more effective. I assumed they would be at their posts, prepared to fulfill their obligations. I saddled Kanthaka and we rode out towards the gate. I expected the sound of the horse's hooves to alert them before we arrived, but Kanthaka did not make a sound. Not one click from his steps. It was as though he was gliding over the earth. When I looked down, I saw hundreds of gods lining the road beneath us, reaching out their hands and catching his hooves in their palms."

I pulled myself up to a seated position and looked at him with my swollen eyes. "The gods were *underneath* you?" I asked incredulously.

"Yes, Your Highness. I saw them myself. Kanthaka galloped across the courtyard without making a sound, each step received by the gods' open hands. No one heard us approach the gates."

"But . . . even if that were true," I was disoriented, "it still doesn't explain how you made it through the gates. The king keeps those locked!"

"You are right, Your Highness. But the gates swung open as we reached them. I tell you, Princess: the gods were *leading* us out, enabling our escape. And it was such a dark night. There was a full eclipse of the moon. We would have been invisible to human eyes anyway. Don't you remember the darkness of that night?"

No, I thought to myself bitterly, I did not remember. I had just given birth. I was not paying attention to the moon.

I wiped my nose with the back of my hand the way I had when I was a little girl. So many competing emotions were tangled inside my head.

I got to my feet and turned around to adjust the sash around my robe.

"Take me to Kanthaka, Chariot Driver," I said as I turned back towards him. "I would like to see him."

Channa looked at me with sad, red-rimmed eyes. "I am afraid that is impossible, Your Highness."

"Why?"

"Because, Your Highness . . . Kanthaka is dead."

"Dead? What do you mean *dead*? I heard nothing of this!"

Channa kicked the floor into a swirl of pink dust. "No announcement was made, Your Highness. The king refused to hear of it."

"But . . . why?" I muttered with surprise. "How can this be?"

Channa did not respond. It was not his place to question the king's royal intentions. Or the lack thereof.

"How did he die? When? Where is he now?" I asked.

"He died the night of the prince's departure, Your Highness ..." His voice trailed off painfully.

I could not imagine a world without that creature in it. He had always seemed immortal to me. Channa, by contrast, looked like a shattered man. I was beginning to understand that I was not the only one with a broken heart.

"Tell me what happened, Chariot Driver," I said more tenderly.

"Well ..." he began with a distressed voice, "Kanthaka was valiant, as always. He was swift and powerful as he charged his way out of the palace compound. We ran through the night, clear across the entire kingdom! He didn't take a moment to rest or drink a bit of water. He just ran and ran. As though it wasn't just the prince escaping anymore. He was running for his life."

He paused to look up at me. "You know, Kanthaka always hated being confined here. No one but the prince was capable of riding him. He never belonged here, bound by our chains."

Siddhattha never belonged here either. I looked away as the emotions rose to the surface again.

"When we arrived," he continued, "the prince jumped down without even waiting for me to help him. He walked towards the forest without looking back."

"You mean he left? Just like that? Without even saying anything?"

"He tried to. At least I think he did. It's impossible to know what another intends. He seemed so determined, but I could not let him go. I ran after him and begged him to return. I had begged him already so many times, but when I saw him take those first steps away from me, I panicked and threw myself at his feet. I begged him all over again, pleaded for him to stay, but his mind would not be changed."

"Where were you when all of this was happening? Where had you gone to?"

"We were at the very edge, Your Highness. The end of the earth as I have ever known it."

The end of the earth, I thought to myself. My husband had not stopped running until the entire world lay stretched out between us. Another knife to the heart.

"What is it like there?" I whispered.

"It is a most terrifying place, Your Highness. When I saw him heading into that forest, my panic became even more terrible. I didn't want him to go in there. Not alone."

I shuddered as I tried to imagine my husband walking alone into deserted darkness. A place of exile. I could not continue the discussion in the stables, facing him as he described the moments that had splintered my heart.

"Go on, Chariot Driver," I started walking out of the stables. "Where is the edge of the world?"

"Well ... it is difficult to say," he answered as he followed me. "I am not sure where we were exactly, but it's bordered by a most wild forest, Your Highness. It's well known amongst the sages. I remember hearing about it as a child, although I never imagined I would see it for myself. It is the haunt of the ascetics. Only those who are prepared to face themselves dare step inside."

We walked into a wide-open field. His description was unsettling. The fresh air wrapped around me with a chill.

"It was dark and eerie," he continued. "I could see a ring of ghosts hovering over the trees, haunting the area. I was terrified, shivers running up and down my spine the whole time. But the prince was fearless. It was where he wanted to be."

We were surrounded by tall grass and pretty wild-flowers. The sun was shining. What a contrast from the place where my beloved now dwelt.

"Once I realized how determined he was, I stopped trying to convince him to turn back. Instead, I just begged him to let me go with him. I didn't want to leave him alone there, Your Highness. I couldn't bear the thought of him in that frightening place without someone to protect him. I begged and I begged, but he refused. He insisted that he had to make the journey alone. There was no way to change his mind. He would not take me with him no matter what I said."

Channa's voice was cracked with torment. I knew all too well what he was feeling. I had begged Siddhattha many times too.

"The prince brought the conversation to a close. He then took out his golden sword and with one quick movement, sliced off his long black hair."

My hands flew to my face.

"I tried to catch the hair as it fell," he continued with an empty stare. "I don't know what I was thinking. I suppose it was shock. Nothing made much sense to me at the time."

My beautiful husband without his long, black hair! I couldn't imagine it. And yet, at the same time, I could already see what it meant. He was cutting himself off from our world entirely. He was not a prince anymore. He was not a husband or a father either.

"The prince then handed me his sword and asked me to bring it back to the king with his respects. He then turned around and walked away."

And like that, he was gone.

Channa and I walked together in silence for a while. It was not appropriate to walk side by side with him, but I did not have enough energy to care. I thought of my husband, alone in that terrifying darkness, wrestling with the questions of his mind. I reached for the Goddess' pendant that hung faithfully around my neck. I put it on every morning before I got dressed and yet I rarely thought about what it meant anymore. The pendant was part of my routine. I never went anywhere without it, and yet I rarely considered it.

But as I listened to Channa and felt the pendant in my warm fingers, I remembered it. I remembered *Her.* My mother taught me that Durga refused to live according to social rules. After she slaughtered Mahisa Asura, she did not retreat behind a husband or hover over a cooking fire. She soared into the Himalayas and settled in a cave to live by her own rules. Free of the rules of others.

Durga.

Her name seemed expansive suddenly. As though it could take up all the space in the sky. I had not thought about her in a long time, despite the fact that I saw her painted on walls and sculpted into statues. Despite the fact that I wore her around my neck every day.

Durga had her own rules and she lived by them fearlessly. She never apologized for her strength, never held onto others to save herself. She was who my mother wanted me to remember, and yet I had dropped her somewhere along the way. I had become a slave to the rules of my station, addicted to the way the king had orchestrated my world. I had become convinced that my husband was the only refuge I had and that without him . . . I was no one at all.

Durga seared herself into my skin, her weapons burning me with their authority.

*

A few peasant women were bent over on the edge of a watery rice field, collecting the harvest into neat bundles by their feet. Their movements were rhythmic and they sang as they worked, pulling rice stalks up and throwing them together like a choreographed dance. My thoughts returned to the time when Siddhattha and I had watched that farmer plow the field, all those years ago.

The women were initially oblivious to our approach, but as Channa and I got closer, one of them caught sight of us and immediately stopped what she was doing. She stared at me for a brief moment and then made a gruff noise that alerted the others. A few of them cried out in surprise and then they all toppled to their knees, mumbling their apologies. Some of the bundles slipped back into the liquid field, but no one made a move to catch them.

I stared at the spilled rice stalks that the water was hungrily swallowing. Siddhattha had had such a strong reaction to the farmer and his labor. He kept talking about how wrong we had been to believe in the truth of social hierarchy. That none of it was real and that we were ultimately all brothers, no matter how far apart any of us might seem. Siddhattha had begun to change after that.

The women were bent over, their knees sinking progressively into the watery earth. Their skin was burned by the sun, just as that farmer's skin had been, and their hands reflected years of hard labor, nails brittle and cracked. My own nails were so clean and delicate by comparison.

When Siddhattha and I had come across that farmer, all I had seen was an ordinary peasant doing ordinary work. I barely noticed him, but Siddhattha had looked *at* him. He had seen him while I had looked right past him. And in the process, he discovered their sameness, their shared humanity.

I stared at the women huddled at my feet. *Were we the same*, I wondered. On the outside, we were worlds apart. But . . .

"Farmwoman," I said to the one closest to me, "please rise."

The farmwoman did not make a move. I tapped her on the shoulder and repeated myself. "Please rise, Farmwoman."

The woman raised her eyes and then immediately threw her gaze back at the ground. Her body was shaking. She seemed incapable of moving, so paralyzed was she with intimidation.

I could feel Channa's indignation mounting behind me. He stepped forward, taking on the role of my personal bodyguard and pulled her up by the arm. I put my arm out to stop him from becoming too aggressive. "There is no need to be frightened, Farmwoman," I said with my gentlest voice. "I would just like to ask you a few questions if it's all right with you."

She did not reply.

Channa intervened. "The Princess asked you a question, Farmwoman. It is your duty to answer."

The poor woman was convulsing with fear at this point. I was about to step back to leave them alone when one of the others stood up and spoke in her place.

"Excuse me, Madame, but she's very shy. She won't be able to answer you."

This one spoke so candidly and with such ease. "I didn't mean to cause her harm," I answered.

"Don't worry, Madame. She's always like that. You did nothin' wrong."

I looked more carefully at the one who was speaking. She had bright green eyes and a small, soft face. Unlike her companions, our differences in station did not cause her to dissolve into a puddle of obsequiousness.

"What is your name, Farmwoman?" I asked, encouraged by the opportunity presenting itself.

"They call me Kisa Gotami, Madame—Skinny Gotami—on account of the fact that my ribs poke out so much!" She pulled her dirty cotton dress against her body to show me. I recoiled instinctively.

"Are you ill?"

"Oh, no Madame. I've always been this way. I can shovel down more plates of rice than anyone, but my ribs never get any cushion around them. My grandma' says it's 'cause I was too fat in my past life, sneaking off with food all the time and never doin' any work, so I was reborn like this to learn my lesson." She chuckled to herself a little and I smiled.

"Do you live far from here?" I asked, not sure where I was hoping to go with the inquiry.

"Just a bit of a ways. In a village east of the town, Madame. It's a nice walk when it's not too hot."

"How long are your days of work?" I asked.

"Excuse me?"

"How long do you work each day?"

She looked confused, and then looked at the others around her. They rose to their feet, encouraged by her example, and consulted with each other in whispered bursts.

Eventually, Kisa Gotami spoke up again.

"My apologies, Madame, but what exactly do you mean by 'work'? I never was too smart . . ."

"Oh," I exclaimed. I thought the question was obvious. "I mean, how long do you spend in the field each day? Or is there another kind of work that you do as well?"

Kisa Gotami scrunched up her face. "Well . . ." she said, "I suppose it depends on how you look at it, Madame. Each season is different. And there are all kinds of work that we women do in a day."

"What do you mean?" I asked.

"Well, in this season, our days start real early, before even the Sun God wakes up. We do our morning prayers—if you want to count that as work of course. We collect water, prepare the food and sweep the floors. Those with babies also have to feed them and wrap them up nice, and they're brought to the grandmothers so that we can come here." She paused for a moment and explained, "I am not married yet, but a marriage is being organized for me soon!" She gave me a wide grin and then continued.

"We walk for a time, up and down hills and over across, until we reach this place. We work 'til the Sun God prepares himself for bed. Then we walk back, over across and up and down the hills again, pick up the children, collect more water, return to our homes and prepare the evening meal. Then we sweep the floor again, wash our clothing and hang it to dry for the next day. We sort out the harvest, pickin' out the bugs and siftin' it clean. Eventually, we go to bed."

She looked at the others, and asked, "Am I forgettin' anything? I'm sure I am, but that's the bulk of it for this season, Madame. The ones with children have a few more things to do in a day than what I just said. But is that what you were askin'?"

"My goodness! You do all of that in a day?" I asked.

"Of course we do. What else is there to do?" she asked in return, apparently baffled by my reaction.

What else is there to do, indeed? What do *I* do in a day?

I must have looked upset, for she soon spoke up again. "Have I done something wrong, Madame?"

"No, no. Not at all. Thank you for answering my questions, Farmwoman. I am sorry to have disturbed your work. I wish you a pleasant afternoon."

The women bowed low to the ground again as Channa and I resumed our walk.

*

A few moments of silence followed as we meandered through the high grass. Then Channa spoke.

"Might I ask you a question, Your Highness?"

"Of course, Chariot Driver. What is it?"

"I am just curious. Why did you ask the farmwomen all those questions?"

I glided my hand along the tall grass as we walked, feeling more contemplative than I had in a long time. The emotional chaos seemed to have abated.

"I . . . don't really know, Chariot Driver. I just wanted an excuse to talk to them, I suppose." I looked at him, slightly embarrassed by that admission. "That must sound rather silly to you."

"Of course not, Your Highness," he replied kindly.

Why *had* I asked those questions, I wondered. The sun was beginning to sink into the horizon. It was time I returned to my chambers.

I kept thinking of Siddhattha's response to the farmer's suffering, of the women bowed low at my feet, and of Durga who seemed to wield her sword against us all. I was not sure what I was looking for.

I was about to take my leave from my faithful companion when a thought occurred to me. "Chariot Driver," I said, "you never told me what happened to Kanthaka. How did he die?"

Channa stopped walking abruptly, as though the question had raised up a wall right in front of him. "You're right, Your Highness. I never did tell you about that. Are you sure you want to know?"

His question unnerved me, but I had come to the stables that day for a reason. It was best to complete what I had started, no matter what the outcome.

"I am sure, Chariot Driver."

"Very well," he said as he started walking again. "It's a sad story."

Channa returned to that dark night. He described his pain all over again, all the ways he tried to convince the prince to let him stay by his side. When it became clear that the prince would not permit Channa to follow him into the forest, Kanthaka was the one to become riled. He neighed and bucked wildly as he watched the prince turn away.

"I tried to hold Kanthaka back, but you know how strong he was. He broke free and raced after his master. He charged towards the forest, neighing so loudly that I felt sure he was calling his master's name. And then something incredible began to happen."

I stopped walking but did not dare face him. I stared at the palace that was looming in the distance like a beautiful cage awaiting its prisoner's return.

"Tell me."

He took a deep breath. "It is an image that I have been carrying with me ever since, Your Highness. A picture that returns to me each night in my dreams. It is, in fact, the very reason I did not take my own life after he left . . ."

"What is it?"

"The sky . . . Your Highness. It began to rain flowers. The whole sky filled with tremendous flowers of every conceivable shape and color. The flowers tumbled out of the sky behind the prince and filled the earth so quickly! Kanthaka was racing towards his master, but the area thickened instantly with those celestial flowers, the size of which I had never seen before on this earth. The forest door was blocked by them—by flowers, Your Highness! No matter how powerful Kanthaka may have been, he was no match for the flowers raining all over him. He pushed and pushed, trying to force his way through the quicksand of petals, but eventually he had no choice but to concede defeat. He stopped bucking and watched as his master disappeared into the forest without him."

Channa's tears were flowing as he spoke, but he did not seem tortured the way he had been earlier. His tears slipped out more gently now.

"I could do nothing but watch that magnificent animal get his heart broken, Princess. When he couldn't push forward another inch, Kanthaka collapsed. Right before my very eyes."

The gods really did ensure that the prince escaped, I thought to myself. His departure was written into the stars.

"Where is Kanthaka now, Chariot Driver?" I asked.

"He lies there still, Your Highness. He took his last breath at the forest door."

Holding on and Letting Go

The king blamed himself. He had received every warning after his son's birth. Every sign pointed to this outcome as a possibility. He should have done more to keep the prince from leaving. The walls should have been higher. The locks should have been bigger. He should have placed more guards at the gate. It was his fault that Siddhattha had left. And now his throne had no successor. He had spent a lifetime worrying that it might happen and the worrying hadn't made a bit of difference. He had failed anyway.

The ancestors would make him pay for that.

"Servant!" he bellowed.

Immediately, the door swung open and servants toppled into the room like hopeful puppies.

"Summon Chief Minister at once!"

"Yes, Your Highness!" they all replied hurriedly. They had not had anything to do in a long time. They were eager to please.

Moments later, Chief Minister rushed into the room.

"At your service, Maharaja," he announced as he hurried forward. He had come as quickly as his old limbs had permitted. Chief Minister lowered himself with well-rehearsed submission, touched the king's feet with both hands and raised them to his head.

He was relieved to have been summoned. Chief Minister had not been able to rest since the prince's departure. He was wondering how the king would survive. He remembered all too well how he had reacted after the queen's death. Could the king face such loss again? And what were the contingency plans regarding succession? There were many concerns rattling around in his tired old head.

Most of all, though, Chief Minister was worried about the prince. Siddhattha had been like a son to him. He felt the loss of his departure as deeply as the rest of us.

"Rise, Chief Minister."

Chief Minister winced despite himself as he took in the king's demeanor. He had never seen the king look so old. How long had it been since they had celebrated something together? Only a few months ago, the king had been full of masculine vigor, but he was an old man now. His skin dripped down his face like melting wax.

"How can I be of service, Maharaja?"

"I have made a decision, Chief Minister. I cannot accept my son's cowardly act. It is time he be brought to his senses."

Chief Minister's heart began to palpitate. He knew what was coming.

"I would like you to find the prince and bring him home."

His intestines knotted themselves into a tight fist. He hated himself for that. Fear was not supposed to be his first response, but he was not a young man anymore. He had a hard time keeping himself upright on a horse these days.

But Chief Minister could not refuse his sovereign lord. There was nothing he wanted more than to please the man who had pledged his life to his kingdom. For years, Chief Minister had served him faithfully, watching this giant of a man carry the burdens of others with stoic dignity. The King of the Sakyas put everyone else first, holding the responsibilities of his station in the shape of the jeweled turban wrapped around his head.

So many kings were disappointments in those days, gorging on pleasure while their subjects sank in the mire that is everyday suffering. Suddhodana was different. He was an incarnation of Rama. He gave his full attention to the obligations of his throne, no matter what obstacles rose to meet him along the way. When the astrologers warned him that his son might leave, he refused to accept it. He took on the stars and fought them with agonizing determination. He had done everything in his power to protect the kingdom he felt responsible for.

Chief Minister could never refuse such a man.

"Of course, Your Highness."

The words reached into the king's heart and softened his anxiety instantly. He knew what he was asking of his faithful minister. He wished that it didn't have to be that way, but there was no alternative. He looked at his friend, at the lines of old age that were written all over his face. He did not want to lose him, but he wanted his son back more.

"I cannot trust anyone else," the king explained apologetically. "You must bring him home."

Chief Minister lowered his head with quiet acceptance. "It would be my honor, Your Highness," he replied. "I will travel to the ends of this earth to find him. I will look for him as though I were looking for my own son. And I will request his return for the love of this kingdom. I give you my word."

The king swallowed slowly. An old friend pledging allegiance to him. A friend who might not survive the journey. His heart ached in so many different ways at once. He knew how much he was asking.

Chief Minister could sense the king's inner conflict.

"My Lord," he continued, "I know you are concerned, but please be at ease. There is still some strength left in these old legs. I will make the journey and I will return. I pledge this to you, before all the guardian deities in this room."

He did not promise to bring the prince home, though. That was more than he could offer. He was all too aware of the depth of Siddhattha's commitment to promise anything like that. But he would go and he would return.

"I am in your debt, old friend," said the king. "This will not be forgotten."

Chief Minister bowed one last time and headed for the door. The king knew he would miss the old man terribly. *Sakka, Lord of the Heavens*, he pleaded, *keep him safe. And help him find my son.*

Chief Minister was almost out the door when the king called him one last time.

"Chief Minister?"

"Yes, Maharaja?"

"Why don't you bring your son Kaludayi with you? I can spare his services for the time being and I am sure he would like to accompany you. He and Siddhattha were great friends in childhood, were they not?"

"They were indeed, Your Highness. The prince's departure has been a sadness for my son too. I am certain he will feel honored by your suggestion. You don't mind losing both of us for a while?"

"It won't be the same, of course, but I am sure the others can take care of your ministerial responsibilities for a while."

"Of course, Your Highness."

The king nodded appreciatively. *At least then he won't be alone*, the king thought to himself.

*

After my visit with Channa and our walk through the fields, I found myself heading for the nursery. I had not planned on it, but somehow my steps delivered me there unconsciously. My decorated feet were spread against the floor as I pondered the closed door that I had so often stared at. The evening was gathering itself into the sky.

It's just a door, I told myself.

I pushed it open and walked in.

A plump nursing maid was sitting on a pile of cushions, rocking my baby into slumber. My son, who had yet to be named, was nestled contentedly against her chest. He had grown since I had last seen him.

"Your Highness!" exclaimed the maid. She began to heave herself up to a standing position.

"No! Please don't move," I replied much too quickly. "You'll wake him."

She stopped in mid-movement, looking like a water buffalo trying to lift itself out of a riverbed. I was amazed that she managed to keep the baby perched in her arms despite the awkwardness of the position.

"I am not staying, of course," I muttered with some embarrassment. "I just came to look. I didn't realize he was sleeping."

I turned around and aimed for my escape, but the plump nursemaid had other plans.

"Princess," she called out before I could close the door. She had pulled herself together and rushed behind me remarkably quickly, the baby still slumbering in her warm embrace.

"What is it?" I was so uncomfortable with myself in that room, particularly as another woman held my son.

"I was just wondering . . ." She actually managed to fidget while holding the baby. "Maybe you want to hold him?"

I was not prepared for that suggestion. Certainly not from her—a woman I did not even know, and a nursemaid at that. It had taken all of my courage to open that door. I did not have enough left in me to attempt more. I took a step back and was on the verge of formulating some kind of excuse when I was interrupted.

"There you are," Queen Mahapajapati declared as she strolled in.

"Maharani!" I exclaimed. "What are you doing here?"

"I come here often," she said as she eyed me carefully.

"Well, I am not staying . . . He's asleep. So I will just come back later."

"Babies sleep all the time. That's no reason to go."

"Yes, well I don't want to wake him." I was backing myself out of the room and bumped into the wall.

"Babies are really easy to hold when they are sleeping. Isn't that right, Nursemaid?" she asked the now-silent woman who was caught between us. "They just snuggle right into your arms and sleep even more. There is no need for you to come back."

The panic was rising. This was not how I wanted things to go. She was invading my space and leaving me with no room to hide.

"We've been waiting for you," she said. "*He* has been waiting for you."

Before I could react, the queen stepped towards the plump nursemaid and took my son into her arms. She then walked over to me, pierced the terrorized shield I had wrapped around myself, and dropped him into mine.

"What are you doing?" I cried. The commotion was drawing him out of his nap. He was starting to squirm. "He is waking up!"

The queen looked at me with formidable clarity. "Yes, Yasodhara. He is waking up. And when he opens those little eyes of his, the first face he will see is yours."

I barely heard what she said. I was trying desperately to figure out how to hold him without dropping him. He was squirming like a fish.

"Yasodhara, when he opens his eyes," she repeated, as she placed her steady hand on my shoulder, "the first face he will see is yours."

I looked up, confused.

"His mother's," she added. Love streaming down her bold face.

I was his mother . . . I knew that, of course. But in some way, I really did not know it at all. Not until that moment.

"But . . . what if he cries?" I asked, pain choking me from inside my throat. "What do I do then?"

"Then he cries," she answered matter-of-factly. "Babies cry, Yasodhara. Adults cry too. It will pass."

*

Weeks passed without news reaching the king's impatient ears. The monsoon had dried out, making room for clear autumn skies. Fresh air floated through the corridors, pushing the wet humidity away. Everything felt lighter after the rains came to their end, but the king did not notice the difference. He remained where he was, tapping his fingers against the Lion Throne, day after day, waiting for his son to come home.

On a windy afternoon, as dust swirled through the dry air, Chief Minister finally appeared at the palace gates slumped on his horse, Old Age crippling him into his saddle. His faithful son was walking beside him, holding the reins. The guards were taken aback by the brokenness of the man. They stepped aside with quiet reverence to let him pass.

Silence followed the two men as they trudged down the familiar path, no one daring to say a word. Servants and gardeners who would have normally whispered rumors to each other in a moment like this, simply bowed their heads as his horse clopped by. Yarns of gossip had filled in the details of this story long ago and no one felt the need to add more. It was clear to everyone that Siddhattha had not returned with Chief Minister. The pain etched into the old man's dying face reflected his failed mission.

The doors to the Throne Room loomed over the old man's bent body. He motioned to the servant to announce him.

"Come!" he heard echoing against the walls.

Chief Minister took a deep breath, whispered a prayer to Abhayadevi, the Goddess of Fearlessness, and then dragged himself across the threshold, leaning on his son for support.

"Chief Minister! What happened to you?" the king cried as he catapulted himself out of his throne and off the Royal Podium to his friend's side. He helped him to a cushioned seat that materialized suddenly beside him. An invisible servant scuttled away.

"My old friend! What have I done to you? What happened?" the king asked with spilling concern.

Chief Minister gave himself a moment to settle down. The hurt was in every one of his bones, making it difficult to sit cross-legged. He carefully folded one leg over the other, adjusting his knees with his stiff hands, twisting around on the pillows until he could find a position he could bear. When he was finally settled, Chief Minister looked up at the king who was standing over him with a look of urgency.

"I am very sorry, Maharaja," he said as he dropped his eyes and pressed his palms together. "I failed. I could not bring your son home."

The king did not move. He just stared at the old man sitting at his feet, as though he could not absorb the words that had just been released. He stretched his neck and looked up at the vaulted ceiling, trying to find a place for his sight to land.

"Forgive me, Your Highness," Chief Minister repeated. "I wanted to serve you one last time, but the gods would not permit me."

Kaludayi stood stoically behind his father, guarding him. Holding him with filial devotion. Holding in the pain he felt as he listened to his father admit to his own defeat.

The king would have stared at the ceiling forever, but it would not change his son's decision. Tossing social decorum away, the king dropped to the pillows by Chief Minister's side instead of returning to the height of his throne.

"I believe you, old friend."

Warm broth was poured into cups of finely decorated pottery, steam rising like prayerful incense. The two men sat quietly as the broth worked its age-old magic, warming them in just the right way. They sipped and they contemplated. Hints of fresh coriander wafted through the air.

"Did you see him?" the king finally asked. "Did you see my son?"

Chief Minister put his cup down and carefully tugged at the pillows under his seat, adjusting himself with the awareness of fragility that comes with age.

"I did see him, Your Highness."

"What was he like?" he whispered. "What did he say?"

Chief Minister looked up at him with tender eyes.

"He was like the sun, Your Highness. He was beautiful."

The minister had not expected to say those words aloud, but the words seemed to have a will of their own, as though they longed to be spoken.

"I don't quite know how else to describe him," he continued, speaking as one old man to another. "I know how much your heart longs for him, how deeply you wish for him to return. But . . ." his voice trailed off.

"But?" the king asked quietly.

"But . . . he does not belong here anymore, Your Highness. He stands apart now. To be honest, he seems to stand above like the sun. Shining and strong, and truly . . . beautiful."

The king took a deep breath as he looked at the strapping young man who stood protectively behind his ailing father. Kaludayi was still as a statue, standing on strong legs behind his breaking father. The king had spent so much of his life trying to force his son to become the son he wanted, to stand behind him and prepare to take the throne when it was time. He had dedicated his life to trying to bend the universe to his command, to make the stars direct his son onto a different course. But the stars had refused and he could not be angry with them anymore.

His son was beautiful. Maybe that was enough.

Fatigue poured into Suddhodana's bones. He looked at his old friend and recognized his own frailty. He was so tired of fighting the stars. He did not have that kind of endurance anymore. He took another sip of the warm broth and tried to imagine Siddhattha like the sun. It was not hard to do.

"What did he say?" the king asked. The chains of fear that had kept him prisoner since his son's birth were falling to the ground.

"We spoke for a while, and of course he asked about you, your health, the throne. But it was not his words so much as his countenance that affected me. It was his way of being." He looked down at his withered hands and the cup he cradled. "It was the way he held his cup."

"His cup? What do you mean?"

"I mean that he moved differently somehow. He had a pace to his movement that was like ..." Chief Minister searched for the words. "... like a bubbling stream. It was cooling just to be next to him. Just to hear him speak a few words. Or to watch him as he sipped from a cup."

Chief Minister swirled the steaming liquid around its delicate container.

"It was like being in the presence of eternity, Your Highness," he added. "That is who your son is becoming."

Siddhattha was becoming eternity. As soon as the words were spoken, the king knew that they were true. He put his cup down and folded his knees into his chest, the way he had when he was a little boy.

"I can no longer hold onto him, can I?" asked the king.

"No, Your Highness."

"It is time that I let him go?"

"You did everything you could to keep him here, but he was not meant to stay. Perhaps you always knew that?"

The king raised his eyebrows.

"Forgive me for being so direct," continued Chief Minister, "but when time is drawing to its end, an old man must speak plainly. I believe we all knew he would leave, didn't we?"

A deep sigh swept through the king's body as he dropped his knees to the ground and leaned back on his hands. "I suppose we did, my friend."

Change was happening to them both, almost as though Siddhattha's presence was changing them from a distance.

"What will happen with the throne, Your Highness?" Chief Minister asked, his practical mind focused as always.

The king thought for a moment and then his face burst into a mischievous smile.

"You know, I asked my son that very question before he left. Do you know what he said?"

Chief Minister shook his head.

"He said that the throne would take care of itself. That it always does."

The two men smiled knowingly at each other. There is a time for everything in life. Including a time to let younger men worry on your behalf.

20

Out the Gates

I spent more time in the nursery after that day, returning regularly and allowing myself to learn how to be with my son. Nursemaid was a kind teacher, patiently explaining the realities of babies to me, showing me how to hold him and how to calm him when he cried. I had so much to learn, and I was letting myself try.

One day, Nursemaid showed me how to make a sling out of a shawl and carry the baby against me the way village women do. She wrapped the cloth around my torso and slipped my son in against my chest, his little feet dangling out from underneath. I wrapped my arms around his bottom and felt his closeness melt the edges of my heart. As soon as I mastered the wrap-around myself, I began to wander the palace compound on my own with him. One day, I decided to go further and I wandered right out the main gates.

The guards were caught by surprise and one of them tried to intervene.

"Apologies, Your Highness, but you are not supposed to wander out on your own. Can we help you with anything?"

The guards had become an ordinary feature of my life. I barely noticed them anymore—or the limitations they represented. But for some reason, on that day, I looked at them and then I looked right past them into the open on the other side.

"Your concern is appreciated, Soldier," I said with all the regality I could muster. "I will return soon." Before they had a chance to respond, I walked right by. They knew—as did everyone else by then—that the very reason for their posting was to keep the prince *in*. But the prince had gone.

I tapped my son nervously as I walked into unconfined space. There was so much land, so many possible directions one could take. Abhayadevi's temple lay directly ahead, but that would land me in the priest's territory. He would have me covered in ash and dipped in prayers the moment he set eyes on me, trying to wash the stain of sadness away. The town was on the other side of the temple, but that was equally out of the question. If I was not assaulted by crowds or attacked with reams of gossip, I would at the very least become lost in the chaotic maze.

Too much time had passed and it would have all become unfamiliar. I felt the pull to return to the safety of the palace walls, like a prisoner who had grown accustomed to her chains.

I was just about to turn back when I realized I was on the edge of a road so familiar, my feet had found the way without consulting me.

"This is the path I used to take as a child!" I exclaimed to my slumbering son. "Every morning, I would tear out of my house and run to the palace to play with my cousins. I traveled this road more times than I can count!"

He opened and closed his eyes to the rhythm of my voice.

"I haven't seen my parents' home in many years." I counted the time on my fingers ... "Thirteen years."

I followed the bend in the road and my house came into view, setting off a wave of fluttering heartbeats inside my chest. My old home—my place of refuge for so many years: I had longed for it from the day I left, but I had chosen Siddhattha and accepted the consequences of what loving him entailed.

I lost my home the day I married, more than most brides ever do. My parents came to the palace to see me, visiting during special occasions and participating in royal festivals as we had always done, but eventually my mother became ill and my father stayed behind to take care of her. I lost access to them both then, and when she died, it seemed as though everything from that time died too. My childhood receded into the past with nothing left for me to hold on to. When my home came into view, I was surprised to discover how familiar it still was to me, and how deeply it called my heart. I didn't think I would remember what it looked like anymore.

The magical asattha tree was still standing by the front door. As I got closer, I could discern the shape of a person sitting on a bench beside it. He was sitting by himself, his body hunched forward.

"Father!" I cried as I broke into a run, squeezing my son against myself to ensure he would not slip through my arms.

My father pulled himself up and shielded his eyes from the sun as he watched me racing towards him.

"Is that you?" he asked, utterly dumbfounded. I threw myself into his arms, my baby squished between us.

"Daughter! What are you doing here?" he marveled as he spoke through the tangles of my hair.

I could not speak at first. I was holding on so tight.

"How did you manage to leave?"

"I ... don't know. I just left. I started walking, and my legs carried me here."

Servants came pouring out of the house to welcome me. The baby was pulled out of my arms with great excitement, each servant eager to shower their little visitor with coddling attention. My father barely had a chance to see his grandchild before the little one disappeared into the house.

"Come inside, Daughter. I will have a cup of honey milk brewed for you just the way you like it," he offered.

I looked at the doorway and could not imagine stepping through it without my mother there.

"It's nice here by the tree. Do you mind if we stay outside?"

He smiled, deepening the layers of wrinkles around his eyes. He lowered himself back onto the bench and patted the seat beside him.

"How are you, Father?" I asked as I sat down. He looked so frail and gray.

"I am adjusting," he answered. One of his hands was shaking. I took it into my own and held on. "The house feels empty without your mother."

"I understand," I whispered. "The palace feels empty without my husband ..."

He tightened his grip around my hand, a silent note of recognition. "But you have a son now," he said with a bit more brightness. "So it can't be that empty."

"No ... It's not that empty anymore."

We sat quietly on the bench together after that. We had not seen each other in a long time, but the quiet communicated all we needed to say. Whenever his hand began to shake, I reached over and held him until he was calm again. I could feel death hovering. My childhood was receding with every breath he struggled to take.

"I am sorry I have not come to visit you, Daughter," he whispered. "I wanted to, many times. But the road is long and the palace seems lifetimes away. I wanted to reach you, but ... I just couldn't."

"Of course," I replied.

Looking at him, I realized how true his words were. Not even a carriage ride would be possible for his old bones anymore. He was waiting for death now, waiting to join my mother in their journey for next worlds.

His fatigue was showing and I could see that it pained him to keep upright.

"I should get back to the palace," I offered. "People will worry."

"Of course," he replied.

"I will come back to visit, though," I promised. "Now that the prince is gone, I think I can."

His eyes filled with intertwining emotions—relief, loss, regret, and many others I could not read. It seemed as though he was pouring a lifetime of truth into the space between us. I held the silence for him until he broke it when he looked away.

I got to my feet and was about to call the servants for my son when my father interrupted.

"Wait. I just remembered something."

He took his walking stick which was lying on the ground by his feet and slowly trudged his way towards the house. He called to a servant by the door, mumbled a command, and was soon provided with a package. He turned around and made the long journey back to the tree, leaning on his stick with one arm and carrying the package under the other. He was wheezing by the time he reached me.

"This is for you," he gasped. "Your mother saved it for a tree offering, but ..." He could not catch his breath. He lowered himself onto the bench, his body folding into itself as he heaved.

I got down onto my knees and placed my hand on his lap. "Take your time, Father."

His chest rose and fell many times, as though it was searching desperately for all the air it had lost. Eventually, he quieted.

"Open it," he said as he gestured to the package.

I unwrapped the cotton cloth and found a brilliant piece of red silk with gold trim.

"It's for a tree offering," he explained. "She was going to use it for our trees in the back. She made prayers for your welfare as often as she could get herself there, but she never managed to use this piece. She died before ..." A lump in his throat. "I was hoping to get this to you, so that you could pray in her place. If you bring it to the palace, the prayers will be closer to you."

I touched the material to my cheek, missing her more than I knew how to express.

A servant brought my son back, while another offered to help me with my wrap. I wound myself back into its fabric and was about to tuck him in when I realized something.

"Father, you haven't had a chance to hold your grandson. Would you like to?"

He seemed to have been taken by surprise. He looked down at his trembling hand. "It's probably not safe ..."

I reached for him, knowing all too well what the pain of separation was like. I had finally learned that it was better to close the gap than maintain a distance.

"What if I help you?"

Before he could refuse, I lowered my son into his shaking arms. I got back down onto my knees and held my father as he held his grandchild for the first time.

*

We approached the palace compound as the sun was setting. I was singing a song my mother used to sing to me, caressing my son's little head along the way, my heart oscillating between wholeness and loss.

I went straight to the Peacock Garden. It greeted us with quiet dignity, the haunting whispers of the trees swaying softly in the breeze. I had to steady my heart for a moment as I breathed in the garden of sacred memory.

I walked to the outer edge and found the tree I was looking for. She was guarding the vastness of the kingdom below and stretching Her limbs right up into the sky. A bench was placed beside Her.

Strips of red silk had been tied around Her and She was painted with layers of red dye. Garlands of bright orange marigolds hung from Her branches, along with a small bell that tinkled gently in the wind. I took a few steps around Her and noticed a mask that had been placed against Her trunk. It seemed as though it had been placed there to give the Goddess a face for us to see. The mask was beaten by the weather, most of the paint having been burned away by the sun, but it was still beautiful. I stopped and touched the mask with my forehead.

I circumambulated the Tree-Goddess three times with my palms pressed together and my son wrapped in my shawl. When I was done, I pulled him out of the wrap and held him up to the tree.

"This, my darling, is a great being," I explained to him. "She has the spirit of the Goddess inside Her."

I leaned him in so that his forehead could touch Her too. I then took out the red silk my father had given me. "We are going to make an offering to the Goddess," I continued explaining to him. "With this gift, we are asking Her to see us and keep us safe."

And to keep your father safe, I said to myself, *wherever he is.*

I circumambulated the tree one more time, wrapping the material around Her strong trunk as I walked. When I was done, I pulled my son in closer.

21

Devadatta

I was in one of the guest rooms, putting together a flower arrangement for the dignitaries who would be visiting that day. I had chosen a combination of different colored water lilies that I was placing in a brightly painted yellow vase. The sun was streaming into the room through the open window, tiny dust particles flittering gaily through its rays. My son was swaddled in a cloth blanket, sleeping peacefully on the bed as I worked.

"There you are!" I heard behind me. "I have been looking everywhere for you!"

The hair on my neck shot up at the sound of his hard voice. I did not need to turn around to see who it was.

"When did you get back?" I asked, trying to sound casual, with my back still turned.

"Just now. I came straight to you," Devadatta replied.

I continued adding flowers to the arrangement, but one of the stalks snapped in my hand. I threw it to the side.

"How nice."

I heard him shuffling around and turned to see what he was doing. He was unfastening the leather strap across his shoulder that held his sword. He dropped the long weapon onto the bed, only a few hands' breadths from where my baby slept.

"What do you think you are doing?"

He stretched out his arms and ruffled his hair as though he were walking into his own personal chambers.

"I have been traveling many days, Yasodhara. I am quite tired. Just dropping some of the weight I have been carrying."

"I would rather you didn't. You should go home for that."

"I don't want to go home. I am here to see you. Why are you being so cold?"

"I am not being cold. I would just rather be alone. I am sure your parents are eager to see you after all your time away."

"As I said ..." his voice became harder. "I don't want to go home. My parents can wait."

I knew what this was about: the throne was empty and Devadatta had come to claim it. I banged the flower-knife against the table and turned towards him. "I know what you want and I am not interested."

He retreated automatically, my flash of fire having caught him off guard. "I don't know what you are talking about," he replied. "All I want is to be here with you in this time of need."

"I don't need anything from you."

He looked sheepish for a moment, but when he noticed that my hands were trembling, his confidence climbed right back up to the surface.

"Has it ever occurred to you that your needs are not at the center of the ten-thousand universes?" he asked as he began to creep towards me again. "Maybe *I* need *your* support at a time like this? You must know that you are not the only one facing loss right now, Yasodhara. I have lost my cousin and my prince. Maybe *I* could use some comfort from *you*?"

"I don't quite believe you are feeling a sense of loss, Devadatta."

"Why not? Loss does not belong to you alone," he replied with a sharp edge.

I picked up the flower-knife again and tried to resume the work he had interrupted. "Please leave me alone, Devadatta. I don't have the energy for this. And you have no business being in a bedroom alone with me."

Devadatta glanced at the bed. "You're right ... Why don't we change the subject?" he took another step forward. "What are you doing with those flowers?"

I exhaled slowly, trying to calm myself down.

"A delegation from Kosambi should be arriving this evening and I want to prepare the room for their arrival."

He closed the distance between us with one more step and covered my hands with his. "You do realize that you are still the future queen of this kingdom, don't you? With or without Siddhattha, that throne is yours. There is no reason for you to be doing the work of a servant."

I ripped my hands free, causing the bangles on my wrists to clatter against each other. I pulled a wicker stool that was within reach and threw it between us, utterly affronted by the audacity of physical contact.

"You seem a little nervous," he gloated as he tossed the wicker stool aside.

My eyes darted instinctively towards my son, lying helplessly on the bed. The door seemed out of reach.

And it was closed. I hadn't noticed him doing that.

"You must be lonely without a husband ..." He was creeping towards me again like an animal hunting its prey. "You should have a husband and the kingdom needs a royal couple on the throne ..."

"Cousin, think about what you are saying," I tried to reason with him. "I cannot remarry. Nothing you are saying makes sense."

My son began to cry. Devadatta was stepping into me now, cutting off all possible escape routes.

"I am making perfect sense, dear cousin. All I have to do is take Siddhattha's place ... There are many roads to the throne, but I think *you* present the most interesting option."

"You could never take his place!" I cried with mounting desperation. "No one would let you! You're mad!"

"Don't tell me that you are still loyal to him, even after he abandoned you! Can you be honest with yourself just once? You venerated him your entire life, but he walked *away* from you, Yasodhara! Siddhattha abandoned you and left you without any protection. He left you to the wolves to pursue some stupid quest in the forest!"

Devadatta was slipping into my fears and pushing them into the center of the room.

"He never abandoned me!"

"But he did. Look at you! You are alone! If he really loved you, he would have stayed! I would never do that to you!"

I pushed Devadatta so hard that I managed to throw him off balance. "Even if you were the last man alive, I wouldn't marry you!" I screamed.

That brought Devadatta into a dangerous rage. He grabbed me by the neck and pushed his body against mine, forcing me backwards. I hit the table, causing the vase I had been working with to crash to the ground. My baby's cries were becoming panicked.

"You need a husband, Yasodhara, and I need the throne!" He tried to kiss me, his grip tearing my necklace off from under my clothing. Durga's pendant clattered onto the floor. She was sitting on her mountain lion, weapons shining in each one of her many hands.

My hands scrambled blindly behind me to find the flower-knife I had been using earlier. As soon as I felt it, I wrapped my fist around the hilt, brought it forward and stabbed Devadatta in the hand. He howled with pain, clutching himself as blood spurted all over him.

"You witch!" he yelled at me. "I am going to kill you!"

His fist flew into the air when Queen Mahapajapati burst through the door. She did not require more than an instant to understand the situation. She grabbed his raised arm, wheeled him around, and together we pushed him right out the open window. He screamed until he hit the ground, two stories below. We heard a thud, and then there was silence.

*

Mahapajapati had my son in her arms as she led the two of us out of the room.

"Servant," she commanded behind her. "Make sure to clean up that mess."

Moments later, we were safely bundled up inside her chambers. She asked her maidservant to bring blankets and drinks of fermented barley. I sat down on the seat she directed me to, dazed by the suddenness of all that had just happened.

"Are you all right?" she asked as the cup was delivered into my shaking hands. She waved her maidservant away and asked to have the door closed. The baby was swaddled on the rug between us, fast asleep again.

"I . . . think so." I leaned against the wall and stared ahead of me. I could not quite wrap my mind around what had just happened. Devadatta had attacked me. He wanted to take the throne by taking me. He was about to hurt me . . .

"I never thought I could fight back that way," I said, almost to myself.

My mind was blank with shock. It had all happened so fast. But I *did* fight back. I was rather impressed with myself for that.

"You know, once when I was a little girl, Devadatta and I got into a terrible argument," the memory returning slowly. "I tried to fight him, but I failed." It was a memory retrieved from a thousand years ago, or so it seemed. "I let my pride get in the way and he ended up laughing me off the field."

Mahapajapati listened.

"When I got home, I ran into my mother's arms and cried my heart out. It was then that she told me about Durga for the first time. She told me that women have power. She said that our power is not necessarily in our muscles, but that it is in our bodies and that it is fierce."

"She was right," the queen answered.

"I feel like I understand a little bit of what she meant now."

I closed my eyes and searched for my mother's face in my mind. Her beautiful eyes and dark skin. Her long black hair that she combed with unhurried grace. I reached for my pendant . . .

"My necklace!" I whispered with panic. "I have to go back to that room!"

I was about to get up, but Mahapajapati put her hand on my knee. "I have it right here." She reached into her folds of her sash and brought out my personal protector. The chain was broken, but I could repair that.

"She suits you," she said and placed it into my hands.

"Who?"

"The Goddess."

I closed my hand around the pendant. I could feel Durga's energy pulsating through me. The elders were right about her.

"I thought I would be falling apart."

The queen leaned back and looked at me with a studied expression. "What do you mean?" she asked.

"I have heard stories of men attacking women the way Devadatta just tried to do. I have feared it. I am sure every woman has. It is an obvious fear to have, isn't it?"

"It is," she replied quietly.

"Each time I imagined the situation, I imagined myself falling apart afterwards."

The baby stirred a little. I picked him up instinctively and brought him close.

"Do you think it's wrong that I've imagined it?" I asked as I patted him.

"No. Most women have probably spent some time imagining it. If we fear something, then we are bound to imagine it. Fear and imagination go together."

She refilled our cups and stirred in some dried cane juice. The liquid was still warm and it absorbed the crystals easily.

"I guess that's true. I never thought about it that way before."

"So why did you imagine yourself falling apart?" she asked as she handed me one of the cups.

"It always seemed like the worst thing in the world to me. I was sure that if a man ever tried to do that, I would . . ." My voice trailed off uncertainly. I turned the words around in my mind for a few minutes.

"I think I imagined that if it were ever to happen to me, if ever a man even tried, I would want to die," I finally admitted.

"I see . . ." she replied with another studied gaze. "You would certainly not be the first woman to feel that way. So how *do* you feel?"

"I . . . I don't know. But I am not falling apart. And I don't want to die."

I caught the flicker of a smile at the edge of her lips.

"Indeed."

A knock came at the door.

"Come."

Her tone was regal and commanding in a way that I had not noticed before. Mahapajapati had been invisible when I had first arrived at the palace, but now she was the fully embodied Queen of the Sakya Kingdom. How had she managed that?

"The king would like to know if you will be joining him for the evening meal, Maharani," the servant asked with head bowed.

She looked at me inquisitively, assessed me, and made a decision without consultation.

"We will skip the evening meal," she decided. "Please send the king our apologies. We will see him in the morning."

The maidservant accepted the message she was instructed to deliver. I leaned back as the door closed quietly, relieved at not having to appear anywhere for the time being.

"Mother-in-Law?" I asked tentatively.

"Yes?"

"Do you think Devadatta will be all right? It wasn't too big of a fall, was it?"

"Oh, no," she answered lightly. "No need to worry on his behalf. I heard him yelling obscenities under the window as we left the room."

The story did not go further than I feared it might have.

"And I don't think he will be coming back anytime soon. After what he just tried to do, he is not likely to show his face here again. The king would have him beheaded and he knows it."

"So he is gone . . ." I whispered, exhaling. "Just like that?"

"Yes. Just like that. If he returns, he would have to face an inquiry. I would make sure of it. Devadatta will have to go elsewhere to make his life now."

It was over. But the memory of him and his actions would stay. I replayed the details in my mind. The blade sinking into his hand. His blood dripping down his arm, staining his clothing and splattering onto the floor. The certainty that he would kill me (or worse) if I did not reach him first. Pushing him out the window and feeling the weight of his body lift off the ground.

Durga's power flew right out of me when I needed it most. My mother would have been proud.

Splendor

One morning, while we were sifting through the baby gifts we had recently received, Mahapajapati announced that it was time to have my son named.

"It's too soon," I replied dismissively.

"It isn't soon at all, Daughter. Your son is more than a year old already. The Goddess needs to see him."

She unwrapped a package and pulled out a magnificent bronze casting of a plow. It was tiny—the whole thing fitting in the palm of her hand—and it came with two water buffalos attached to the end of it. The buffalos' collars were decorated with tiny jewels and the plow was studded with turquoise. The man guiding the plow had a lovely expression on his face.

"Will you look at that?" she marveled. "I have never seen its equal. Who gave this?"

The craftsmanship was superb, but I was distracted by the conversation below the surface. "I don't remember ... but I don't think it's necessary to have him named yet. You know, some children live for years before they're named."

"Perhaps, but those children are not princes and heir to a throne. This child needs a name."

Without my husband? Without my parents, both of whom had now passed on? I wasn't prepared to perform this ritual by myself.

"And you will not be on your own, Daughter, if that's what is worrying you. I will be right beside you."

*

The naming ceremony followed the tradition of the elders. An elaborate procession led us to the royal temple while our faithful subjects lined the road. There were musicians and dancers and every version of fanfare accompanying us. The king rode an elephant while Mahapajapati and I were transported together in a carriage, swaying to the rhythm of the many beating drums.

I looked down at my son who dozed against my shoulder and wondered what kind of name he would receive.

Mahapajapati was reminiscing about Siddhattha's ceremony, some thirty years ago, recalling the sudden outburst of monsoon weather that flooded the road immediately after. Most of all, she talked about his name: Siddhattha. *He Who Would Attain It All.*

"Siddhattha was never meant to stay with us in the palace. He was supposed to do what he is doing right now," she concluded.

"I know," I replied absently.

I had heard the stories many times. I had even gone to look for the astrologers once myself. I wanted confirmation of the narrative that was haunting my life, but I was too late. They had all died by then. The stories were all that was left. Oral traditions that suggested he would leave home life, despite his wife and son.

"When someone is destined to leave, nothing can make them stay," she added gently.

That may be true, but the charts never declared that he could not take us with him. It was one thing for a man to leave home to pursue a higher quest, but it was something else altogether for him to leave his family behind. That was the part that I could not come to terms with. Rama took Sita with him.

I peeked through the slit in the curtain and watched the commotion outside. "The charts also said that he might have stayed," I mumbled.

The queen looked at me, perceiving me in ways I did not want to be seen.

"But he didn't, Yasodhara."

We arrived at the temple and were greeted by our new young priest. He wore the sacred thread across his bare chest and his lower body was wrapped in crimson silk—the Goddess' color. He was barefoot and beaming with his newfound authority. Our previous priest had retired to the forest, leaving this young one to inherit the royal role.

"Welcome, Your Highness!" he declared as he bowed with obsequiousness.

The sound of his voice catapulted me back into the past with surprising force. Although I hadn't recognized his face, I now knew him to be the priest who had sat outside my room for weeks after I had given birth, trying to chant my pollution away.

I assumed a look of neutrality and watched as the young priest performed the rituals the way he was supposed to. He was less halting and insecure than he had been a year ago, his mantras recited with more fluidity, but I was far from feeling transported. Our previous priest was able to conjure magic each time he reached into the sacred fire with his words, but this one produced none of that effect.

Every once in a while, he lifted his voice dramatically as though he was trying to impress us, but that just made me cringe instead.

Partway through the ceremony, the priest slipped behind the curtain of the inner sanctuary to prepare the Goddess for her viewing. He recited as he worked, hidden from view, but we could hear clumsy movements and the clanging of pottery as though he was bumping into her with his tools. Eventually, he drew the curtain with a grandiose wave of his arm and Abhayadevi was revealed.

She was as beautiful as ever, festooned with colorful flowers and draped in bright red cloth. I could smell the sesame oil that had been rubbed over her black stone body, making her sparkle in the flickering light of the priest's oil lamp. I bowed at her feet with the required prayers on my lips, my son in my arms, her tall, graceful body looming over me.

The priest descended the steps and blessed each one of us with sacred ash. And then without warning, he announced my son's name.

"He will be called Rahula," the young priest decided.

Whatever positive impression he might have generated with his efforts was dissolved instantly.

"*Rahula*? But that's not an auspicious name! Why would you suggest that?"

"He was born during an eclipse, Your Highness," he replied, apparently unruffled by my indignation. "He was born in the planet Rahu's shadow. There is no other name to give under such circumstances."

My maternal protectiveness rejected his explanation ferociously. "We cannot give him that name. I am sorry, Brahmin, but I refuse."

A name was a powerful indicator of the path ahead. Siddhattha's name had directed him his entire life. It was why he left us all behind. I could not allow my son to be handed a name like that.

The priest spoke more gently now. "Princess, I understand your concern, but calling him Rahula is the best course of action. He was born under a powerful planet's shadow. Rahu is not one to be trifled with. You must honor the planet that has claimed him. To do otherwise is to invite Rahu's wrath."

The king and queen were watching our interaction quietly, giving me room to negotiate, but eventually the king intervened.

"Daughter, listen to our new priest," he counseled. "He may be young, but perhaps he is right about this. We must give the boy the name that is most true for him."

"How can you agree to this?" I asked as I wheeled towards him. "How can you agree to having your grandson named *Rahula*? Haven't we been through enough?"

I did not know that the anger was still with me. I had quieted down in the past months, finding a routine I thought I could live with, but the moment this name was announced, all the hurt had returned. The stars refused to give me peace.

"Child," the king replied, "we have all struggled, but I think that is precisely why we should accept this name. Many years, ago, when Brahmin announced Siddhattha's name, I was terrified. I didn't want my son to *attain it all*. I wanted him to become king. I did everything I could to make his name untrue. I fought the stars for years trying to make them do as I willed, but I learned the hard way that you cannot fight them."

But I want to fight them, was what I wanted to reply. I want to protect my son.

"Do you know what my favorite plant is?" he asked, changing course.

I stared at the king blankly.

"My favorite plant? Do you know which one it is?" he repeated.

"No . . . I don't think so," I replied.

"It's a lily that Chief Gardener calls the mahmeda," he answered with a smile. "The mahmeda plant produces long lines of delicate white bell-shaped flowers."

I tried to imagine it, but didn't recall seeing it anywhere.

"That lily is in my private garden; it's planted along the outer walls." He smiled softly and added, "It grows in the shade."

I wasn't sure what that was supposed to mean.

"Not everything must be of the sun, Daughter. Those beautiful flowers are children of the shade. And that shade plant is healing. Cook uses its stalk to make a brew when I am ill. The mahmeda has a lot more to offer than it seems." He paused and put his hand on my shoulder. "Let your son be Rahula, Daughter. He will grow strong under the banner of his own truth, just as you are strong under your own."

"My own?" I asked.

"Yes, Daughter. You are Yasodhara—*She Who is Full of Splendor*. That is your name. It is your banner and your story. It is who you are and who you continue to become."

I looked away, embarrassed.

"I don't think there is much splendor left in me, Your Highness." There was still so much sadness and confusion inside me. I had such difficulty letting go.

"Oh, but that is where you are wrong, Yasodhara. There *is* splendor in you." He lifted my chin with his finger the way my father used to do. "Your splendor is all around you. You might not feel full of splendor these days, but it is there. I can see it in your eyes."

Mahapajapati stepped forward and put her arm around me. "He is right, Yasodhara," she said. "Don't trouble your son's chart by trying to hide him from himself."

"It won't work if you do," the king added. "I should know. It will just bring trouble to your household instead."

But he was being named after a planet of darkness . . . I could not wrap my head around that. I looked down at his sleeping self in my arms. He was already so much bigger than he used to be. Soon he would be walking.

"Daughter," the king continued, "if you allow him his real name, and if you allow him to follow his path, something beautiful will come of it. Let him be himself."

I looked up at the two royals who were on either side of me, holding me with their strength. They had loved and lost so much, and yet here they were, right beside me, encouraging me to let go.

Rahula, I repeated to myself uncertainly.

*

The sky was heavy with humidity. I was alone in my room, passing time by watching it pass me.

I decided to venture into my wardrobe. I normally left that arena to Neelima who took great pride in orchestrating its contents, but for some reason, on that dark afternoon, I felt drawn to explore it for myself.

I pulled open the heavy gilded doors and was greeted with an explosion of shimmering color. Row after row of beautiful silks twinkled luxuriously. Many of them were studded with jewels that shined like little stars. There were scarves to match every outfit and other scarves that did not match anything at all, but were there for creative interference. Sandals trimmed with gold and speckled with shimmering stones lined the floor, some of which I had never even seen before. It was all so much more than any one individual could reasonably require in a lifetime.

I stared at this dazzling display and felt, to my own surprise, deflated. When I had first come to the palace, I was thrilled by the many gifts I was showered with. Foreign dignitaries and royal visitors arrived regularly bearing treasures that were the currency kingdoms traded in. The gifts were delivered to the royal family drenched in the hopes of political advancement. I was excited by all of it then, but I was not excited anymore.

My fingers drifted over the shelves. *There is not much for me here now,* I thought to myself. I no longer had a husband to delight and social functions did not inspire me to make an effort.

I was about to turn away when something caught my eye. On the top row, folded neatly in a corner, was something turquoise that felt vaguely familiar. Curious, I reached onto my tiptoes and pulled the piece down from its perch. A long cascade of silk tumbled over me, falling on my head like the waters of the Ganga as they crashed onto Shiva's head. I caught the material in my hands. White cranes were painted along its edge.

Memories flooded. I had not seen the piece in ages. It was the one my mother had bought for me all those years ago. She had purchased it in the market and kept it under her bed until I became a woman. It had cost my parents a small fortune.

I remembered my mother's face as she pulled it out of its package, beaming with pride. She chose it because the cranes reminded her of Shakuntala's story—a story I loved to listen to as a child. She thought it would make me feel safe as I ventured into unfamiliar territory for the first time.

So much tender effort had gone into that one outfit, for that one event. And now here I was with shelves dripping with decadent pieces, most of which had never been worn, and none of which told a story the way that one had. I stared at the contents of the magnificent collection and felt empty. Why would anyone have so many fancy clothes when they only have one body with which to wear them? And what difference does any of it make in the end? I looked at it all and knew what my next step was supposed to be. I had enjoyed making myself beautiful for my husband, but I did not have a husband anymore. The royal wardrobe had done what it was supposed to do when it was supposed to do it, and that time was gone.

"Maidservant," I called out.

"Yes, Your Highness," she answered almost immediately from behind my chamber doors. "What can I do for you?" She found me stepping away from the wardrobe as I was closing the doors.

"Would you like to change? Can I get something for you?" she asked with her usual helpfulness.

"No, Neelima," I answered. "I have no need of anything from in there."

She looked at me curiously, apparently sensing a change already. "Actually, you *can* do something for me," I said on second thought.

"Of course, Your Highness."

"I would like you to fetch me two dresses made of white cotton cloth."

She had not expected that. She stared at me for a moment.

"Oh . . . Of course," she finally replied. "But may I ask what for?" White cotton clothing was exclusively reserved for certain types of people.

"Well . . ." I considered the words before I spoke them. Saying them would be the first step into a new life. I sat down on my bed and pondered the change.

"I am no longer a young bride, Neelima," I explained. "That part of my life is finished." I fiddled with the jeweled bangles on my wrist. They seemed clunky and slightly ridiculous suddenly. I pulled one off and looked at it in the light.

"Your Highness, what are you doing . . .?"

"My husband is gone, and I don't want to continue living as though he is on his way back." I put the bangle down and began to work on the next one.

"I am a widow now."

"No, Your Highness!" Néelima screamed as though the word itself had attacked her. She threw herself at my feet and covered my bangles with her hands.

"Neelima, I don't think there is anything to be afraid of. It will be all right."

"How can you say that, Your Highness? Widowhood is a curse!" she cried desperately. "Please don't take the word, Your Highness! If you call yourself a widow, they will throw you out of the palace! Terrible things will happen to you! Please take it back!"

For many women, that was indeed the outcome they faced when they lost their husbands. The word had terrifying implications.

"No one is going to turn me out of here, Neelima."

She knelt at my feet, shaking with fear. I could see that she was trying to calm herself, but she was struggling. "What is going on? Why are you reacting this way?"

"My mother was widowed when we were young," she whispered. "It was awful what happened to her . . ."

She never spoke of her life.

"My father died very suddenly, in the middle of the night. He wasn't sick before. He woke up with a cry and then died. No one could understand why, so some of the villagers said it was my mother's fault . . . I don't remember all of it, but I remember being afraid. And missing my father . . ." She wiped her running nose with the back of her hand. "After that, life became really hard. No one would talk to us and we became so poor. We were hungry all the time. People said my mother was bad luck and they would turn their faces whenever she passed. Sometimes they threw things at her. Sometimes it was worse . . ."

Many women found themselves shut out from the world because others said that they had to be. I could imagine the details without her having to fill them in.

"I don't want that to happen to you, Your Highness," she begged. "You don't deserve that kind of life!"

"No one does," I answered quietly as I placed my hand over her own. "I am sorry your mother suffered that way."

"Please don't let yourself become a widow, Your Highness. Your husband is still alive. You don't need to say it!"

"I know how frightening this all sounds, but truth is better than falsehood. And it is certainly better than false hope. My husband may still be alive, but he is not alive as my husband anymore. A life of renunciation is a life of social death. You know that. He *chose* death. The moment he walked away, he made me a widow. That is the way of things and I need to accept it. Living on false hope will hurt me more than that word ever could."

Her look of terror was subsiding.

"I am a widow now, Neelima. It's the truth."

She dropped her head and laid it on my hand.

"You are brave, Your Highness. I don't think I could ever be as brave as you."

I didn't feel brave. I was just hoping I could be. Hoping that I had the courage to stand up once I stepped outside in the clothing of widowhood.

She picked herself off the ground, adjusted her clothing, and sighed.

"Would you like help with your bangles?" she offered.

"I would like that very much."

For the next hour, Neelima and I worked together to remove the many bangles that decorated my wrists. Some of them slid off easily, but others had been with me since my wedding day and were much more difficult to coax.

"I think oil will help," she suggested, and she ran to fetch some.

We worked through them, one bangle after the next. She massaged my hand until my thumb was folded as far into my palm as possible, and then we squeezed them off, one at a time. It was a long and painful process, my wrists and thumbs becoming cramped, my skin becoming bright red. I was learning the hard way that shackles don't fall by themselves.

The last of the bangles now remained. Siddhattha had placed it on my wrist himself after we married. It was made of thick glass and it was studded with white jewels. After pulling at it for some time, we finally had to give up.

"I don't think this one wants to come off," I said. "It's much too tight." I was rubbing my hand, trying to release the tension in my joints.

"What would you like to do?" she asked.

"I don't know. Do you have any suggestions?"

"Well . . ." she paused and scratched her chin. "I guess we could break it."

I looked at her, slightly stunned by the suggestion. "You mean, smash it while it is still on my wrist?"

"I have seen it done. It's possible."

Smashing my husband's gift to me ...? I had to admit that it was a fitting gesture. But it was much fiercer than anything I had prepared myself for. I reached for my pendant as I considered. *What would Durga have done?* I wondered.

She never would have married in the first place.

The Return

"Come, darling! I want to show you something! Get dressed!"

I shared everything with Rahula. He was seven years old and the center of my world. We spent our days together, going for walks and telling stories about the gods and goddesses of our time. Each morning was a new adventure.

"Where are we going this time, Mother? What did you find?" he asked, his curiosity mounting.

"You think I am going to ruin the surprise? Not on your life! Finish getting dressed and I will show you."

He scrambled to get his clothing together and tried to throw his scarf around his neck in a quick movement, but it got tangled and he had to pull it off and start over again. I smiled as I watched his beautiful little eyebrows knit themselves together with concentration.

He grabbed the first pair of sandals he could find. "Let's go!" he hollered as he hopped on one foot, trying to pull the strap as he hurried for the door. There is nothing quite like the joyful exuberance of a seven-year-old boy.

We walked from one garden to the next using the maze of tree-lined passageways that were bursting with chirping birds.

"Mother, look! The sloth moved! He was in a different tree yesterday!"

I laughed. "I think you are right, darling. It looks like he made quite a journey last night. He will probably need to sleep for a week to recover."

Rahula giggled appreciatively.

"So, tell me where we are going!" he asked again, bouncing up and down like a grasshopper.

"We will be there soon. Patience."

We were making our way through the passageways until we reached the edge of the Peacock Garden. We passed the Goddess-Tree and rounded the cliff, following the path until it began to slope down the hill.

"Are we allowed to go this way?" he asked, as we maneuvered our way down.

"We are not going much farther. Don't worry."

The landscape became drier as we descended. There was less greenery and more rocks.

"Mother, what's that little mountain up ahead?" he asked as we approached a dry mound of earth.

"That, my darling, is precisely what I wanted to show you. I found it yesterday."

I watched as Rahula's eyes took in the strangeness of the artifact we had come to explore. It was taller than him and a few hands-breadth wide. Neither of us could have gotten our arms around it. There was a series of holes in the mound, each one about the size of my palm. The earth of the mound was so dry it looked like it would crumble at the slightest touch.

"What is it?" he asked.

"This is something quite special, my son. It is a dried-out termite mound."

He jumped back a few paces. "A termite mound? Are you serious?"

"I am quite serious."

"Are there still termites in there?" he asked.

"No, I don't think so. When it dries out like this, it means the termites are gone."

He exhaled and took a step forward.

"But I wouldn't get too comfortable here if I were you . . ."

"Why?"

"Because cobras usually build their nests inside once the termites have left."

Rahula jumped back and raced behind me for cover. "This is dangerous, Mother! Why are we here?!"

"Because," I said, as I pulled him gently to my side, "these places are the haunts of great beings. The termites dig tunnels all the way down into the underworld, summoning the Serpent-Spirits up. The cobras are the physical manifestations of spirits that belong to somewhere else. We must honor them when they appear."

"But they're dangerous!"

"Yes, they can be. Anything that is powerful is dangerous, so we must be careful, but we must also always honor."

I felt my mother's voice coming from inside me, as though I was growing into her, becoming her with time. The teachings I was offering my son were the kinds of teachings she had offered me.

I pulled a few flower garlands out of my bag and handed one to him. I deposited the flower garland at the foot of the mound, bowed with my palms pressed together and whispered my prayer. I then invited my son to do the same.

"We can walk around it now," I suggested after he had placed his garland next to mine.

"Do you mind if I just stay here and watch?" he asked, clearly still a bit worried.

"Of course."

I walked around the mound three times, throwing flower petals and grains of rice as I went. When I was done, I packed up my things and began the walk back up the hill, my shining son by my side.

"Mother, what makes the Serpent-Spirits special? Is it just because they come from the underworld?"

It was a good question and I took a moment to think about it. I picked a pink flower from the tall grass and placed it behind my ear.

"Well, all beings are special in their own way. Whether they come from the underworld or from the heavens above, every kind of being deserves to be honored, but Serpent-Spirits are special ... I suppose because they are so often misunderstood."

"What do you mean?" he asked.

"Dangerous creatures are usually misunderstood. People fear them because they are dangerous, and fear often leads to cruelty, so dangerous creatures can suffer quite a lot, and we don't worry about them when they cry because they are strong. But tears are tears, no matter who sheds them."

"But if they are dangerous, we have to protect ourselves from them!" he declared with the absolute authority of a seven-year-old.

"Yes, we do," I replied. "But protecting ourselves is one thing. Attacking is something else. We must always be careful around powerful creatures, but we also need to honor them."

Rahula looked puzzled, so I offered an example.

"Do you remember the story of Surpanakha?" I asked.

"The demoness in the Ramayana?"

"That's the one. She was powerful, so Rama and Lakshmana had to protect themselves from her, right?"

"But they didn't just protect themselves. They were mean to her."

"Exactly, and that's the difference. Powerful creatures have fire inside them and that is something for us to honor. We cannot run from them because they frighten us. We have to learn how to face them."

"And that's why you brought me to see the mound?"

"You learn quickly, my little one."

He smiled with pride.

As we made our way back to the palace, Rahula asked me one last question.

"Mother, if we are supposed to learn how to face power, does that mean that I can finally go hunting?"

"The answer to that question continues to be no," I answered with a smile.

*

I returned to my room to wash up before the midday meal. I was sore from the walk and asked Neelima to massage my feet. She used lavender oil, which put me to sleep almost instantly. When I woke up, it was to the sound of a stampede in the hallway. People were rushing around just outside my door, anklets chiming with hurried movement in every direction.

I wondered what all the fuss was about and looked around the room for my white shawl, but Neelima flew through the door before I made a move.

"What's going on out there?" I asked, scanning the room for my missing fabric. "Is the palace on fire?"

The sounds were growing in intensity. Too many people were running around without a reason I could identify. Even when we had festivals in the palace, the upstairs apartments remained relatively quiet. I got out of bed and started throwing the pillows around, searching for the piece of white cotton I used to cover my shoulders.

Neelima, however, did not move. She watched as I shoved pillows and blankets around, not even offering to help.

"Maidservant, where's my shawl?"

She did not answer. Eventually, I stopped what I was doing and looked at her, an orange pillow dangling in my hand.

"Neelima?"

"Someone is here, Your Highness."

The way she said it gave me pause. The walls around my mind began to rise up protectively.

"Is that what all the noise is about?"

She nodded.

The sounds of exuberance on the other side of the door increased. I could hear laughter and animated talking now, and I could even detect the smell of food reaching into the room from under the door, but the kitchen was on the other side of the palace.

I put the orange pillow down. "Who is here, Neelima?" I asked. My heart was making strange leaps inside my chest, as though my body knew what was happening before the rest of me did.

"It is the prince, Your Highness."

"The prince?" I repeated, unsure of what she meant—or at least unprepared to consider the looming possibility . . .

She stepped towards me with a bowed head. "It is *he*, Your Highness. Prince Siddhattha. Your husband has returned."

The room began to spin and I thought I was going to lose my balance. I put my hands on the bed to keep myself steady. This wasn't possible. He was gone. He had left more than seven years ago. He could not have returned. He wasn't allowed. I looked down at my white clothes in horror. I was a widow!

"What is he doing here?" I mumbled almost inaudibly. Desperation seemed to have stolen my vocal chords. "He's not supposed to come back . . ."

She looked at me with loyal tenderness and seemed to want to reach out for my hand. She didn't, but I could feel her wanting to.

"There were rumors, Your Highness," she said instead. She was not going to withhold the truth from me now. "People say that the king has been sending messengers to the prince for a long time. Every few moons, he sends someone to the forest to beg him to return."

"The king has been doing *what*?"

Neelima understood my disorientation.

"The thing is that the messengers never came back."

"Why not?" I asked, trying to keep up.

"We didn't know at first, but it seems that when the messengers met him, they no longer wanted to leave."

The smell of fried breads and curried chicken wafted into my room uninvited. How many people were gathering down there?

"They say that the prince has achieved something extraordinary, Your Highness. That he has attained something that has not been attained in ten-thousand years." She took a deep breath and added with a reverential tone, "Your Highness, they are calling him a Buddha. An Awakened One."

A Buddha? Is that what was meant when they described him as eternity . . .?

"They say," she continued, "that his presence is so beautiful, everyone who approaches him is affected. Every messenger falls at his feet as though intoxicated. That's why they don't come back."

"So then . . . How is it that he has come back now?" I asked, trying to make sense of all the new information.

"Minister Kaludayi volunteered to bring him back. He promised the king that he would return with his son if the king promised to grant him permission to follow the Buddha after he did. The king agreed and Minister Kaludayi succeeded. He went into the forest to find him and convinced him to return."

The sounds of boys racing through the hallway faded in and out of the background of my mind.

"Siddhattha is back ..." I whispered. "Do you think he is going to stay?" I asked, as though she would have the answer.

Apparently, she did.

"I don't think so, Your Highness. They say that the king just wanted to see him. To hear what he has to say. To have *darshan* with his son one last time."

The whirl of emotions that I thought I had conquered rose to the surface with dizzying speed. I didn't know how to face this. I had gotten used to living my quiet, white-clad life, but this ...?

"Your Highness, Minister Kaludayi is with the Buddha in the courtyard right now. Actually, many of the family members who had disappeared over the past few years are there. They have all become the Buddha's followers. And they have all come home."

Missing pieces were falling into place. One cousin after another had walked out of the palace to seek a life of renunciation—more than I had ever thought was natural—but I never realized it was to follow Siddhattha. They had all abandoned the material world for something else. Now Kaludayi would leave too? I never imagined that it was something they were doing together, that they were meeting each other on the other side.

"Your Highness," Neelima insisted, "you must come to the courtyard. Everyone is there."

She stood up and waited for me to move.

He was here. *My husband was here.* I looked down at my white clothes. But he was not supposed to come back.

"Where is Queen Mahapajapati?" I asked. "Does she know?"

"She does, Princess. She has arranged for the women to have a separate audience with the Buddha. It will take place very soon. You must come!"

I thought I had conquered the inner chaos of my mind, but his return sent me spiraling. I was not ready. Neelima opened the door and waited for me to lead the way out.

"No," was all I could say.

*

I stayed where I was, on the edge of my bed, lost in thought. I could hear the festive sounds of community in the palace courtyard. There was so much giddy excitement surrounding the prince's return, but was he still a prince? I wondered how he was being greeted. And how I was supposed to greet him.

I wanted to see what he looked like.

I remembered a discreet window that overlooked the courtyard not too far from my chambers. I got up, steadied myself, and searched again for my shawl. I found a corner of it peeking out from under the bed. I folded myself into it and opened the door into the hallway that was buzzing with energy.

"Mother!" Rahula cried out as he glided into me.

"Darling! What are you doing here? I thought you were taking a rest."

"I had to come find you. There's a party in the courtyard with all kinds of people dressed in orange. I think we are going to have a second adventure today!"

Rahula's eyes were shining with enthusiasm. How was he going to react to the discovery of his father for the first time? The sharp wings of resentment pierced my heart with their blades.

I took a deep breath and focused on my son's immediate needs. "Someone special has arrived, my sweet one. A great teacher."

"Let's go and see!" he pulled my hand toward the stairs.

"No!" I cried, as I dug in my heels.

He stopped and turned toward me. "Why not? Everyone is there!"

"Because . . ." I looked for the right explanation. "It would not be appropriate to disturb them right now. But if you want, we can watch from the window at the end of the corridor. Would you like to do that?"

We had often used that window to spy on important dignitaries as they arrived.

"Sure," he agreed easily. "Let's go see from there." He filled my hand with the warmth of his own and I clasped it.

We walked over to the window and I placed myself to the side so as not to be seen. Rahula stuck his head out as only children can do, leaning over the ledge to take in the scene at the other end. I put my hand out protectively to ensure he did not fall forward.

"Oh Mother, you have to see this! There are so many people down there!"

I was so close to Siddhattha now that I could almost feel him, but I did not dare look yet. My heart was beating so hard that I thought it was going to beat right out of my chest. Rahula's feet were not even touching the floor. He was dangling, his stomach folded over the edge, enjoying the sights in the courtyard below him. Eventually, he lowered himself back to the ground.

"That man at the center . . . is he the teacher you were talking about?"

I kept my back against the wall to avoid being seen through the window and closed my eyes. I was taking deep breaths, trying desperately to calm myself down, but my heart was too agitated. There was no way out of this. I clenched my hands, shifted towards the window and willed myself to open my eyes.

There he was. Shining like the sun, just as others said he did.

He looked like a blazing ball of fire in the middle of the courtyard, but he did not make anything around him seem faded by comparison. On the contrary, he seemed to bring the entire courtyard to life with him. He sat so calmly, his hands folded neatly in his lap, gentleness radiating all around him. He was listening to the person seated in front of him. The person—I think it was one of our servants actually—had his head bowed. He was speaking to him through a veil of tears.

The scene had a timeless quality about it, as though it had taken place before and it would take place again. I became absorbed in the moment of it and everything inside of me finally slowed down. *I could see him*, for the first time in seven years. I was looking at my beloved and he was more beautiful than he had ever been before.

I smiled with my whole self, the way I always had when I saw him. But a moment later, the smile faded as I recognized what Neelima was trying to tell me earlier: he wasn't my beloved anymore. He had become someone else.

I looked down at my clothes again, at the white that I was wearing. I was still a widow after all. Even though he was right there in front of me, my husband was gone.

"Who is he?" Rahula repeated eagerly. "Have you ever seen him before?"

I looked at my sweet, loving son. He was in awe of the scene and his eyes kept returning to the one who held center stage. What was I supposed to tell him? What was the answer to the question in his case? If *I* had lost Siddhattha, Rahula had too.

"They are calling him the Buddha, my son. An Awakened One."

I watched his features as they processed the information. He was such a thoughtful little thing.

"Can I meet him?" he asked innocently.

"I . . . I don't know."

"Why not? It looks like everybody else in the palace is getting to meet him! Even the women!"

The men were beginning to take their leave as the women waited patiently for their turn to sit at his feet. Mahapajapati was at the head of the line, shining gloriously.

I looked down at my son and felt the jagged edge of life's injustice. A boy needed a father, but this boy did not have one. He never did, and yet his father was right there on the other side of the window, a few steps away, acting like a king even though he had left the throne behind.

Even though he had left us all behind.

"Mother, do you know him?" he asked carefully. "Tell me who he is."

I sighed and lowered myself to my knees to be at eye-level with him.

"Darling," I whispered as I took his sweet hands into my own, "he is not a stranger to me. Nor is he a stranger to you. That man ..." I peered towards the window with Rahula's eyes following me, "is your father. He was my husband many years ago."

He looked at me, his eyes as round as saucers, and then he turned back to the window and stared at the man who sat at the center of the courtyard with the whole world prostrated at his feet.

"*He* is my father?"

"Yes, darling."

He turned towards the scene and examined it with even greater attention than before. He gripped the marble siding for support.

"What should I do?" he asked.

"I don't know. I have been wondering the same thing. Perhaps you want to introduce yourself?"

"And say what?"

What does a son say to the father who left him?

"Maybe you have a question you would like to ask him?" I suggested.

He thought about that for a moment. "Well," he said, "I guess I do have a question."

"What is it?"

He furrowed his brow. "If he is alive again, will I still get to be king?"

That was the last thing I expected him to say. He didn't understand succession law under such circumstances. Inheritance was irrelevant to a renunciant. Of course, the throne was still Rahula's, but I could see the logic. Rahula had been raised under the weight of the throne's dominating presence, just as his father had before him. Rahula was a practical boy and it was a practical question for him to ask.

"If that is your question, then you must ask it," I replied tenderly. "Go and ask him about your inheritance."

*

I watched my son walk away from me, pangs of maternal heartache beating against my chest. Rahula had not invited me to come with him and I had not offered to join. This was something he had to do for himself and my place was not beside him. That fact alone was pain enough.

I could have joined the women for their audience with him, but I did not want to. In fact, I could not imagine any public setting that I could accept in which we would meet. It was still unclear to me *how* he was being greeted. Did the king still think of him as his son or was he hosting a foreign dignitary?

Siddhattha would never be a foreign dignitary to me, no matter how famous he became. Even if everyone in the world prostrated themselves at his feet, I refused to see him as someone else. I would not lump myself in with the masses in the hopes of catching a faint glimpse of him. And I was still angry. He had abandoned all of us when we needed him and then he came home and was hailed a hero, while I remained invisible and forgotten. He always did what *he* wanted to do. He made the decisions that suited *him* and I was left behind to pick up the shattered remains. I was expected to be the dutiful wife, to accept whatever he offered or took away.

But I did not want to be the dutiful wife anymore. Even Sita eventually said no. She asked the Earth Goddess to release her rather than continue meeting the demands of a husband who kept taking.

I turned away from the window and went back to my room. If he wanted to see me, he would have to come find me himself.

Overcoming Obstacles

I sat by the window in my room watching the trees sway as I listened to the sounds of movement outside my door. Neelima had not come back; she was probably still enjoying the after-effects of her audience with the man who was once my husband. I pulled spaciousness apart like yarns of wool in my hands.

There was a knock at the door.

I took a few deep breaths and stared out the window as a hawk swept by. I hoped it was a good omen. When I was ready, I went to the door.

"Blessings, Yasodhara."

He was more beautiful than ever. Tall and graceful, with his shoulders pulled back like a well-trained archer, and eyes so dark they looked like pools of eternity that I would have gladly fallen into rather than spend another moment apart from him. With a cry I did not even hear myself make, I collapsed to the floor and covered his bare feet with my face, clinging as though I was drowning and he was my raft.

Others shuffled into the room with quick steps and swarmed around me like protective bees. I closed my eyes and tightened my grip, sobbing into his feet with my hair splayed out like a puddle.

"Let her be," he said to them. "She has my permission. She was my wife once."

An uncomfortable silence ensued as their bodies loomed over mine. I dared not look up.

"You may leave now," he said. Without a word, their bare feet moved away and the door closed behind them.

Siddhattha kneeled down beside me and put his hand on my shoulder, causing me to shudder.

"Please get up, dear Yasodhara."

I nodded as he helped me to my feet. I was desperately embarrassed, but there was nowhere to hide. I followed him to the sitting area by the window.

"Are you all right?" he asked gently.

"I think so . . ." I replied, the emotions swirling. "What happened to your hair?" I asked.

"I cut it."

"Oh . . ." Channa had mentioned that, but I had forgotten. I folded my fingers into knots, unsure of what was supposed to happen next.

"Why are you here?" I asked.

"The king has been asking to see me. He does not have much time left."

"What do you mean he does not have much time left? He is in perfect health," I argued almost immediately. Why was I arguing?

He did not argue back.

I kept twisting my fingers around themselves. How was this conversation supposed to go? What does one say to a man who was socially dead but physically alive? How does one address a husband with a shaved head? Was it wrong that I still loved him?

It would have been easier if I didn't.

"Are you allowed to be here?" I said instead.

"What do you mean?"

"I mean . . . I am a widow now. Haven't you noticed?" I pointed to my clothing. "We are no longer married."

"No, we are no longer married, Yasodhara," he replied.

"So is it appropriate for you to be here? In my chambers, as though we still were?"

He sat with stillness, as though he was part of the forest he lived in, rooted like an ancient tree to the Earth Goddess.

"You would not come see me and I would not leave without seeing you, so I came here. But you are right: people might talk."

"You realize that when people talk, it is rarely about the man. If people talk, *you* will remain blameless, while the whispers will follow me like a shadow."

"Would you rather I leave?"

No, I did not want him to leave, but he was exasperating all the same. The urge to fight was overwhelming, as was the urge to throw myself into his arms and fall against his strong chest. My body ached with loneliness, and my heart ached for him. I jumped to my feet and turned towards the window, pushing my palms against the hard marble frame.

"You made me a widow," I repeated with my back turned.

"There was no other way."

I pushed my nails into the stone. Why was there no other way? Why couldn't he have stayed? Or at least taken us with him?

"You left us behind, without even saying goodbye," I whispered.

He remained silent after that last accusation, leaving me time to stare out the window and quiet the hurt.

Swollen white clouds were gradually filling the sky. It had been a clear day earlier, but the sky was changing. The clouds seemed to be appearing out of nowhere, as though they were being painted over the blue by a celestial artist who was conjuring them out of nowhere. One cloud after another was being stamped over the blue sky until they were everywhere ... I looked down and saw the clouds filling up the space below too.

I rubbed my eyes, unsure of what I was looking at. This was not natural weather by any stretch of the imagination. The clouds were not darkening and there was no wind to carry them, but everywhere I looked, the clouds were being plastered over the blue. It made no sense. When I looked below my window again, I could not see the ground.

"Husband ..." I whispered. "What is happening?"

He stood up to join me as a great white eagle sliced through the clouds with a screech of power, followed by a flock of loud black crows, which frightened me. Soon birds of all kinds were sweeping by the window, as though we were sharing the sky with them and not grounded in a palace on the earth.

"It feels like some kind of magic is happening ..." I mumbled. I stuck my head out further and tried to see if I could catch a glimpse of the ground through the clouds, but there was nothing.

"Are we ... floating?" I asked, bewildered.

He smiled at me with that familiar mischievous grin I loved.

I could not even begin to understand how or why any of it was happening, and it did not matter. The world had receded, and with it all the gossipmongers, palace politics, and royal loneliness I had grown accustomed to navigating. With growing excitement, I reached out and touched one of the clouds. The whiteness trailed between my fingers and disappeared before I could hold on.

"Shall we take a stroll?" he offered.

"Where? Out there?"

"Yes. Out there."

I nodded with a great big smile, giddiness lifting me up. I suspended all of my questions as we clambered onto the sill together. Without warning or a hint of concern, Siddhattha stepped right out into the blue expanse and hovered in the air in front of me with a wonderful smile on his face. I laughed, pitched my worries to the side and followed him right out.

It was glorious! I stood in the sky beaming with delight! My hands moved around the air, feeling its quality, exploring the vastness that sparkled bright. When I looked back towards the window, the palace was gone.

"How is this happening?" I asked.

"Does it matter?" he asked in return.

A great thick cloud meandered by and we jumped on. Although it was nothing but a shimmery veil of whiteness, it was somehow able to carry us. I kept trailing my fingers through it, wondering how it managed to be empty and full at the same time.

"There are still questions you want to ask . . . Or things you would like to say," Siddhattha observed as he picked up the thread of our conversation.

"What? Here?"

"Where else?"

"Oh . . ."

A great red bird with blue tail feathers flapped its way pass.

"There is a question that has been haunting me since you left . . ."

He waited for me to gather my courage, as though we had all the time in the world. And in a way, floating on a cloud in a sky far from everything, we did.

"Was it difficult for you to leave us—Rahula and I?" I finally managed to ask.

He looked down at his hands, as though there was something there for him to hold.

"It was," he admitted. "It was very hard."

"And you could not take us with you?"

"No."

"But *why*?" I asked pleadingly, the pain returning in an instant.

"Because . . ." he looked back up at me. "I was too attached. To you. To our son. To everything. I had to walk away if Awakening were ever to become possible. If you had come with me, I would never have been able to let go."

"Why not?" I could not let my question go.

"Because Yasodhara, I was too attached," he repeated patiently. "I loved you and Rahula for my own self. I had to learn to let go of that kind of love if I was going to find the answers I was looking for. I did not want to love you more than everyone else. I wanted to learn the kind of love that went beyond individual preferences. The kind of love that did not come from suffering. I could not find that while staring at you."

"But all love comes from suffering," I argued. "You wanted the answer to suffering, but you caused suffering to all of us in order to find it! That doesn't make any sense to me! You could have just stayed here. It would have been so much simpler!"

They were the words I had been desperate to throw at him for seven years. I looked away and stared into the shining white space.

"You could never get over those water buffalos . . ." I added under my breath.

He seemed taken aback by this memory. "No . . . I guess I never could."

I wished we had never gone into the woods that day. Perhaps then he would have stayed.

"But it wasn't just the water buffalos," he said as though he could read my mind. "I could not stay shielded from suffering. The king tried to cover my eyes, but it was only a matter of time before I saw the world for myself. You would not have been able to cover my eyes either. It was not your fault that I left."

That was what Mahapajapati kept saying, but I did not believe her. I wanted more control over my life than that.

A glittering gold carriage drawn by colorful flying horses suddenly appeared. It seemed to be moving along an invisible track in the sky, carrying four Great Gods who were waving at us exuberantly as they passed. One of them kept trying to climb over the other three, pushing his hand over their heads to get a better view.

"Who are they?" I asked, slightly amused despite myself. The clambering god almost fell out of the carriage, but the others yanked him back into safety while reprimanding him with wagging fingers.

"Old friends," he replied enigmatically.

I waved as they disappeared.

The clouds looked like seats of sparkling white pearls now, and hints of shimmering blue were starting to appear behind them. The sky was becoming a tapestry of jewels, lighting us up with its brilliance.

"Siddhattha?" I had one last question I wanted to ask before the show came to an end.

"Yes?"

"What does it feel like?"

"To be Awake?" he asked.

I nodded.

"It feels like this."

*

The palace re-appeared in the sky and the cloud stopped by my window.

"I suppose it is time to return . . .?" I asked, not really wanting to let the moment end.

"It is."

He helped me to my feet and I stepped through my window. I rubbed my eyes again and found myself back where I had been before. The magic was done.

"Yasodhara?" It was his turn to ask a question.

"Yes?"

"Rahula has asked to come with me."

That was not a question.

"I will provide him with the education he is ready to receive."

"Oh no ..." I felt dizzy immediately and could not bear to look up at him. Did he really just say those words? "Please don't do this to me again," I heard myself beg.

He did not react. He knew there was more coming. My heart cracked out loud.

"There have been so many tears because of you!" I sobbed with frustrated tears. "There is so much pain inside my heart that echoes with your name. You're hurting me *again*. How is *this* the answer to suffering?"

"Yasodhara," he said tenderly, "you cannot hold onto Rahula forever. He is seven years old. He requires training."

"Seven is not so old! And his training doesn't require that he leave home. He can do his training here! Or he can do it later, but not now! Not this way!"

"But he is ready, Yasodhara."

I dropped my hands onto my lap as I felt my hold on life escape me. What would I do without Rahula?

"You can't take him. Think about what you're doing," I pleaded. "Not just to me, but to the kingdom! Your father is depending on him to take the throne now that you have gone. Are you going to have the throne stripped of its heir a second time? Will you do this to *all of us* a second time?"

"The kingdom has many potential candidates for the throne. The king has not even invested in Rahula's training yet."

"Maybe," I answered, "but Rahula believes the throne will be his. Will you take it away from *him*?"

I turned my back and folded my legs into my chest, hugging them with all my strength. I could feel him reaching out to me without touching me. He was so close and yet so very far away.

"Yasodhara, I am not taking anything away from him. I am offering him an opportunity. He asked me for his inheritance when he came to see me and this *is* his inheritance. This is what I have to offer him. Everything else is impermanent, subject to change, and cannot be depended upon. Only the teachings that lead to freedom are of value. When he asked for his inheritance, this was my answer."

He was impossible to argue with. I turned around and looked at him with the fire of motherhood in my eyes.

"You want to take him with you, but to where? To the forest, to sleep on leaves? How will he survive? What will he eat? Who will take care of him the way he needs? He's just a boy!"

"But he is ready to learn how to become a man. I will take care of him."

"Not the way I would," I declared. "You cannot take care of him the way a mother would."

He sighed, as though trying to pace himself as I rode my emotional crest.

"I know you love him, Yasodhara," he said eventually.

"Then why are trying to shatter my love?" I demanded.

"You know that I am not trying to shatter anything. But *you* will shatter it if you hold onto him when he is ready to go."

He was not going to soothe me through this. He was being serious with me, and his seriousness felt harsh. The walls of my room were closing in on me.

"Yasodhara, have you ever thought about what his name means?" he said as he changed direction.

"What?"

"His name," he repeated. "Have you ever thought about what it means?"

"Of course I have. I was at the ceremony." Without you, I wanted to add, but I withheld. "He was born under Rahu's eclipse. He is of the darkness."

"True. But there is another meaning to his name. 'Rahula' also means 'obstacle.'"

I remembered hearing that once . . .

"After Rahula was born, I came to see the two of you in your room. You were fast asleep and I didn't want to disturb you. You were both very tired."

I did not know that he had come to see us before he left. I thought he had walked away without even a glance in our direction.

"I stared at you both for a long time," he continued, "and I wanted very much to hold our son in my arms, but I knew that it would wake you if I tried. I also knew that if you woke, I would lose the courage I needed to leave, so I let you both sleep, too afraid of what would happen if either of you woke up."

He paused quietly for a moment, as though sitting with the memory required that he give himself time.

"And then a word came to my mind," he said. "Rahula. *Obstacle.*"

I dropped my turmoil and looked at him with incredulity.

"You thought of his name before the priest had even considered his chart?"

"I did. His birth created an obstacle. Both of you were obstacles. If I lingered, I would never achieve what I knew needed to be achieved, and so I left, without ever touching my son or saying goodbye to you. I could not risk the obstacle overtaking me. I had to leave and cut the bonds that caused suffering if answers were ever to be found."

But I love those bonds, my heart cried out. Those bonds are what make life worth living! Why did he want to cut those bonds so badly? Why couldn't he just let them be as they had always been? Families were made of bonds. That was the way of things. The way things had always been.

"Bonds cause suffering, Yasodhara," he answered as though I had spoken out loud, "and the answer to suffering needed to be found. Not for myself, but for all beings. For you and for Rahula and for every living being in this world."

"But you caused suffering to find the end of suffering," I repeated, incapable of letting the paradox go.

"The bonds we were holding onto caused suffering. The bonds you are holding onto still."

I wasn't holding on, I told myself stubbornly.

"When you love only those to whom you are bound," he continued, "your love is limited and small, and it grows claws with which to grip. That kind of love turns into hatred in an instant when you least expect it. The bond a mother has for her son is the kind of bond we should all feel for every living being. But when it is limited to her offspring, it is poison waiting to spread."

My heart twisted at his words. I knew he was not telling me that I was poisoning my son, but he was telling me that if I did not let go, if I continued to hold onto him as though he was the answer to my hurt, I would destroy us both.

"Let him go, Yasodhara."

"You ask so much of me, Siddhattha," I replied.

He nodded.

"It's too soon. I am not ready to lose him."

"You will not lose him, because he was never yours to own. People do not belong to each other, Yasodhara. Not even children to their mothers. No one is ever ours to lose."

He was going against everything I had ever known. In our world, people *did* belong to each other. Children belonged to their parents and wives belonged to their husbands. Families belonged to their tribe, and tribes belonged to their kingdoms.

And yet, there he was, sitting before me, saying those very things and speaking those words so plainly. He was overthrowing the elders, overthrowing my world all over again.

And he shined like the sun.

"There is a time for young boys to be carefree and playful," he continued. "To sleep beside their mothers and nestle in their arms, but there is also a time for young boys to leave their mothers. Rahula is seven years old. He needs proper training and instruction. It is that time."

Mahapajapati had been saying the same thing all along. She had been trying to convince me of this for many moons, but I would not listen. She was concerned about my attachment and warned me that I was hiding in motherhood. Just as I had once hid from it.

I looked at Siddhattha and realized how similar he and Mahapajapati had become. They had even started to look alike as they aged. They had similar eyes and a similar way of speaking. They held themselves with a similar grace.

"I don't want to let go," I said one last time.

"I know," was his reply.

25

Departures

The palace felt hollow after Siddhattha left with Rahula. I woke up in the mornings with no one to take care of. I spent my time looking for something to occupy me, but nothing held my interest. I had no responsibilities. No one to go on adventures with. My husband was gone and so was my son. I had servants preparing my meals and arranging my things, caring for me every moment of every day, leaving me with nothing to do at all. I walked the corridors of the palace waiting for something to happen, for someone to need me in some way, but no one ever did.

Mahapajapati, on the other hand, grew bolder by the day. Somehow, she had things to do. I could not understand how she did it. She grew into magnificence as her hair turned gray. When the king fell ill, she tended to him lovingly. Whatever resentment either of them had experienced in their marriage no longer mattered. They were at peace with each other and he died in her arms a contented man.

The ministers placed a distant relative on the throne and everything fell into place, just as Siddhattha said it would. Mahapajapati had fulfilled every one of her obligations to the kingdom and now she was free to be herself again. She took on the white clothes of a widow and they suited her. She walked through the last stage of her home life without anything holding her back. Each time she passed me in the hallways, I took a moment to watch.

One morning, I took a walk through the fields by the royal stables. Women often came in from the villages to harvest the land, but there should not have been anyone there that day. It was the in-between season, after the fields had been planted but before the harvest came in. Someone, however, was moving through the tall grass further ahead.

Curious, I approached. The person didn't seem to be going anywhere. She was stumbling around in circles, directionless. She was carrying something in her arms. I should have kept my distance, but there was something about her that struck me as familiar, so I crept closer until I was only a few steps away. The woman never noticed I was there. When she turned towards me, we both jumped in surprise.

"Kisa Gotami!" I cried. "Is that you?"

Kisa Gotami stopped in her tracks like a startled animal.

"I don't mean to frighten you. We met a number of years ago, in this very field. I am Princess Yasodhara. Do you remember?"

She was disoriented. She should have dropped to her knees out of deference to my station, but I don't think she knew what I had said. She just stared at me, her arms wrapped tightly around the bundle she was carrying.

A few years ago, when we had first met, she had been alert and fearless. She seemed to have aged one hundred and eight years since then. Her clothes were also strikingly different. When we first met, she wore the clothes of a peasant. Now she wore the clothes of a noble woman, but they were torn and tattered and stained. As though she had been sleeping in them outdoors. Her hair was wildly disheveled and knotted.

"Kisa Gotami, what happened to you? Are you all right?"

She did not answer.

I looked at the strange package in her arms that she was holding. "What do you have there?" I inquired as I reached out. She whipped away from me and growled like a wild animal. She then lowered herself into the grass, apparently prepared to pounce.

I should have retreated and called a guard to attend to her. She was clearly unsafe, but for some reason, I didn't. Her suffering reached straight into my heart and caught it.

I kneeled down beside her.

"Kisa Gotami, I won't hurt you."

She did not answer.

"Would you mind if I sat here with you for a while?" I asked. "We don't have to talk. We could just sit."

She stared at me, probably amazed that I hadn't run from her, and then gave me an almost imperceptible nod. Relieved, I settled in the grass and watched her settle in beside me.

We did not speak for a long time. She was far away inside herself. Although I had no idea what had happened to her, her pain felt familiar. I knew what it was like to feel lost. To disappear into hurt and not know the way back.

The silence grew comforting. She still clutched her package, but she was calmer. The sun dipped into the horizon and the sky transformed into a magnificent collage of colors. I thought back to the magical moment Siddhattha had conjured for me just outside my bedroom window. How we had walked on emptiness and traveled on clouds. I hugged my knees to my chest as gratitude washed over me.

"Kisa Gotami," I ventured again, "would you tell me what happened?"

She looked up at me cautiously, her eyes swamps of anguish.

"I . . . think so . . ." she finally replied. She was coming back from wherever it was that she had gone.

She moved her tongue around in her mouth, as though trying to waken it from its slumber.

"I came from a poor family, Madame," she began. "But I was happy. I had my sisters and cousins and friends. We did fine. But one day, not long after we met in the field that day, a wealthy man chose me for his bride and he took me away."

She took a breath. I had a feeling she had not spoken in a long time. She tightened her grip around the bundle.

"I got some nice clothes and lived in a nice house," she continued. "And I didn't have to work in the fields no more. I kinda' missed that—being with everyone and gossiping while we worked—but I couldn't tell no one that because they were all jealous of my new life . . ."

She paused again. I looked up at the sky and watched the evening birds take flight.

"My husband was pretty mean actually," she explained with more force. "He hit me lots, but I didn't love him, so I tried to think that it didn't matter. I never really expected I would love my husband. But then one day I became pregnant, and I had a son . . ."

Her voice broke and she stopped. My eyes were pulled towards her package again. A strange smell emanated from it.

"Go on," I urged her tenderly.

"He was the most perfect little thing you ever saw. Everything was better after he was born. Even my husband was kinda nice to me for a while. And so I was happy. I thought I would be all right. But then . . ."

Thick tears down her cheeks.

"My baby died. I've been wandering around ever since."

The loss of one's only child . . .

"Kisa Gotami," I said quietly, "please tell me what you're holding in your arms."

She looked up at me with her sad, sad eyes.

"You'll think I'm crazy if I tell you . . ." she sniffled.

"I promise I won't."

She held me in her stare, trying to decide whether she could trust me. Finally, she moved her arms forward and pulled back the blanket . . .

"Oh my goodness!" I cried out as my hand flew to my mouth. There he was. Her baby. Dead in her arms.

Quickly she covered him up again and tucked him back in. "I just didn't know what to do, Your Highness! I didn't know where to go. I don't wanna go back home. I don't wanna go anywhere! I just want my son to be alive. I want him to come back!

"But he can't come back . . ."

"But they were going to bury him! I couldn't let them stick him in the earth all by himself! He'd be so cold! So I grabbed him and ran. What else could I do?"

I pleaded with Kisa Gotami, begging her to come back with me to the palace. I promised I would take care of her and that I would take care of her son, but she wouldn't hear of it. When it became dark, she scuttled away. She was not ready to let her son go. The grief was calling for her return.

*

I walked back to the palace in a solemn mood. Kisa Gotami's state was precisely what Siddhattha had warned me of. Attachment can destroy us. We have no choice but to let go. If we refuse to do it ourselves, death will do it for us. One way or another, we will eventually all have to let go.

I walked slowly through the corridors towards my chambers, remembering all the times in my life when I was called to let go and refused. Even as a child, I had fought my parents to avoid growing up. I didn't want to let go of my youth. I didn't want to let go of my freedom or of the way things were. I fought change whenever it approached me. And I fought the future, hoping that if I tried hard enough, it would not become what it was destined to be. I had always thought that the king was mad for fighting the stars throughout Siddhattha's childhood, but how different was I from him? How many of us are capable of letting anything go?

Siddhattha had tried for months to tell me that palace life was not his to live. He sat with me, talked to me, held my hand as he struggled with the call he heard inside. He told me in every way he could that he would have to go, and yet I refused. I wanted him to stay.

When Rahula had come of age, Mahapajapati had told me the same thing, and I again refused to hear. Holding on to the people I loved was the only way I knew to survive. How different was that from what I just saw in Kisa Gotami?

She was holding onto her son just as I had held onto everyone around me. Was I like a crazed woman with a dead baby in my arms? The thought sent a chill down my spine.

I entered my room and sat down on the bench by the window. I watched the leaves fluttering in the trees outside. Every once in a while, a leaf would fall and drift to the ground. A tree would never try to catch the leaf and stick it back on. Why, then, had I spent my life doing just that? I kept trying to catch the pieces that were falling away to stick them back where they had been. But fallen pieces don't stick back on. Even trees know that.

There was a knock at the door and before I could answer, Mahapajapati sailed in.

"I am leaving, Daughter," she said without ceremony.

"What? Where?" I was not expecting that. Truthfully, I was not expecting anything.

She sat down beside me. Right where Siddhattha had sat with me a few moons earlier.

"Daughter, I have done everything that I can do here. My role as queen is complete."

There was a new king on the throne who would eventually bring in a new queen. What did either of us have to do in the palace anymore?

"I have decided to follow in the Buddha's footsteps. I am going to go look for him in the forest and ask him if he will grant me ordination. I want to join his community."

I pulled back with surprise. "What do you mean? How can you join them? They're all men out there," I exclaimed.

"I know. But I see no reason why women cannot join them. We also have a need for freedom. Why would he say no?" she asked.

Because we are women, was what I wanted to answer.

But I didn't. She was right. He should say yes.

My eyes flickered for a moment and I suddenly thought I was seeing the Goddess in her face. I imagined her with shining weapons in eighteen arms and a mountain lion under her seat. Was this the fearlessness my mother had been trying to teach me? Was this what Durga looked like in human form?

"But what if he says no?" I asked, more out of curiosity than anything else. "What will you do then?"

She looked at me candidly. "Yasodhara, I am too old to worry about that. I long for freedom and I am prepared to seek it, no matter what the cost. I cannot waste time worrying about the possibility that it might not go as planned."

She *was* the Goddess. I reached for my pendant as I thought about the many ways power can manifest itself. We must be careful, but we must honor it all.

"So I am leaving," she said. "And you are welcome to come with me. I leave at sunrise, with nothing more than the clothing I will be wearing. Everything else I leave behind."

She smiled at me lovingly and then reached over to kiss me on the forehead. "If I don't see you tomorrow, take care of yourself."

*

All night I tossed and turned in my bed. I could not sleep. When the stars began to recede from the night sky, I stepped out of my bed and my foot landed on something hard. I looked down and found the little tree Siddhattha had carved for me years earlier. It must have gotten lost under the bed.

I picked it up. He had made a tree out of a piece of wood. He had made something back into itself.

I had my answer.

I lay the tree on my bed and placed my Durga pendant beside it. I then wrapped my white shawl around my shoulders and walked out of my room. I walked down the marble staircase, through the palace courtyard, and towards the front gate, my pace picking up speed with each step.

When I arrived downstairs, I found hundreds of women from all around Kapilavatthu standing together at the palace threshold, Mahapajapati standing tall among them.

"Who are all these women?" I asked when I finally reached her. "What is going on?"

"The word spread that I am going to ask the Buddha for ordination. They have all come to join me in my request."

I looked around and saw all kinds of faces. Young and old. Family members and strangers. Servants and noblewomen. I recognized Neelima and waved at her. She waved back enthusiastically. It was the most extraordinary gathering of women I had ever seen. And we all stood together, waiting for Mahapajapati to take the first step.

Off to the side, I saw one face I thought I would never see again: Kisa Gotami's. I don't know how she had heard or what had happened, but there she was in her stained clothes, still clutching her dead baby in her arms, standing with the rest of us. She was going to try for freedom too.

Tears dripped down my face with more gratitude than I had ever felt before. We were going on a quest. Mahapajapati began to walk.

And I walked right behind her.

Acknowledgments

Writing acknowledgments for this book has been more daunting than usual. This may be because this book has been many years in the making (although most books tend to work that way), but I think it may also be because this book has come to mean so much. I never anticipated how much love I would come to feel for the characters here and all the attachments I find myself bound by.

Even more surprising was to discover how much I came to love the process of creative writing. Although I have always enjoyed academic writing, there can be something predictably formulaic about it. With this book, I was able to let go and it was an unexpected delight. Indeed, I soon found myself incapable of *not* writing, grabbing five minutes between meetings if that was all I had available, just so I could open the book on my computer and tinker with a line or two. I even remember once becoming so absorbed by the process that I completely forgot to go to class. Twenty minutes passed before a few sheepish students appeared at my door, asking if class was cancelled. This book has taken me far away, to a time and place I have devoted my academic career to studying, but that I don't think I ever quite loved the way I do now.

There are so many people to thank. I begin with David Shulman, to whom I am indebted not only for Surpanakha, but also for introducing me to one of my heroes—Wendy Doniger—who then serendipitously introduced me to Ravi Singh at Speaking Tiger, who published the first edition of this book.

This new edition would not have been possible without Lucy Carroll and Lalle Pursglove at Bloomsbury, who championed this project and supported me every step of the way. My thanks also go to Cynthia Read at Oxford University Press for her ongoing encouragement; John Strong and Charlie Hallisey for their support (which means the world); Naomi Appleton, Andy Rotman, Damchö Diana Finnegan, and Rajini Obeyesekere—each of whom offered invaluable comments at various points on this journey. Thank you to Maria Heim, Kristin Scheible, Karen Derris, and Natalie Gummer for being wonderful girlfriends in what can otherwise be a rather institutional boy's club; and forever gratitude to my Buddhist Studies homegirl, Amy Langenberg.

I also thank my McGill family—the precious friends I am so glad to have shared my graduate years with. They carried me through many an existential crisis. Jackie Du Toit and Jason Kalman (my academic siblings), Lara Braitstein, Rowshan Nemazee, Barbra Clayton, Melissa Curley, Jessica Main and eventually (joining us at the end of those years) the indomitable Rongdao Lai.

My friends outside the academy have been just as important to this process, providing me with their friendship, encouragement, and a warm cup of coffee when nothing else would do. In particular, my gratitude to Holly Wheatcroft (Gilgamesh!), Nancy Berman, Rachel Levine, Selena Liss, Megan Spriggs, Marcus Alexander (and Charlie Keeper), Edie Ledany, Kim Kujawski, Anne Plantade, Seth Shugar, Wendy Garling, and Claire Rothman.

Last but certainly not least, my crazy family. Like many from the Middle East, my family is a boisterous tribe that moves like a tidal wave. I cannot thank any one member without thanking them all. I don't know who I would be without them. I thank my grandmother Sheila, the queen of the tribe, for lifelong inspiration. I dedicate this book to her. My four mothers (her four daughters), my uncle, and the eight siblings who are really cousins but are really siblings anyway (LVG Agenda). My parents and my sisters who cultivated my storytelling tendencies, and Becky, who told me stories I was much too young to understand (because her stories were true, even though they weren't).

Finally, to Sebastien and Darshan: you are my heart. Thank you for everything.

Notes

Note on Transliteration

The point of transliteration is to limit the corruption a foreign script may otherwise create. Diacritics are therefore used to ensure a more precise reading. 'Yasodhara,' for example, would traditionally be spelled 'Yaśodharā' in Romanized Sanskrit, demonstrating a *sh* sound on the *s* and a lengthening of the last *a*.

For the purposes of this book, however, the general reader would probably be better served with a more simplified experience, so I dropped the diacritics entirely. My apologies to Pali and Sanskrit readers who may find the experience disorienting. The decision was taken with the best of intentions.

I have chosen to use Pali rather than Sanskrit in this work, Pali being a more likely language used by the characters of this book. The Buddha's personal name is therefore 'Siddhattha' rather than 'Siddhartha.'

Prologue

Many sources make reference to the fact that **the Buddha took Rahula with him to the forest** after his return to Kapilavatthu (see notes to Chapter 24), but none of these sources describes the actual scene of separation. The Prologue was, therefore, the product of my own imaginings.

Although it did not influence my decision at the time of writing, I realize now that a useful parallel can be drawn between this scene and Shankara Acarya's renunciation at a similar age. In this case, however, Shankara was the one who wanted to become a renunciant (instead of having the decision be taken for him), but his mother had to be coaxed into agreeing (Shankara convinced her while caught in the jaws of a crocodile, so the story goes . . .). The theme of maternal heartbreak in the face of child renunciation is a familiar one in classical Indian narrative traditions. For Shankara's hagiography, see Isayeva (1993).

The monks are described as wearing orange rags. Early Buddhist literature is not consistent regarding monastic dress, but reference to robes made of discarded material (rag-robes) appears repeatedly in the different Vinaya traditions. Monastic clothing eventually becomes an important preoccupation in the literature, with detailed discussions about what is permissible, what is forbidden, how many items may be owned, and how to care for the items a monastic might have. The rag-robes were exchanged for nicer materials as monastic history developed (although the rag-robe tradition continues for some). For a discussion of Vinaya regulations, see all of Schopen's work, but specifically his article, "Death, Funerals, and the Division of Property in a Monastic Code," (1995). See also Schopen's discussion of a fascinating scene from the *Lalitavistara* where the Buddha exchanges his well-worn rag-robes for a death shroud—taking the tradition of discarded materials even further (Schopen 2006). For the rules concerning care of robes, see Ann Heirman 2014.

When Yasodhara touches her son's hair before they part, she recoils when she realizes that his hair will soon be shorn. Although it is not obvious how renunciation would have been experienced at this early stage in the tradition's development, or if head shaving was even practiced by monastics yet, there is no question that head shaving eventually came to represent a powerful cutting away ceremony. Once the head was shaved—theoretically at least—the renunciant was no longer a son to his mother. He had become a monk. For a discussion of monastic ordination in the earliest strata of the tradition, see Kloppenborg (1983). For a discussion of more contemporary practices (and a counter-argument to the notion of radical family separation), see Samuels (2010).

Chapter 1: Beginnings

Yasodhara is not the focus of most Buddhist sources. There are, therefore, many missing pieces to her narrative, which will become increasingly obvious as these notes progress.

Yasodhara's parents are not consistently featured in the literature, and when they are, they are not consistently named. In the *Mahavastu*, for example, Yasodhara's father is called Mahanama (2:73). Elsewhere, he is known as Supabuddha (*Mahavamsa* ii 19). According to the *Lalitavistara* (1:215) and in early Tibetan accounts, he is known as Dandapani (Rockhill, 20).

I made the decision to go with Dandapani, because Supabuddha as a name risked confusing readers (given the 'buddha' part of his name), while Mahanama can be mistaken for a different character by the same name in the literature. Dandapani seemed to be the easiest choice.

Pamita, by contrast (Yasodhara's mother), is a name I chose.

There are no descriptions of **Yasodhara's birth** in the literature (to my knowledge). One detail, however, repeatedly surfaces: that **both she and the future Buddha (her future husband) were born at the same time.** This is commonly referred to as their co-natal status and is a regular feature of the Pali Commentarial tradition. See Horner (1979) for a list of Pali references and Walters (2003) for some discussion. Worth noting here, however, is the fact that the future Buddha and Yasodhara are not *only* co-natal. They take rebirth together in their last lives, but they also shared many previous lives together as husband and wife. Their relationship is therefore a very long multi-life relationship, not confined to their final narrative. See Walters (2014) for a discussion of their interdependence, along with Sarah Shaw (2018) for a focus on their past lives together.

With regards to the Buddha's birth, many of the details referred to are key elements of the traditional narrative. **Maya, the Buddha's mother, is regularly described as leaving for Lumbini** just before she gives birth. See, for example, *Jatakanidana* (52) and *Buddhacarita* (1.6). It is not clear in most texts why she chose to do this so close to her delivery date. I provide an ambiguous answer of my own: the goddesses of Lumbini were calling her. For a discussion of Lumbini, see Bareau (1987). For a discussion of possible explanations for her decision to visit Lumbini, see Sasson (2007).

An important feature of the Buddha's birth narrative is the fact that **Maya dies seven days after she delivers.** Indeed, this is described in the literature as one of the rules for all Buddhas. See *Majjhima Nikaya* 123 for a list of these Buddha-rules and Strong (2001) for a discussion of how these rules fit into the larger Buddhist narrative (what he calls "the Buddha-life blueprint"). For a discussion of Maya's death, see Ohnuma (2012) and Sasson (2013b).

The scene with the astrologers is not as clear-cut as I have made it seem. At times, the prediction is delivered by the famous sage Asita (for an example, see *Lalitavistara*, 1:150ff), whereas other sources have the news delivered by a group of unnamed Brahmins (*Buddhacarita* 1.30ff), or even named Brahmins (*Jatakanidana* 56). Sometimes the prediction is straightforward (he will become a religious teacher), whereas in other cases the news is two-pronged (*either* he will become a religious teacher *or* he will become a great king). In this book, I have chosen to present the either-or version, but I have added my own justification for this ambiguity (something that does not appear in the traditional accounts): the chief astrologer provides two options because he does not have the courage to tell the king the truth.

For discussion on divination practices in the Buddha's biography, see Sasson (2015). For further discussion, see Fiordalis (2014).

Chapter 2: Monsoon Rain

Yasodhara's naming ceremony is not part of the hagiographical tradition. Indeed, there is no evidence that any ceremony like it was practiced for girls, but I developed one in the hopes that girls did in fact have some kind of ritual life outside of marriage. Rituals ebb and flow, and many of the early rites are surely lost to us now. This means (at least in the context of a novel) that there is space to imagine where facts fail. There is, however, one ritual that continues to be practiced in the Kathmandu Valley specific to girls that may serve as an example (or inspiration). See Lewis (2013). For a discussion of traditional Brahmanic rites of passage, see Michaels (2015).

Mahapajapati is regularly cited as having been Maya's sister. She is beloved in the tradition for many reasons, not the least of which because she raised the future Buddha as her own after her sister's death. According to the *Mahavastu*, the king fell for Maya but could not marry her before her six older sisters were married. He, therefore, asked the father for all seven girls, took Maya and Mahapajapati for himself, and sent the other five to his five brothers (1:356).

After Queen Maya died, the *Lalitavistara* describes an elaborate return journey home from Lumbini Garden, with each of the five hundred noble Sakyan families offering a dwelling place to receive the young prince along the way. The king allowed his son to stay in each of their homes on his way back to the palace, but he could not find a suitable woman to take his wife's place. He then chose Mahapajapati, although why he chose her is not explained (1:149). There is no coronation ceremony described (although I cannot imagine there wasn't something done to recognize her new role in the palace).

The *Buddhacarita* is particularly brief about this important decision, stating simply that the queen (Maya) died and then "his mother's sister, in majesty equal to his mother, brought up the prince . . ." (2:19). Following the tone generated by these texts, I have decided to make Mahapajapati's choice as replacement queen a background affair. See Ohnuma for a discussion of Mahapajapati as a 'leftover woman' (2012).

Regarding **the temple ritual** alluded to in the text (but not really described): the *Mahavastu* claims that when the child was brought to the temple, the infant turned himself towards the goddess' feet first (rather than put his head to her feet) because, as the goddess herself explains in the story, had his head touched her feet, she would have shattered in seven pieces. Because he is cosmically higher even than her—a goddess—it is not appropriate for him to bow to her (2:26). I took the goddess' name (Abhayadevi) from there. The *Jatakanidana* also presents the infant prince turning himself feet forward, but in this case, it is towards a sage named Kaladevala, rather than a temple deity (54). The *Lalitavistara* provides a more elaborate rendition of the temple scene, with all the statues of the gods rising from their places and bowing to the young prince (1:175) as he entered the temple.

Sakka is one of the names of the god known as Indra. He is a prominent character in the Rig Veda and appears repeatedly in early Buddhist sources. He is known as the lord of gods and is in charge of the rains—hence his role in monsoon delivery. See Delavan Perry (1885). One of the most sensuous descriptions of the monsoon I have come across is by Suketu Mehta. His description of the flirting rains is masterful. See his book, *Maximum City: Bombay Lost and Found* (2004).

The Buddha's hagiography generally describes the king as shielding his son from suffering, but little is said about *how* he came to this decision. In the *Jatakanidana*, the king asks his advisors how to avoid losing his son to religion and they matter-of-factly explain the connection between suffering and the religious life (57). I don't think this version of the story holds well. People don't usually cling to a radical decision unless they have come to the decision themselves in a profound way. I, therefore, created **the scene with the ox-cart** to bring the king to the realization himself.

Chapter 3: Adjustments

The hagiographies do not describe visitors from foreign kingdoms coming to the palace, but India has a long history of trade pointing as far back as the Indus Valley Civilization. In this case, I chose to imagine **trade with Zhou envoys** (from today's China). Despite its warring history, the Zhou Dynasty ruled much of China during the period of Yasodhara's life and therefore seemed like a good fit. For an overview of early Chinese dynasties, see Ebrey (2010). For an excellent history of trade between China and India, see Liu (1995).

In this chapter, I introduce some of the important characters in the Buddha's family, especially **Ananda** and **Devadatta**, who are described as brothers in the *Mahavastu* (3:176). Both Ananda and Devadatta become the Buddha's disciples. Ananda becomes his most faithful attendant, while Devadatta becomes his fiercest opponent and eventually tries to split the monastic community. For a discussion of each of the Buddha's main disciples in the Pali tradition, see Nyanaponika Thera and Hecker (1997).

The lion is an obvious metaphor for royalty the world over. Many sources describe the king's seat as being a **lion throne** and some of our earliest Buddhist iconographic representations include a kind of lion throne. See DeCaroli (2015). In Buddhist literature, the Buddha is often associated with lions. He makes his lion's roar with his declaration to achieve Awakening; whenever he lies down, he is described as taking the lion posture; and many of Asoka's pillars are crowned by lions on top. The *Milindapanha* (400) provides a detailed explanation of the lion's qualities and instructs monks to be like a lion in those ways. See Horner's translation (1996).

The scene of the young prince stomping on the throne is a scene my son actually dreamed up when he was about six years old. I had asked him what he would do if he had free access to an entire palace and he answered without hesitation, "Obviously I would jump on the throne!" That seemed right to me.

The reference to **Krishna jumping on Kaliya's head** is a famous Puranic legend in which the poisonous multi-headed serpent Kaliya rose out of a river and attacked Krishna. He responded by jumping on the serpent's many heads until Kaliya begged for mercy. The story can be found in the *Bhagavata Purana*, Book X. For a translation, see Byrant (2004).

Chapter 4: Durga

Nanda is often identified as having been the Buddha's younger stepbrother. In one Pali commentary, as cited by Malalasekera, Nanda was born only a few days after the Buddha (Mahapajapati being one of the king's many wives, even before she took the role of "replacement queen"). When I first began writing this book, I assumed that Nanda was a few years younger than the Buddha, given the immature character he is often associated with. It was only after completing the first draft that I realized my mistake. I then made the creative choice of keeping the text as I had imagined it. Nanda is famous for having been particularly vain, even after becoming a monk. He was reprimanded by the Buddha for wearing ironed robes, painting his eyes and using a fancy begging bowl (*Samyutta Nikaya* 21.8). He even considered giving up monastic life to chase a beautiful woman (*Udana* 3.2). Ashvaghosa produced a book-length poem about Nanda's love affairs; it is translated by Linda Covill as *Handsome Nanda* (2007). All of these associations rendered Nanda much younger in my mind, and thus he stayed that way in this book.

The early literature has preserved a number of characters named Nanda, both male and female (the female version has a long *a* at the end). One of the female Nandas may have been the Buddha's stepsister, but her character is not developed. I have therefore chosen to leave her out of the family biography I have created here. For a discussion of the Buddha's possible stepsister Nanda, see Collett's excellent contribution (2014).

Durga is one of the most important goddesses on the Indian subcontinent. It is not clear how old the legend of her killing the Buffalo Demon is. The story as I relate it here was not in written form during the Buddha's period (earliest evidence begins in the first or second century CE), but oral traditions are sneaky and usually reach further back in time than confirmation allows. See Kinsley's chapter on Durga for discussion of her role in Hinduism (1988). Some have suggested that Durga's trail can be traced all the way back to Harappan civilization. See Asko Parpola's book, *The Roots of Hinduism: The Early Aryans and the Indus Civilization* (2015) for a good overview of the possibilities.

The birth goddess goes by many different names. Depending on location and time period, she may be Hariti, or Bemata, or someone else. She is a complicated deity, because birthing is dangerous and does not always deliver a happy outcome. **Midwives**, meanwhile, are often associated with pollution and low-caste status— mostly because they deal in blood—but they are also dangerous and slightly feared because of their own fearlessness in the face of such profound liminality. Two important books on midwifery and birthing worth considering include Rozario and Samuel (2002) and Van Hollen (2003).

Kaludayi is an important character and future disciple of the Buddha. Sometimes he is known as Udayi, while at other times he is Kaludayi (dark Udayi). He is described in Pali sources as having been the son of one of the king's ministers, a good friend to the prince in his youth, and he eventually became a minister himself (*Jatakanidana* 86). The scene of his mother's death is not part of the tradition, but was a way for me to create further context to Yasodhara's world and introduce Kaludayi at the same time.

Chapter 5: Festival Day

Menstrual taboos have a long history in South Asia (along with everywhere else in the world) with many ritual variations. Indian narratives make reference to confinement during menstruation, such as Draupadi's separation in the *Mahabharata* during the famous scene of the dice game (see Hiltebeitel 1980). In western Nepal, confinement in menstrual huts (*chhaupadi*) continues to be practiced, although it is far from the romantic experience I have presented here. A less extreme isolation practice continues in Sri Lanka, but specifically in reference to a girl's *first* menstruation. See Winslow (1980). One of the earliest texts to identify menstruation as dangerous is the pivotal legal treatise, *Law Code of Manu*. See Olivelle's translation (2009). Although there is a desire to see rituals as static and changeless, research suggests that rituals have a much more fluid history, so it is really impossible to know how a ritual was practiced from one period to the next (or one household to the next). For a discussion of ritual change, see Lincoln (2000). For a discussion of the purity/pollution dichotomy in religious discourse, see Douglas (1966) along with Langenberg's later discussion (2016). For a discussion of Buddhist appropriations of female pollution, see Langenberg (2017).

The story of **Shakuntala** was made famous by the Sanskrit poet, Kalidasa. It is a great love story with heartbreak and confusion running through the core of it (despite the happily-ever-after ending). There is no tradition of Yasodhara encountering this story, but it seemed like a natural fit for her. The story of Shakuntala being guarded by birds in her youth does not appear in Kalidasa's work. That scene appears in the *Mahabharata* (Adi Parva, section 72). The birds who guarded her were called *shakunta*, which is how she received her name.

Both the **plowing festival and the meditation under the rose-apple tree** are regular features of the Buddha's hagiography, but there is much variation. In the *Buddhacarita*, for example, the prince has his experience under the rose-apple tree after watching random farmers plow a field (5:5ff). There is no festival in this account, but in the *Jatakanidana*, the story unfolds in the order I have presented here, with a plowing festival followed by a meditation under a rose-apple tree while everyone is looking elsewhere (57). For a discussion of this scene, see Bareau (1974) and Sasson (2013a).

Chapter 6: Surpanakha

The *Ramayana* is one of the great Indian epics, with as many tellings and variations as imagination will allow. I have referred to this story throughout the book, in part because it is a wonderful story worth incorporating, but also because of its many resonances with the Buddha's hagiography. For an excellent discussion of the endless variations of this beautiful narrative, see Ramanujan (1999). For a lovely retelling of the *Ramayana*, as told from Sita's perspective, see Chitra Banerjee Divakaruni's novel, *The Forest of Enchantments* (2019).

The scene played out in this chapter of the book is a pivotal moment in the narrative. In Valmiki's Sanskrit rendition, **Surpanakha** is a much less sympathetic character than she is made out to be in Kampan's later Tamil version, which I have chosen to follow here. For a translation of Kampan's version, see Hart and Heifetz (1988). The main protagonist, Lord Rama, is often idealized as a perfectly dharmic king, but there are scenes in the epic that suggest a more complicated reality—the scene with Surpanakha being undoubtedly one of these. See Shulman (1979) for a discussion of this complexity, and Erndl (1991) for a discussion of Surpanakha specifically.

I must thank David Shulman for inspiring this chapter. I had the privilege of hearing him give a talk on a *Kudiyattam* performance of this scene when he visited McGill, and his description of the experience has stayed with me ever since. In a *New York Times* piece, he describes the experience of watching 130 hours of *Kudiyattam* performance as life changing. Although most of us rush ourselves towards death, *Kudiyattam* insists "on carrying through a natural rhythm without compromise, without cutting corners, without rushing on to something else that is waiting with its own demands" (2012). I am certain I have not captured the *rasa* fully, but I remain grateful for the inspiration.

Tree worship is a practice found throughout South Asia. Some trees are associated with contemplation, others with death and rebirth, and others still with fertility. Some trees become famous for their relationship with important events or specific miracles—the most famous in Buddhist circles undoubtedly being Mahabodhi (the tree under which the Buddha is said to have achieved Awakening). When a tree is deemed sacred, it becomes part of the community and is decorated with tenderness. A beautiful discussion of tree worship can be found in Haberman's book (2013). One of the most tender examples of tree worship to have recently developed in Buddhist communities is the practice of ordaining individual trees to protect them from deforestation. See Darlington (2012).

Chapter 7: The Choosing

The Choosing is one of my favorite scenes in the Buddha's hagiography. It certainly appeals to my romantic side, ringing of fabulous fairy tales familiar in every part of the world.

The scene appears in a number of early Sanskrit hagiographies, but in small doses and with much variation. The *Mahavastu* sets the scene in a royal park and does not explain the reason for the ritual distribution (2:73). The scene opens with the prince handing out jewels to maidens when his gaze suddenly falls upon Yasodhara. He gives her the necklace from around his neck and she responds (rather audaciously) with, "Is that all I am worth?" He laughs and gives her his ring too.

The *Mulasarvastivada Vinaya*, by contrast, sets the stage in the throne room in front of the Lion Throne, and this time the scene is specifically aimed at finding the prince a wife. All the jewels have been given away by the time Yasodhara ascends the steps. The only piece of jewelry the prince has left is his signet ring. The prince shows it to her and she takes his hand—and presumably his ring at the same time. For a translation and discussion of this scene, see Finnegan (2009).

The *Lalitavistara* provides a similar account, but in this case, she does something even more striking: he tries to give her his ring and she refuses, explaining that she has more than enough jewelry (217).

Chapter 8: The Peacock Garden

Gardens feature prominently in early Indian literature. Both public and private gardens were tended to lovingly, and the sources are replete with descriptions of the many kinds of trees and flowers used to fill them with. The Buddha's palace is regularly described as having had gardens with different colored lotus ponds (*Angutara Nikaya* 3.38). The *Mahavastu* likewise describes a variety of gardens and adds that the palace was surrounded by gardens facing each of the four directions (2:117). In his discussion of gardens in ancient India, Dasgupta (2016) describes a king embellishing his city with gardens, temples, and wells, with "as much love and care as [he] would when adorning his beloved wife with adornments" (137). The Peacock Garden is a garden I made up, but the notion fits in well with the general love of gardens evident in the literature. See also Ali (2003) and Basham (2004).

The issue of the **prince's lack of training** is an important theme in the Buddha's hagiography. If the prince was shielded from suffering, then he could not have been pushed very hard or trained in any way. This is a problem the hagiographers were obviously sensitive to, because the literature tackles it directly—not only to maintain some logical consistency to his narrative, but also to dispel potential charges made against the Buddha by competing religious schools. In the *Jatakanidana*, this concern is presented as a thread of gossip that eventually reaches the king (58). In the *Mahavastu*, the issue of the prince's lack of education is raised by Yasodhara's father after the two chose each other for marriage. So serious is his concern that the father does not want to give his daughter away (2:73). Her father tells the king that the prince has grown up around women and "has made no progress at all."

The *Lalitavistara* resolves this problem by having the prince know everything intuitively: he does not require learning or training because he has mastered all the arts himself. When he goes to school, for example, he asks the teacher which of the sixty-four different scripts he should study, and then proves to have mastered them all. Thankfully, his teacher laughs good-naturedly and marvels at the young man before him (Bays, 1:189–191).

I alluded to this issue earlier in the book (Chapter 4), when Devadatta makes fun of Siddhattha for not having been trained. Although that scene was made up, it was inserted to illustrate what must otherwise have been an ongoing problem in the prince's life. If Dandapani was concerned about the prince's lack of training after the Choosing, it could not have been the first time anyone had mentioned it.

Chapter 9: The Competition

The legend about King Sihahanu (the Buddha's grandfather) and his final battle is not a legend associated with this particular king, but should sound familiar to readers of Buddhist history as its legend belongs to the historical king Asoka who ruled India in the third century BCE. There are many legends associated with Asoka, but one of these is that he gave up warfare after looking at all the dead soldiers left on the battlefield. He became religious (possibly Buddhist) thereafter. Since this is a very important legend in Buddhist circles, I decided to incorporate a reference to it here. For a discussion of some of these Asokan legends, see Strong (1989).

The competition for marriage (*svayamvara*) is a tradition found in many early Indian narratives. Sita (in the *Ramayana*), Kunti and Draupadi (from the *Mahabharata*) are among the many women who have been publicly competed for. In the Buddha's narrative, the scene is played out in a number of hagiographies and includes many exciting details (depending on the version consulted). The *Jatakanidana* provides a very brief description, but we are told that the prince did manage to demonstrate his archery skills in twelve ways that other archers did not match (58). In the *Mahavastu*, the prince demonstrates his extraordinary abilities before the competition has even begun by tossing a dead elephant that was blocking the road over the seven city walls (2:75). In the *Lalitavistara*, the competition is much more elaborate than what I have opted for here, with the prince competing in a very long list of categories that includes writing, astrology, mathematics, wrestling, archery, running, swimming, riding elephants, chariot driving, feats of strength, use of a lasso, striking heavy blows, games of dice, poetry, grammar, painting, drama, instruments, dream interpretation, and more (234).

The story of **King Sihahanu's bow** is not quite as I have told it here. According to the *Mahavastu*, the prince took his grandfather's bow (where he got the bow from is unclear) and threw it into the middle of the arena. He then challenged his fellow contestants to try to draw the bow themselves. Each contestant tried, but none of them was strong enough. The prince then picked it up, drew the bow and shot spectacularly with it (2:76).

When I first sat down to write this chapter, I remembered the story as I have told it here, with the bow being planted in the earth and no one being able to retrieve it.

After completing the chapter, I returned to the texts and discovered that I had gotten the story quite wrong. I had confused King Arthur and his miraculous sword retrieval with this narrative.

I was about to correct my mistake when I thought better of it. If this book is an exercise in hagiographical writing, then part of the experience is (consciously or unconsciously) about weaving together old stories with modern yarn. Storytelling is, moreover, nothing if not at least a little spontaneous. The prince has, therefore, become slightly King Arthur-esque here. And that is just how stories go.

By the sixth century BCE (the period associated with the Buddha's life), the northern gangetic plain had urbanized significantly, with a series of cities and small kingdoms establishing themselves along river lines. One of the most important kingdoms at the time was **Kosala**. The Sakya clan was in fact not a major kingdom (more likely a small chiefdom), eventually massacred by Kosala near the end of the Buddha's life (at least insofar as the Dhammapada Commentary is concerned). See Ghosh (1973) for an overview of early kingdoms and city life in ancient India; also Thapar (1991). For a discussion of Kosala (and its relationship with Magadha—the kingdom that eventually swallowed Kosala), see Kosambi (1952).

The discussions that form **the debate section of the competition** are not in the hagiographies, but each of them is rooted in early Indian literature. The political strategy proposed by the prince comes from the *Mahaparinibbanasutta* (*Digha Nikaya* 16). Here, a king asks the Buddha if he should invade a neighboring kingdom and the Buddha responds with the kinds of questions posed in this chapter as his response.

The second debate topic (on "heavenly matters") does not come from a Buddhist text. It is, rather, one of the central concerns of the *Chandogya Upanishad* and the salt-water exercise is used therein (6:13). The point is not to credit the Buddha with this important Upanishadic passage, but to invite key teachings of the Buddha's period into conversation. For a translation of the *Chandogya Upanishad*, see Roebuck (2004).

The last part of the salt-exercise, however (when the argument concludes on the question of *tasting* truth), is inspired by more than the *Upanishads*. In the *Chandogya Upanishad*, a father teaches his son that Brahman cannot be separated out of anything the way salt cannot be removed from water. But the issue of *tasting* Brahman (which is assumed in the text but not specifically articulated), comes from a conversation I had years ago with an old friend who is the Sheikh of a local mosque. I asked him how he could be so sure God existed. His answer was, "because I can taste the divine." It was the most beautiful answer I had ever heard.

Chapter 10: Wearing the Red Line

The sacrificial fire is one of the most enduring features of Indian religion and manifests in almost every ritual context. It is reasonable to assume that a sacrificial fire was also used during the Buddha and Yasodhara's wedding rite. There is continuity regarding fire ritual in some respects, but there is also evidence of significant variation. How the fire ritual would have manifested in the Buddha's time is therefore unclear, leaving imagination much room to play. For a discussion of ritual change, see again Lincoln (2000). See Payne and Witzel (2016) for a wonderful collection of essays on the varying manifestations of fire ritual.

The wedding ceremony is one of the key rites of passage in Hinduism—especially for women, who in some contexts are not deemed fully initiated into the tradition until they are married. Wedding ceremonies in India can be extremely elaborate affairs lasting many days (if not weeks), with variations across time and place. See Michaels (2004). It is not clear how Siddhattha and Yasodhara would have been married. The hagiographies do not describe the event—they only tell us that it happened. Marriage rites according to early Indian sources could be performed in a number of ways, from "marriage by capture" to the gifting of a bride to the bridegroom. See Pandey (1949) for an overview. Obviously, this story would make little sense if Siddhattha "captured" Yasodhara forcefully (particularly after their mutual choosing), so I have opted for a more egalitarian method. A collection of essays on marginalized marriage narratives by Harlan and Courtright (1995) reveals some of the many variations we might find on this theme.

The issue of **Yasodhara's fertility** has not received much attention in modern scholarship, but if we accept the idea that Yasodhara and the Buddha were co-natals (see notes to Chapter 1), that they were married at sixteen, that he made his Great Departure at twenty-nine, and that their son was born the night he left, then according to that timeline, they would have been married twelve years before she finally conceived.

According to the *Mulasarvastivada Vinaya*, the Buddha's son was conceived on the night of the Great Departure (instead of being born on the night he left), which means that she would have been childless even longer (see Strong 1997). Not to over-psychologize the Buddha's narrative (and diminish its cosmic quality, among other things), but I cannot help but wonder if this childlessness had any effect on the Buddha's increasingly philosophical focus.

Chapter 11: Soil and Suffering

The prince's encounter with suffering is a key moment in his hagiography. According to some tellings, he encounters **farmers plowing a field** and their suffering affects him deeply. The *Buddhacarita* provides a haunting description, with the young prince out for a ride when he comes across this scene. Seeing "the men plowing the fields, their bodies discolored by the wind, the dust, the scorching rays of the sun, oxen wearied by the toil of pulling the plows, great compassion overwhelmed that great noble man" (5:6). He then gets off his horse and begins to pace as he realizes how wretched the world is with all of its suffering and death.

The *Mahavastu* provides a different scenario, but with a similar intent. Here, the prince watches a farmer working when the plow overturns a frog and a snake. A young boy nearby grabs the frog to eat and throws away the snake. This stirs the prince deeply (2:45).

None of the early tellings includes Yasodhara, probably because this is an experience the future Buddha needed to have on his own. But since this is *her* story and since this is a creative project, I decided to have her there for this pivotal moment in his life. They were, after all, co-natals and partners over many lifetimes. By including her here, it also provided me with an opportunity to explore the growing chasm that will separate the two characters as the story progresses.

Birth hierarchies, often limited to discussions of caste in popular discourse, have a long and complicated history in India. Although the idea goes back at least to the Rig Veda, it is unclear how these traditions were interpreted at each stage of development. A number of early passages in the Pali Canon present the Buddha as challenging the supremacy of Brahmins in his community. This has led some to interpret the Buddha as having been "anti-caste," but the situation was probably more nuanced. Occupational divisions were likely well-established by the Buddha's period, but we don't know how far the divisions extended and whether they affected issues like commensality (a major concern in contemporary discussions of caste) or marriage. See Thapar (1991) and Bailey and Mabbett (2003). For these reasons, I have preserved caste distinctions throughout the book, but kept them relatively vague.

When the prince describes what the experience felt like for him, he describes it as an **earthquake.** The texts do not describe his experience this way, but earthquakes play an important role in his larger narrative. Whenever an important moment happens in the Buddha's lifestory, an earthquake accompanies it, marking his development with a cosmic response. For a discussion of earthquakes in the Buddha's lifestory, see the *Milindapanha* (113).

Chapter 12: News

The hagiographies do not tell us anything about **Yasodhara's pregnancy**. There are stories of her being pregnant for an inordinately long period of time (according to the *Mulasarvastivada Vinaya*, she was pregnant for six years, but there are narrative explanations for this that need not concern us here; see Strong (1997); see also, the *Bhadrakalpavadana* translated by Tatelman). We don't know how she felt about becoming pregnant after so many years of childlessness, who she told first, or how she went through the experience. This is not surprising, given that the hagiographies are focused on telling the Buddha's story—not hers. Yasodhara was, after all, just playing a supporting role.

The dream she has in this chapter is a famous past-life narrative familiar throughout the Buddhist world. It is known as the *Vessantara Jataka* and has numerous tellings. It can be found in the Pali Canon as Jataka 547 (see Appleton and Shaw's translation); it is one of the stories recounted by Arya Sura in his Sanskrit collection called the *Jatakamala*; and it is referred to in every list of the Buddha's past lives, such as the Sinhala *Thupavamsa*. The *Vessantara Jataka* is not limited to textual renditions, but is also depicted, recited, performed, and ritualized. See Collins (2016) for an excellent collection of articles on the *Vessantara Jataka*. Also Sarah Shaw's article (2018) where she considers Yasodhara's role specifically.

Yasodhara does not dream the *Vessantara Jataka* in any of the traditional tellings, but since she is part of that past-life narrative (she was Vessantara's wife), the story belongs to her as much as it belongs to him. I thought her dream was a fitting way to include a reference to this important tale.

Chapter 13: The First Sights

The Buddha's horse, **Kanthaka**, is one of the most beloved animals of the Buddhist imagination. We have seen that Yasodhara is co-natal with the Buddha, but she is not alone in this category. Seven beings/objects are said to be co-natal with him. Included among these is both Channa and Kanthaka. Both of these characters are deeply tied to the Buddha, following him from one lifetime to the next. Kanthaka is the one to carry the Buddha as he makes his Great Departure, and, as we shall see, he dies of heartbreak after the Buddha leaves. In the *Vimanavatthu*, Kanthaka proudly introduces himself with a reference to his esteemed co-natal status, declaring, "in the superb city of Kapilavatthu of the Sakyans, I was Kanthaka, conatal with Suddhodana's son" (*Vimanavatthu* 81.15). See Ohnuma (2017) for more on Kanthaka. Although these stories belong to the realm of myths and legends, the idea that the prince had a special connection with his horse is entirely reasonable. Govindarajan's research on animals in Kumaon reminds us of the importance of relatedness that has surely always existed between humans and the animals they care for. See her book, *Animal Intimacies* (2018).

Channa, the Chariot Driver, is also an important companion in the Buddha's lifestory. He is likewise co-natal with the Buddha, follows him dutifully wherever he goes, and is said to have become so attached to the Buddha, that when he became his disciple years later, he could not achieve Awakening. See Malalasekera's entry (1997). The story about Channa's village and childhood is made up.

The story of the **Four Sights** appears in probably every telling of the Buddha's life, for it functions as the inspiration that finally sets him on his way. The texts present the circumstances surrounding the sights differently, and some texts include additional material (for example, the *Buddhacarita* adds a scene of sleeping harem women in his room prior to departure; see *Buddhacarita* Chapter 4), but all sources maintain the tradition of his having seen the Four Sights. In some tellings, the Buddha sees them all at once on the same day (*Digha Nikaya* 14), while in other texts he sees them over a period of a few days (*Jatakanidana* 61). In the *Buddhacarita*, he sees three sights, then has his meditation under the rose-apple tree, and then encounters the fourth (5.16). In some tellings, he leaves the palace with the king's knowledge and blessing (*Abhiniskramanasutra* 107), while in others, it is unclear how he has managed to slip away.

The gods who send the sights down at the appropriate time are indeed part of the Buddha's traditional hagiography. Gods and guardian deities are described as having surrounded the Buddha from the moment he entered his mother's womb, to ensure he makes this final leg of his multi-life journey safely and reaches his goal on time. When he is ready to make his departure, the deities are right above him, watching over him and sending him the signs he needs to take his final steps. See, for example, *Jatakanidana* 59 or *Lalitavistara* 241 for evidence of deity-intervention.

Chapter 14: The Fight

Many seem to assume that the past—even the ancient past—was sterile and prudish. Women did not argue with men, people spoke formally, teacups were always made of china. But this is a Victorian assumption that does not represent the entirety of human history. Early Indian literature is much more textured than any simplistic presumption we might want to make; it has passion, tenderness, fury, and everything in between. To assume sterility is to limit Indian literature in an astounding (and devastatingly ignorant) way. I therefore decided that, although there is no "**fight scene**" in the early sources, there very well could have been. And it was inspired not just by the texture of early Indian storytelling. It was also inspired by my Syrian-Egyptian-Lebanese grandmother (to whom this book is dedicated). Arab women are similarly limited to specific roles in popular imagination. They are expected to be docile and subservient, and they are certainly not "supposed" to argue with their husbands, but my grandmother always finds a way to have her voice heard. She says what she needs to say, when she needs to say it. She is much bigger than any of the little boxes conceived for her. Just as I assume Yasodhara to have been. And Indian writers to have appreciated.

Chapter 15: In the Arms of a Tree

Yasodhara's request that he take her with him seemed like a natural request for her to make. In countless narratives, men go into retreat *with* their families—and not necessarily without them. Rama took Sita with him into exile, even though Lakshmana (his brother) left his wife behind. The Pandava brothers of the *Mahabharata* took their wife Draupadi with them, and in the Buddha's past life as Vessantara, he took his wife with him too. There are, of course, many stories of ascetics leaving their wives behind, but my point is that it could have gone either way. It makes sense for her to have at least asked.

As I explained in the notes to Chapter 13 above, each hagiography arranges the Four Sights differently. In some texts, the Four Sights are delivered at once, whereas in others, the first three are delivered together and the **Fourth Sight** takes place later. I have chosen to follow the *Buddhacarita*'s pattern and have placed the Fourth Sight separately from the other three.

The image of **the monk's footsteps** was inspired by the closing scene of a BBC documentary called, "The Long Search: Footprint of the Buddha," as it follows a monk doing walking meditation in the forest. There is a close-up of the monk's feet that is hauntingly beautiful.

The mask attached to the tree is a practice described by Haberman (2013) in his book on tree worship in India. The masks he encounters in his research are primarily linked with neem trees in contemporary Banares, but the practice is so loving and personal, I can well imagine it extending beyond any one particular context. Haberman insists that the mask helps devotees connect to the goddess; it enhances her personhood in the shape of a tree.

Chapter 16: Departure

As noted above, the early literature does not provide any details about how Yasodhara experienced her pregnancy (with the exception of the legend about a six-year pregnancy). **Her delivery** is, therefore, something I had to imagine for myself. Given the context in which she found herself (with her husband on the verge of leaving), I felt compelled to imagine it as having been a very difficult birth.

The conversation between Siddhattha and the king appears in a number of texts. In the *Buddhacarita*, the prince goes to see his father before his departure and the king begs him to reconsider. He tells him that it is not his time to renounce because he is young, "the mind is fickle" (5:30) and "he is not used to solitude" (5:31). The prince eventually says that he will stay if, and only if, the king can guarantee four things for him: that he will never die, that disease will never strike, that old age will never overtake his youth, and that he will never lose his fortune (5:35). A similar conversation can be found in the *Lalitavistara* (1:301ff).

The prince's response about his **house being on fire** is referred to in the *Buddhacarita*, when he tells his father not to hold him back, "for it is not right to obstruct a man who's trying to escape from a burning house" (5:37). This metaphor takes on a life of its own in later Buddhist literature. In particular, it is at the root of one of the most important parables in the *Lotus Sutra*, when a father contemplates how to save his sons from a burning house. See Chapter 3 of Watson's translation (1994).

Mahapajapati's character in this telling deserves a comment here. Mahapajapati becomes a very important character in the Buddhist tradition, not only because she raised the prince after her sister's death, but also because—years later—she leads a group of women into the forest to be ordained. She therefore becomes a hero in her own right, and according to an important contribution by Walters, she may have been the Buddha's female counterpart once the monastic orders were established. See Walters (1994) for this argument.

Despite this heroic conclusion to her story, it is unclear what Mahapajapati's life was like during the palace years. Maya is idealized in the literature, which must have made Mahapajapati's life in the palace difficult by comparison. I have, therefore, decided to paint her as a background character, regularly overlooked—especially by the king—until she finally pulls herself out of the shadows and shines on her own. Once again, see Ohnuma for a discussion of Mahapajapati as a 'leftover woman' (2012).

Siddhattha's defense of Nanda as having more potential than the king realizes is an important ingredient in the larger narrative. As mentioned above (notes to Chapter

4), Nanda struggled with sensual desire throughout his life. Even after he followed the Buddha and became a monk, he struggled, but the Buddha did not give up on his sibling. Instead, he worked with him until Nanda finally freed himself of his attachments. This is why I have Siddhattha defending Nanda here. The method the Buddha chose to teach his brother, however, was to create an illusion of beautiful women turning into corpses so as to replace desire with disgust. See in particular Liz Wilson's important book, *Charming Cadavers* (1996) for a discussion of this theme.

Chapter 17: Sadness

The *Law Code of Manu* identifies **birth as a polluting event** (5:61ff), a theme that continues throughout Indian literature in a variety of forms. It is not obvious what ritual would have been performed to cleanse the area of Yasodhara's afterbirth, but it is reasonable to expect some kind of ritual event. See again Langenberg (2017) for discussion of how this has been appropriated into Buddhist narratives, as well as Van Hollen (2003) and Sasson (2009).

The Great Sadness is an obvious reference to what we know today as Post-Partum Depression. The term does not appear in the early hagiographical literature, but it made sense to include it given Yasodhara's general experience of loss after the prince's departure. As we shall see in the coming chapters, Yasodhara is described in many early tellings as having experienced profound sadness after he left. Since he made his departure the night she gave birth, I could not help but imagine that she experienced some kind of post-partum depression. Although I am basing this interpretation on contemporary understandings of post-partum depression, I don't think we are the first to identify it. To be honest, I think we have come to the discussion rather late in the game . . .

Chapter 18: Tapestries

Yasodhara's pain after the Great Departure is recorded in a number of sources. The future Buddha was on a heroic adventure that would (according to Buddhist doctrine at least) save the world, but the hagiographies regularly remind us that his departure broke many hearts in the process. In the *Buddhacarita*, Yasodhara challenges Channa for having taken her beloved away and even accuses Kanthaka for having been complicit in this betrayal (8.31ff). Later tellings elaborate on this theme, such as the *Bhadrakalpavadana* (translated by Tatelman) and the twentieth-century Newari poem, *Sugata Saurabha* by Chittadhar Hrdaya, in which she accuses

Channa of the betrayal only to realize that he is just as devastated as she is. She then wanders aimlessly through the gardens they used to frequent together, lamenting her loss. See Lewis and Tuladhar's translation (2010). Obeyesekere explores the history of Yasodhara's laments in a very important book on the subject and describes how her sadness has become the source of funeral liturgy in Sri Lanka (2009). Perhaps one of the most striking tellings comes from the ex-Dalit poet, Hira Bansode. She opens her poem with a cry to Yasodhara, in which she says, "O Yashodara! You are like a dream of sharp pain, long-life sorrow." See Zelliot for a translation and discussion (1992).

The gods intervene during the Great Departure in a number of ways. The *Jatakanidana* describes Kanthaka neighing loudly with joy as he charges across the road and the gods muffling the sound so that no one hears it (62). In the *Buddhacarita*, by contrast, Kanthaka keeps silent, clenching his jaws so to avoid making noise (5.80). In both texts, along with many others, gods catch his hooves in the palms of their hands (*Jatakanidana* 62 and *Buddhacarita* 5.81). In the *Lalitavistara*, the gods silence the noise of the city and plunge its subjects into a deep sleep, so that the prince can make his great escape. All of these details serve to remind the reader that the cosmos was an active participant in the Buddha's narrative.

When they reach the closed gates, the *Jatakanidana* tells us that the prince was prepared to push his valiant steed over the gates if necessary. Chandaka, in the meanwhile (who is clutching Kanthaka's tail) is likewise ready for a jump, as is Kanthaka the horse, who tells himself that he will jump if required. But just as all of these heroic thoughts are circulating, the gods appear and **swing open the gates for them** (63).

Indian storytelling often sends its ascetics into the **forest** for some period of time. Forests were places of danger and power, filled with insects, animals and all kinds of unseen creatures. They were not for the faint of heart, especially 2,000 years ago, when they must have been immense—nothing like the small strips of trees we tend to call forests today. Indeed, each time I tried to imagine a forest for this book, I found myself reaching the limits of my imagination. I knew the forests of my world were nothing like what they must have once been. The manga series, *Buddha*, by Osamu Tezuka (2014) does an especially nice job of engaging the forest in his series. For a discussion about the power of ascetics (and by extension, their ability to face the forest), see Carl Olson's book, *Indian Asceticism* (2015).

The image of **the prince cutting off his hair** is an important moment in the Buddha's hagiography. As mentioned in the notes to the Prologue, hair cutting has tremendous significance as a symbol of renunciation. Of course, unshorn hair can also serve as a symbol of renunciation, with ascetics letting their hair grow wild as an alternative means of representing their departure from householder life. For an excellent discussion of hair in South Asian culture, see Hiltebeitel and Miller (1998). The scene of the prince cutting off his hair can be found in many early Buddhist reliefs; for textual descriptions, see the *Jatakanidana* (65), the *Mahavastu* (2:165), and the *Abhiniskramanasutra* (144) for examples.

Kanthaka's death is one of the most tragic elements of the Buddha's Great Departure. In some accounts, Kanthaka returns to Kapilavatthu with Channa (*Buddhacarita* 8:1ff), but in the *Jatakanidana*, he dies broken-hearted after his master has abandoned him (65). The flower petals overwhelming him is not part of Kanthaka's death story, but is a detail that arises elsewhere in the *Jatakanidana* that I wanted to incorporate. A bit earlier in the narrative, while Kanthaka is carrying his master into freedom, the text tells us that the sky was filled with deities showering the prince with their offerings. Flowers and garlands were poured over them as they made their way out. Normally, so the text explains, Kanthaka could cover the distance of three kingdoms in one night; he could even cover the distance of the universe end to end had he so desired. But on this night, his progress was impeded because of all the flowers that filled the road around him and reached up to his flanks (64). In this telling, I chose to combine the imagery of both scenes into one, having him die at the forest edge in a sea of flowers. Poetic license is my justification.

Kisa Gotami is an important character in the Buddha's lifestory. I reserve my notes for her when she returns to the stage in the closing chapter of this book.

Chapter 19: Holding on and Letting go

A number of sources tell us that **the king commissioned two ministers to find his son** and bring him home. This mission did not succeed (at least at first). The texts do not tell us who was sent, so I inserted familiar characters here for the role. As we shall see, Kaludayi will eventually accompany the Buddha home for a visit, but at first, none of the king's ambassadors manage to convince the Buddha to return.

In the *Buddhacarita*, the king sends two of his councilors (8:82) to look for the Buddha. The *Abhiniskramanasutra* likewise tells us that two ministers were sent and includes a long and very emotional conversation between the Buddha and the visiting ministers. They try very hard to convince him to return, but the Buddha remains steadfast. The two ministers return to the palace, unsure of what to tell the king (161ff).

Chapter 20: Out the Gates

The scenes in this chapter were created for continuity; they are not part of any of the traditional hagiographies I am familiar with.

Chapter 21: Devadatta

I debated a long time about including the scene of **Devadatta's attack on Yasodhara.** Although Devadatta is vilified the Buddhist world over (the *Lotus Sutra* presents an alternative representation, but it was produced as a counter-argument to an established tradition and thus ultimately functions as further evidence of Devadatta's vilification), Pali sources do not go so far as to imagine him assaulting Yasodhara after the departure. This scene will be shocking to some readers as a result.

In certain Sanskrit, Tibetan, and Newari narratives, however, Devadatta *does* assault Yasodhara, which makes sense given his unabated thirst for power and her state of vulnerability. See Finnegan for a translation and discussion of this scene in the *Mulasarvastivada Vinaya* (2009), along with Tatelman (1998) for a translation of the dramatic Newari version.

In most versions of this tale, though, a co-wife helps Yasodhara fend off the attack. One draws blood from his hand, while the other tosses him out the window. I decided not to include stories about co-wives in this telling and to focus on Yasodhara exclusively (the co-wives are not consistently named or identified in the literature, nor do they play important roles in most cases, so the focus on Yasodhara was fair to my mind). I chose to replace the co-wife with Mahapajapati. If anyone was strong enough to toss an assailant out of a window, I think it would have been her.

Devadatta does not make further appearances in Yasodhara's life after this scene. Eventually, he joins the Buddha's order, although when he chooses to do this is unclear. If any narrative logic is to be expected, I think it would be safe to assume that he renounces after this failed attempt at seizing power. Soon enough, however, Devadatta will try to seize the monastic order from the Buddha. He will fail in that endeavor too.

Chapter 22: Splendor

The gift of a bronze casting of a plow is inspired by a piece on permanent exhibit at the National Museum of India in New Delhi. It belongs to a collection from the

Indus Valley Civilization and is a striking example of ancient Indian art. This story takes place much later, and I, therefore, imagine the gift as being more sophisticated than that which was produced during the Indus Valley Civilization, but I could not shake that bronze piece out of my head, so I included it here. For a study of the Indus Valley Civilization and its crafts, see Chakrabarti (2006).

Rahula's naming ceremony is not part of the tradition, but a ritual must have been performed. With regards to the meaning of **Rahula's name**, consensus has not been reached. There are generally two theories to explain it: either it has something to do with the planet Rahu (as I have presented in this chapter) or it can be interpreted as having something to do with an obstacle (that theory will be referred to in Chapter 24). For a discussion, see Crosby (2013).

Reference to the **Ganga falling over Shiva's head** is an important Puranic legend that can be found in a number of sources. See, for example, the *Siva Purana* (5:38), and Doniger (1973) for a discussion.

Yasodhara's decision to appropriate her status as a widow and the paradox it represents is beautifully articulated in the *Buddhacarita*: when the ministers find the Buddha in the forest and beg him to return to the palace, they describe Yasodhara as an "anguished wife who is widowed although her husband is alive" (9:27). The Newari *Bhadrakalpavadana* describes her shedding her royal attire for a life of widowhood: she puts off her colorful garments, trades them in for white cloth and eschews all adornments and oils (Tatelman 202).

The notion that **a renunciant becomes socially dead** emerges out of interpretations of the *Samnyasa Upanishads*, rendering the wife a widow as a result. See Olivelle's discussion and translation (1992). See Nagarajan (2018) for a discussion of women and auspiciousness (and by extension, the loss of auspiciousness in widowhood). See also Vidyasagar (2012) for a discussion of widowhood in early Hinduism and a nineteenth-century challenge to some of the practices attached. See also Shanti Mishra's novel, *A Widow's Gift* (2008) for a touching exploration of widowhood in contemporary Nepal.

Chapter 23: The Return

Serpent-deities, traditionally known as nagas, are important mythological beings in early Indian narratives. They generally occupy space below the earth, but some are also said to inhabit the sky. They are protectors of the Buddha, his relics, and his order, but they are not always safe creatures to interact with. They are unpredictable and fiery. For a discussion of nagas in the early Buddhist imaginary, see DeCaroli (2004).

Termite mounds are often worshiped in South India and Sri Lanka today, but evidence suggests they have served as ritual sites throughout the subcontinent from the Vedic period onwards (see Irwin 1982). As mentioned a few times in these notes, rituals are rarely static and change continually with time and place. Termite-mound worship has been performed with a wide range of interpretations, but they are often associated with nagas, fertility, and even ancestor worship. See Rigopoulos (2014) for further discussion.

Along with the first two messengers sent by the king (see notes to Chapter 19), there is also a narrative tradition that **the king continued sending messengers to find his son** and bring him home, but none of them returned. See Rockhill for a reference (51), as well as the *Jatakanidana* (86). Kaludayi now plays his big part in the story: after having sent out nine thousand men to summon the Buddha (at least according to the account provided by the *Jatakanidana*), none of whom returned, the king asks Kaludayi to try. Kaludayi agrees, but on the condition that he may receive permission to become a monk thereafter. The king agrees and Kaludayi brings the Buddha home.

The many male family members who followed the Buddha into renunciation form the beginning of the Buddha's sangha. We have already gotten to know Ananda and Devadatta, both of whom become disciples. Anuruddha (who we briefly encountered) and Nanda (the Buddha's stepbrother) eventually also join the community. See again Nyanaponika Thera and Hecker (1997) for character sketches of some of the Buddha's primary disciples.

Mahapajapati's request for the women to see the Buddha separately appears in the *Mulasarvastivada Vinaya*. See Finnegan for a discussion and translation (2009). See also Rockhill (58). Mahapajapati broaches the subject with the king, explaining that the women would like to hear the sweet teachings of the Buddha and proposes taking them herself after the men have had their time with him. Permission is swiftly granted. This scene is important because it reveals Mahapajapati as a burgeoning leader in the community—a role she will grow into with increasing strength.

There are different versions of **the Buddha's return to Kapilavatthu**. In a number of tellings, the Buddha greets the community in a grove outside the palace. According to the *Mahavastu*, the king made the journey to the grove with a host of Sakya nobility walking behind him (3:116). A wonderful side-note included in this text is the concern the Buddha felt about how the greeting would be played out. As the greatest being in the universe, he could not stand up in the king's presence (because he was higher than the king), but he knew how proud the Sakya people were and did not want to offend them by remaining seated in front of the king. He, therefore, opted for levitation as his alternative: he lifted himself into the air and greeted his father from there! The text tells us that Yasodhara was part of the entourage at this time.

The *Sugata Saurabha* has the king hearing about his son's return from others and he rushes out to find him. He sees the Buddha begging for alms in the street and becomes "dumbfounded for a while" (213). The king forgets to speak at first, but then recovers and tells his son that a man of his pedigree should never beg. The Buddha gives his father a teaching and the king's heart softens. They return to the palace together, hand in hand, "together they went, like the hand and the spun yarn of the spinner near the spindle" (216). According to the *Abhiniskramanasutra*, the Buddha is first greeted while residing in a grove. Then the king invites his son for a meal at the palace and **Yasodhara watches him from a window** (360). I have simplified the story here and placed the Buddha in the palace courtyard right away.

According to a number of tellings, **Yasodhara was the one to tell Rahula that the Buddha was his father**. In the *Jatakanidana*, this is played out quite directly—she tells him that the Buddha is his father with little additional context provided (91). In the *Mahavastu*, however, a royal declaration forbids anyone from revealing this fact to Rahula about his father on pain of death. Yasodhara refuses to abide and valiantly tells her son the truth (3:258), regardless of the threatened consequences.

Yasodhara's line, "go and ask him about your inheritance" will be familiar to many readers. In the *Jatakanidana*, Yasodhara tells her son to ask his father for his wealth and treasures so that he might become a king himself (91). In the *Abhiniskramanasutra*, she tells her son to ask without any explanation why (362). The *Mahavastu* provides two different versions of this scene. In one, she sends Rahula with a plate of sweets and tells him to ask for his wealth. In a second version, however, Rahula himself clings to the Buddha's robe as soon as he learns that he is his son and declares that he will follow him into a life of renunciation (3:262), never even asking for his inheritance. See Crosby's chapter for further discussion (2013).

Yasodhara's refusal to join the others in the courtyard is narrated in a few sources. According to the *Jatakanidana*, she justifies herself with the statement, "if there is any virtue in me, my lord will come to me himself; when he comes to me, I will worship him" (90). This expresses some of the complexity she must have felt as the abandoned wife, as she tries to reclaim some of her dignity. In the Thai poem, translated by Donald Swearer as "Bimba's Lament" (1995), Yasodhara cries with pain and sadness in front of her father-in-law. The king relays this to the Buddha, telling him that if does not visit Yasodhara, she will die of a broken heart (549).

Chapter 24: Overcoming Obstacles

This was, without a doubt, the most difficult chapter to write. Although I could write Siddhattha's character before he reached Awakening, I struggled with his character once he became the Buddha. **How does a Buddha talk?** And even more daunting, how exactly did this particular conversation go? Many texts allude to there having been some kind of conversation between the Buddha and Yasodhara, but none of them tells us much about how it went. This scene is part of the Buddha's traditional hagiography, and yet it remains apart at the same time. As though the authors did not know how to get close to it.

The few texts that do allude to the content of their discussion were, unfortunately, often unkind to Yasodhara about it. The *Mahavastu* (3:142) describes Yasodhara trying to seduce the Buddha during their meeting. Even worse, the Buddha later explains that this was not the first time Yasodhara tried to entice him: in a past life, she did the same thing. In other words, according to the *Mahavastu*, this was a pattern.

Other texts, however, tell us that as soon as she saw him, **Yasodhara fell sobbing at the Buddha's feet** and clutched his ankles. See the Sinhala poem the 'Yasodharavata', translated and discussed by Obeyesekere (2009). See also Bareau's article on Yasodhara for further discussion (1982).

The scene of the couple floating on clouds does not come from any of the traditional sources. After months of pondering the question of how this scene should play out, I finally decided that it required some playfulness. Buddhist literature is filled with fantastical teaching moments conjured by the Buddha for the benefit of his audience. I decided that this moment required something to that effect. It is a scene inspired by Buddhist storytelling, but the product of my own imagination at the same time.

The Buddha's reference to having visited Yasodhara and Rahula on the night of his departure comes from the *Jatakanidana*: just before leaving, he goes to her room and finds the two of them sleeping, she with her hand resting on Rahula. He thinks to himself, "If I remove the queen's hand and take my son into my arms she will wake up, and that will prevent my journey. I will come back after gaining Enlightenment and then see him" (62). This is, to me, one of the most painful moments in his hagiography. We feel his longing for his family and the paradoxical pull towards renunciation at the same time.

The reference to **Rahula's education** was referred to in the Prologue. It is not clear how Rahula's departure into a life of renunciation would have been interpreted at the time, since he was the first child to be ordained into the Buddhist community (his age later becoming the minimum requirement for novices). In ancient India, high-caste male children were often initiated into the Vedic tradition by a guru who would provide teachings away from home. Although I cannot be sure, I suspect that Rahula's departure from home functioned as a kind of socially acceptable educational opportunity and I chose to explain the Buddha's decision to take him into the forest this way. I otherwise cannot see the logic behind Rahula's departure at this stage. For a discussion of education in ancient India, see Scharfe (2002).

Chapter 25: Departures

I made a few creative decisions as I neared the end of this book to bring loose threads together. One of these decisions was to bring Kisa Gotami in to help carry us to the finish line.

Kisa Gotami made an appearance in Chapter 18. She is a well-known disciple of the Buddha with a very sad story to tell. There is no evidence that the two women met prior to their ordination, but her story is certainly well anchored in the tradition and I decided to include a reference to it here. Kisa Gotami's verses can be found in the *Therigatha* (213–223). The commentator Dhammapala narrates some of her story in the *Therigatha Commentary* (175ff). For a discussion of Kisa Gotami and motherhood, see again Ohnuma (2012) and Collett (2016).

Mahapajapati's departure marks the beginning of a female sangha. She leaves the palace with five hundred Sakyan women in tow, and together they ask the Buddha for ordination. The Buddha, however, does not receive her request well. He refuses her three times, thereby sending Mahapajapati into temporary limbo (having renounced the palace, she cannot go back; but because he refused her, she is left with nowhere to go). Eventually, Ananda intercedes on her behalf and helps her gain a second audience with the Buddha. This time, the Buddha accepts her request, but it will come with heavy conditions attached. For a textual source, see in particular the Pali Vinaya account, found in Cullavaga X. For a translation, see Horner (1997).

This moment in Buddhist history has left many readers puzzled and has generated a number of responses. See, for example, Sponberg (1992), Wilson (2002), and Blackstone (1999). The Buddha's decision to limit women's ordination status with these heavy conditions has led to a number of painful consequences that continue to affect women's ordination status in certain Buddhist contexts today. For an excellent collection of writings on this topic, see Mohr and Tsedroen (2010).

It is for this reason that I have Yasodhara appear shocked at Mahapajapati's audacity. She asks her how she can join the order when they are all men, and Mahapajapati responds with, **"I see no reason why women cannot join them . . . Why should he say no?"**

Study Questions

1   The author uses Buddhist texts from all over the Buddhist tradition, but which one is the "right one"? How does a religion operate with so many different sacred texts at its disposal?

2   Given that there are so many sacred texts throughout the Buddhist world—texts from India, China, Japan, Sri Lanka, Nepal, etc.—is it possible that the West will eventually produce its own sacred Buddhist material?

3   Does the author have the "right" to tell the story in her own voice, with her own interpretations?

4   Siddhattha left his wife and newborn son (and his father and his kingdom and his horse) without looking back. How does he get away with that? How do Buddhists look up to a teacher who left so many behind? How did you feel about his departure?

5   Why couldn't Siddhattha become the Buddha at home, with Yasodhara beside him? Why did he have to leave to become the Buddha?

6   With this story, is Buddhism declaring that it is in an either-or situation? *Either* one seeks Awakening, *or* one remains at home as a householder, but never both?

7   Who was Yasodhara really married to? An ordinary man who achieved Awakening, or something "other?"

8   Why are there gods in the sky pulling strings? What does this say about the story?

9   What are your thoughts on the Bleeding (menstruation) and the concept of pollution so often associated with it?

10   After Yasodhara gives birth, she falls into what her mother calls the Great Sadness. We have only recently begun to discuss post-partum depression in the contemporary context. Is it possible that women would have known what this was in classical India? Would they have had their own language for it?

11   Was it realistic to depict Yasodhara fighting with her husband, as happens in the chapter entitled, The Fight? Do you expect women in classical India to have been meek and subservient? If so, why? If not, why not?

12   Kanthaka, the horse, dies of heartbreak. Is this entirely fantastical or do you think animals can experience attachment and abandonment this way?

13   The Buddha returns to Kapilavatthu to see his father (the king). He then takes his son back to the forest with him, to provide him with his "inheritance"—the

teachings that will free him from suffering. But bringing a child into the forest to follow the same regimented lifestyle that adult monks pursue is a complicated decision. Do you think children can live like monks? Buddhist monastic rules are eventually tailored to meet some of the needs of children living in monastic community; rules are likewise established about parental consent (so that children cannot leave home without it) and full ordination is limited to adulthood (child monasticism is therefore temporary and not binding until full vows are taken later in life). Would these kinds of rules be enough? What benefits (and challenges) can you imagine child monasticism might generate? Would you have wanted some monastic training in your youth? Would you have hated it?

14 What do you expect will happen with the women's departure at the end of the book? What might this ending say about women's aspirations in classical India?

15 Do you ever feel like abandoning everything and walking away?

Further Reading

Primary Sources in Translation

Ācariya cariya Dhammapāla. *The Commentary on the Verses of the Therīs: Therīgāthā-Aṭṭhakathā*. Translated by William Pruitt. Oxford: The Pali Text Society, 1999.

Appleton, Naomi and Sarah Shaw, trans. *The Ten Great Birth Stories of the Buddha: The Mahānipāta of the Jātakatthavaṇṇanā*. 2 vols. Chiang Mai: Silkworm, 2015.

Ārya Śūra. *Once the Buddha was a Monkey: AryaŚūra's Jātakamālā*. Translated by Peter Khoroche. Chicago: University of Chicago Press, 2006.

Ashvaghosa. *Handsome Nanda*. Translated by Linda Covill. Clay Sanskrit Library. New York: 2007.

Aśvaghoṣa. *Life of the Buddha (Buddhacarita)*. Translated by Patrick Olivelle. New York: New York University Press, 2008.

Bays, Gwendolyn, trans. *The Lalitavistara Sūtra: The Voice of the Buddha*. 2 vols. Berkeley: Dharma Publishing, 1983.

Beal, Samuel, trans. *The Romantic Legend of Śākya Buddha: A Translation of the Chinese Version of the Abhiniṣkramaṇasūtra*. Delhi: Motilal Banarsidass, 1875.

Berkwitz, Stephen C., trans. *The History of the Buddha's Relic Shrine: A Translation of the Sinhala Thūpavaṃsa*. New York: Oxford University Press, 2007.

Bhikkhu Bodhi, trans. *The Connected Discourses of the Buddha: A New Translation of the Saṃyutta Nikāya*. 2 vols. Boston: Wisdom, 2000.

Bhikkhu Ñāṇamoli and Bhikkhu Bodhi, trans. *The Middle Length Discourses of the Buddha: A New Translation of the Majjhima Nikāya*. Boston: Wisdom, 1995.

Bryant, Edwin, trans. *Krishna: The Beautiful Legend of God (Srimad Bhagavata Purana Book X)*. New York: Penguin Classics, 2004.

Geiger, Wilhelm, trans. *The Mahāvaṃsa or the Great Chronicle of Ceylon*. New Delhi: Asian Educational Services, 2002.

Hart, George L. and Hank Heifetz, trans. *The Forest Book of the Ramayana of Kampan*. Berkeley and Los Angeles: University of California Press, 1988.

Horner, I. B., trans. *Milinda's Questions*. 2 vols. Oxford: The Pali Text Society, 1996.

Horner, I. B., trans. *The Book of Discipline (Vinaya-Piṭaka)*. 6 vols. Oxford: The Pali Text Society, 1996–1997.

Hrdaya, Chittadhar. *Sugata Saurabha: An Epic Poem from Nepal on the Life of the Buddha*. Translated by Todd T. Lewis and Subarna Man Tuladhar. New York: Oxford University Press, 2010.

Jayawickrama, N. A., trans. *The Story of Gotama Buddha (Jātaka-nidāna)*. Oxford: The Pali Text Society, 2002.

Jones, J. J., trans. *The Mahāvastu*. 3 vols. London: The Pali Text Society. 1976–1987.

Kalidasa. *The Recognition of Shakūntala*. Translated by Somadeva Vasudeva. Clay Sanskrit Library. New York: New York University Press, 2006.

Olivelle, Patrick, trans. *Saṃnyāsa Upaniṣads: Hindu Scriptures on Asceticism and Renunciation*. New York: Oxford University Press, 1992.

Olivelle, Patrick, trans. *Law Code of Manu*. New York: Oxford University Press, 2009.

Rhys-Davids, C. A. F. and K. R. Norman, trans. *Poems of Early Buddhist Nuns (Therīgāthā)*. Oxford: The Pali Text Society, 1997.

Rockhill, W. Woodville, trans. *The Life of the Buddha and the Early History of his Order, Derived from Tibetan Works in the Bkah-Hgyur and Bstan-Hgyur*. New Delhi: Asian Educational Services, 1992.

Roebuck, Valerie J., trans. *The Upanishads*. London: Penguin Classics, 2004.

Swearer, Donald K. "Bimbā's Lament." In *Buddhism in Practice*, ed. Donald S. Lopez, Jr., 541–552. Princeton Readings in Religion. New Haven: Princeton University Press, 1995.

Tatelman, Joel. "The Trials of Yasodharā: A Translation of the *Bhadrakalpāvadāna* II & III." *Buddhist Literature* I (1998), 176–261.

Vidyasagar, Ishvarchandra. *Hindu Widow Marriage: An Epochal Work on Social Reform From Colonial India*, trans. Brian A. Hatcher. New York: Columbia University Press, 2012.

Walshe, Maurice, trans. *The Long Discourses of the Buddha: A Translation of the Dīgha Nikāya*. Boston: Shambhala, 1995.

Watson, Burton, trans. *The Lotus Sutra*. New York: Columbia University Press, 1994.

Woodword, F. L., trans. *The Minor Anthologies of the Pali Canon, Part II: Udāna (Verses of Uplift) and Itivuttaka (As It Was)*. Oxford: The Pali Text Society, 1996.

Secondary Sources

Ali, Daud. "Gardens in Early Indian Court Life." *Studies in History* 19.2 (2003): 221–252.

Bailey, Greg and Ian Mabbett. *The Sociology of Early Buddhism*. Cambridge: Cambridge University Press, 2003.

Bareau, A. "La jeunesse du Buddha dans les Sūtrapitaka et Vinayapitaka anciens." *Bulletin de l'école Française d'Extrême-Orient* 61 (1974), 199–274.

Bareau, A. "Un personnage bien mystérieux: l'épouse du Buddha." In *Indological and Buddhist Studies: Volume in Honour of Professor J. W. de Jong on his Sixtieth Birthday*, ed. L. A. Hercus et al., 31–59. Canberra: Faculty of Asian Studies, 1982.

Bareau, A. "Luminī et la naissance du futur buddha." *Bulletin de l'école Française d'Extrême-Orient* 76 (1987), 69–81.

Basham, A. L. *The Wonder That Was India: A Survey of the History and Culture of the Indian Sub-Continent Before the Coming of the Muslims*. Third revised edition. London: Picador, 2004.

Blackstone, Kate. "Damming the Dhamma: Problems with Bhikkhunīs in the Pali Vinaya." *Journal of Buddhist Ethics* 6 (1999): 292–312.

Chakrabarti, Dilip K. *The Oxford Companion to Indian Archaeology: The Archaeological Foundations of Ancient India*. New York: Oxford University Press, 2006.

Collett, Alice. "Therīgāthā: Nandā, Female Sibling of Gotama Buddha." In *Women in Early Buddhism: Comparative Textual Studies*, edited by Alice Collett, 140–159. New York: Oxford University Press, 2014.

Collett, Alice. *Lives of Early Buddhist Nuns: Biographies as History*. New Delhi: Oxford University Press, 2016.

Collins, Steven, ed. *Readings of the Vessantara Jataka*. New York: Columbia University Press, 2016.

Crosby, Kate. "The Inheritance of Rāhula: Abandoned Child, Boy Monk, Ideal Son and Trainee." In *Little Buddhas: Children and Childhoods in Buddhist Texts and Traditions*, edited by Vanessa R. Sasson, 97–123. New York: Oxford University Press, 2013.

Darlington, Susan M. *The Ordination of a Tree: The Thai Buddhist Environmental Movement*. New York: SUNY Press, 2012.

Dasgupta, Nupur. "Gardens in Ancient India: Concepts, Practices, and Imaginations." *Puravritta: Journal of the Directorate of Achaeology and Museums* 1 (2016): 133–151.

DeCaroli, Robert. *Haunting the Buddha: Indian Popular Religions and the Formation of Buddhism*. New York: Oxford University Press, 2004.

DeCaroli, Robert. *Image Problems: The Origin and Development of the Buddha's Image in Early South Asia*. Seattle: University of Washington Press, 2015.

Delavan Perry, Edward. "Indra in the Rig Veda." *Journal of the American Oriental Society* 11 (1885), 117–208.

Divakaruni, Chitra Banerjee. *The Forest of Enchantments*. Delhi: Harper, 2019.

Doniger O'Flaherty, Wendy. *Śiva: The Erotic Ascetic*. Oxford: Oxford University Press, 1973.

Douglas, Mary. *Purity and Danger: An Analysis of Concepts of Pollution and Taboo*. London: Routledge, 1966.

Ebrey, Patricia Buckley. *The Cambridge Illustrated History of China*. New York: Cambridge University Press, 2010.

Erndl, Kathleen M. "The Mutilation of Śupaṇakhā." In *Many Rāmāyaṇas: The Diversity of a Narrative Tradition in South Asia*, edited by Paula Richman, 67–88. Berkeley: University of California Press, 1991.

Finnegan, Diana Damchö. *For the Sake of Women Too: Ethics and Gender in the Narratives of the Mūlasarvāstivāda Vinaya*. PhD diss. University of Wisconsin-Madison, 2009.

Fiordalis, David. "On Buddhism, Divination, and the Worldly Arts: Textual Evidence from the Theravāda Tradition." *Indian International Journal of Buddhist Studies* 15 (2014): 79–108.

Ghosh, A. *The City in Early Historical India*. Simla: Indian Institute of Advanced Study, 1973.

Govindarajan, Radhika. *Animal Intimacies: Interspecies Relatedness in India's Central Himalayas*. Chicago: University of Chicago Press, 2018.

Haberman, David L. *People Trees: Worship of Trees in Northern India*. New York: Oxford University Press, 2013.

Harlan, Lindsey and Paul B. Courtright, eds. *From the Margins of Hindu Marriage: Essays on Gender, Religion and Culture*. New York: Oxford University Press, 1995.

Heirman, Ann. "Washing and Dyeing Buddhist Monastic Robes." *Acta Orientalia Academiae Scientiarum Hung* 67.4 (2014): 467–488.

Hiltebeitel, Alf. "Draupadī's Garments." *Indo-Iranian Journal* 22 (1980): 97–112.

Hiltebeitel, Alf and Barbra D. Miller, eds. *Hair: Its Power and Meaning in Asian Cultures*. New York: SUNY, 1998.

Horner, I. B., "The Buddha's Co-Natals." In *Studies in Pali and Buddhism: A Memorial Volume in Honor of Bhikkhu Jagdish Kashyap*, edited by A. K. Narain, 115–120. Delhi: B. R. Publishing, 1979.

Irwin, John C. "The Sacred Anthill and the Cult of the Primordial Mound." *History of Religions* 21.4 (1982): 339–360.

Isayeva, Natalia. *Shankara and Indian Philosophy*. New York: SUNY, 1993.

Kinsley, David. *Hindu Goddesses: Visions of the Divine Feminine in the Hindu Religious Tradition*. Berkeley: University of California Press, 1988.

Kloppenborg, Ria "The Earliest Buddhist Ritual of Ordination." In *Selected Studies on Ritual in the Indian Religions*, edited by Ria Kloppenborg, 158–168. Leiden: Brill, 1983.

Kosambi, D. D. "Ancient Kosala and Magadha." *Journal of the Royal Asiatic Society* 27.2 (1952): 180–213.

Langenberg, Amy Paris. "Buddhist Blood Taboo: Mary Douglas, Female Impurity, and Classical Indian Buddhism." *Journal of the American Academy of Religion* 84.1 (2016): 157–191.

Langenberg, Amy Paris. *Birth in Buddhism: The Suffering Fetus and Female Freedom*. New York: Routledge, 2017.

Lewis, Todd and Christoph Emmerich, "Marrying the Thought of Enlightenment: The Multivalency of Girls' Symbolic Marriage Rites in the Newar Buddhist Community of Kathmandu, Nepal." In *Little Buddhas: Children and Childhoods in Buddhist Texts and Traditions*, edited by Vanessa R. Sasson, 347–373. New York: Oxford University Press, 2013.

Lincoln, Bruce. "On Ritual, Change, and Marked Categories." *Journal of the American Academy of Religion* 68.3 (2000): 487–510.

Liu, Xinru. *Ancient India and Ancient China: Trade and Religious Exchanges AD 1-600.* New York: Oxford University Press, 1995.

Malalasekera, G. P. *A Dictionary of Pāli Proper Names.* 3 vols. Oxford: The Pali Text Society, 1997.

Mehta, Suketu. *Maximum City: Bombay Lost and Found.* New York: Vintage, 2004.

Michaels, Axel. *Hinduism: Past and Present.* New Haven: Princeton University Press, 2004.

Michaels, Axel. *Homo Ritualis: Hindu Ritual and its Significance to Ritual Theory.* New York: Oxford University Press, 2015.

Mishra, Shanit. *A Widow's Gift.* Varanasi: Pilgrims, 2008.

Mohr, Thea and Jampa Tsedroen, eds. *Dignity and Discipline: Reviving Full Ordination for Buddhist Nuns.* Boston: Wisdom, 2010.

Nagarajan, Vijaya. *Feeding a Thousand Souls: Women, Ritual and Ecology in India – An Exploration of the Kōlam.* New York: Oxford University Press, 2018.

Nyanaponika Thera and Helmuth Hecker. *Great Disciples of the Buddha: Their Lives, Their Works, Their Legacy.* Boston: Wisdom, 1997.

Obeyesekere, Ranjini. *Yasodharā, the Wife of the Bodhisattva: The Sinhala Yasodharāvata (The Story of Yasodharā) and the Sinhala Yasodharāpadānaya (The Sacred Biography of Yasodharā).* New York: SUNY, 2009.

Ohnuma, Reiko. *Ties That Bind: Maternal Imagery and Discourse in Indian Buddhism.* New York: Oxford University Press, 2012.

Ohnuma, Reiko. *Unfortunate Destiny: Animals in the Indian Buddhist Imagination.* New York: Oxford University Press, 2017.

Olson, Carl. *Indian Asceticism: Power, Violence and Play.* New York: Oxford University Press, 2015.

Parpola, Asko. *The Roots of Hinduism: The Early Aryans and the Indus Valley Civilization.* New York: Oxford University Press, 2015.

Pandey, Raj Baley. *Hindu Samskāras: A Socio-Religious Study of the Hindu Sacraments.* Banaras: Vikrama, 1949.

Payne, Richard K. and Michael Witzel, eds. *Homa Variations: The Study of Ritual Change Across the Longue Durée.* New York: Oxford University Press, 2016.

Ramanujan, A. K. "Three Hundred Ramayanas: Five Examples and Three Thoughts on Translation." In *The Collected Essays of A. K. Ramanujan*, 131–160. New Delhi: Oxford University Press, 1999.

Rigopoulos, Antonio. "The Construction of a Cultic Center through Narrative: The Founding Myth of the Village of Puttaparthi and Satthya Sāī Bābā." *History of Religions* 54.2 (2014): 117–150.

Rozario, Santi and Geoffrey Samuel, eds. *Daughters of Hāritī: Childbirth and Female Healers in South and Southeast Asia.* London: Routledge, 2002.

Samuels, Jeffrey. *Attracting the Heart: Social Relations and the Aesthetics of Emotion in Sri Lankan Monastic Culture.* Honolulu: University of Hawaii Press, 2010.

Sasson, Vanessa R. *The Birth of Moses and the Buddha: A Paradigm for the Comparative Study of Religions.* Sheffield: Sheffield Phoenix Press, 2007.

Sasson, Vanessa R. "A Womb with A View: The Buddha's Final Fetal Experience." In *Imagining the Fetus: The Unborn in Myth, Religion, and Culture*, edited by Vanessa R. Sasson and Jane Marie Law, 102–129. New York: Oxford University Press, 2009.

Sasson, Vanessa R. "The Buddha's Childhood: The Foundation for the Great Departure." In *Little Buddhas: Children and Childhoods in Buddhist Texts and Traditions*, edited by Vanessa R. Sasson, 75–96. New York: Oxford University Press, 2013(a).

Sasson, Vanessa R. "Maya's Disappearing Act: Motherhood in Early Buddhist Literature." In *Family in Buddhism*, edited by Liz Wilson, 147–168. New York: SUNY, 2013(b).

Sasson, Vanessa R. "Divining the Buddha's Arrival." *Religion Compass* 9.6 (2015): 173–181.

Scharfe, Hartmut. *Education in Ancient India*. Leiden: Brill, 2002.

Schopen, Gregory. "A Well-Sanitized Shroud: Asceticism and Institutional Values in the Middle Period of Buddhist Monasticism." *In Between the Empires: Society in India 300 BCE to 400CE*, edited by Patrick Olivelle, 315–347. New York: Oxford University Press, 2006.

Schopen, Gregory. "Death, Funerals, and the Division of Property in a Monastic Code." In *Buddhism in Practice*, edited by D. S. Lopez, 473–502. Princeton: Princeton University Press, 1995.

Shaw, Sarah. "Yasodharā in Jātakas." *Buddhist Studies Review* 35.1-2 (2018): 261–278.

Shulman, David. "Divine Order and Divine Evil in the Tamil Tale of Rama." *Journal of Asian Studies* 38, no. 4 (August 1979): 651–669.

Shulman, David. "Creating and Destroying the Universe in Twenty-Nine Nights." *The New York Review of Books*, December 9, 2012.

Sponberg, Alan. "Attitudes toward Women and the Feminine in Early Buddhism." In *Buddhism, Sexuality and Gender*, ed. José Ignacio Cabezón, 3–36. Albany: SUNY, 1992.

Strong, John. S. "A Family Quest: The Buddha, Yasodharā, and Rāhula in the Mūlasarvastivāda Vinaya." In *Sacred Biography in the Buddhist Tradition of South and Southeast Asia*, ed. Juliane Schober, 113–128. Honolulu: University of Hawaii Press, 1997.

Strong, John S. *The Legend of Aśoka: A Study of the Aśokāvadāna*. Delhi: Motilal Banarsidass, 1989.

Strong, John S. *The Buddha: A Short Biography*. Oxford: Oneworld, 2001.

Tezuka, Osamu. *Buddha*, 8 vols. New York: HarperCollins, 2014.

Thapar, Romila. *From Lineage to State: Social Formations of the Mid-First Millennium BC in the Ganga Valley*. New York: Oxford University Press, 1991.

Thich Nhat Hanh. Old Paths White Clouds: Walking in the Footsteps of the Buddha. Berkeley: Parallax, 1987.

Van Hollen, Cecila. *Birth on the Threshold: Childbirth and Modernity in South Asia*. Berkeley: University of California Press, 2003.

Walters, Jonathan S. "A Voice from the Silence: The Buddha's Mother's Story." *History of Religions* 33.4 (1994): 358–379.

Walters, Jonathan S. "Communal Karma and Karmic Community in Theravāda Buddhist History." In *Constituting Communities*, edited by John Clifford Holt, Jacob N. Kinnard and Jonathan S. Walters, 9–39. New York: State University of New York Press, 2003.

Walters, Jonathan S. "*Apadāna*: Therī-apadāna: Wives of the Saints: Marriage and Kamma in the Path to Arahantship." In *Women in Early Indian Buddhism: Comparative Textual Studies*, edited by Alice Collett 160–191. New York: Oxford University Press, 2014.

Wilson, Liz. *Charming Cadavers: Horrific Figurations of the Feminine in Indian Buddhist Hagiographic Literature*. Chicago: University of Chicago Press, 1996.

Wilson, Liz. "Red Rust, Robbers, and Rice Fields: Women's Part in the Precipitation of the Decline of the Dhamma." Buddhist Studies Review 19.1 (2002), 41–48.

Winslow, Deborah. "Rituals of First Menstruation in Sri Lanka." *Man* 15.4 (1980): 603–625.

Zelliot, Eleanor. "Buddhist Women of the Contemporary Maharashtrian Conversion Movement." In *Buddhism, Sexuality and Gender*, ed. José Ignacio Cabezón, 91–107. New York: SUNY, 1992.